500

9

COME TO ME

SIN SORACCO

Ithuriel's Spear

The Green Arcade

San Francisco

ACKNOWLEDGMENTS

With respect for the people who will change the world for the better—
People working against climate change. Occupy Wall Street. Black Lives
Matter. Workers, dreamers and wild hopeful dancers.

For this book—Andrew Ahn, Patrick Marks, Gent Sturgeon, Tia Resleure,
Francesca Rosa, Jim Mitchell, and mi padrino Carlos. I am honored that
you are in my life. Thank you.

Come to Me
Sin Soracco

ISBN: 978-1-943209-08-8
Library of Congress Control Number: 2015960979

Cover art and frontispiece by Gent Sturgeon

10 9 8 7 6 5 4 3 2 1

Ithuriel's Spear is a fiscally sponsored project of Intersection
for the Arts, San Francisco
www.ithuriel. com

The Green Arcade
1680 Market Street
San Francisco, CA 94102–5949
www.thegreenarcade.com

A joint noir of Ithuriel's Spear Press

and The Green Arcade Press

Pomba Gira, come to me!
Bloody fate, sweet destiny—
Pomba Gira, come to me!

The woman stiffens, turns around, blind, spinning out of control, eyes rolled back, limbs trembling. Her outstretched hands open and close, grasping, capturing only air.

In a white flash several doves circle high into the night. They disappear into the moon.

Shivering, the woman lets the people dress her as they sing to her, they slip the red skirt trimmed with black lace over her hips.

She picks up her whip, her black fan.

Flames start up in her dark eyes, in the slash of red lipstick, in the sudden whip crack.

"Pomba Gira, please help us!" Bookmakers streetwalkers transvestites lost souls murmur, "Pomba Gira, you are so lovely."

She accepts rum and gold-foil-wrapped chocolates from them.

"Pomba Gira, please help us!" Petty thieves card sharks late night stalkers whisper, "Pomba Gira, you are so clever."

Common dealers sleight of hand squealers call for "Champagne for the Lady. Another song for the Lady."

She struts among them stiff-legged, her proud eyes unseeing. She uses a long silver holder to smoke a sweet tobacco cigarette, she condescends to bless the dancers with the smoke. More drums! Stronger! Sing louder... Dance. Dance!

"Give me give me give me—"

"Give your very best to the wife of Eshu."

"The Queen of night! The Queen of Hell! Her pleasure is the dance—her laughter, endless desire. Bloody fate, sweet destiny, my beloved Mistress Pomba Gira, come to me!"

Vinha caminhando a pe para ver se encontrava a minha cigana de fe—

CHAPTER ONE

Magdalena Carvalho, renamed and reborn as "The Gypsy Woman Oleander," stood on a San Francisco street corner, humming. She held a plate of cornmeal and a bottle of rum in her hands. A glowing point in the darkness, she was a boldly sexual woman brightening the starkness of the urban desert. Raising the rum bottle to the night sky in cheerful salutation, she took a healthy swallow.

A small boy danced at the top of the hill. A black giggling roly-poly creature, he somersaulted down the street toward Oleander.

The streetlights dimmed.

The lights weren't usually so unreliable, but the neighborhood wasn't wealthy. These things happen.

Shadows stretched across garage doors, pooled up against fences, leaked away through missing boards.

Oleander crouched down by the gutter, her solid body radiating, a hot shadow within the greater shadows, she poured out half the rum, sprinkled the cornmeal in a circular pattern. Singing: *Eshu-oh. Elegbar-ai-yey. Eshu ohhh—*

The streetlights got brighter.

Maybe a cloud moved away from the moon?

Oleander smiled at the small child rocketing down the hill—an odd hop and he stood tall before her, transformed into a grand figure in a wide brim fedora, vintage tuxedo, mirror shades and red tennis shoes. He bent down to greet her. Pulling her up, he hugged her, kissing her on the left on the right on the left. Formal. Ceremonial.

The streetlights blinked. Off. On again. Fragile light dimming. Dimmer.

Oleander handed the tall elegant man a cigar, held the match for him. Every gesture graceful. They stood close together in whispered conference. Comfortable and intense.

Ever since Oleander started having corner confabs with her nebulous pal, the predatory hustle had ground to a halt in the neighborhood. The scammers and grabbers, the folks who just want to get over, get off get down get ahead get naked get loaded—they simply didn't work those few blocks any more. The newest set of tough missionary crack dealers vacated the area just hours before; nervous spit coagulating in the corners of their mouths, they told each other how this strange dude came up to them, not saying a word. One of them said he wore a tux, flashed a gun, another swore he was in sweats, carried a blade, the other one said he wore a baseball jacket, talked on a silver cell phone. His face was thin, thin, skull thin and cold. They all agreed they wouldn't be back.

The streets were silent. No wind. No motion.

Sudden footsteps, thudding with determination, broke the calm of the night. A small woman straggled up the sidewalk puffing under the weight of a ten foot palm tree she'd recently boosted from in front of a hotel. It wasn't quite what she had in mind when she started out that evening, but the snotty doorman returned from his break three minutes early. Sometimes you go for whatever you can get.

While Gina appeared to be a delicate little woman— tangled hair obscuring heavy-lidded eyes, sharp pointed nose and a sweet pouting mouth—she wasn't particularly fragile nor was she especially gentle, nor stupid. However, she was perfectly glad to let anyone make those assumptions, in fact she encouraged it. She blended, she faded into the situation; her ability was not so much to be invisible as to be unremarkable.

Of course just then, trundling a palm tree down the street, her habitual camouflage wasn't working. She raggedly hoped that this sort of late night palm tree transport maybe happened around here a lot? She dropped the palm tree, pushed her hair back, a rough gesture, her eyes flashed out with bitter intelligence. From between the fronds of the palm she surveyed the neighborhood as she caught her breath. It wasn't a particularly warm or cheerful place at night, she wished she could be somewhere else. But she couldn't, she suffered from obligations.

As she lifted her tree Gina caught sight of the woman on the corner: a steamy babe talking to herself, waving a bottle of rum, sucking on a huge cigar. The hair on Gina's arms raised up.

The streetlights went out.

Gina didn't mind the dark, there'd been more than one occasion she'd been grateful for the cover; those days were, for the most part, gone. Involuntary retirement: a nasty combination of broken bones, torn ligaments and handcuffs. She had fallen off a ladder during a badly planned robbery. She didn't talk about it.

Huffing, Gina hustled across to the opposite side of the street with as much grace as she could sustain under the weight of the palm tree. She heard the woman laugh, saw her turn. The beautiful crazy woman looked right over at her.

Tucked up small behind the palm tree, Gina scowled. The sweat chilled on its way down her spine. The woman beckoned to her.

No way. Eyes forward, Gina shook her head. Not even gonna look across the street again, get herself all twisted up in someone else's dream. End up in the shit again. In an uncertain world that much was a lead pipe certainty. Times like this Gina always made it a point not to see whatever it was she didn't see.

Gina knew a lot about crime, she wasn't afraid of crime, she had a graduate degree in crime, she understood crime from motivation to modus op; but whatever was going on here—ah, this loopy street corner hoodoo stuff—not so much.

A quick set-to-it double time jaw clenching block later, panting, Gina put her tree down, peeked back along the street. No one around, a look up the street, down the street, nothing. She entertained herself with speculations: The madwoman was lurking in the shadows, a dusky demon conjure woman out to get her, gonna jump her. Steal her palm tree. Right. Things that go bump in the night. "Shit." Gina muttered, "Whatever happened to simple crime? Rob the rich? Another tradition gone to hell." That's why, Gina grumbled, she ended up boosting palm trees. Wouldn't be right to show up empty handed.

Gina made a snorting noise, took a couple deep breaths, shook her arms to relax the tension, opened and closed her cramped hands. Ground her teeth against the pain.

Hadn't always been like that. Well, of course not. No one could live with pain like that all the time. The pain came and it went. The past half year she'd spent chasing down quack remedies: water therapy, gold salts, mega-vitamins, mini-minerals. *Pain is good for you, it's a learning experience, an indication of energy blockage. Open Up. Ooooopen up. Ooga wooga.* Then there was the no-meat no-dairy no-salt no-sugar no-caffeine routine; but Gina didn't want to Attain Sainthood in this lifetime, she only wanted to stop the pain. One infamous trance medium hissed at her to Visualize Health, told her to put fifty dollars in an envelope and—Gina had taken the old charlatan's fringed lamp, her crystal ball (it turned out to be ordinary glass) and the black table cloth with the silver stars and moons.

When she realized the pain wouldn't kill her, she decided the damn cures just fucked up her style. She lived with the pain. Banged some heroin when it came her way. Beat hell out of the alternatives.

Gina sat on some handy uninhabited front steps, used the back of her hand to wipe the sweat off her forehead, wrapped her arms around the palm, and grumbled: *I'm no good at this.* Gina swore softly as she got up, hefted her burden and trudged up the dim street.

CHAPTER TWO

Situated on the Northeast coast of Brazil just beyond the disintegrations and rubble of a big city, a decaying artist colony collapsed in a sprawl along the beach, shimmering in the heat. The hot wind blew pieces of sea-spattered garbage through the streets. In the back alleyways skeletal cats pawed listlessly at piles of rubbish, scattering abruptly at the passage of the tall cool white man.

James Collier floated along the edges of the world, culling anything beautiful that looked like profit. He was a man who always paid less than the most reasonable asking price for such treasures as came to his notice. It was business that caused James to wander through the remote labyrinths of Brazil, and business pushed him down the narrowest darkest alley of his search. The scavenging cats recognized James as a fellow predator.

The alley ended abruptly at the workshop of one of the area's more famous artists. There was no identifying sign on the premises. Old Vicente was an unsociable man, but inside his filthy shack he created masterpieces, unveiling them to the world in his own good time. James leaned against the wall opposite the workshop door, smoking a cigarette.

A gnarled shadow crouching in his workshop, Old Vicente murmured and rested one of his callused hands on a golden statue's lustrous enameled black hair, his small red-rimmed eyes glanced at her, away, and back again, unable to resist, covetous of his own creation.

No one, no one in all of Brazil had seen anything like her.

The locals called him Old Vicente since his wife left him seven years ago, although he hadn't yet reached his middle years; neither his strength nor talent waned, but his bitterness drained him of youth. He stepped back from the statue, the product of anger distilled into glowing metal.

No one would ever see anything like her again.

The ferocious figure stood more than three feet high, she was poised with one foot forward, one hand extended

7

as if in greeting, or warning. Her sinister smile was sweet as blood.

Vicente's statue was of Pomba Gira, a lusty Brazilian deity, the fabulous one who holds the heart of Eshu-the-Gatekeeper. She was hollow, cast of aluminum enameled with glass and gilded with Dutch gold; each ear had an uncut emerald set as an earring; more brilliant but less valuable gems and jewels highlighted her hair, her fingers, her toes, the handle of her whip. Old Vicente had made her more shapely than the most lascivious Nepalese dakini, her breasts were high and seductive, her belly rounded, her hips full, her thighs strong, her calves and feet as delicate as a young girl's. She was a Cigana dancer, a fortune teller, a slut. She was powerful beyond censure, wise beyond understanding. She was Pomba Gira, dark Queen of the Cross-roads.

As Vicente gazed at his work, his mouth twitched, the statue really looked like his wife, the same proud tilt to the chin, the curve of her cheek. Magdalena Carvalho was a practitioner of Macumba, a spiritual tradition formed from the melding of philosophies from Africa and the Americas. Magdalena had been baptized as the Eshu's wife, Pomba Gira. Baptised and married to be a proper wife to Vicente, a devotee of the Eshu himself. They were well mated. But Magdalena Carvalho da Silva was of an independent turn of mind. She left him, moved north then still further north, finally to California and out of his reach. Until now.

He'd heard that she'd changed her name, how the woman had even "divorced" him up there in the North. A man like himself, with connections all over the world, well, he was not so easy as all that to divorce. It took some time to arrange what he needed. Magdalena Carvalho had learned from Vicente himself, the master, how to change, how to hide—but he'd found her anyway. He knew Magdalena Carvalho da Silva, no matter who she called herself, would come back to him when she felt the pull of his magic. She would be confused in her heart, tormented in her spirit and she would turn to him. Who else? The magical force he let loose with his statue would be intimate, irresistible, calling her home. He was still, divorce papers or no papers, her husband.

Carefully laying the hollow statue on its side in a nest of
tattered black blankets, he stuffed a wad of noxious roadside
sedges slathered with palm oil deep inside it; after that, thirteen
ripe black berries of the Deadly Nightshade were tossed in, with
muttered imprecations, one at a time. "And finally, a heart for
you." He used three rusty nails to tack fresh mimosa leaves—
the sensitive plant, curling with every touch—around the still
bloody heart of a recently sacrificed black pigeon. He placed
this deep up into her belly. The plug was woven with leaves
from the golden brugmansia plant, called La Reina de Noche—
Queen of the Night, and mud from the little graveyard at the
edge of town.

Before he soldered the bottom plate he drew a *pontu riscado*
using a pinfeather from the shattered pigeon. He dipped the tip
in the rapidly thickening blood, drew jagged lines, curling and
etching his demands into the foundation of his lovely statue.

He covered her, stepped back, admiring: even hidden under
the blankets, it radiated power.

He looked at the Rolex on his wrist, an abrupt elegant
motion, surprising in such a weather-beaten man. It was time to
go pick up the black rooster, the imported champagne, a pack of
sweet tobacco cigarettes—only the best for his insatiable Queen
of Hearts. Old Vicente was going to dance the statue, give it
a soul, that night at midnight. He shivered in anticipation, his
revenge was well begun, his triumph assured.

Vicente didn't stop to lock up his little shop, no one would
touch anything in there, no one dared even look inside beyond
the forbidding wooden door strapped with cold iron, the
bloody black cock feathers nailed to the frame at the top were
lock enough. Everyone in the old quarter knew him for what
he was: embittered sorcerer, abandoned husband, superb artist,
and a vicious master in a *roda de capoeira*.

Vicente paid no attention to the pale cosmopolitan man
who lingered at the mouth of the alley. As Vicente passed him,
the stranger leaned back against the whitewashed wall, one leg
bent up. This casual white man said hello, his sharp acquisitive
eyes gleaming. Vicente didn't return his greeting.

CHAPTER THREE

The sand stretched flat gray and deserted in the cove at the north end of the beach, the waves rolled in, thick and colorless. The mutton fat moon shed a faint light on the man hunching to the crossroads at the edge of the shore.

Along this Brazilian coast nobody sleeps at night, the world reverberates with samba music, booze, wild talk, the flash of teeth, of bottles, of babes, of blades, of warm flesh and great sad eyes. But this end of the beach was silent. Empty.

Empty except for Vicente and his bundles. Further back on the road, if Vicente had only looked in that direction, outlined against the sky, the slender form of the pale stranger.

Old Vicente set about his preparations at the crossroad with methodical gestures: One red votive candle, its flame a tiny beacon against the dark, was set at the edge on the seaward side, the long curving street pointing to it as if the road were an arrow. A red rose, a travel-size bottle of open rum and a small pack of gold-tipped cigarettes on top of a small box of wooden matches completed his design. He spit some of the rum in a wide spray around this arrangement, he hummed, he did a capoeira *ginga* stepping back and forth facing back up the street. Back and forth, a challenge to whoever/whatever might be interested in his business. Smirking, he gathered up the rest of his paraphernalia and hopped down from the jagged seawall onto the flat shore.

The stranger ambled along the road above, a cat, a secret, a whisper in the night, nothing more.

Vicente laid out an empty bowl, a plate with some fruit, a coconut, several more cigarettes, another box of matches, a bottle of champagne and a couple large bulging sacks. These things he placed on the sand, carefully, measuring the distances between them by some internal necessity.

A large bundle stood in the center of this array. He whipped the blanket off. She glistened, she glowed, she sucked all the faint light into herself and gave none of it back, she was the source and the destination of all that might shine in that night.

Vicente reached in his hip pocket, pulled out a flat flask, took a great mouthful of rum, spit it out in a circle of fine spray. A couple swallows, then he put the flask back in his pocket and lit a cigar. Squatting on the sand he seemed a statue himself, although an utterly dark one.

His cigar nearly finished, Vicente reached out for the bottle of champagne, opening it with a sharp jerk on the cork. He stood up, grabbed one of his bundles and extracted a huge nearly comatose black rooster. He splashed the champagne on the rooster causing it to jerk in irritation. In a quick fluid movement he unsheathed a long wicked blade and sliced the angry rooster's head completely off. He bled the champagne-drenched corpse into the bowl. The body of the rooster was laid, with an odd bobbing reverence, at Her foot. Vicente lit another cigar, blowing the smoke over the twitching corpse, over the bowl of blood, still puffing sharp circles of smoke, he tilted the bowl over Her head, pouring out the blood. The blood continued to pour, hissing and sloshing, covering the luster, dimming the fire. Sticky and slow, the cock's blood slurried out of the bowl onto Pomba Gira, pooling at Her feet.

Vicente grabbed the statue, the rooster's head, the platter of fruit and spun in crazy circles down to the waves. His feet lifted and pounded in a strange parody of dance, he bounded deeper into the ocean, alternately dipping the statue into the waves and raising it to the moon.

A wailing chant came from Vicente's mouth, an eerie sound smudged by ocean waves, fighting its way out of some not quite physical center, piercing the heart of the world.

Eons passed as he and Pomba Gira writhed in the rising surf, until Vicente was thrown back on shore, unconscious. His statue floated like an air-filled ball, graceful, upright, golden in the quieting waters.

The stranger ran up past the unmoving man and into the bay. He grabbed for the statue one-handed, his grip slipping off a metal shoulder as if it shrugged him away. He stepped deeper into the water and picked it up, both his arms wrapped around it. It seemed to bleed onto his linen suit jacket but he didn't stop to wipe himself clean. Dripping, not pausing to see if the man laid out on the sand was even breathing, James clung to the slippery statue and staggered up to the roadway.

As the sound of scrabbling footsteps receded into the distance, Vicente rolled over and sat up, shrugging himself back into himself. He walked, not too steady, back to his little ceremonial circle, dropped four opened kola nuts onto the sand. Lit a final cigar.

The nut pieces fell two sides down and two sides up, dark and light. The pattern of blessed balance gleamed on the dull gray sand. Vicente smiled as he slung the cock's body to join its head somewhere far out in the sea.

CHAPTER FOUR

Breathing hard, Gina pushed open the double glass doors, she entered the lobby ass-first pulling the palm along behind her. The place was all faded glory, bordello red walls and slow, sensuous sad music, not Muzak, it was more Gothic romance—no, wait! Jailed and jilted lover: False heart made you spend all your money honey. There was a dusty display case in front of some ascending stairs. Along the right side, book cases, and on the left a time-scarred mahogany bar sagged in derelict splendor. Books and baskets of trinkets and decks of cards were scattered along the tops of everything. Instead of liquor bottles on the bar back there were rows and rows of glass candles, jars of dried herbs and a faded poster of a pit bull puppy: LOVE ME.

Squatting imperiously at the far end of the bar was a huge oak file cabinet. It looked to Gina to be a couple hundred years old. Its top was occupied by an incongruous state-of-the-art professional cafe-style Italian espresso machine. Gina calculated wholesale cost at a couple grand. She peered into the open top drawer of the cabinet, it held a battery of tiny white cups and saucers, the second drawer was closed but labeled Cream, sugar, chocolate, cinnamon, etc. No non-dairy. No aspartame. You drink my coffee, you 'Do It Right.'

Gina could hear machinery humming invisibly behind the bar, she looked around, no one was watching her so she sidled closer, stood on her tiptoes and levered up herself to see around behind the bar. It was what she did: Check out the premises, never know what might be found. She glimpsed one serious cash register, two multi-line phones, and a tiny obnoxiously up-to-date computer chugging away, attached to one of those printer/ fax/ scanner/ whatever/ copier things.

She tapped her short fingers on the bar top, a small frown between her eyes, a speculative smile on her mouth. The gentle wafting of incense, the wailing rip-your-heart-out voices, the old fashioned junk-filled display cases were clever mis-directions for some very modern business of hopefully clandestine operation. She licked her lips.

The front door bell jangled, a man came in, looked around apprehensively, saw Gina and pulled back into himself. Startled turtle reflex.

A slender young woman wearing a tiny gold cap and white sweats swiveled through the lobby. Knotty muscles. Nice bones. Greek profile. Brown sugar skin. Oh lord. Gina's knees, never the sturdiest part of her, melted.

The pretty girl hardly glanced at the man or Gina and her palm tree.

The man started to speak.

The girl smiled with professional disinterest, "One moment, please." Exit lobby, stage left. She disappeared into what seemed to be a kitchen. Terrific ass.

The small print on the poster read: 'Stop dog baiting. Adopt a bull terrier. Get a new best friend.' Before Gina could ask the pit bull in the poster if the pretty girl might qualify for a new best friend, her thoughts were interrupted.

Several other women crossed the lobby wearing head wraps and not particularly clean white skirts. The women nodded to Gina, ignored her palm tree, grabbed herbs or something off the shelves behind the bar, went back into the kitchen. More busy women came and went, up the stairs down the stairs—doing mysterious things. None of them were Frankie. Gina couldn't imagine Frankie floating along in one of those odd virginal white costumes. She was completely uncomfortable—the palm tree was no help.

Two black women, tall and short, chattering irritably, wearing the long white skirts, their heads wrapped in lavish white scarves, burst into the lobby from the kitchen:

"Oh Thea, you can't taste anything anyway you smoke too much."

"So what if I smoke?"

"Lissen up, Queenie, you people put too much goddam pepper in everything, burned your taste buds off ages ago."

Thea retorted, "What people? Who people?"

"Your nose so fucked up from all those years snortin coke you dun know pepper from hairspray."

"Damn! I kill you if you mention dope again. I really will."

"Yeah. You an who all else? Besides, you never have made pigeon pie right."

"Have so."

"What?!"

"What?!"

Hands on hips, glaring, deep into a conversation they obviously had sing-songed many times before, neither one of them paid any attention to the other people in the lobby. Queenie was tall, slender, regal, and she bent rather lovingly over the dark round woman she addressed with a throaty growl as Thea. There were edges of a smile in their voices, but they played it serious. Hissing,

"You think you know everthin about everthin now don't you?"

"Well, yes I do because, darlin, I do."

Both of them turned for a moment to Gina, as if to assess her appreciation of their argument.

Gina straightened up, scratched her cheek. She ran her rough hands through her knotty hair, looked around trying to figure out how to look inconspicuous there in the lobby at everyone's first communion. Ignore the crazy women. Act like she didn't maybe know some of them from one jail or another. She figured she might know them, figured it be best she didn't know them so she stared at her toes wondering: Why in Hell Frankie decide to take refuge here? Although the cooking harpies didn't sound like virgins, they were still in those weird white virgin outfits. What's with the white clothes? Who lived in this place anyway? And was hair bad? She nearly asked them.

The click of footsteps came from the hall above the stairs.

Sling-back spike heel shoes. Peek toes. Making that click-slippery sound which always reminded Gina of sex. Gina didn't turn around.

Deep voice, filleting through the fishwives' banter: "Go on, both of you. Upstairs with that crap. Nobody wants to hear it."

They whirled up the stairs in a flurry of garlic, rosemary, and the sharp smell of barbecue. Laughing. "That got us outta there." Gina heard the slap of hands, like a high-five.

"Good evening." Satin ribbon voice. Rich. Perfume.

Gina turned.

Curves. No jiggle, this woman was solid. Red. Orange. Smoldering. She moved as if she had great legs under her long skirt. "I'm Oleander." The woman's voice reached into all those secret places. She had long wavy dark maybe burgundy wine color hair curling out from under a red and black head wrap. If this was the Mother Superior, Gina was up for the church service. Oh yeah.

For a moment Gina thought she'd died and gone to heaven? No. For a moment Gina thought the woman looked familiar, like the hot crazy woman dancing at the corner? Oh but no, honey, Gina wasn't going there.

The man cleared his throat, stepped delicately closer to the woman and whispered, "Can you help me? They said you could help me?" He frowned over at Gina.

As if Gina gave a sweet damn what the little lecher needed. She frowned right back, then remembering she was a guest in that place, she got small again, the corners of her lips pouted down, her eyes drooped, her shoulders curled in, she pulled her hand along one of the palm tree fronds. Fading.

The woman motioned the man to the end of the bar by the cash register, they mumbled, she reached back and got a candle, a bundle of herbs. Her every motion was musical.

He handed her a pile of money, nodded, nearly bowing, and hustled himself and his little sack out the door.

"So? You brought me a palm tree?"

"Yeah. No. Uh. Well. I mean it's a palm tree. But it's not for you." Gina didn't know what to say, not an unusual situation for her, but after all this time spent not knowing what to say she figured she ought to be better at not-saying, but she wasn't. "I could get you one too if you really like it?" She sputtered. "I never go anywhere without my palm tree, it's the custom in the old country?"

Oleander's mouth curled up.

Gina took a breath, tried again, "Frankie, er...Francine's cousin gave me this address as the rooming house where she stayin? She move here couple months back?"

Gina thought, but didn't say: I used to be a friend, a good friend, before Frankie got sick, pushed me away—screaming with the first fever, puking, yellow as a banana.

Gina plunged forward, "I brought this palm for, for, her? You know?" Pause. "Or well, maybe I should leave it in the lobby here? And come back when it's more convenient?" She wasn't about to take it with her out into the cold hostile streets of San Francisco. Carry a palm tree, sleep safe in any corner of the world? Gina waved her square calloused hand at the empty lobby as if there was something going on there. And she thought as she gestured that there probably was something— she just couldn't figure out what the hell it might be.

"You can leave it there. Frankie's not home right now, but she'll be back pretty soon. She doesn't get around much anymore, you know?"

Gina knew.

"It's a nice palm." Oleander's voice was as light as a tropical breeze, "Noticed you carrying it up the street earlier."

"Oh." The madwoman. Uncomfortable smile. "I didn't want to intrude."

Oleander's red, red lips twitched, "I don't let anyone intrude, ever. So don't worry about it." Oleander was good at what she did, thank you very much for noticing. Some days she called it diplomacy, other times, creative financing. Other times—never mind.

The brown sugar virgin all in white, oh rose bud lips and ebony eyes, pushed back into the lobby, complaining, "Oleander! The stew's too hot, Queenie puts in too many red peppers."

Queenie barreled back down the stairs to confront the youngster, hands on hips. Glaring. Statuesque as Mother Africa, "Not too many peppers. That tough ol bird need serious spicin." Her voice held a lilt, a prison grown assurance that Gina recognized. Gina ducked her head smiling, the young girl must be a brave woman to complain about this queen of cooking.

Oleander said, "Add potatoes, they'll suck up the heat."

Disappear all back into kitchen, Lovely Ladies in White, bickering about pigeons.

Gina was trying to get a handle on the place. Everyone but the divine Oleander was all in white, or at least once-white, what with the goop from kitchen duties all down the front. Some of them maybe had hair, some of them didn't. All of them had head rags. So it was either personal choice or chemo? Was Frankie staying in one of those getting-set-to-die hospice places? Were these women nuns? Not hardly. She didn't know why, but hair must be bad. She touched her own snarls. Well, she wasn't gonna shave her head just to finagle a place to sleep. Besides the all-in-white-style was cult creepy. They did not sound like choirgirls. They did not move like virgins. Who were they trying to kid?

There was a clattering and giggling from behind the kitchen door and a screaming, "Oh no! Rita! Don't do that!"

A small silent puppy, looked like the one in the poster, pushed out from the Kitchen of the Screaming Virgins. She snuffled in Gina's direction, gave a tiny puppy wag and trotted off to investigate her palm tree.

Gina swallowed. "You suppose I should wait?" Stumbling over the words. Time was when she was welcomed/expected wherever Francine was. That time was long gone.

"Coffee's always on. Have a cup. Settle in, get comfortable." Waving at the couch by the bookcase on the right wall. "Make yourself to home."

"Right." Sure. Whatever you say. Home. Ha. Gina filled a tiny white cup with coffee tar, three spoons of sugar, and listened to the computer-gizmos clicking. She wished the cool little pup would come over to play with her, tell her what was the deal in that weird old place.

CHAPTER FIVE

Couple miles to the southeast of Oleander's house, deep off in Hunter's Point, Ellis—one very drunk young man— stumbled towards his Aunt Lou's unhappy home. His thin brown face was battered on the left, the deep brown eye on that side was partially closed. He groaned as he bent over to peel off the garbage clinging to his shoe. Everything jumped around his head when he looked at the world from his bent over position.

Ellis straightened up in front of the grungy brick apartment building, peered at the steps, reluctant to go up. With that pained puzzled non-curiosity which only the very drunk have, he noticed a ragged old man crouched at the top of the stairs. Smoking a fat cigar. Ellis called, "Hey, what you doin up there?" The demon kept shifting in and out of focus.

The old man stood up, stiff, he'd been waiting a long time. Shaking his grizzled dreadlocks, the demon lifted his big shoulders in a small shrug as if settling his bones. "Took you long enough." A red-eyed glare. "You drink with everyone except me."

Ellis wobbled forward, his mouth lightly open. "I don't know you." Querulous.

"You think you better'n me?" The demon bounced down the stairs grinning, took a swallow out of his rum bottle, smacked his lips. Shoved the bottle at Ellis. "Best drink in the world."

Ellis reached for the bottle. Too slow.

The demon pulled the bottle out of his reach, "What you give me?"

Ellis, unsure of the etiquette of negotiating with phantasm, snapped, "Ain't gone give you nothin." Snatched again at the bottle. Didn't connect.

The old man took Ellis by the arm. "Come on. We got places ta go. Things ta do."

Ellis tried to pull back. "Wait a damn minute." The old man's wrinkled hand was stronger than it looked.

"What? You doin something so important you can't walk wit me for awhiles?" As if insulted, the old man let go of Ellis's arm, took a couple steps. Casual, matter-of-fact voice, "Cops waitin for you upstairs."

Ellis jerked, he couldn't remember much, there might be something the cops could be interested in. Damned if he knew what though. "I didn do nothin." Long-suffering whine.

"That's the problem." The demon's red-rimmed eye seemed to wink. "You comin or stayin?"

Before the bottle was empty they were deep into the barren urban desert on the rotting edges of the bay. The weed-choked lots surrounded by collapsed fences demarking the property lines of paint-peeling wooden houses with porches that sagged had faded away. They were in a dim industrial wasteland with defunct warehouses and abandoned machinery. The traffic was local, sporadic. It was raining.

The old man leaned against a broken gate in a ruined chain link fence, crossed his feet. Ellis noticed the old man wore bright red sneakers, seemed an odd choice, but maybe that's what old people wore. Ellis wouldn't know, he'd been mostly drunk for what seemed like all his life. He began, for the first time in a long time, to wonder about many things. The demon's gap-toothed smile was sinister.

"Know where you are?"

Ellis looked left, right, not much there. "No. Somewhere in HP, I guess." Ellis's head throbbed something terrible, he wondered what the hell he was doing wherever the hell he was. Besides playing the percentages. And losing.

The old man cackled. "So. So." He tipped the empty rum bottle against the fence. "Long walk back to where you come from." He pushed the gate open. "Long way back to where I come from too. Come on in."

Ellis, abandoned to the desolate street, watched the old man disappear into the shrub-choked yard. "Shit." His steps muffled, he followed a path covered with old leaves and rubble, upended bottles lining both sides, it led him around a large gray warehouse to a well-raked patch of dirt. A tiny pressboard shed sat to one side, yam vines scrambled around the edges. It was absolutely silent.

The demon popped out of the shed. "But then, this place as good as any other." Waving his arm. "Sit." There was no place to sit except on the ground. "Sit. Make yourself comfortable. We have a lot to do." He handed Ellis a lit cigar.

Ellis waved his hands in front of his face, his stomach churned on the smoke, bitter fluid pushed up his throat. "It's fuckin wet out here. And that thing stinks."

"Got a lot to learn. Sit your butt down. Smoke."

No way to defy the old man's glare. Ellis sat on the damp ground, smoked.

"There are things in the world money can't buy." The old man's voice was compelling; as he spoke, he examined every corner of the young man's understanding. He spat in disgust. "You one stupid disrespectful young human." Contempt curled like smoke.

"What I do?" Voice rising. Ellis came out with his automatic response, "I didn do nothin."

"Right. Problem's always bin what you didn do." The old man stood up. "First thing. You need to learn to pay respect." He hustled Ellis back down the path. "Pay attention to what you do. Be respectful. Salute the guardian at the gate, now. You just walk by him before, came in like you own the place. But you don't. This time you greet him correctly."

Ellis looked around for some 'him' to greet. No one. The rum bottle the old man had left at the gate seemed to be full again.

"Drink a little rum, pour a little on the post, bow forward, say: 'Thank you'."

Ellis, frowning, drank, poured, bowed to the post. In a strangled voice he said, "Thank you." Stupid rotten post.

"Now. Over here. Like this." The old man pushed Ellis down flat on the ground in front of him. He touched his shoulders, left and right, delicate, grabbed his shoulders and picked him up into a hug, "Ben'dic-cion."

"What? Benediction? What you mean?" This old fart was no priest.

"Ha." The demon glared at him, "One day you understand then you know what it is to be respectful." His gnarled hand grabbed Ellis by the shoulder, lifted him in the air.

Ellis, terrified, drunk and confused, was dropped on the ground as if from some great height; he crouched there, mouth open in shock, panting. Ellis shouted, "Hey! Stop!" He put up his hands to protect his face. Rolling away from the old man's kick he began to dodge the old man's strange attack.

The old man tagged him, left and right, top and bottom. Ellis swung, but the old man wasn't there and he got tagged again. Ellis picked himself up off the ground, curled his fists tight, planned a left jab, right uppercut— and pushed air. He finally just started to copy the guy, squatting, one leg out, swaying right and left, while the mad old man wailed like all the nameless dead in a high wobbling voice.

Ellis lifted the bottle when it was handed to him, spilled a little at the foot of the post—shifted right, shifted left, lifted the bottle, drank and made a full circle with the trunk of his body, saying, 'Thank you'. Fall over.

"Hey don't spill any of that rum! Stand up. Roll forward. Don't spill. Shift ya weight. Drink and thank the gods for takin such good care of you as to bring you here to the gates." The demon howled, "The gates to the rest of your life!"

Ellis sat back on his haunches, he was not grateful for one single damn thing. He considered just getting up and running away but the muscles in his thighs were jumping from exhaustion, he was afraid he'd collapse. Crawling away just wouldn't cut it. He growled, "I still don't see what the point of all this is."

"That's the way we do it."

"Huh?" Disoriented, he still could raise a small tentative rebellion, "Who is this 'we', old man?"

Grim cackle, "You and me. You and me. We as like as like can be."

The old man, the demon, was standing upside down, balanced on his head, grinning evilly and waving the rum bottle. "Stubborn. That what you be. Stubborn and hungry and stupid."

"Tired. That what I am. And drunk. Who the hell are you, anyway?"

"Who the hell!" The demon repeated it, gesturing obscenely, a grotesque capering figure right side upside downside up. He contorted forward, his face a glare of glee, "I'm your godfatherrrrr." A rolling jump into gales of baleful laughter.

"No way." Ellis remembered back when his mom was still alive, but unwelcome in Aunt Lou's home. There was Aunt Lou screaming in the kitchen about Satan, slamming plates, yelling about how his-mom-was-a-slut and not welcome in her home ever ever and how Aunt Lou's own sainted dead brother never shoulda married that woman. Oh yeah and how Ellis was lucky she'd taken him away from all that—that nasty foreign filth. Then back to Satan again. Aunt Lou always went on how Ellis was gonna end up dead or in jail. Unless he forgot everything about his mom. Went to church. Accepted Jesus as the Only Way. Got the best grades. Kept his clothes clean, even when he worked at the garage. Was properly grateful.

Gratitude! 'Say thank you' slamming him in the teeth again. It all came rocketing back. A god-forsaken godfather? A connection to his mom? "No way."

"Way." The old demon chortled at that, "Well. It's a bright balmy night. You'll sleep outside tonight, eh?"

"Fuck that. It's raining." Ellis held his head with both hands, barely keeping it from exploding into the sky with an alcoholic pop.

"Tomorrow you can start work fixin up my old Caddy. It's a honey. Proud old thing, alls it need is a new engine. Some body work. I got a line on a new engine—we might jus put that in right away. Of course, tha's after you pull out the old engine. Give the ol girl a lot more power. That be good, hey?" He smacked Ellis on the shoulder, snorted in amusement. "You work on cars, now don't ya?"

"Some. Yeah." In fact, before he decided to spend his life drunk as a lord, Ellis had been pretty good with machines. But it'd been awhile. "Never said I wanted any part of this."

"Actions. Actions. Don't matter said, not-said. You in it now." Rubbing his hands with a wicked back-ass-wards cheerful shrug. "Tomorrow you rig up the A-frame and winch. Gonna take finesse to cut off the ole bolts, they're rusted in there tight. Yes. Yes. You got any finesse? Lotta things just rust right up if they not used. Eh?"

Ellis flexed his hands. Hadn't got them greasy in awhile. He liked the smell of motor oil. He liked cars. He just didn't much like the old man.

"Everything take time," the old man said. "This kinda thing need a firm hand." He spat, turning his head to the left. "Ain't nothin firm about you. If you not careful, you end up just a drunken old blob." He licked his lips, speaking slowly, "Good at nothin, good fa nothin." He laughed at the look on Ellis's face. "Got no cause to be insulted at the truth, you."

Ellis staggered to the edge of the cleared space, kicking at the scruffy yams, muttering to himself: "Old fool. Got me thankin things that ain't there, for nothin they ever did for me anyway." He spoke directly to the old man, "You expect me to go around talkin with spirits?"

"They's worse conversation."

"Next thing I'll be killin chickens and hoppin round like a savage."

The old man's eyes glinted into the distance. "Relax. You worry like a old lady with a paper asshole."

CHAPTER SIX

Years ago, when Gina came back into the city on short notice, she'd just gotten out of jail, once again fresh-hatched, impressionable as a gosling. Ribs on the barbecue weed in the pipe beer in the cooler. Friends around sun's out who cares getting high feeling good. Free at last. Praise the Lord, free at last.

Her lover, Francine, still healthy then, was tall blonde and rangy, flexible as a rope, dressed in skin tight leathers and denim. Every dream come true. Frankie had stopped dancing long enough to announce they were gonna free the buffaloes corralled in Golden Gate Park to honor Gina's release. "Mine is a romantic soul," Francine said.

"Who's gonna take care of all them wild animals? Feed em, keep em out of traffic?" Gina was sure Grand Larceny Zoo Keeping was the wrong way to start off her parole.

"It'll be okay, Gina. It's a token gesture."

"Fucking buffalo." Gina's mouth had wiggled from the effort not to laugh. Gina waved her hands around, her blunt clever fingers spread in exasperation, "People won't put up with buffalo."

"You have no imagination, Gina. No appreciation for theoretical thinking. Don't know nothing about allegory. Metaphor. Analogy. Art. That your problem."

Gina, slurping her first beer in a year, said, "Ah shit, Frankie, don't tell me my problems. You think words are magic, to say them is to own them." Gina filled her mouth with stolen meat, chewed awhile, finally: "Metaphor is NOT as good as reality."

Francine hadn't bothered answering. "Okay. What we needa do first is declare the neighborhood a actual free-buffalo zone. A refuge. A urban buffalo sanctuary." Graceful arms outstretched, "Bring us your cold, your hungry, your buffaloes longing to be free." Francine said, "Welcome home, Gina. Oh Gina, welcome home."

This time, Gina wasn't sure how big a welcome she'd get. Been a long time. Long time no see. No hear. No nothing. All of a sudden her palm tree peace offering didn't seem quite the thing. She stood behind the palm, peering through the fronds as Francine crossed the lobby. Francine seemed translucent, fragile, she was dressed not in white but in black and green. Gina was relieved to see that she seemed to have all her hair. Frankie's smile was as shining as she remembered it and her voice seemed as strong,

"Hey now, Gina, didn't know you went in for horticulture."

Diffident. "Whore culture always been a special interest of mine." Gina tried to be clever for Francine, habit is hard to break. Wanting to please. They didn't touch.

Francine giggled, pushed her fingers into the palm searching for Gina's face. "Oh Gina, you are so thoughtful."

Gina scowled, the palm tree was a last resort kind of thing, seemed an okay idea, just okay, not great, not SO thoughtful. Oh hell, never mind.

They finally connected, fingers touching through the palm fronds, then each stepped away from it, looked the other up and down, blaming their awkwardness on the tree.

"Ah. You're looking good. Um. You have hair."

Francine's laugh was deep, happy. "Oh, Gina, don't confuse yerself when you ain't even been here a minute."

Gina muttered, "Well, there are certain odd things... which along with the flocked red wallpaper are like, um."

Francine stepped towards the stairs in the back. "Hah. It's not that complex." She didn't elaborate on just how it wasn't 'that complex'. "Come on up, girl. Leave your leafy friend down there until we find a place for it." She held the hand rail as she started up the stairs. "If you remember, my house always pretty full up with stuff." Francine lifted her hand off the railing for a moment, "Stuff in progress. Stuff stuck half-way. Done stuff with nowheres to put it. You know." She gripped the rail again and pulled herself up the stairs.

When they got to the first floor, Gina noticed the handrail continued down the hall against the wall, past several doors to a wavy glass door at the end. Someone had taken the time to make moving around easier for someone who, someone who— Gina watched as Francine stopped at the first door, one hand still on the rail—someone who would probably never dance again. Gina swallowed hard.

Francine opened her door with a flourish, held it for Gina.

Gina got stuck in the doorway, shifted her weight, surveying the premises. One room, filled. Window opposite the door, couch bed below it. Navajo blanket on the couch. Two doors on the left wall. The other walls were covered by shelves of books, esoteric tribal wall hangings, elongated wooden masks, bright primary color lithographs. A huge pine worktable jutted into the room. Hot plate, soldering iron, scraps of copper and splotches of melted solder, a leather hide, carving knives. A huge machete. Gina saw these things, wished she hadn't come. "You got your place fixed up nice. Not so different from what I remember."

"I've gotten more diverse." They struggled through the crowded little room. Francine pointed at the couch. "Park yourself over there on the bed and I'll make some tea."

"What's this?" Gina picked up a glass candle with a paper picture on it of a man on a great steed, sword high in the air. "You still into this stuff?"

Francine laughed, took the candle out of her hand. "Yes. I'm still. Don't you start. Try to see things from my perspective." Francine put her thin arm across Gina's shoulders, whispering spooky-voice, "From the viewpoint of the walking dead."

"Jee-zuz Frankie." Gina shuddered. "Don't start your ownself." Shrug away. "Walking dead, my ass. You're going to live forever. Years an years."

Francine flicked her fingers: Up yours with the years and years. "That doesn't sound good to me anymore."

"What? The alternative to years and years sounds worse to me." Gina's mouth slipped into a pout. "You're always throwing shit around like that, I never can throw it back at you." Because Frankie's smarter. Taller. Sicker. Gina patted her pockets for a cigarette, forgetting she had decided that morning not to smoke anymore. "Well, shit." Turning full circle in the room. Searching for the proper phrase. "Smacks of ethnic confusion." She nodded to herself. Yes. "Superstition. Incorrectly applied metaphor." She was proud of herself—it was Frankie always talking about metaphor, simile, analogy. Whatever the hell.

"I got your ethnic superstitions." Frankie held out her pale arms, tracks pitting the skin over her veins. "And your inappropriate metaphors. There's no doubt in my mind I'm a skinny white broad." She raised an eyebrow. "The issue isn't race, it's survival. Hey, I'm more a dead person than I am a white one. I'm in the market for whatever works."

"Whatever works? Salvaaation?" Gina's voice dropped, wobbly: "Send ten dollars an put yore hans on the teevee. Hunh. So explain to me how burning candles to Celia Cruz is the way to go?" She indicated a candle with a paper label of a strong brown skin woman leaning in the doorway of a cantina/bar.

Frankie laughed, "The Cult of Celia? Um, not quite."

"It's simply a puritanical desire for control: Clean livin no smokin no screwin no drinkin. Fuckem. I thought you had enough of that with jail? Oh. No swearin neither. Cults like this demand an obedient, brain-dead audience for their bad carney magic tricks. Shit. Act like they got the moral upper hand. Dayam, there's nothin admirable about denyin pleasure. Bunch of stuck-up grumpy frustrated assholes swooshing around in white clothes." Gina glared at Frankie. "And generally bald."

Frankie stopped her. "No. This isn't a cult. It's a spiritual path that millions of people are walking. And it's me and the Angel of Death walking along here, and together we not doin too bad. But I can see the end. Tryin not to worry. Not to worry un-duly. Unduly." Her eyebrow arched up in a challenge.

"Yeah well, I just got here and I don't want to break down just now." Gina wiggled her mouth, drooping, tears in her throat. "So, don't tell me what it's like yet. Okay?" Last time they were together Gina offered to stay with Frankie forever, care for her when it got bad—You and Me and Me and You— but Frankie said: "I'm doin fine, You the one's fucked up, girl. Don't bother about me. I-can-take-care-of-my-self."

Frankie turned on the hotplate under the tea kettle. "You ever find anyone who could fix the pain?" She got herself out a bag of opium poppy seeds. "I only go for the real thing."

"We talkin weekend miracles?" Gina flexed her right hand. "Sure, I found cures. That's what I was looking for, right? Cures up the wing wang." Grimace. "Those cures are worse than the disease. I gave up on that shit. I been looking for work again, you know?"

A long time ago they had sworn their future forays onto the wrong side of the law would be transcendental: They were very tired of getting caught. "We agreed, remember? We'd make the streets safe for buffalo."

"Thought you'd quit the life?"

"Who? Me?"

They both quit petty larceny (it really wasn't all that interesting or successful), turned their skills in another direction. Francine recognized the strange potential in all kinds of decorative objects, Gina was practical. They used their combined skills to retrofit things with hidden compartments: Want a secret pocket in a Gucci belt? Euro-spa hair spray can, fake portable computer? Hollow-core door, earplugs noseplugs buttplugs art deco rugs. We talkin about Italian boots, handmade suits, Borgia poison rings, Chippendale cabinets. How about some tabletop versions of monumental pre-Colombian statuary, hollowed out just-so.

"Stash Art. For the upwardly mobile paranoid professional." Gina looked hopeful. "Made with love and skill. We could still do it. Hey, our work would come with a guarantee: If you get busted with one of our stashes, we try to put bail together. Everyone needs someone on their bond."

Frankie had written a manifesto announcing that art and crime were two sides of the same coin. Buffalo nickel.

It was coins they'd never had enough of.

Frankie said, "I don't think so."

Gina said, "I thought you'd devote your life to aesthetics? Anarchy and Art? What happened?"

Frankie said, "I didn't find any great curative or spiritual content in it."

"In aesthetics? Of course not. I coulda told you that." Gina watched Frankie prepare two cups of tea, opium seeds for herself, peppermint for Gina, "My thing's never been aesthetics at all. Anesthetics is what does it for me, remember?"

"Well, today you get peppermint. It's not time for you to be anesthetized."

"We were good together weren't we, Frankie?"

Gentle. "Yes, Gina. We were. Until we weren't any more." The kettle whistled, Frankie poured. They sat in silence.

It had been good—until Francine was diagnosed with Hepatitis C and a bunch of other things Gina never did understand. There was probably AIDS in there too—just to add some more modern horror to it all. Then Gina fell off a ladder while she was ah—climbin for a cure.

Frankie said, "All we did was fight."

"Okay. Okay. So we won't do that."

Handing Gina her tea, "Right. But what will we do?"

"Well. I hoped I could crash here?" Gina screwed up her face. "Doesn't look like that's gonna work. I have hair and none of the clothes I own are white."

Frankie said, "On the floor tonight, but tomorrow you got to check your other options. We usually have a guest bed here but there's a woman stayin here… Less able to take care of herself at the moment than you are." She paused, "Two kids and a husband who likes to punch her."

Gina didn't know how to take that, just because she was without a place to stay didn't exactly mean she couldn't take care of herself. Or did it?

Frankie sipped her tea, playing for time. "The house here is peculiar. Um. Everyone works together on all kinds of things you probably wouldn like."

"Try me. I like vestal virgins as much as the next dyke."

"Oh Gina, put a bag on it." Frankie got up and walked, brittle as a dried twig, over to the left hand door, "Here's the loo. Shower's down the hall where the glass door is." She smiled, gentle. "Mostly it's pretty clean. There's around a dozen of us livin here right now."

Gina thought again about the railing along the hall—was this place a hideout for the sick, the lame, the down and out? Virgins? Or mothers? Or what then? She didn't get the place at all. "Frankie? Are you a virgin?"

"What?"

"Well, okay. Have you ever fucked a guy?"

"Huh? Probably."

"What?" Frown. "You mean you don't know!?"

"Well." Serious thought, wrinkled brow, the whole deal. "I probably did. And it probably just wasn't very memorable," Frankie replied.

"No memory? Nothing?"

Trying reeeal hard. "Nope."

"So. It doesn't count if you can't remember?"

"Who's counting?"

"Whoever dresses your housemates up like vestal virgins all in purest white. Except where there's tomato sauce and relish all down the skirt."

"Those are in their *yawo* year. Or they're making ritual food. Or they might be in hiding. Or—any number of reasons." As if that answered everything. "Listen, when we finish our tea, I'm going to rest for awhile. You go on downstairs, tell Oleander you're crashing with me for the night. You probably shouldn't mention you'd like to stay longer until you find out more about us."

"I don't have no white clothes, I won't buy no white clothes and I'm not shavin my head. My hair, tangled bird's nest that it is, is my crowning glo-ory."

"Such as it is. Why don't you see if you can ingratiate yourself with the household? Offer to help with supper? Or somethin."

CHAPTER SEVEN

That evening after circle sparring with the old man and getting kicked because he couldn't successfully duck out of the way one too many times, Ellis called a time out, "What's that you chant? Where you from anyway? Sometimes you talk about events in places no one else has ever been."

The old man laughed at him. Not a pleasant sound. "Too far for you to imagine." He stared at the night sky. "Even the stars are different there."

"What? You from outer space?"

The old demon cracked up, crouched and cackled and flipped over in a slow broken legged cartwheel. "Okay. Sure. That's just what I'm tellin you."

Never out from under the mocking red eye of the old man, Ellis learned how to mold fiberglass into shapes that imitated metal car parts, how to weld a nearly smooth seam holding two, three, four odd pieces of metal together. He didn't learn patience, or humility. This lifetime might not be long enough for him to approach either of those two skills. He was introduced to the spirits of the living, of the dead, the demons and gods who rode the old man, he made the acquaintance of the Eshuas, and the shadow, he learned a little about the Orishas, and about the necessity for retribution. Obligations. And the stupid dance fighting.

"Get it right. Get it right, pay attention." Long steps side to side. "Ginga." Balance on one leg. Balance on one arm, upside down. "Do it." Crescent kick high. Scuffing kick low. "Sweep me off my feet," the old man hollered, falling down laughing as Ellis unsuccessfully flung himself around. "You don't pay attention, it come out wrong, you always fallin down round you own ears." The man cackled, pushed him. Ellis swung, wild. The old man placed his foot directly in the center of Ellis's chest, shoved. *"Bençao."* Ellis went flat on his back. The old man stared down at him unsmiling. "Ben'dic-cion. We call that a blessing."

Air gone from his lungs, Ellis lay on the ground wheezing like a fish on the dock.

They sparred and drank most of the night, every night in the yard, except Mondays. On those nights they went to a deserted crossroad at the edge of the bay, there they danced and drank, the old man whispering strange demonic chants, they both got very tall or very small—tiny enough to curl inside a walnut shell.

And then they went back to the warehouse to spar. Ellis never could lay a finger, hand or foot on the man. There were times when the old man didn't seem to be so old anymore, as if he put on the old man routine like a suit of clothes. As Ellis fell down the wily sorcerer bounced up, as Ellis bent over the glaring flame of the torch or gooped layers of fiberglass into precise curves, the other man stood tall and straight. Ellis crawled and the man danced. "That's how it is. You got so much to learn."

Some afternoons the man tinkered away in one of the rooms in the abandoned building doing things that Ellis never saw. Humming and chanting and carrying on. Ellis didn't care, he was too consumed with retaining his own balance, glad enough that the old bastard was occupied, giving him a respite from constant criticism. Ellis was just trying to do his best, do what he was told. Upside down or not. After all there was plenty to eat and drink. Stories. Maybe something of his mom. He didn't know. Beat staying at Aunt Lou's. He bet she didn't even notice he'd gone. Except for maybe if the police came round lookin for him. Fuckit.

It hadn't taken Ellis long to fall back into the rhythm of car mechanics. Engines, transmissions, brakes, all these were second nature; under pressure his old talents came back. Having the old man teasing, challenging, threatening every moment of his life, however, was nearly more than Ellis could stand. At first he drank to escape the old man, then when he found the old man right there with him, even fallingdown upsidedown drunk, then he drank because it seemed to make the curvings and curlings of the exercises easier.

Shifting in and out of focus, everything was more complicated, convoluted and backwards than Ellis figured it needed to be—he spent hours keeping tiny feathered balls up in the air while he was standing on his head. Stupid.

When it came time to work out the wiring schematics Ellis knew he was gonna blow himself or the car up. Didn't much care by then. Either way.

Instead of final sweet oblivion, the ignition fired up. The new engine growled, the headlights worked, the dashboard lit up, the turn signals and the brake lights did their thing.

The chicken sacrifice. Damn Ellis grumbled, I knew it would come to this, probably helped. At least Ellis hoped it helped, otherwise there'd been a whole lot of blood and nasty tearing of feathers and for what? Even when it was barbecued, the damn bird was as stringy as the inside of a baseball.

The limo hadn't been washed in decades, "Didn't want it to get too proud." It rumbled like a monster, crouching, eager, powerful, unmoving in the back yard. Ellis didn't know how it handled, never having been allowed to drive it.

He wasn't even allowed to work on it once the engine turned over, the old man kept him busy doing the strange set of exercises—with even weirder contortions than he'd made him do the very first night. "Hey, is this some Super Fly kung fu?"

"Nope. Not kung fu. This is done to music when it's done right."

"Super Fly done it to music."

Red eyed, the demon glared at Ellis, "It's the art of treachery. Started by your ancestors long ago when they were slaves." Ellis wasn't ready for some black-power lecture, so he stared up at the sky. "Massa thought we were dancin. But what we were doin was, we was practicin the art of treachery." The demon did a lazy 'au', the cartwheel turn at the beginning of a battle, he squatted in front of Ellis, challenging, "This martial art is called capoeira, but you're so bad I wouldn't insult our sacred tradition by giving any name at all to your half-assed form."

Ellis staggered up to spar with the old man, they fought, dancing, cartwheeling over each other until Ellis crawled out of the circle, defeated again.

At night on his little cot under the stars if it was clear or in the warehouse if it rained, sometimes Ellis dreamed that he was cruising down the street in a big black car, a big fancy black car. It turned into a kid's plastic toy car with fat wheels that you move down the street by pushing with your feet. He was just as happy, making *rrrrmm rrrmm* noises, zipping along at a great clip in his toy car when he careened right past an angry policeman. So he flipped the man the bird. He snap-snap snapped his way under a railroad crossing gate and thumpa-thumpa across the tracks moments before a huge train screamed by. He stood up on the far side of the tracks, put the car in his pocket and turned to the furious cop. "Yessir?" he said. Cool as cool. But when the cop accused him of hijacking the train and stealing some weird shit, he got really confused and woke himself up.

That morning when Ellis rolled off his cot the Cadillac limousine was gone.

"Dayam." Ellis stood on the broken steps of the little shack, staring around. Stood, as if stuck there, struck there. Shocked and stupid. "Where'd the limo go? Man, I worked my butt off on that car and then it just disappear?" He pounded on the door of the shack. "Hey! Old man! This ain't right, you hear me?"

"I guess this'll have to do." With a sudden snap, the demon came up behind him and tossed a string of red and black beads over Ellis's head. Not a casual gesture. The necklace weighed more than it should. "Time for you to get gone. This place closin down." The old man turned and trotted out to the street. "C'mon hurry it up. Landlord be here soon and we best ain't be here."

Ellis followed, swearing to himself. "I knew it come to this. I bust my fuckin balls." He was working himself up into a righteous fit. "My fuckin balls. And then I just get tossed out."

The demon fished in his pocket, pulled out some car keys, registration papers, red taxi medallion. "Here." He tossed the keys. Ellis caught them more out of reflex than desire. "I got to show you a couple things then you can have it."

The Caddy was parked in front of the broken gate. It was sleek, shiny black, no longer dusty. The demon popped the trunk. "See, this here part opens up into the back and under the seat so you can carry stuff without anyone knowing it's in there." He peered up at Ellis. "That's your work there. You better hope it's good. Your ass in the sling if it ain't." He opened the back door. "See, you can get to it through here too." The seat lifted up, smooth as smooth. "And these door panels all pop off with those nice little compartments you welded up behind." He waited for Ellis to respond.

Ellis just stood there, scowling.

"All I want's for you to answer a call now and then, do a couple errands for me."

Ellis turned his head, looked at the old man out of the corners of his eyes.

The man grabbed Ellis's unresisting hands and shoved the papers and the medallion into them. "Take it to the address here. The lady's name is Oleander, I'm an old friend. I owe her. But don't tell her about me. Be a surprise when I show up. Tell her you'll run her errands. Do a real good job. I'll be checking on you. You come when I call, okay?" He fumbled in his pockets, came up with a tiny black cell phone, crinkled up his eyes pretending he was too near-sighted to see if it was working. "Here."

Ellis protested, "Wait a minute waitaminute now old man." He shuffled the stuff from one oil-stained hand to the other. "Hang on here just a minute now." He said, "I ain't yo bitch."

"Ain't that always the way. Teach em everything ya can, they still trip over they own feet." The old man left him, going back up the path and beginning to fade into the ragged mess of plants. He didn't turn around as he added, "Up to you now." He turned the corner, out of sight.

Ellis hollered, "What's up to me? Who the hell is Oleander?" He listened. Nothin. Not even wind in the ratty leaves. "Who the hell you think you are?" No answer. Ellis took a few steps down the path, hit a solid wall of silence. Not a breath, not a rustle.

Ellis edged back along the little path, through the tumble-down gate, he bent and grabbed the rum bottle, took a swig and sprayed it into the sky. His eyes narrowed as he glared at the long black limousine parked at the curb. He pulled down his mirror shades, opened the door and slid behind the wheel.

CHAPTER EIGHT

"Okay, Frankie. I peeled potatoes with a bunch of giddy broads, heard a lot of boring conversation about goddesses." Exasperated. "Frankie, tell me, is this a time warp here or what? Goddess-chat in the kitchen? Listen, it just is all so—so—"

"Appropriate?"

"No! Shit. And the divine Oleander, cruisin in and out, spreadin joy and sweet cheer—"

"And you, droolin and mumblin, causin whatever kind of chaos you can, simply because you don't get it?"

"What!?"

Frankie directed her clear gray eyes at Gina. "The simple version is that Oleander runs the little store in the lobby, you know, lotions, potions, candles, herbs, pills to cure all your ills. She's one of those people you go on about. The charlatans. Except she's not. She for real. And this her house. She is mother to all of us."

"Mother. Right. I never met anyone less motherly. The woman is sex in motion."

"Mother. Like in leader, you know? And this house is more than a place to live, it's, um, it's, well, it's a spiritual thing."

"Right. A nunnery for crazy girls. Lead by the hottest Madam Mother Superior in the City."

"Yeah. But you're not gonna do your novitiate here. Where will you go? What will you do?" Frankie's face was all slanted sadly to one side.

"Told you. I'm looking for work. You know how it is. I'm not on the street yet."

"I didn't think you would be."

"Ha. Shows how well your mind's workin. Last town I was in gave me the legal chills, you know. So now I'm here. But this town doesn't have no easy livin zone for poor people. Hell." Gina didn't want to go on. "Skip it."

"Stubborn as you ever were. What if this was my last week on earth?"

"You be delighted to share it with me." Gina snapped, "And since you not gonna share it with me, it ain't the end times, so cut the crap. Besides, according to all the literature your last week will be spent in a deep coma." She was angry enough to cut to the chase: "What's the latest doctor prognosis?"

"I'm bloody gonna die, you stupid girl. Is that what you wanted to hear? You want details?"

Solemn. "Yes. Give."

"Oh, hell. I'm a little rocky today. Can't remember details." She looked at her hotplate, the set up. Motioned at the syringe. "I only use when it gets real bad. It got real bad about an hour ago, and I can't seem to hit a vein?"

Gina placed her hand, so, the needle, so. The vein, tired from pushing the thin blood around the thin body, rolled away at the touch of the point, a feeble furtive snake with a skin like steel. Gina placed one finger on the opposite side of the vein, holding it still, gentle as a mother, she was the one who placed the point, she the one to depress the plunger. Familiar.

Frankie's smile was as bright as a birthday girl. "Yep. That did it for me." Exultant. "I'm not just a knee jerk reaction machine to the dictates of doctors." A slow shuddering breath, smiling, contented. Her face blurred, seeing, not seeing, it didn't matter, she shone like a new pearl. "I'm with the program now." She looked up at Gina, a false glow of health back in her cheeks. Francine's hand clenched, middle finger raised, a small snicker. She grabbed a bottle of pills, milk thistle seed, popped a handful in her mouth. Knocked them back with a mouthful of tea. "My liver's already Swiss cheese. They tell me nothing anyone can do will change it. So I do what I can. You want?"

But Gina shook her head 'No', licking her lips. "Thanks, not today." The death wish, always present with heroin, was suddenly too close to the surface.

Frankie grinned, punched Gina in the arm. "I meant do ya want some milk thistle." Sly, "Ain't your liver hungry?" She relaxed back against the cushions. "Take a lot more her-ron than that ta kill me. And it will. When I'm good and ready. But for now, I'm still real curious to see what's going to happen next, you know? Be-sides, if I want to go out gooo-od, got to get me a whole lot more in my stash." She chuckled, without humor. "I have no intention to let hepatitis or any HIV shit rule my life. Damn, I hate to shiver and puke. You help me won't you, when I'm ready? Like, if I only get half dead or something, you make sure? When I'm dead," Frankie said, "I intend to be that way for awhile."

Gina turned away. She wasn't all that eager to help anyone commit suicide, her breath jammed in her throat; she wanted to remind Francine that killing wasn't right up there with the things she was eager to do. Not looking back at Francine, she said, "Sure Frankie. You can count on me."

"Good. Now remember: No coma for me. And then, I got things to do when I'm dead. And I don't want no reincarnation as a sea turtle or a member of some other charming but endangered species. Promise me."

Gina turned around. Frankie's eyes were large, unavoidable. The strange trusting sincerity of the heroin high.

"Promise you?" Gina's gaze wandered around, taking in the room, the crazy decorations, how everything was arranged to show it off to its best advantage as Francine sat or lay on her couch, most days all day, most nights all night, getting what pleasure she could from the memories—whatever—that her collection of bizarre things evoked. Gina shoved her hands deep in her pockets. "How can I promise that?" She pursed her lips. "Termites and cockroaches aren't endangered. How about one a them?"

The memories were ragged, sharp like broken coke bottles.

"Fuck you, Gina. I haven't been awful enough to come back as a cockroach. Maybe when I'm ready, I'll consider a buffalo suit."

Gina shifted position, as if she were in a play, now one person, now herself. "Come back as the missin link?" Shifting. "Or did someone already do that? Nope. That's why it's called missin."

"We're all the missin links. Doing battle for the spirit."

"Spirit? What's spirit?" Caught up in spite of herself. "Like here in this weird place—you got ha'ants or what? What's the difference between spirit and soul? I mean, well, I mean, assumin there is such a thing. Things."

"I don't know. Soul is maybe what each of us has, you know, what makes us part of the greater human soul?" Musing.

"But spirit, now. Spirit is what's great in the world. And it's dangerous when it's defiled."

"Defiled?"

"Yes. I think what we do is we choose for the spirits to work for good or for evil.

"What's good? What's evil?" Gotcha.

"There are no limits, what we choose is what is."

"Crap. Our choices haven't manifested to fit our desires. Nobody gets what they want."

"Oh but sometimes ya get whatcha neeeeed?"

"Come back as a buffalo?"

"Better that than a feedlot cow."

Gina slid in and out of herself, wishing they could just agree that Frankie wouldn't die yet, that she'd live for years and years.

"Speakin of feedlot cows, go on down and get some food for yourself, Gina. I'm not hungry just now."

"I'm not goin down there to eat with a bunch of crazy women, not without you to correct my table manners anyway." Arms folded.

"It'll be fine. Go on." Francine rolled her head back. "Besides, if you're even thinkin about stayin here at all, you have to learn to deal with the, ah, Cult of Celia." She watched Gina pout over toward the door. "Actually," she whispered, just at the edge of hearing, "It's more like, you know, Santa Marta?"

"What's with the Catholic confusion now? Fuck you, Frankie, I'm out of here. Look, as long as they take good care of you, I'm sort of fine with it, you know? Just don't you dare go on about your spiritual analogies, cross-religious fertilization. And," Gina sputtered, "one more mention of some bee-you-tee-ful allpowerful allseein allknowin sexy mama goddess with the pomba boom bam name and I'ma break some heads open. With or without the intervention of a saint."

The door slammed. Just before Francine closed her eyes she realized how glad she was that Gina hadn't changed. There had to be some constant thing in her life as she approached the end of it. Smiling, she thought she could bet her next bag of heroin that Gina would remain the hard-headed bitch she'd always been. Behind that cherub mask she was still solid. Gold.

CHAPTER NINE

Oleander leaned against the old mahogany bar, she took the pins from her hair, dragged her long fingers through it, pulling it in thick ropes down her back.

La Favorita, the tiny pit bull puppy, sat at Oleander's feet, watchful, proud of doing her job well. She'd gotten to growl at the big loud man, and her lady hadn't said not to. This pleased her very much. Her ears were up, her short tail out straight behind her ready to pound the floor with joy if someone she liked said 'hiya'.

They had both been relieved when Raymond finally left. He was a huge sloppy man, brown-green ugly, perverted and too smart. The owner of a small import-export company and curio shop, Raymond visited them once or twice a month for a consultation. He wouldn't use the phone line, he claimed he needed to look at Oleander while she told his fortune, he preferred her hair pinned up, formal. She catered to his whims when it suited her.

Oleander didn't actually like reading the cards for Raymond—she tried to be careful how she thought about him but she kept coming to the conclusion that Raymond was actually some big slimy green thing scraped off the bottom of a pond—which made the interpretation of cards like The Moon problematical. She grinned to herself.

Raymond's interest in fortune telling was entirely a matter of profit not prophecy; he refused any spiritual counsel even though he knew Oleander was privy to an impressive cache of strange and useful information. Just that evening, upon hearing her warning, he'd said, "How you get your information isn't any business of mine. What I do with it shouldn't concern you." Smug in his sense of his own superiority, the red gleam in her eyes caught him off guard.

Oleander set her jaw, "Stick with that attitude, Raymond, and you will never ever get my advice again."

He had made a sort of *urp?* sound. Oleander had continued, standing to glare up at him, "Money does not buy my concern.

If I tell you something, you will treat it as precious. If I advise you in your affairs, your conduct reflects on me." She strutted away from him and back again, "And I will never," dramatic pause, "accept an ugly reflection. Do you understand?"

Raymond liked to insinuate to people that Oleander's debt to him was still largely unpaid, he assured curious people, "Oh yessss, we go way back."

"We both know I've saved your fat butt more times than you can count." Oleander was still grinding her teeth at him, "Listen good now, Raymond—this whole deal stinks."

Raymond nodded: Yes, Oleander. He didn't say what he thought. If it wasn't for him, Oleander would still be on the streets, most likely hustling her fine ass for red beans, rice and rum. Indignant, he recalled that he was the one who helped her get her first legal US passport and then the legal title to her shop and rooming house. And what thanks did he get? A mad harpy screeching at him to pass up a sweetheart-easy-moneymaker.

According to Raymond's figuring, their working relationship was a simple one. He provided a certain cachet to the poor gypsy woman's con, she was grateful that he listened to her mystical pronouncements. "Oh my dearest girl, I only follow your advice out of courtesy."

The perplexing woman laughed in his face. "Right. Raymond, if you actually followed my advice you would be far wealthier than you are, I haven't called it wrong yet. But you insist on playing the money game using your own faulty magic. Greed-driven hunches. You continue to second guess me and always," she looked at him with huge sorrowful eyes, "always come up losers when you do."

"Oh come on, Oleander, I'm asking about potential problems with a shipment of artifacts from Brazil." He had been gruff. "Simple. I asked if you saw any problems. You went nut city on me."

Oleander had seen mention of some iffy Brazilian art shipments on the traders' network. She was always interested in any news from Brazil, so she'd followed it closely. When Raymond came in with his Big Deal Brazilian Coup, she pulled the cards with more than her usual curiosity. The cards were absolutely clear: Stand back. Danger. Serious complications involving extreme risk. She didn't tell Raymond that it looked like some kind of personal rather than financial risk.

Raymond had shrugged. "My man down there's got a good eye but he's no expert on Brazilian goods. Won't know what he's got. I'll skim the cream. He may even have some of your husband's work." Raymond kissed the tips of his index and middle fingers.

Sharp. "He's not my husband anymore." Oleander reminded him, "It's stupid to spend your money on a fortune teller if you won't listen to her."

People who have no talent for it get annoyed that someone would feel virtuous pride in their skill with the cards, or the crystal ball, or with any of the hundreds of other traditional diviner's options. On balance, Oleander did far more good than harm, and she was generally aware enough to choose the good, or choose the harm. There were no accidents. Oleander calculated exactly what the balance due was on virtually everything in her life, to the smallest gold nugget, or whatever. When the time came around, she never hesitated to pay up, nor did she pause when it was time to call all the bets in.

She would be graceful. Put her hair up in a sophisticated twist. Pull the cards for Raymond. And she would be very careful what she told him.

She said, "You are clever, but seldom wise." She knew all of his business connections, even had the import numbers for most of the shipments he'd falsely declared to be "old clothes" and "books". Tipping her head back to grin at the ceiling, she reflected that she often bought and sold to the same clients as Raymond—but she actually did deal in old clothes and books, as well as recycled computer parts and school furniture. That international trade gave her contacts that were useful far beyond money. She sold necessary goods at a very slim margin of profit to schools and hospitals in Brazil, thus making herself a steady income as well as helping the poorest of the poor. It was something she'd promised herself to do when she ran away.

And those contacts kept her informed about her ex-husband. "Don't push me, Raymond." She could put him out of business with a couple phone calls. Put him further out than that with another kind of call. She'd rather keep the arrangements as they were.

He had smiled in his greasy superior way, slipped an extra twenty in her pocket. "Just tell me if there's anything in this shipment I ought to pick out special for you."

Oleander turned up the Lightning-struck Tower card, said, "I don't think so." That's when La Favorita got to growl without a reprimand.

The reading left Oleander uncomfortable, itchy, with a feeling of nebulous menace. There had seemed to be more in the cards than just trouble for Raymond. She checked her watch, there was a little time before anyone else would need her.

She went behind the bar, sat down on the low stool and pulled the computer keyboard into her lap. Tapping carefully she logged into one of her databases, constantly updated it kept track not only of her own business—for which many people were grateful—but with a few keystrokes she gained access to another linked network. She hadn't realized when she first put the system together that it would be so useful. Her friends in far places kept her informed of many things—current prices, cultural changes, bills of lading, custom certifications, import duties. There it was: One of Raymond's agents, James Collier, a man she didn't know, was bringing in crates of old clothes, household goods, tourist trash and other items of no particular interest. From Recife. Hah.

She marked it for tracking and returned the system to its innocuous duties of monitoring her little shop's inventory.

She flipped the lock on the front doors, pulled the plush red/black curtains over them, the sign 'closed for awhile' swung into place. She pushed at the first of the red panels to the left of the bar, saying, "Rita, stay." The pup flattened out on the floor, her large head between her paws. Oleander stepped into the secret closet. With the panel shut, it was impossible to notice there was a closet there. La Favorita looked around the lobby for something to growl at, firmly on guard.

Inside the closet a lascivious lime green paper skeleton reposed by the door, one arm draped across the top of the frame. Faint Christmas lights glowed from the upper reaches of the ceiling, the walls were covered with sequined cloth worked with magical designs, cobwebby faces leered in the corners. Dried vines small shrines incense burners candles sandals cupboards without handles, knives swords wands shields cups, pots and more pots, baskets bones cauldrons dusty books in toppled piles.

Oleander could barely turn around in there. She knocked three times on the door frame, knelt on the floor, patted a cowry-lipped cement head and lit a stick of incense from the flame burning in the red and black glass candle. She hummed a simple melody, took a sip of rum, sprayed a fine mist over the small lumpy cement head.

The cowry mouth in the little cement head opened wide to gulp the rum, the cowry eyes squeezed shut in pleasure. The cement hissed as it absorbed the liquid. *Eshu-o Elegbara-aye.* Mischief maker. Gate keeper. Tranca-rua who shuts off the steets. The elegant man of the cross roads.

Oleander gave the little cement head her full attention, slowed her breathing, tried to clear her mind—the thought came: *Someone's been making fingernail tea again.*

It was as good an observation as any.

She spoke out loud, in English, not her native language, not Brazilian-Portuguese, not Yoruba, not Lucumi, but the language of the new land where she lived, "Why is everything so itchy all of a sudden? Has all my work, all our work, been just an exercise? Something to keep me occupied while you set me up? Set all of us up for some big fail? What's up with that, hey?"

The phone rang outside at the desk. No one would pick up while she was working in her altar room—the answering machine took the message.

"What now? What now? I spent too many damn years running, and finally build us a safe haven." She grabbed the rum bottle, "Not just for me, you know." She took a deep swig, continued more to herself than to the little door guard, "I dreamed of safety for all of us. And now," she swore, "I'm not going to lose it because some greedy asshole's fuckin around with things he don't understand."

She slammed the rum bottle on the floor.

The blinking light on the private line greeted her when she emerged.

Before checking it she looked around the lobby, sensitive to any changes during her absence, not sure what it was she expected to see: An omen? A big sign declaring 'Oleander is Right Right Right. So there'?

She saw the world's bravest dog waiting for her notice. "Good girl. Good girl."

She played back the message: "Vicente gone from here. Maybe he looking for you? They tole me notta tell you, but I thought you oughta know." The voice was flat, distorted by the miles between the origin of the call and its destination. She didn't recognize it. It spoke in an accented English, and it hissed in a nasty insinuating way.

"What the hell?!" She poked the machine to delete the message, instead it began to replay that snakey voice once again.

La Favorita whined, poked Oleander on the leg with her cold black nose: I'm here. Don't worry.

Oleander smiled at the little creature; she'd rescued the pup from some people who beat her—trying to make her tough—intending to breed her and breed her until she dropped dead from exhaustion and a broken heart. Oleander knew from tough, from beatings. From broken hearts and too many children. She seldom spoke of her life in Brazil, never of her childhood in Argentina—she didn't remember much of that anyway. Memories came in small doses, packed with a lot of regret. Most people learned not to question any tantalizing glimpses they might get. Oleander presented herself as Romni. People thought that was far more mysterious than a run-away Argentine whore. Showed what little they knew. Now it seemed that her ex-husband was once again, she almost shivered, trying to scare her. She shrugged, "Bastard. Scare away if you've nothing better to do. I'm safe away from you here." She half-smiled, moved once again with the confident gestures of a woman comfortable with herself.

She glanced up to see Gina coming down the stairs. "Ah." An all-purpose noise.

"Ah, yerself." Gina twisted her hands around each other, caught herself, shoved them in her pockets. "Sometimes life stinks, ya know?" She squatted down low to the floor and held her hand out for the pup to chew on. The puppy, polite at an early age, sniffed it carefully and wagged its tail very decorously.

"Her name is La Favorita, and she's very very brave. She's only a few months old but she's very very smart." The very-verys were directed at the pup, who sat up looking brave and smart. "After you've met her a few more times you might be allowed to call her Rita." Oleander pushed an espresso cup toward Gina. "Have some coffee." She was careful, talking up one side, down another, practically taking Gina's pulse, a living tension-o-meter. "Don't worry about Francine. She's tougher than any of us."

Sad smile. "Oh yeah, you right about that." Gina said. "I'm not worried about her anyway. I'm worried about the rest of us. Shit."

Oleander nodded, "Of course." She started laying out a deck of regular playing cards in a line, left to right. Two of diamonds, Jack of clubs, six of hearts: Troubling news, regrets. It could have meant Vicente, maybe when he was young, before he turned—she would not think of him or the stupid phone message. It could be referring to Gina, or even to someone she hadn't yet met. "Frankie wrote to you soon's she moved in here. What took you so long, anyway?"

"Uh. Nothing, really. Just a sense that I, uh, be in the way." Gina flexed her hands. Staring at them she continued. "Well. I hadda get outta jail first, yunno?" Gina shrugged, not looking up. "Guess you wouldn't understand what it's like to lose the one skill you ever had." Shaking her head. "I mean it be like you couldn't..." She finally looked at Oleander, "couldn't do whatever it is you do."

"Indeed?" Oleander had many skills besides fortune-telling. She watched Gina squirm. Snapped down the five of hearts: Loss. "Of course it's easier. For Frankie. Not you." Five of diamonds: Mistake in judgment. Whose? "Well, Frankie's glad to have you back, even if she don't say so." Five of clubs: More stupid trouble. "We been expecting you for awhile." Her words had nothing much really to do with the cards; she couldn't believe she'd gotten that annoying phone message. A crease appeared between her brows. Five five five five. Ugh.

The beautiful sugar girl, dressed in a different set of white sweats, her head wrapped in a clean white turban, came hurrying into the lobby, stopped to watch Oleander lay the cards out. Eight of spades. "Ooooooh girl." She cut her eyes over at Gina, shook her head.

Oleander folded the deck back together into one pile. "Julia, you don't know from ooooh girl. Get goin. You serving dinner this evening."

Julia ignored her, flirting with Gina. "Hey. Thanks for helpin in the kitchen." Pretty girl wrinkled her long nose. "I really don't much like it, but since I'm working with Oshun for this year before I can formally take Pomba Gira properly," chattering, "I mean, since the life I led, Oleander doesn't think it's good for me to get Pomba without a year of working with Oshun, she's sweeter, you know?"

Gina didn't know. Not even a little.

"Anyway, I have to get back to work in the kitchen." She rolled her eyes over at Oleander, where she met a human blank wall, so she turned back to Gina. "I'm not so good at figurin people's saints, you know, but I bet you're not any kind of Oshun at all. Am I right?"

Gina barely kept incomprehension and irritation from showing. She concentrated on the pretty girl's lovely nose. "Uh. Yeah. Right. I'm not an Oshun." Whatever that might be, she wasn't it. It sounded sort of awful. "Cookin and cleanin are things I never got the hang of."

"I'm with you there. But besides learnin to not-cook, I'm also learnin to read the cards too. But first I have to get palm reading down—want me to do you?"

"What?" Gina's mouth slipped into a lopsided grin. *Do me? Of course. Why, thank you very much.*

"I could also give you a hand massage?"

"What?" That seemed to be Gina's stock response.

Oleander barely held back her laughter.

Julia didn't notice. "It's really relaxin. And it revitalizes the abundant energy throughout your whole body. Listen,

I've got these special oils, chamomila, calendula, lavender and—"

Gina stopped her. "Thanks. But I don't think so." She fidgeted. Get my palm read? Hands done? What's this revitalization crap? Should I find out what the hell 'chamomila' is? What an Oshun is? Should I ask her? Do I care? She shrugged at the cards, at Oleander, at the pretty girl. Time to blow Dodge. "Errrr, I gotta go. See ya." Not quite the sophisticated exit line she'd wanted.

"Dinner's ready. Where ya off to?"

"Got to start work in awhile. Place over in North Beach." Didn't turn around. "The Lizard Lounge." Maybe pretty girl would stop by for a drink. Maybe they'd find something to talk about. Maybe she was way under-age. Maybe nothing.

"Hey. That's a famous place!" Maybe Julia was easily impressed. It was a piss hole. "How cool to work there! Lotsa famous people must hang out there."

Oh no. Wrong move. Anger flamed across Gina's face, old reactions flared up: Famous people! Just before Gina had come to see Francine, she found an acquaintance running the bar. Lethal Jack suggested that she fuck him for a place to stay, she suggested he consider how much longer he'd like to live, he shrugged, tapped a happy rhythm on the bar and told her she could crash in the basement if she'd swamp out the place.

Fuck famous people. Rip their eyes out eat their hearts spit them out—Gina stopped, she was a civilized woman. Her voice was level. Bland. "I'm the swamper. The after-hours janitor." Once, a long time and many shitty straight jobs ago, Gina tried to believe all work was equally valuable, equally squalid but what she learned was shame in pointless thankless menial jobs. "No famous people there when I'm there. Just their shit."

Julia fidgeted.

"Like cleaning up's all I'm fucking good for! Human excrement. Puke." Bitter. "Sorry." It wasn't an apology, just a word. "Famous don't count for much with me." She jammed out the door.

Julia stood there with a hurt look on her face.

Oleander tapped the cards back into a pile. "Julia. Don't get too taken with Frankie's old friend." Oleander put the cards down. "That girl is so busy trying to avoid what she can't avoid, she's dangerous."

Julia waited.

"And she's a danger to herself too." Oleander half-smiled. "But that is nothin new to her, so don't tell her, okay Julia?"

CHAPTER TEN

Julia rushed out after Gina to apologize for being thoughtless. Or something.

Too eager. Julia skidded to a halt as she opened the front door.

Parked on the street directly in front of Oleander's house was an old black Cadillac limo. A skinny brown dancer kind of guy was rummaging in the glove compartment. Nice ass. He backed out, papers in hand as Gina raced by. He showed his teeth, a flash of gold in a brief smile. "Hey."

Gina didn't even glance at him.

Ellis looked up the steps and saw a slender vision *all shining in white raiment*—even as he thought it, he recognized that was a cheesily poetic reaction. He shrugged at himself, took a breath. Low groovy voice: "Well, heyyyyy." He pushed his shades up onto his forehead. Gave her the professional once over, up and down, down and up. And then again as he took a step towards her. "You live here?"

The skinny guy was flirting with her. "Yeah." Julia was not giving him anything.

"Well, that's great. This right where I'm supposed to be, then."

"How you figure? This house for women only."

"Oh?" He wasn't deterred. Smiling. "Oh good. Sounds like my kind of house."

Julia stepped back, lifting her face to the light. "Oh. I dunno about that. Looks to me like you a dude." She watched Ellis raise his eyebrows with a classic *no shit* expression. "We got rules, you know? No men except in this store lobby part."

Grinning. "Seems to me that might be against the law."

Julia, smiling in spite of herself said, "What your business here anyway?" She looked closer at the fellow, skin the color and smoothness of polished teak, dark glasses, dark sweats, pouting mouth, red tennis shoes. She couldn't guess his age after all. He was either much younger than he seemed, or much older. Hah. Street smart? Nah. Men never measure up. She blocked the door, but not with any big determination. "Besides, we closed. Come back when the store open."

"I tha new chauffeur." Grand gesture at the limo. "And that my ride." Ellis made a flourish with his hands and a small bow, the red and black beads fell out of his sweats. "Name's Ellis, and I'm at your service."

"Oh." Julia stared at his beads. "You're one of us?"

He looked down at the beads splashed against his white tee shirt. "Oh. Yeah. Sure." He was, if nothing else, determined to stay on top of things.

"Well, come on in. Oleander will be glad to meet you."

"She will?"

Oleander came outside, stepped in front of Julia, hand out, saying, "Hold up there, youngblood." La Favorita's deep warning, coming from an invisible source behind Oleander's skirts, was ferocious.

Ellis stepped backwards as La Favorita growled forward. He saw that while she sounded dangerous, she was very small. He puffed himself up, carefully preening, posing. He didn't know what he expected when he drove up, from the looks of the dilapidated old pile he'd figured they'd be overjoyed to have his services. Maybe even give him a cozy berth. But Oleander seemed—seemed, ah, formidable. And her little doggy too.

Julia introduced him. "This here's Ellis. He goin to be our new chauffeur."

Oleander didn't even look at her, "Oh? What's the matter with our old chauffeur?"

"Who? Do we have one?"

"No, Julia, we don't." Gentle exasperation. "Because we don't need one." Oleander's eyes bored into the center of Ellis's chest, just about melting his red and black beads. "You are?"

Ellis wiped his hand on his pants, surprised at how sweaty his palms were, "Yes'm. Name's Ellis. Like it says there on the registration." Hand extended, palm up, to shake.

The pup pushed between them.

"Thank you, Rita. But I can handle this one."

La Favorita leveled the classic pit bull's gaze at Ellis, she moved one large puppy paw forward an inch: One false move, dude, your ass is mine.

"Good girl."

Ellis tried to outstare the pup. Like many others, he discovered that it's simply not possible, those steady almond eyes seemed to have no thought in them other than not-blinking. Or perhaps ripping your heart out. Hard to tell, the pup was still so young.

Oleander took his hand in hers, examined it. "Well. Well." The ability to easily intimidate was second nature to her. "Ellis, what really brings you to my door?" She didn't relinquish his hand for a few moments longer than seemed necessary. Long enough to confuse.

"Here's the registration papers, all made out. To you. And to me." He handed her the papers but kept the medallion in his pocket. "Straight up legal."

She showed exactly no reaction as she read through the document. "You do know what this is about, don't you?"

Ellis was feeling more than a little deflated. "Old guy, lives a couple miles south, out in the warehouse district?" Pause. He remembered that the old demon had told Ellis not to mention him. He remembered that the bastid had not told him one word, not one word, about the formidable Oleander or what he would encounter when he brought the limo to her. He did say she was an old friend. Or something. Fuck the old demon anyway. "Well. He knows you! Sent me all the damn way up here to bring back your limo." He struggled against the tide of Oleander's indifference. "Said he just moved up here from somewheres else?" Going down for the third and final time: "Says he owes you? Mean old sonofabitch?"

Oleander tipped her head to one side. Nothing was supposed to surprise her. Nothing ever did. Or at least that was the original deal she cut with the universe those many scary years ago when she was simply running and hiding, hardly living. She didn't quite know how to react, she assumed that what she was feeling was, in fact, surprise. She didn't like it. She didn't like him. She decided not to let him out of her sight.

"Well, come in, Ellis The Chauffeur." She did a gliding stroll into the lobby and over to the bar. "Julia? Would you get Ellis some coffee, please?" Dropped the papers on the bar counter.

"Oh, sure." Julia glanced at Ellis again. The measuring tools she'd used in her life before moving into Oleander's house—how much would they pay and were they vicious—perhaps weren't appropriate to this guy. "What you take in your coffee?" The fellow hadda Cadillac so he hadda be worth something.

"Nothing. Thanks." Ellis knuckle-tapped carefully on the doorjamb. Stepped inside, grabbed the tiny cup of syrupy black goo from Julia, squeezed it, burned his fingers. His flirtatious smile wobbled.

"Are you the limo's only driver?"

"Yes, ma'am."

"And since you're the only driver of that vehicle, are you also responsible for maintenance, insurance, gas and speeding tickets? Or did you think I would handle all that?" Sword point right at the base of the throat. Oleander debated about shoving it right through his stupid neck. She kept her face bland as she thought about his words 'old dude says he owes you'. Bloody hell.

"Um." Ellis coughed on his coffee. He'd never even thought of that. What is it with all these people? Suspicious. Rampant paranoia. For no reason. Here he was offering a great service—well, he didn't know exactly what he was actually offering but it should have seemed to them like a great thing. Shit. "Well." He could feel Julia's speculating gaze. He swallowed again, the coffee burned all the way down. His other hand went, all unconscious, to his chest, where the strand of black and red beads the old man flipped over his head seemed to burn as fiercely as the coffee. He wondered what they signified to these strange women. "This old man, he's like my godfather, you know? He tries to teach me a whole lot of things. He finally says, like, I don't learn so good from him and that I should go see you and help you out and you'll teach me more what I need to know." It started out pretty good but wobbled off into the upper registers near the end.

Silent, Oleander watched him.

Ellis shifted his weight, left right left, dancing like the old man taught him. He wanted to get out of there. Wondered, not for the last time, what the hell he thought he was doing. He said, "I figured you'd understand and straighten it all out for me."

Oleander smiled. She'd straighten it out alright. Send this demon spawn right back to one of the lesser hells that had burped him into her life. "Julia, you've got dinner to serve. Yes?"

Sorry to leave the room, Julia nodded, winked at Ellis and scrammed.

"Ellis. You're not goin to tell me what game you're playin, are you?" She paced away from him so she wouldn't have to see him blather some silly response. With her back to him she said, "You know this old man's name? No?" She turned again and stepped up to him. "It's always better to have the viper close, isn't it?" He leaned back and away, his eyes big. "Where I can watch you. Rather than leave you loose somewhere in my garden."

Ellis said, "Yes'm. I'm not no snake though."

"We'll see. You don't go anywhere in this building but this lobby. There's a loo around back off the alley where you can wash up. You're responsible for your chariot out there—and you will be respectful to everyone here." She glared at him. "Do you understand me?

"Yes'm." He stepped back a pace. "Thank you ma'am." He tottered out the door staring fixedly at his limo, not daring to breathe. Wondering what he was thanking her for anyway.

.

CHAPTER ELEVEN

Lethal Jack said, "I dunno. I don't think you should crash in the store room. Cold down there. Crawly things. You better come on home with me after all."

"No way." Gina glared at him, her eyes flat and narrow.

Jack said, "Didn't think you would, oh well." He shrugged and wiped the bar down, "I just don't know that ten bucks an hour, four hours a night will pay for what you need? Besides, I like this place kept real clean, yunno?" He walked over to pop the pinball machine into action. "Sparkling."

"Yeah right, Jack. I know." Gina scratched her cheek so he couldn't see her mouth curl down. "You really got a problem with me crashin in the basement now?"

"Nah. I guess not. Just don't put your gear in anyone's way. Yunno."

"Yeah right, Jack." She ducked down the stairs. Flicked the light on, pushed and pulled at some stinky piles of junk to make a space for the toolbox she'd just picked up. She was moving a carton of twenty year old register receipts, she figured the old bastard was planning to re-date them for the IRS, when she whistled in surprise. A rotting cardboard box filled with something that clinked and sparkled: pieces of a filthy broken crystal chandelier. *Mm-hm, mm-hm, and that's the way she likes it.* She occupied herself for about fifteen minutes—it would have taken less time if her body hadn't been so damn stiff and creaky. If she hadn't been afraid Jack would catch her. If she had a decent light to work by. Even so, the thing wasn't in such bad shape, the final loose pieces could be attached on later. It looked pretty damn impressive to Gina.

She hoped Oleander would find it equally fine. Let her pay for a bed with a crystal chandelier. Who could refuse? So, when Lethal Jack actually decided to push their arrangement beyond Gina's limits—she figured it was only a matter of time, or booze—she'd cruise out of this piss hole, and maybe by then Oleander would be, ah, bribed enough to let her crash for awhile in her big old crazy girls' rooming house. Would that be an improvement? Gina didn't know. She wasn't shaving her head to find out.

Gina piled her chandelier in a canvas sack, poked her head up from the basement. Jack was involved, arms on the bar, chin tucked in, muttering out the side of his mouth to a big sloppy ungraceful man in a five hundred dollar overcoat. Famous person number one for ya, Julia.

No one noticed the little janitor scurrying out of the bar.

Ellis climbed out the passenger's side of a big black Caddy just as Gina approached Oleander's. She shifted the sack to her right side, checked out the skinny dude—one false move and she'd smash his face in with it. Better: She'd sell it to him. Thirty, forty dollars. Get something else for Oleander.

"Looks like you could use some help with that."

Gina glared, tried to catch her breath. After all, she stole the damn chandelier by herself. She snapped, "Well then, open the damn door up there for me."

The girl was funny. "You live here, too? Maybe I oughta introduce m'self. M'name's Ellis. This my ride. Numbah twenny one. And I'm tha official chauffeur for this here establishment. Even if I'm not allowed past the stupid lobby. You need a ride, just ask for me." Thumb to chest. Then he held his hand out to her, palm up.

For a long minute Gina ignored him, after all she was holding a forty pound chandelier she'd just carried for blocks. At last she shifted it around ("Please God, don't let me drop it.") and gripped his hand. They shook. Wary and solemn.

"You needa be careful, walking around alone at night. People around here think they slick. They about as slick as rubba-cement in a tube of KY jelly."

Gina shrugged. "People everywhere think they slick. But," sarcastic, "I'll keep the warning in mind." She pointed to her chandelier. It chinked in its sack. A cosmopolitan sound. "So. An antique chandelier, worth hundreds of dollars. You wanna buy it? Sixty dollars? A deal, cheap, just for you?"

He laughed. "Thanks. I'll get the door for you."

"Three blocks earlier it woulda bin cheaper, but."

"Another time. Another light fixture."

"It's real crystal." She looked at him. No sale. "Oh hell, get the door." They entered the lobby together. Gina pointed at the light bulb swaying from the center of the room, "It'll look real fine right there." She lifted her shoulders, rolled them like a boxer getting ready to go a couple rounds. Ladders again. She hoped her luck with the temperamental things had changed. "Take me only a little while to put it up there if I hadda ladder. You got a ladder in that long car of yours?"

"No. But I bet there's one around here somewhere. It's just that I can't go looking for it. Out of bounds, you know?"

"I'll keep that in mind." Her mind was getting full, what with the young stud's ideas and all the chandelier parts. She felt his eyes on her back as she put the awkward tinkling sack on the floor, she looked around for Oleander, she fussed with her present, unhappy. The dude stood there as if he belonged there and she didn't. "Um."

Julia came into the lobby, scrutinized the two of them, mumbled, "Oh. Hi," and backed into the kitchen.

They both admired the good long lean look of her as she disappeared. Then glared at each other.

Oleander made her entrance. She seemed taller than she had before. Taller and somehow dangerous. Her chin pointed at the sack. "For me, this time?"

Gina flushed at the sound of her voice—damn the woman anyway—fished in the sack, pulled a rope of crystals out. It was twisted, battered and filthy. She swore to herself. How come these things always seemed like such a good idea until the presentation? She said, "Doesn't look like much right now, but I can make it grand." She ducked her head. Oleander probably had people bringing her crystal chandeliers all the time. "If the ceiling and wiring up there's adequate, I can hang it for you," Gina fumbled in her pockets for the six-inch drops that went on the corners, "and attach these." Like a little kid. "I thought it'd suit this room?"

"Thank you. It will be lovely." Staring at the ceiling as if imagining just how lovely it would be.

Ellis edged toward the kitchen and Julia.

COME TO ME

"Good night, Ellis. If we need you we'll call."

Gina looked back and forth between the two of them. "Right. Maybe I'll go up and see how Frankie's doin?"

Oleander compressed her wide mouth against a smile, something funny about Gina. Guileless? Not hardly. "It's late, but Francine doesn't sleep much at night anyway. I'll ring her bell." She turned toward the back of the counter. "You, young man, aren't going in that kitchen so quit edging toward the door." She nodded to Gina, "Go on up, honey. The lady expecting you."

"Oh. Right. Good. I'll check the wiring and all in the morning?"

Oleander didn't answer. Gina forced herself not to run up the stairs.

CHAPTER TWELVE

After the deep warm red of the lobby the street was bleached, the white glare of the streetlights sucked all color out of everything. The air was heavy, cold, moving into the corners and freezing them solid. Ellis sat on the fender of his limo, shivering and smoking. He watched Gina trudge down the steps. "Hey, girl, you get your light fixture hung up widdout me?"

"What you doin still out here? It's one in the morning." She stared at him like a pointer, focused on his cigarette. "It's cold. You got another one of those?"

Grouchy. "I'm on call. I could be needed at any moment." He pointed to the cell phone in his pocket. Pulled out the pack of cigarettes. "That's me. Ready. Willing. And able." He frowned, held out the pack to Gina. "Like she couldn't just come to the door, you know?"

Gina took two cigarettes, nodding her thanks, putting one carefully behind her ear for laters. "What you do then, Ellis? Hang around here all night waiting for a call?"

Decision. "Nah. Come on, I'll give ya a lift. Where ya wanta go?" He opened the door. Talking to hear the sweet sound of his own voice. She didn't move to get in. "No? What'sa matter? You prejudice?" Grin. He had the ability to charm anyone. Everyone. Except Oleander. Nah. He charmed her, yes he did. He remembered the earlier grueling scene with Oleander as a-piece-a-cake, he remembered that he'd completely overwhelmed the lady. A lot of people remember their encounters with Oleander wrong. She liked it that way.

Ellis held the door open for Gina, proud that he was going to give his first limo customer a ride.

Gina didn't get in. She said, "Prejudice? Against you? Nah." Silly boy.

Nodding his head. Up down. Once. "Good. So come on. Try me, you'll like me!"

Mocking. "Oh Ellis, you have no idea." He probably had too many ideas. "Listen Ellis, I'd love to stay and talk to you but I gotta go grovel at my stupid job." Her voice lifted with all the ardor of a kitchen table preacher. "Work is uplifting. Work builds self-confidence. Self. Reliance. Self. Satisfaction."

"Yeah right. For the people who make you do the work."

Gina stuck her tongue in her cheek, ran it along her teeth thinking maybe she'd found a kindred work-hating spirit. "Mmhm. Now, that's the truth."

Oleander popped her head out the door: "Yo. Ellis. You wanta come up here a minute, please?"

Gina thought his boss was a lot more attractive than hers. "Hah. She caught you slacking off."

Oleander looked at Ellis, but seemed to include both of them as she spoke. "Watch yourself around Julia. She's preparing for her initiation." She paused. "That means she is in a state of ritual purity." One eyebrow arched up.

Gina thought that sounded stupid. Or kinky. Ellis didn't look like he had any better understanding of ritual purity than she did. Gina backed away, not touching that conversation. Nope. Bald girls in filthy white skirts, reinstalling virginity. Like the first go-round, maybe it hadn't been taken? "Ritual purity. Right." Gina nodded, her head bobbing with lack of sincerity. "Gotcha. I'm outta here."

As she backed away, Gina thought that her legal gig cleaning toilets and swabbing crapped up bar floors would make ritual purity sort of irrelevant. Straight jobs were always stupid, this one was just more awful than most. Less pure. There was so much more—purity—in simple fucking thievery. Jeez. Compare the two: toilet bowls and cash registers. She looked back over her shoulder to see Ellis frozen on the steps, his mouth half-open as if there were words in there but none would hop on out. Purity? What the hell?

Oleander said, "Initiation is a step towards grace." She stared at him. "Oh Ellis, close your mouth. Initiation is something, even though you carry those beads, you seem to know nothing about. Maybe it's time to start your own year of initiation? How willing are you to earn the right to wear those beads?" She pointed at his heart.

Ellis looked down at his chest, the red and black beads, then at her finger.

"I'll give you something easy, Ellis Tha Chauffeur. How long does it take for you to get from here to the airport? What is the fastest route at this time of the night? During the morning rush hour? At five o'clock in the evening? At nine, ten, eleven o'clock at night? Where is the nearest hospital? Night vet? Drug store? Hardware? Organic food store? Botanica?"

"What?" Ellis said it again, "What?"

Implacable. "Please," Oleander could afford to be polite, "Please have the answers for me by tomorrow, noon."

Ellis backed away, a slight frown between his eyes. He thought longingly of his old life where he was mostly loaded a lot and fell down a lot and got beat up sometimes and maybe he did some things which may have been horrible but since he didn't remember them so good, life back then was easy. Sort of a snooze. He remembered it fondly. Anyway, the people he was encountering recently were all mad. Timed trips around the city? Preparation for initiation? My sweet ass. And there was no fuckin way to time anything at five in the evening before noon tomorrow. Nuts. The whole lot of them. Nuts. "Sure. Sure thing, Oleander. I'll do it right now. Yeah."

Driving back towards the old man's shack—which he'd said he was vacating, but where else would he be anyway—Ellis made up his mind to get some answers. The old man never gave him any answers, just this upside down inside out drunken revel song and dance shit. Not good enough. He took the black and red necklace off his neck and flipped it over the mirror. There.

He came to a four way stop, so he stopped. There were no cars at the other stop signs but he stayed stopped. He sat there in his big ol black Cadillac and felt a strong desire for a cigar. For a little rum.

Tap. Tap. Tap. Tap tap tap. Tap—

"Okay! Okay! Stop with the scary noises already." He got out of his cab, looking tough, he was a tough dude and he was ready. Ready to the left, nothing. Ready to the right, nothing.

Ellis jumped six feet in the air when he saw the skeleton on the hood of his Caddy. "Shit!"

The skeleton slid off, stood tall, and then taller, he wore a very nicely tailored tuxedo, a little old fashioned but it had been quite elegant in its day. Or night. "Hello?" The voice was low and mellow. Cultured. It sounded like one of the uncles Ellis had loved when he was little—tired and generous, whispering of memories.

Ellis pushed his face forward, said, "Hello?"

"I've got a cigar someone left for me, but no light. Have you a light?"

Ellis was no professional when it came to dealing with ghosts, but he'd learned enough to know that it was wisdom to either run screaming bloody murder or to be very polite. "Certainly." His hand shook when he held out the lighter but he was determined to be debonair. "Here you go, sir."

In the flame the face wasn't skeletal, just thin. A tall thin ebony man who needed a light for his cigar. That's all. Ellis relaxed a bit.

"You don't have any rummmm, do you?"

The sweat which had begun to dry poured forth again. Ellis backed around the car, something racketing around his brain reminded him that the common wisdom was 'don't turn your back on them'. He said, "In the glove box. I'll get it." The whatever/whoever was standing too near, standing everywhere so Ellis couldn't just pop in the car and peel out of there. He got out the rum. *You pays your nickel, you takes your ride.*

"While you're at it, please get me those beads off the mirror. I need to look at them."

"Certainly, sir." *Aaaaugh. Take the damn things they're yours, oh anything you want sir please just don't kill me, I have a wife and three little children at home.* Grabbing his courage in his hands along with the rum and the beads—his hands were full although the courage didn't really take up much space—he handed the man the beads, opened the rum. The courage dribbled onto the pavement.

The man took a deep drag off the cigar, his deep chanting filled the sky with smoke, the sound hiding the waning moon,

"Red for the blood in your veins, for the blood that has been spilled to feed the black black earth, the treasures of the night, the things we hold dear and the things we will lose, the noose that binds day into night, spins wrong into right." One thin hand clicked the circle of beads like a rosary, the other spun the red cigar tip in front of Ellis's eyes.

There was great laughter then. And a pounding as if huge drums were resonating in the sky. The wind came up and blew the two of them around and around.

In the lonely silence that followed Ellis bent to retrieve the empty rum bottle, turned bending again to pick up the stub of the cigar, he slipped the paper ring onto his finger, then he bowed down to the other two empty corners of the crossroads. With odd jerky motions he climbed back in his cab. "What the hell?" He touched the beads at his throat.

He drove back to Oleander's place pulling back up in front as if he'd never gone anywhere.

The lights were still on in the lobby. He watched Oleander shut the place down for the night. The lights went off. He sat behind the wheel of his car staring straight ahead.

Oleander checked the room key list, everyone was home. Followed by La Favorita, she double-locked the doors, dimmed the light, thought how nice the chandelier might look, shook her head and surveyed the street. Ellis was in his limo, sitting still as a cadaver. Good.

Leaving Rita on guard, Oleander slipped once again into her private altar room.

She fed her Eleggua friend by the door some rum and lit a small sweet cigar, she glared at him and said, "You sure do like to mix it up, don't you?"

Fifteen minutes earlier she'd gotten a call from Raymond, wanting to come over again, bring her some money, wanting to see her, wanting to thank her, wanting wanting. The upshot was that he seemed to believe that in spite of her warnings, his proverbial ship was about to come in. His voice bellowed over the phone, "Money!" he howled. "Monnnney!" He was so full of himself he gave her the flight number, time and the name of his courier—James Collier. Still trying to rope her into the deal.

She'd stopped him, "Oh Raymond, you remember what I told you? This whole thing stinks."

He'd chuckled, "We shall see. We shall see. James hasn't failed me yet." He hung up with a smug belch.

She wrote the flight number down. And "James Collier". She slipped the paper under the little cement head of her Eleggua in her secret room, muttering, "Hey Eleggua! You're already involved in this so you sit on it tonight and give me the best advice." She took a quick hit off the cigar, blew the smoke directly at Eleggua, "The best advice for me, for my house, for my loved ones so we can live well." This was an old threat, but it always worked, "And make good and sure we continue to have the health, freedom, time and money to share our good fortune with you." As she was leaving she muttered to Eleggua, "I don't need allegories or riddles. I need answers."

When Oleander reappeared La Favorita bounded around the room hunting spiders. And teasing ghosts. That was part of her job. They went through the kitchen, out the back door, Rita pee'ed, they came back in, Oleander triple-locked the back door. They went up to bed.

Next day, after racing to the airport through rush hour traffic, ramming the car through every gear, Ellis's cell phone rang. No surprise, it was the old man. Ellis said, "Hey. Oleander's one tough piece of work." His voice slid higher, a teenage whine, "She expect me to pay for everything."

The old bastard chuckled. "Don't worry. I got a job for you. Pay ya good for it. Cover all your bills. Airport pickup, Friday night midnight. A white man, tall, thin, probably have lots of luggage. Name James Collier. I tell yas more when ya come by. Same place as before but don't go inside." The old man breathed for awhile, waiting for Ellis to say something. "I'll meet ya at the gate. Even have some money for you then. Pay your gas and all."

And the secretive old fart hung up.

Ellis called him back, "Gimme the fuckin flight number. The airline. Somethin so I can find the dude. Jeez."

The demon cackled. "Flight 1783 from Miami. Midnight. He has a crate—grab that. I want it." The phone went silent. Ellis glared at it.

When he got back to Oleander's, a tall skinny woman was sitting on the steps with Julia. They both stood up. The woman standing at least a foot taller than Julia was rather beautiful, in a been-out-in-the-weather too long kind of way. "Hey, hey."

"Hey, yourself. You know how long it takes to get to the hospital from here?"

"Nope. But if that's where you need to go—" He smiled, mirror shades flashing in the sun, "We about to find out."

The women climbed in the back seat, made appreciative noises, introductions, "Frankie, this is Ellis. Ellis, Frankie. She's my older sister." Ellis looked in his rearview, no way they were related, one was junky chalk white, the other was tropical dream cream. He didn't say a word.

"Hey, there's no button back here for the windows? Roll the windows down?"

He said, "Whole point of riding in a limo is that no one can see you. You are secrets on the move. Special folks, different, invisible—privileged. If ya rolls the windows down everyone can see you."

"But that's just it. I want everyone to see me ridin inna long black Cad-il-lac."

Grumbling, Ellis obliged. People just didn't get the mystery of his cab. The basic magic of the machine. But he was obliging. Figured that's what a real limo driver would be. Obliging. He didn't much like the sound of the word so he rolled the windows back up. They were quiet in the back seat except to give him directions.

"This is it." Frankie's voice was strong, almost virile, certainly nothing he expected from her fragile appearance. "Please don't wait. But if you can, come back in about an hour? We'll only be about that long, I think."

"Sure thing. Then we'll go for some coffee?"

"We'll see."

"Oh yes! That would be great! Maybe we can go to the Lizard and see if Gina's there?"

Frankie pressed her lips together. So that's where Gina was hanging out. "We'll see."

Ellis drove off whistling. It had taken him fifteen minutes to get to the hospital, twelve to get back to Oleander's place. It would probably be about a half hour south to the old man's shed—good to know even if Oleander hadn't asked him about that. He wasn't sure but it was maybe forty fifty minutes to the airport. And the dude he would pick up there. Shit. He didn't understand. He figured Oleander would let him in on it one of these days. Or she wouldn't. Because it was all bullshit. She could take that initiation shit she'd talked about and shove it.

When Ellis entered the lobby, Oleander was involved with a couple women who seemed to want to have babies. Or not have babies. Or get money out of some poor dude because they were or were not going to have his/or not his/child. Ellis sat on the couch trying to look as if he wasn't listening.

They moved to the far end of the bar. A dozen women passed through the lobby, ethereal and efficient. The smells of cooking mixed with the incense in the lobby. It was altogether sort of comfortable. Ellis relaxed. Like he was at a weird movie maybe.

The customers eventually left happy, clutching paper bags filled with candles and herbs and powders and Ellis couldn't see what all else. He was thinking that Oleander had herself a good little scam going.

Oleander shut down her little shop and grabbed her purse, ready to go on some secret errand of her own. "Did you find out what I asked you?"

He reported. "Can't get you the times for later in the day because it hasn't gotten later in the day yet. You want to go somewheres?"

"No place I need you for, but thanks." She paused by the doors. "But since you're Tha Chauffeur, I do have a job for you. Friday night I want you to meet a plane coming in from Miami. Pick up a man. Take him where he wants to go. Notice everything about him and come back here right away, no matter how late. Tell me everything you find out." Her eyes were hot. He got the feeling she could peel his skin off, scouring his very bones to find out what it was he knew. Or didn't know. He thought maybe dealing with the Old Man was easier.

"What man? There millions of em." Friday night. This was not coincidence. Ellis felt the heat go right to the base of his spine and coagulate into ice. He felt like his breath had been stolen. His voice hit the higher ranges by the end of the sentence, "How can I find out anything if I don't know who I'm supposed to find?" He wasn't whining but he bobbed around as fast as his confused mind could manage.

Soft. "There's only one American Airlines flight coming from Miami Friday midnight."

"Great." Ellis grumbled, "Two-Three hundred people."

"Eighty seven."

"Eighty seven?" He waited, but she wasn't giving anything up. Finally, he said, "How'm I s'posed to know who to pick up? I'll get the wrong guy, find out all sorts of deep secrets, you'll tell me I jammed up the wrong jerk?"

"You told me you're the expert." Looking at him out of the side of her eyes. Checking her watch. "Oh come on, Ellis. He'll have a lot of baggage tagged with 'Brasil'. Probably looking shifty." Hand flip. She fed him a little more from the quick vision she'd gotten when she laid out the cards for Raymond. "Tall. Pale. Probably thin and twitchy."

"From Miami? From Brazil? Which is it?" Choking. Thinking fast. "Tall and twitchy? Hey. Everyone in the airport is twitchy. What? He's some Samba guy? The guy's a coffee baron humping his own beans? Come on, Oleander, what he got that's such a damn big deal?"

"You will find out." Implacable. "You're the expert finder."

"When I got something to work with."

She turned away. "You will find the guy. Name's James. Take him where he wants to go. Then we both know what so special about him."

Imitating. "Then we both know." Getting up. Brushing down his pants. "What if I can't find him? What if I don't give a damn?"

La Favorita popped out from behind the bar, dove for his ankle. Ellis danced away.

"You said you can find fish in a storm ditch. Think of this as proving your point."

Ellis spread his hands in exasperation. La Favorita followed him to the door, growling. He considered a swift well-placed kick. The sly puppy sat down then, pink tongue hanging out of its mouth, and yawned. Teeth like a crocodile, jaws like grim death. Her little eyes glinted at him. He decided he'd be better off making friends. "Okay. Later. I got to go pick up Julia and that long drinkawater. We're going out for coffee." He raised his eyebrows, carefully, suddenly aware of a newer frost in the air.

"Ellis, if you want to find out things about this house, you would do best to ask me."

"Uh, sure thing, Oleander." Not likely, you secretive bitch.

"Good." You are a sly little bastard.

Ellis gunned his limo back to the hospital, he'd pry some information out of the other two women or he wasn't the clever dude he knew he was.

"So," he said as Frankie and Julia climbed in, "Ready for some coffee?"

"Not today. Doctors and hospitals just seem to take it out of me. Please just bring us back to the house."

Ellis drove and thought, both at top speed. When he let them out, he called to Julia, "Maybe you have time for some coffee?"

"Sure."

Well there. Julia liked him even if everyone else thought he was, thought he was—well whatever they thought it seemed like it didn't matter to Julia.

"Sure. Come on in and we'll talk here."

It wouldn't be private but it got him back in that weird house. Legit. Ellis walked ahead of both of them, cool and in charge. He opened the door for the ladies.

Inside, after Frankie tottered up the stairs, tiny cup of black goo in his hand he began his pitch. "Interestin buncha women livin here, hey. What's the story with all of you?"

Julia was very proud of all her friends and happily told him every funny story she could think of. Leaning forward, beautiful eyes glowing, she regaled him with tales she'd heard about Frankie and Gina in the days before they split, about Thea and Queenie and their convoluted lives in and out of prison.

About Rhea who had wanted to be a professional boxer, and all the rest of them. But no information, nothing about Oleander. Nothing about herself.

CHAPTER THIRTEEN

The stranger's name was James Collier. He was pale and slender, he had a deceptively droopy posture, his small eyes were set far apart, his peripheral vision therefore, was excellent. A crooked nose, a long jaw, a smile disarming and lopsided. He was blessed with a sharp mind, a cutting wit, and he had never developed any sympathy for the general run of humanity. He was like a Cardinal in the Church, a pampered diplomat—he was a special kind of merchant.

James had to let a couple of the porters help with his multitude of packages, suitcases and the crate. A mother snake with her eggs, he propelled one hand truck himself and watched the porter drive a top-heavy cart through the terminal to the curb. James congratulated himself on his foresight, planning, cleverness. His papers had been in order, colorful stampings and pompous phrasings all too official and impressive for anyone to question, so he'd slipped his packages, containing several months of careful purchases adding up to a large taxable sum, past the vigilant troops of the US Customs with a minimum payment and examination. After all, it wasn't drugs.

He was well pleased, he timed his return exactly when his condom supply ran out. Besides, he picked up some good pieces along with the usual array of ethno-junk. His best find was the statue, a representation of some secret Brazilian deity. James didn't know the actual name of the goddess, the name he got from checking with his sources was something silly like Bombadier, but since no one up here knew anything about her anyway, he could call it anything he wanted. The craftsmanship was of the highest quality, its beauty was astonishing—if you liked sexy gold statues. After he added hints of blood and bondage, it'd be worth a small fortune.

There were several other smaller obscure idols in his luggage, he hadn't decided which ones he would flog off to Raymond, if he would sell them as a set, or separately. He didn't know if he'd work out of the hotel or find his own display space. The sale of some of the better pieces, he decided, would be by sealed bid. People liked to believe they were members of an elite bunch. As they would be, if they could pay his prices.

The moment James hit the curb a young black man rolled up in a dark limo. The fellow hopped out with a little sign: JAMES COLLIER. James waved him over thinking that Raymond was on the job. Good man, Raymond. Greedy, but this was a generous gesture.

"Hey. James? Your chariot awaits." Between Oleander and the old man he had about half the information he needed: James Collier, nick the big crate, take him where he wanted to go, call the old bastard, tell Oleander. A completely crap set up. Like everything else.

James saw the fortuitous arrival of perfect transportation as his good luck continuing to smile upon him. "Many thanks." Before he let Ellis touch any of his luggage he inquired, "Will a twenty get me to the center of town?"

"Get ya where ever ya wanta go, James. Unless you want to go further than that. Then it'll maybe cost ya more." *Ha-ha*. Ellis kept an expression of fatuous good humor on his face as James pushed him out of the way so he could handle the largest crate, placing it himself, too carefully, on the back seat.

The man watched Ellis load the rest of it into the trunk, counting and fussing.

"It'll all be fine, sir. This machine is de-signed to give the smoothest ride no matter where anything is." Ellis got a sharp look from the man then, gave him a hard moment of doubt, he licked his lips steadied his voice, "Looks to me like you've got some things here that are pret-ty important." He insinuated that his passenger was himself pret-ty important.

James flopped in the front passenger seat. He held his hands open, thumbs touching to form a square. Sincere. Pedantic. Going to let this poor cabbie in on some of the important things he'd learned in the course of his important life. "Arriving is only part of the pleasure. It is the journey itself which is the key to ultimate satisfaction."

Patronizing bastard. Arrogant creep. Cultural pilferer. *Yaaaargh*. Ellis wondered why people squinched up their mouths like that when they talked, why they said such obvious things with such slurping glee, as if they were the only ones who thought at all. Mostly he wondered what was in the important-untouchable crate in the backseat. Guns? Dope? Either one was common, easy and boring. The market for them was always there, always unpleasant. The old demon probably sold all kinds of contraband.

Ellis wondered if he was being set up. Made no sense, all this trouble just to slam him around. Of course the people he was dealing with were so utterly nuts, anything was possible. Ellis smiled as he cruised through the post-midnight city, headlights yellow blots against the heavy darkness. Empty lots around the airport gave way to factories, more freeways. The lights of the city were pale in the distance. He offered his passenger a choice of thermoses and bottles: "Hot coffee? Black tea? Scotch? Ice tea?"

The man went first for the coffee. Then the Scotch.

"So. Have a good trip?" Ellis was careful not to seem too interested.

James puffed his cheeks out with satisfaction. "Yes. Yes." Counting profit, counting impressions, discounting the taxi driver. Sucking down his Scotch.

"Glad to be back though, huh?" Ellis steered carefully into a sleazy section of town; whatever was on the backseat was HIS, he just hadn't secured it yet. "Which hotel?"

"Ah. The Criterion. You know where it is?" James slumped back in the seat, exhaustion overtaking him.

"Sure." A glance at his tired passenger made Ellis think the man wouldn't be too great a challenge. With a flourish Ellis turned the meter off at eighteen fifty, "Ways to go yet."

James started to express gratitude when a look of acute pain, maybe panic, crossed his face. He curled over, groaning. Embarrassed. "I don't believe I will make it to the hotel without... ah, without—Where's the first bathroom, eh?"

Oh, great blessings from above bestowed on us ungrateful sinners. He heard his mother's Catholic voice singing in his head. Then he remembered the old demon and his set of spirits and hummed a little thank you to them: Oh, praises and rum shall be given unto the mighty Eshuas in whom all goodnesses abound. In case any of them might be taking an interest in what he had in mind.

He knew he couldn't depend solely on the gods of his ancestors, so Ellis had dosed the coffee, the Scotch, the teas with MiraLax, just in case the gods were busy elsewhere, or didn't perhaps approve, he'd made certain he'd have a chance at the big crate. He'd do all right. "Oh dear, sir. This isn't the neighborhood for casual pissing."

James groaned.

"But if you can hold on there's a bar three blocks up?"

"Go! Go!"

James dove out the door as the limo coasted to the curb, Ellis said, "Hey, James. This a no parking zone. I'ma have to move."

James hollered, as he grabbed the bar door, "Drive around the damn block then."

Ellis drove. Just like the man ordered.

In certain circles, at one time, before Ellis became a total drunken loss as a human being, he had been famous for his uncanny ability to make the best of circumstances. James didn't know that. In any case, it wouldn't have done James much good since he was shitting his brains out in the filthy john of a filthy bar.

Ellis dusted off and revived his famous versatility; the unusual compartments under the back seat, along with a plethora of scrap metal piled behind a service station made his task simple. And quick.

He pulled the crate onto the midnight concrete, pried open the lid, out came the whatever-the-hell-it-was that was so important—an unwieldy thing in a padded sack—into the crate went a rusty cam shaft and some bolts that looked like they came from some bridge or something, who knows, he didn't care, *pafpaf* the crate was nailed shut. The whatever-it-was/oh man he didn't have time to even peek at it/went into the compartment under the back seat where it fit like the compartment was made for it, now wasn't that interesting/no nothing was interesting except getting back on the damn road.

James was just emerging from the bar as Ellis drove up, smooth, smiling and Johnny-on-the-spot.

James didn't talk much for the rest of the ride, which was short. He also didn't tip Ellis. But Ellis, good hearted little black cabbie that he was, didn't seem too put out about it. Touched his forehead and wished sir a pleasant stay in the city.

Sir just growled, clutched his groin and directed the hotel bellhop to bring all his luggage up to his room.

CHAPTER FOURTEEN

The panting bellhop needed the largest trolley to bring all of James's luggage and miscellaneous packages up. James lay on the bed in a pool of sweat. Some left-over tropical fever. The price of adventure.

Soon as the man left, James rolled over and drank from the fifth of Scotch he'd grabbed from the limo. He clawed his way to an upright position, poured a good shot down his throat. Waited for the warning rumbles in his stomach. Nothing. Good. Whatever had hit him in the cab had been temporary.

He looked around the room for something with which to pry the crate open. He ripped the nail on his middle finger in a useless frenzied scrabbling at the boards. He stared impotently as a little blood dripped on the carpet. He stuck it in his mouth then finally wrapped his finger in toilet paper. *Wounded in pursuit of art.* The frustration prompted him to add another couple thousand dollars to the price of his goods. He started to flop back onto the bed but his intestines forced him into the bathroom. Where he remained for the rest of the night. Staring at his slightly bloody finger. Plotting revenge. He blamed Raymond.

In the morning he called the front desk to bring him a tool. A long bladed tool. A sword? Pliers? Hammer? Saw? "For Christsake! I need to open a crate. You must have something!"

It was a first class hotel. A snobby young man in funereal clothing brought him a crow bar and left James to his pleasure.

James pried the crate open. "Oh my Gawd! It broke!" He grabbed at his chest, fearing a heart attack. He squeezed his head, stopping an explosion. He flung all the metal parts and rubbish in the crate out onto the floor. He poked his fingers in every crack. He made a strange *woe-oh-woe* noise the whole time.

This part of his reaction ended with him careening around the room smashing into things and muttering multisyllabic curses. He grabbed the bottle of scotch and rushed to the bathroom. He passed out.

He woke up with an ache in his jaws, his mouth tasted like a sneaker full of shit.

He checked in all the other packages: no statue. The other trinkets he brought back did not please him any longer.

He called room service.

Room service arrived, wrinkled its snooty butler's nose, with great dignity intoned, "Most likely there will be a surcharge for the damage."

"Damage? Damage?" James turned the icy blades of his eyes on the man. "I've just discovered that an extremely valuable piece of art has been stolen and you have the nerve to stand there yelping about damage?"

"I never yelp, sir. Would you like your coffee in a cup or should I simply pour it on the floor?"

James's proverbial good luck, the luck that travels with every rich and successful collector of *objets d'art* may have begun to turn. The turning however was slow, and not recognized in its entirety.

James heard phantom aristo voices: *Sooo hard to get good help these days.* "Get the hell out of here."

James marshaled the facts: he couldn't know if the statue actually made it out of Brazil, but he had to assume it did, else it was lost to him forever. The plane change at Miami—well it might have been stolen there. Miami was a cesspit. He began shallow breathing again. So, any one could have taken it at any time when it wasn't under his direct care. That didn't narrow the field. Worse: He couldn't go to the police since he never actually declared it, his situation would go from delicate to criminal.

He needed to call fucking Raymond anyway, he riffled through his address book, looking for the number. A sexy gold statue had an undeniable allure, but Raymond would be interested in the rest of the stuff too. The man had no discernment.

He paused in his pacing. First he must assert his right to the statue if it hit the local market. With careful maneuvering Raymond might be able to track it—the man was connected to every thief in the city. On the whole damn west coast. If it was somewhere on the west coast, James drank some more Scotch and dialed Raymond's number, he would find it.

CHAPTER FIFTEEN

"Look, Frankie. I don't know how to tell you this but your Gypsy Queen from Abilene is putting you on with this Pomba the Great Goddess business. She made it all up." Gina had gone to the library and looked up "POMBA" on the internet, just to see who was who or what was what; she came up with dozens and dozens of hits; at first she'd figured Frankie's wild goddess thing might be legit, until she found out all these websites weren't for worshipers of the mystical mysterious black and red goddess at all: Parents Of Multiple Births Association. She should have known.

"Oh?" Francine wore a black shirt, red leggings, and eye makeup from the dungeon queen's back shelves.

"Don't 'oh' me, dammit. I'm serious. If she's such a Romni, where's her big family? It's mandatory that all the Roma have these big families, even ones that don't have big families and travel around continuously have these big old safe houses and some family comes by to crash. So where's her family? Hah. Just like I said, you been captured by a cult!" Francine looked like she was going to 'oh' her again, so Gina plowed ahead, "Look, I'll give you that Oleander's one of the sexiest women on earth. And folks here cater to your every whim. Don't interrupt. This is supposed to be a no-drug household? Right, half the women here are working some Oleander version of the twelve steps, kind of like a clean-up-and-dance thing. And here you are banging away—but these broads don't mind. It's bullshit. Secret ceremonies, weird white clothes, shaved bald heads! It's a cult for Chrissakes."

"Not exactly for Christ's sake."

Gina made a noise like a teakettle.

Frankie said, "You want information or you want to simmer?"

Gina set her jaw. "Give."

How much to tell, how much to save, how much to put it? Francine sat on her couch, patted the place next to her. "I guess it would have been better if I ran it all down to you when you first showed up but I thought that if you hung around for awhile you'd see how valuable this place Oleander set up is."

"You thought I'd get brainwashed like the rest of you." Arms folded across her chest.

"It's too late for me to be brainwashed, my mind was spin-dried and then some a long time ago. And I often wonder if you got a br—never mind. If you will just stop bumping up and down...." Francine paused, spoke softly, spinning it out. "This place is a refuge. A safe house. Just like you say Roma always have. For Oleander, for me, for all the women here. Every one of us was running from something, hiding from something. Oleander set this house up in honor of her patron saint. The one in charge of hopeless causes, protector of street people, whores, junkies, losers of all kinds. Pomba Gira."

"I been alla them people and more. Never seem to me we gots no patron saint. Spend our whole lives just fallin through the fuckin cracks with no safety net." Scowl. "Maybe that's where the brainwashing lies, in the believing."

"Don't believe in anything? It's all brainwashing? That perspective sucks the meaning from the words. Besides, you're mixing metaphors."

"I don't give a good goddamn."

"Falling through the cracks is not a safety-net type of falling. High wire act would be more appropriate."

"This is a conversation we've had before, and I'm not in the mood. I think you need to get your skanky ass out of here." Keep Frankie talking. Keep her occupied with small things. It's the insignificant parts of life that keep death away. "You don't need this weird-ass shit. You've never needed it." *Come away with me, Frankie my love, some place where you won't be sick. Where you won't ever die.*

"Maybe there are people who need to believe, and that's me, and then there are other people who don't. Or maybe it's just that you get so damn much more pleasure out of distrusting everybody than you think you'd get out of one tiny little belief."

"One leads to another and next thing you know I'll be bald or worse."

"Gina? You've already been worse."

"Yeah. So?"

"So. Come to our midnight ceremony for Pomba Gira tonight. You're certainly well enough defended so we won't be able to Get You."

"Is the irresistible Julia going to be there?"

Francine rubbed her nose, "Julia is off limits."

"Right. I knew it. You guys are a cult. A bloody conspiracy. It's a dark plot to frustrate me into full compliance with some anti-sexual program. Buncha deviants. That's what you are."

"Julia is fulfilling her promise to refrain from sex in preparation for her initiation."

"That's entirely fucked."

"And, while it might do you a lot of good to get laid—after the life she's lived, it wouldn't be good for her to break her initiatory promise."

"Crap. After what life? She's barely legal."

"She's not even legal. Not merely age-legal, but legal-legal. Julia had her own client list by the time she was fourteen."

"Client list?"

"Top of the line. Her brother wanted a piece of the action. It seems he thought that since she was selling her snatch professionally, as family he ought to get it for free. She didn't agree. He insisted. She sliced him up. He died. Anyway. Like all of us, she's avoiding the long arms of the law by living here. New name, new—"

"Hairdo?"

"That's part of it."

"Come clean."

"There's nothing to come clean about. We are Oleander's family. Most all of us are here just because the rest of the world is inimical—"

"Inimitable? Like not to be imitated? Or unfriendly? Wellll, he-elllll, either way, I fit right in. I've been in-imacalitized by the world plenty."

"You think you'd be happy here?"

"At Oleander's Nutty Girls' Home? Hah. I'll be delirious with joy. I promise I won't touch your precious little Julia." She crossed her fingers. That way the promise didn't count. "Really. Just let me have a little corner room with a sink and a couch and a window and a door I can actually close. And no Lethal Jack peering around at me too early in the morning looking to see if I'm undressed before he gives me the night's clean up wages. Oh man, people are such pigs."

"Be back here well before midnight. Remember that Pomba likes red and black."

Gina stood up. "I ain't gonna make it to the party tonight. Whoever she is, she's certainly not very adventurous in the color department."

"Get."

*   *   *

Ellis sweat his way through the post midnight streets wanting to stop and examine what he'd pulled out of the crate and stashed under the seat. On the other hand, and this confused him, he didn't want to stop, his sole overpowering desire was to drive. Drive fast. He slowed down, hands shaking on the wheel. Who was in charge here? His foot slammed back down on the pedal.

He had very few options about which way to jump with this thing, and one by one he rejected them. He had a feeling his Aunt Lou wouldn't be all that thrilled to see him again, let alone stash his ill-gotten gains (the exact words she'd used in the past). Besides, if the old man was some kind of relative—and there was a family resemblance if only in their mutual ability to swallow down rum by the case—Aunt Lou's was right where the demon would look for him.

The only thing Ellis was clear about as he barreled around the corners was that he wouldn't be bringing the whatever-it-was to the old man. Ellis figured he'd grabbed it fair and square, he was going to find out just what the hell it was, and then exactly what-the-hell he did with it was his own good self's goddamn decision. Nobody else's.

He'd been sleeping in the limo since nobody was giving him enough money to get his own place—he would have complained about car-camping (not that anyone would listen) but it wasn't all that uncomfortable really—besides, the mobility would come in handy if the old man started looking for him when he didn't show up with the Whatever.

Ellis finally managed to pull over to the side of the road in front of a couple office buildings with trees. Nobody around. He peeled back the wrapping from the package. Gold. Solid gold.

He got back in the car and drove. He felt like he was the driver of some big shot get-away car, letting the Caddy's new engine whack itself to the top RPMs. At a stoplight he noticed a big red and black purse sitting on the seat next to him. He stared at it long and hard. Where the fuck did that come from? No way James left it. He reached over, tried but couldn't open it. He looked up from fumbling with the latch and there he was driving again, sixty-seventy, one hand on the purse, one hand on the wheel, seventy five, then there was a tall voluptuous woman standing in the middle of the road, hands on hips, scowling directly at him. "What the hell?" He slammed on the brakes, the car fishtailed, he pulled over to the curb surrounded by vicious laughter. He was breathing heavily. He wiped the sweat out of his eyes, rolled down the window and peered out at an utterly empty road. "Damn."

There was a sharp click-click of stiletto heels approaching from the rear, but nothing except starlight in his mirrors. A brandy-crusted woman's voice muttered in the shadows right outside his window: "Give it to me."

He fumbled at the purse, finally undid the clasp, a huge flare of green light burst out of it. "Holy shit!" His eyes watering he flung it out the window. There was no one, nothing there— he confronted a great emptiness. His foot slammed on the gas, as he screeched away he saw a tall woman with red red lips and black black eyes in his rear view mirror. She shook her fist at him, there was the sound of satin ripping, smoke from an expensive sweet cigar drifted through the cab, then the thick cloying fragrance of full blown roses.

He pulled up in front of Oleander's building, the lights were still on behind the heavy red curtains in the lobby. He sat there for a minute, dumb and sweating. Wondering if the old man would suddenly come up behind him. Probably not, he had a feeling the old man wasn't that keen on being caught nosing around Oleander's.

He looked at the alley on one side of the building which led back to the loo and a utility sink where he'd wash up in the mornings. It was dark back in there. But he had to do something. So yeah, what he'd do is... yeah. He'd walk back there right now and knock on the door and talk to Oleander all in private. Yeah. He'd tell Oleander that he picked up the guy from Miami and he was an arrogant creep. Nothing about the gold statue.

Or. Maybe he wouldn't tell anyone anything.

Or he could hand it over to her? No.

He'd take it and disappear. Disappear.

He sat there in front of the building, shaking.

.   He could hear music thumping against the glass of the front doors, pounding against the windows of his cab, thudding around in his head. Did these mad women never sleep?

His stomach went funny, he had nothing especially convincing to say to Oleander. To anyone. What? He got hijacked by some voluptuous babe who smelled of roses and cigars? But then, he told himself (Be brave, Oleander's only a dumb gypsy, be brave) she hadn't given him much to work with. Maybe he'd tell her he missed the connection. Maybe he'd say the guy was just some old fart looking for babes. Maybe he'd say —

He got out of the car, still running maybe-he'd-say through his mind.

He peered through the crack in the curtains into the lobby. The crazy broad Gina was up a ladder hanging the damn chandelier. In the middle of the fuckin night. Francine and Julia and most of the other women who lived there were padding around eating and drinking. Stuffing their faces, arms around each other. The music was going full blast, some kind of heavy breathing sexual wailing, Oleander was holding the ladder, everyone had their backs to the door. Paying no attention to anyone who just happens to push their nose against the window. He thought about leaving. He thought about knocking. He pushed his nose against the glass.

Gina was saying, "Well, I'm not sorry I missed it. I had negotiations about my sleeping accommodations again." She cut her eyes to Francine.

Francine shrugged: I refuse to let that be my problem. "Well then, don't miss the next one. It's next Friday night, outside. It will be a really big deal. You'll hava ball, I promise."

Gina's eyes cut to Oleander.

Oleander lifted her hands palms up, small lift of her shoulders, "All the rooms here are taken just now." Although with Thea looking at a parole violation and Queenie likely to follow, just so's they'd be together for the year or whatever down time, there might be. Oleander would worry about all of that in the morning. "Please try and come to our party next week?"

"Okay. My misfortune in the sleeping department's not your problem." Big pause, no one contradicted her. Sigh. "Well, anyway, I just want you to know I read some about this trance business on line and I don't get it. You know, the whole eyes rolling around in your head, muttering, spinning, out of your mind with no substance abuse necessary." She put a screw into the ceiling bracket, fished around for her screwdriver. "I mean, what's the point other than a cheap high?" She stopped looking for the screwdriver, scowled down at Oleander. "On the other hand, if it's supposed to be re-li-gious...." Holding the chandelier with one hand while she waved the other in loopy circles around her ear. "Is all this 'excuse me I'm out-of-my-body for the moment, I'm-busy-being-someone-else' business really necessary?"

"Yes. Come to our celebration and you'll see." Or, Oleander thought with a small smile, or perhaps you won't see. "Dancing is one of the ways humans connect with the sacred. It's a subtle thing."

"Ah, Gina never understood allegory, let alone subtlety." Francine was smoking one of those fancy-ass red paper cigarettes with the snazzy gold filters.

"Right. One thing I'm not, is subtle." Gina glared around at them. "Never seem to have the time."

Queenie, once again joined at the hip to Thea, spoke to the smaller rounder woman, saying softly, "There's somethin soooo subtle about a great piece of ass." She smiled down at Thea's cleavage.

Her partner responded, "Good music, every body's beautiful." They exchanged a long hot look, turned away and boogied up the stairs.

"Just who you lookin at, beautiful?

"Oh darlin, no body but you."

"Better be the stone truth now."

"May that chandelier drop on my head if—"

"Don't be sayin shit like that."

Rhea, the boxer or body builder or whatever she was—all gold skin tight muscles wrapped around sleek bones—twinkled up at Gina. Her hair was a shiny blue-black halo sticking out at all angles. She said, "Hang er high, *hermana*. Gonna look sharp." She sort of wiggled a little, twisted to show off her ass in some black leather hot pants.

Gina muttered, "This is supposed to be religious? I don't get it."

"Just hang the damn chandelier."

"Okay." Gina fidgeted with the lamp, decided to get some of her own back, after all, she was as much of a craftsperson as these tranced-out sluts, "Now listen up, *mijas*. I'm going to let you all in on the real religion: Hidden Places. Known only to the few. The brave."

Francine wiggled the ladder. "The clumsy."

"The people who climb up ladders! Pay attention to things that can be drilled or dug out, or," waving her hand with oratorical glee at the hole in the ceiling, "are already hollowed out." Gina warmed to her subject. "I could rig a stash up here in the ceiling behind where the fixture connects to the electrical box, between the upper floor's joists. Tucked up here, anything'd be safe. Nobody ever looks up here. I mean, it wouldn't be easy to get to or anything, but then sometimes you don't want hidden things to be for daily access. That fancy-ass counter you got would be a real chore to put a couple secret compartments in. But for small secrets, it'd be beyond belief cool."

She reached down for the screwdriver, turned her head and saw a ghost standing on the front steps. La Favorita rushed the door. Gina wobbled at the top of the ladder, nothing to hold onto. Her ladder luck looked to be running out again, she squeaked, "Jeez. What the hell is that?" She gulped. She gripped the screwdriver, some small protection against ghosts. She saw the ghost turn into Ellis, nose pushed against the door glass. "That man tryin to give me a heart attack."

As Rhea went to get the door, Gina sat down on the top of the ladder, chin on her hand, one eye on her chandelier, one eye on Ellis and one eye on Oleander. Gina was good at the three-eye trick.

Ellis rubbed his hands as if he was cold, his shoulders hunched up, his face was twitchy, a sweat sheen highlighted his cheekbones. La Favorita stood in his way.

Gina climbed down the ladder. Either the guy was about to tell one hell of a big lie—lying had always fascinated her, an under-appreciated art form if ever there was one—or he was on drugs, something else which interested her greatly.

Ellis opened his mouth.

The phone rang.

Everybody jumped out of their respective skins.

Oleander stepped over to pick it up, hesitated. Pointed her finger at Ellis, "Stand right there, don't move." Late calls were never good news. The answering machine would get it.

Gina sidled up behind Ellis, whispered, "Saved by the bell or what?"

He stared at her, eyes wide and empty, then turned on his heel and dashed off down the steps.

Francine watched him turn the corner behind their building.

As the door slammed, the machine coughed into life: "Vicente is dead. Vicente is dead. Vicente is dead." The voice spoke that flat uninflected English which indicated a voice-distortion program. "This very night in Recife. Oh oh. Magdalena Carvalho da Silva what will you do now? Vicente is dead."

Creepy. Gina shook it off, said, "Doesn't sound particularly sorry, does he?"

Oleander curled her lip. "Sounds like a load of crap to me." She glared at the machine as if she could see whoever made the call. "Well, Gina," she looked up, "that may be it for tonight. Your ghost seems to have disappeared. Are you far enough along with that thing so it won't fall on anyone's head?"

"Ten minutes. Then I'm going to work. And I'll leave you alone with your guests and ghosts and creepy-assed messages." She looked around the room, wondering who Magdalena Carvalho da Silva might be. "Well, I'm sorry that Vicente's dead if that's what I'm supposed to be, but mostly I'm sorry the message came like that."

"No sorry necessary. That man is not dead. That man is far too evil to die. I'm not sure what this message is supposed to convey."

Rhea said, "In my experience when they say someone's dead it's either true or they want you to think it's true. Either way they expect you to do something stupid."

Oleander smiled. "Yes. Something stupid. Yes." She held the ladder as Gina climbed up to put the finishing touches on the chandelier. "Yes. Thank you very much, Rhea. You too, Gina."

Puzzled. "Hey no problem."

CHAPTER SIXTEEN

Ellis bundled up the statue, waited at the mouth of the alley until that dreadful little dog had been let out to pee, and Oleander had gone upstairs. He thought maybe he could put it in the loo—no one but him ever went in there. Of course the problem was that the statue might have resented that. Or not. Maybe the statue didn't have opinions. Not likely. Solid gold was the foundation of opinionation.

The lights in the kitchen were still on. He tapped on the kitchen door, a furtive scrabbling in the drizzle.

Francine opened the door. "The hell?" Her tired eyes gleamed as she looked from his face to the large package held on his knee and hip, its unbalanced top somewhere above his head.

He was breathing hard, glancing behind himself as he bobbed around trying to pretend like he wasn't holding such an unwieldy package. "Uh. Hi."

Francine pinched her lips. She said, "You're in trouble and you need someone on your bond? Are you mental? You just like to hear me tell you to get lost?"

Ellis gurgled, "Please. Let me in. Please."

Francine, more curious than cautious on every occasion, pointed him to one end of the kitchen. She shut the door, flipped three locks over and pointed to the counter. "Put that thing up there."

Ellis gawked at her, insulted. "Not a thing. It's a magnificent statue."

"I don't give a shit. Put it down. And put yourself on that stool. Hands in your lap." He complied. "Lovely."

Ellis, wise man, didn't say another word.

Francine rubbed her hands together, gently poked the wet sack with one long thin finger, there was a sharp glint of gold, she looked over at Ellis then back at the package. "This doesn't belong to you."

"Yeah it does. Yeah. It's mine." Ellis wiggled.

"Tell me another."

"The real deal?"

"All of it."

"How far back?"

"You best start with tonight and then fill in what's not making sense, back as far as you need to go." Sharp. "But I don't want to hear not one single self-serving goddamn word about no fucked up childhood or how you've been misused by a society that don't care." Glare. "I don't care. And right now I'm the only one you got to impress, you got that?"

Nod.

"So you best figure out right away what I do care about, and don't stray too far off the subject."

"You guys used to build stashes, right?"

"Hide things? Nope."

"Oh come on, Frankie, it's how you and Gina made your living for years." Julia had been very forthcoming about her friends over coffee.

Francine's voice was edged with danger, "You way off topic now."

"You know where there's a large, very safe place?" He chin pointed at the thing on the counter.

"Nope."

"But you could find one in an emergency."

Not a blink. "Nope."

They hunkered down, metaphorical elbows on the table, analogous right hands clasped, waiting for the referee to say 'go'.

"I don't have much time."

"Neither do I, Ellis. Neither do I." Vicious snicker.

"Shit." He grimaced.

"Give it up Ellis. You need me. Best be a gentleman about this." She screwed her face up, skeptical. "You do know what I'm talking about don't you? A gentleman?"

He opened his mouth ready with a nickel-nickel-penny-story. Reconsidered. "Okay. You call the price and I'll pay it."

"You haven't got a pot to piss in or a window to throw it out of. And I always charge whatever the market will bear." She sat back, "Now. Tell me what the market is."

"Uh. I don't know."

Sigh. "Ellis, my man, you're wasting my time. You know, my time? The one thing I haven't got enough of? Cut to the chase or cut on out of here."

He said, "Okay. Unwrap it and you'll see what my problem is."

"Okay, sure. But you better start talking." She listened to Ellis staggering from one untruth to another as she unwrapped the bundle. She whistled. "Creepy. Looks like someone we know." He shrugged. She didn't take her eyes off the thing, just motioned with her hand for him to continue.

When he'd gabbled for a while she asked, "So why didn't you bring her to the old man? Like you were supposed to? Like you agreed? Like he planned for you to do last week when he gave you the pick up?" Or, she thought to herself, all those weeks before that when he was setting you up. Just for this. Whatever it was.

Before he could answer, she went on, "You don't bring it to him you may be blowing your big chance for money. Then again, if he's the way you tell me he is, you probably in so much trouble, money won't matter." She sucked a loose tooth. "Rippin off that man be bigger trouble than you ever had."

He said, "Somethin tells me that statue shouldn go to that old man." Stubborn. "Hell, I stole it. It's mine now."

"He's comin after you. You know that. You leave it here with me—it's gone from you, gone from your memory. You ain't gonna know where it is. It'll be gone."

He groaned. "What other choice do I have?"

"Walk out of here, we forget you came by. Take it where you promised." Small smile. "You know. Do The Right Thing."

He shook his head.

"Then, this Lady here, she's gone. Gone for one month if no one comes looking. Gone for six months or longer if there's one single person even looks at me funny about her. Is that clear?"

"You gotta remember she ain't yours. She just temporary in your custody."

Francine tipped her head, looked pleased with herself. "Get your ass outta here." She unlatched the back door, thinking:

And if she isn't mine now, I'd like to know just who else she belong to. Hah.

CHAPTER SEVENTEEN

Raymond's dark shop was crowded with huge snarling idols, dusty statues cracked with time, caked with grime, the weight of the ages patina-ed on their inauthentic shoulders; carved and painted wooden masks scowled from the walls, broken cabinets overflowed with colored cloth, raffia remnants, cowry covered baskets, tiny stone creatures grinning with malice. Clay horned snakes reposed on the lids of a multitude of strange vessels piled every which way on rickety tables. Ethnic Art. The latest bend in the world beat buying curve.

When the bell rang Raymond didn't move his bulk from his overstuffed chair, he didn't even lift his massive head to survey potential customers. Didn't have to, when they came in his store they were in his domain, at his mercy, he dispensed the goods, or he didn't. He continued repairing a triple rope of glass beads.

The voice was suave, "Hello Raymond, you old fox." Cool international accent. Raymond lifted his head, his heavy eyelids remained at half-mast, he grunted. Interesting that James should arrive at his shop so quickly, so empty-handed. "Hey, James. What'd you bring me?"

"Back at the hotel." A small deprecating gesture. "Some good, some not-so-good." Diffident. "Some missing in transit." He waited a moment before continuing. "I think you will be able to help me with that."

Raymond's eyelids may have lifted slightly.

James had thought his strategy through, very carefully: His statue had to be in the city, he refused to consider it disappearing in transit at Miami. Or anywhere else. Raymond had his statue, knew where it was or else he'd already sold it to someone. In any case, James would get it back or get his cut of the damn money. "You know I've always been interested in unusual artifacts, been collecting em for years." Slick smile. "It's a main passion of mine, this game of chance we indulge in." Man-to-man. "I always manage to pull through, go the full ten rounds, you know that. Tenacity counts for something, a split decision if not a knockout."

James had never been in a boxing ring in his life yet he cultivated the image, the implication that he might have been a welterweight champ, but he was modest about it.

Raymond hissed. His lips trumpeted out, the color of calves liver. "Yessss. A game of chance." He didn't change the sullen expression on his fat sallow face.

James's voice went creamy, "I seem to have a partial set of ritual artifacts. I'm hoping to find the specific piece that's gone missing." He leaned forward, smiling, showing a lot of teeth. "You're the one man who knows this town and where things we're both interested in might have gone off to. Be hidden. Whatever."

Raymond put down the string of glass beads; he didn't trust James. He didn't like his tone. James was supposed to waltz in ready to sell things, then Raymond would denigrate them, talk him into lowering the price, back and forth. Like that. Raymond wondered just what the man was up to.

"I need to find something I've lost. Stunning, extraordinary. Magical." Pause. "Legal provenance is not," James smiled again, lop-sided, "an issue." Corners of his mouth pulled tight. "I'm sure you know what I mean."

Raymond's voice was a growl, as if it needed oil, "No. I don't."

James stepped closer. "There's always good pieces for sale in the city. Un-advertised in a manner of speaking. I want to hear about anything—especially a statue about so high," his fist hovered around his ribs. "You'll get a commission if it's what I'm looking for." Tight. "If it's what I lost. Now you understand?"

"No. I don't understand." Raymond's eyelids lifted for a moment exposing clever porcine eyes, the whites the color of old ivory, then shuttered down again. "How did you lose this stunning thing? A fet-eesh?" He suggested, adding a thick quiver to the word.

"Fetish? Perhaps." James thought of all the kinky cults in the city. If Raymond got hold of it, he might hand it off to some fanatical cult—fine fine but James wanted his cut. James used his soft confidential tone, "There's an electrical charge around an object which has been used in ritual, a charge which can be felt, but not necessarily visible to the eye." There was a note of priestly piety in his voice as he whispered, "But unmistakable to the initiated." Hands raised, not quite ecclesiastical, James didn't want to overdo. "A residue of divinity."

"I heard you studied the subject." Raymond's words were sleepy.

"Magic?" Gruff, modest. "Hoo-doo? Oh. I dunno. I'm a student of sorts. Of all the esoteric arts."

James prided himself on his years of classical studies, the many years he spent feeling superior to people from cultures he referred to as primitive. James studied magic, he talked magic (it impressed the girls) but he didn't DO magic. James knew that no one DID magic, except insofar as they participated in a very complicated set of codified deceptions. Magic was simply a clever sales ploy that existed to raise the market value of artifacts. He looked around the messy shop, maybe squalor made the place seem more exotic, more dangerous than it really was. Attracted stupid people with a lot of money? James frowned at the idea of magic, money and reality in the same sentence. As if finishing a thought too profound for complete utterance, James murmured, "Infinite potentialities."

Raymond scratched his scraggly beard. His hand was work callused, a sallow green brown by nature but stained darker by pine pitch and nicotine. "Don't muck with it m'self."

James settled into his pitch, "All spiritual force comes from the same source, there's no good, no evil, only energy, vast and never ending. Doesn't matter what the objects are, nor from which culture they come, the goal is always the same: manipulation of the universe by strength of will." And so on—a professorial drone. "The point of the exercise is to train ourselves so perfectly that our will and the divine will are one." James leaned forward trying to look deeply and sincerely into Raymond's eyes—a daunting task since Raymond's eyes all but disappeared in rolls of fat. He soldiered on: "We strive to let nothing inhibit the quest." A shine of sweat was becoming visible on James's brow.

Aleister Crowley was probably a bore too. Raymond murmured, "Whatever you say." He'd give James another three minutes, tell him to shove off, come back with money, or goods. Then they'd talk.

"Now, we both know, once you make thirty thousand dollars on a piece of art you get a sense of history. It's a matter of a totally changed perspective." James pulled the figure out of the air, out of the very esoteric ether itself, allovasudden BAM! Inspiration. Thirty K didn't seem outrageous. Of course he was thinking of getting paid that amount, not buying the damn thing back for it.

Raymond shifted. His perspective did change. What thirty thousand dollars on what piece? Whose thirty thou was the dude yammering about? There was a good chance James just wanted to make noise while he still had enough hair left to impress the ladies. Raymond remained silent for a moment, as if he was giving the man's words a lot of thought. "Well. I never thought of it that way." The mention of thirty-thousand extended the three-minute warning period. Not indefinitely, but some.

James paused by a dull metal statue, around three and a half feet tall: a battered yet jaunty black man, squashed top hat on his head, huge sad eyes, a cigar drooping from his mouth, his hands may have been clenched into fists. James sucked in his breath. "This one! What is this one?"

"Did you see the fella I told you about?"

"Yeah. I did. He's the guy who made my missing golden Venus." He turned toward Raymond, one hand reaching out to Raymond, the other pointing, unsteady, at the dusty statue. Raymond nodded, mimicked the way James' hand reached out, levered his large bulk up from the chair, patted his dingy white Nigerian-style crocheted cap into place. Standing up, Raymond Arthur was formidable, his striped sweater pulled tight across an expanse of stomach which was intimidating in its width and solidity. He pirouetted on his tiny slippered feet, graceful, he led James over to one of the locked display cases. "Ritual items. What kind of ritual art? West Africa? Amazon?" His was an eclectic selection, not necessarily authentic, although the layers of dust certainly gave the things the proper feel. "You just got back from Brazil, didn't you?"

"Yessss. You should have been with me. It was quite—quite. Ah."

James took a breath, remembering the scene on that flat gray beach. "Quite diverting." He pointed to a piece in the display case. "Let me see that beaded belt. West African?"

Expansive. "Ah, yes, that's a very special piece. You have good sharp eyes." Raymond opened the case, deliberate motions, lifted out the Yoruba belt. Careful. Fragile red, green and black beadwork, cowries, knotted black fringe. "My cousin is one of the kings over there, he sent this to me special."

"Oh. Is that blood on it?"

The belt was a modern copy of the old style. "My cousin, the king, told me this was used for many years by a famous Babalawo." Raymond had made sure there was the proper ritual appeal by storing it in a plastic bag with a bunch of chicken innards for a couple days after he got it. He turned, holding it out for the other man's examination. It stunk. "It is not, unfortunately, for sale right now. There are some members of a cult here in the City who placed a down payment on it." Classic lift of eyebrows, who knows what secret cults are up to? "Perhaps they wish to take it out of my infidel hands." A small lift of the shoulders then. "I would prefer to sell it to them than suffer some curse, or failing that, some noxious dead beast on my doorstep."

James thought there were enough noxious beasts in the little shop to make anything that might end up outside seem tame by comparison.

"Even though they're very secretive they don't seem to have gone completely over to… the dark side." Raymond watched James react to 'the dark side'. Idiot.

"A cult?" James trembled with suppressed excitement, he felt hot on the trail, he smelled, as it were, the path opening clearly in front of him. "Right here in the City? You sell to them? You know them? Can you introduce me to them? Perhaps they'd let me see their collection?" James was chattering. "Oh, perhaps I could attend a ceremony?" In his eagerness James grabbed Raymond's shoulder, the belt wedged between them.

Ritual magic and bloodthirsty cults, oh boy! Ritual magic and blood—if that's what James would pay for, that's what Raymond would give him. He wasn't sure what had "gone missing", but he would play James until he found out. "They aren't keen on strangers."

James nodded, "Ah." Knowing smile. "I'm willing to pay handsomely for their time." Afterthought. "For your help also, of course."

Raymond nodded. "Of course."

CHAPTER EIGHTEEN

The following morning Ellis staggered out of his limo, blankets tossed into a corner of the back seat, shoes untied. He hadn't slept, just rolled himself up in his blankets, unrolled himself all night long. When the morning light ripped at his eyelids he still had zero bright ideas about how he was going to deal with the situation he'd gotten himself into. The song seemed to go: Avoid the old man. Get his statue back from Frankie—that was such a dumb fuckin move, he should have left it under the back seat. Jeez. He returned to the first verse, adding that he should also avoid Oleander.

He glared balefully at the rain-spattered front of Oleander's building. He must have been mad. The only thing he knew, if knowing could be what the visceral drive in him had become, was that he needed a place to set up his beautiful statue the way she deserved. Maybe a long mahogany bar, like Oleander's, only better, with red and black satin draped all around, and the best champagne and caviar and baskets for people to put money in for her.

While he wasn't exactly delirious—he was afraid to examine his thoughts too carefully—he noticed the strange turn his mind had taken. Too many different mentalities seemed to be fighting for control in his head. He told them all to shut up. He knew what he wanted to do and he didn't question how he knew it or how he was going to do it.

His pleasure in quelling his internal disturbance was short lived. A huge swarthy man minced past him. Ellis watched as the man took off his little cap, spun it in his hands, put it back on his head. Patted his stomach. Sucked his gold tooth. Looked around. The man nodded to Ellis, gave him a rosebud-lips smile, opened the door to the lobby and bowed Ellis in ahead of him.

Ellis, expecting La Favorita to go for his ankles, did the "Oh no, after you," routine. Sure as shit the little pup charged with that huge rumbling growl and those gnashing flashing fangs.

Raymond's voice slid into a drag queen's falsetto: "Get this beast off me!"

Ellis smiled, "Just think what a terror she'll be when she grows up."

Julia was not too quick to call Rita to heel, but eventually she convinced Rita that there was no necessity to kill. Yet. La Favorita sat at Julia's feet, disappointed. First ankles of the morning.

"Thank you." Raymond spoke with a plaintive tone, "When? When is someone going to do something about this awful decor? Always reminds me of blood." Raymond paused, looked behind him. "Ah. Where did the young man go?"

Julia shrugged. Seemed to run into a barrier on the way to speech. A dumb-girl look settled on her face.

Ellis had buzzed back outside with barely a nod. He hoped that Julia wouldn't tell Oleander about seeing him. Even though Ellis belonged there—after all, he was tha official chauffeur, on call at all hours. Day or night. Ready. Willing. Able. Shit. He went back to his limo, watching the mirror in case Julia came out—he could tell her to get Frankie. They'd talk. Everything would get straightened out.

"Ah well." Raymond tipped his big head forward. Looked sincere. "So." Sighed. Looked around for Oleander. "Nice chandelier. New?"

"No. Old. Very old. Priceless." Julia kept herself a couple feet from the repulsive Raymond.

"Well. Got a little, ah, proposition for Oleander." The expected light didn't go on in Julia's eyes. "Something right up her alley, so to speak." Nothing. "I had a bit of good fortune last night, she'll remember, I'm sure. We talked about it at some length the other day. Well, fellow I know is interested in cults, you know. Wants to see a real ritual."

Julia took a step back. La Favorita did too.

It began to dawn on Raymond that he might be talking to someone who was perhaps not all there. A lovely girl, but— something in her family? He headed toward the door. "Okay. Tell Oleander that the guy has monnnnay and he'll be delighted to pay."

Julia scowled at him, not about to pass on any kind of message to Oleander from pond scum. Setting her jaw she said, "You want messages delivered," lift of her chin, "talk to Ellis, out there. He's the messenger boy."

"Oh? That handsome young man? Right." Raymond bowed himself out of the lobby. He trotted his bulk along to the Caddy, calling seductively, "Hey! Hey! Ellis! I got a message for Oleander."

Ellis, sitting in the driver's seat of his limo, stared into the distance. "So?"

"Tell Oleander I got a guy, seems he got bit by the voodoo bug and wants to see a real voodoo ritual. I figure you and I, we can maybe work together, put on a little show, split the take."

Ellis had a terrible suspicion that his life was about to go damn-all-to-Hell. Again. "I dunno, man. I don't know you."

Big meaty paw came through the window, "Raymond. Raymond Arthur. Ethnic Art and Artifacts."

Hardly looking at the man. "Did the guy smell like a cop?"

"Nah-hh." Raymond looked hurt. "You know I wouldn't bring something like that around to Oleander."

Ellis shook his head. "I don't know nothin of the kind."

"I've done business with him before. He's okay. A white guy, but oh well. There's a lot of them, you know. Come by my shop tomorrow." He handed Ellis a card. "We'll talk."

Ellis shook his head. "We'll see. I got things to do."

"Me too. Me too." Raymond tiptoed down the street, climbed into a pale beige Eldorado. Vintage. Pan-African flag on the trunk. Red Black Green. He drove around the block, cruised back in time to see Ellis disappear into the morning rush hour streets, driving like the devil was on his tail. Raymond didn't know if he always drove like that. The boy interested Raymond Arthur. He licked his thick lips. His eyelids clicked to half closed. He sucked his gold tooth.

CHAPTER NINETEEN

Ellis wasn't parked in front when Oleander left her house. She walked briskly by the empty parking spot, tossing only a small worry about Ellis into the world. His preoccupations didn't concern her, couldn't concern her just then, damn, she was in no frame of mind to deal with the petulant Mister Ellis Tha Chauffeur. She rubbed her knuckles into her eyes and rehearsed her role for the interview at the Brazilian consulate.

The building was imposing, with a row of ostentatious cement pillars and glass doors with brassy straps—made Oleander's toes cold. Cold. She had left all things Brazilian behind her when she ran away, she found it odd that the outpost of such a warm country should have steps leading to it which chilled her enough to make her bones crack.

After a few moments of smiling, showing teeth, delicate compliments, Oleander's inquiries were answered, in solemn helpful tones by a manicured secretary with large icy eyes. "Oh yes, Vicente da Silva is dead. Heart attack. These things are always a terrible shock."

The secretary noticed that the woman standing in front of her didn't look shocked, she thought the woman looked angry. She inhaled, a delicate sniff, patted her sleek hairdo, continued with a patronizing edge, "Of course, there is great interest now in his work. It almost always happens that way. But then, Vicente da Silva was well known within certain circles."

Oleander's lip started to curl up, but she controlled herself. "Oh yes?"

"He wasn't merely a peasant artisan with a grudge against society. It's true Vicente has been called a primitive artist," the fashionable woman at the consulate's voice dropped, she practically whispered, "but that certainly carries a hefty price in today's market. And since you're the widow—"

Oleander interrupted, "We are divorced."

"Vicente made it clear in these papers here," shuffle shuffle, "which just came in by courier," she drawled the word 'courier', "that you are the wife, beneficiary and rightful owner of his work."

"As his wife?"

"Well. Yes."

"But I am not his wife."

Exasperation. "It doesn't matter. We will take care of any inheritance details and let you know what's important."

Let me know what's important? You bitch. "Where did this sudden heart attack or whatever it was, happen?"

"In Recife it seems." More shuffling to find the papers for her to sign. "All the information hasn't arrived yet. Of course, it would be simplest if you would simply sign off now, then we could begin the process. Oh, with a team of lawyers of course. To evaluate his works, figure the inheritance taxes, connect you with some trustworthy dealers and set up an auction?"

Taxes due? Trustworthy what? Auction? Oh that bastard. Oleander didn't respond.

"I guess this is all quite sudden. A great loss. My deepest sympathies." Realizing that Oleander hadn't made any gesture of either sorrow or of willingness to sign the papers, the secretary tapped the papers with a pearly fingernail, "It would be good if we could expedite the process with your signature now."

Oleander still didn't respond. She let the officious little bitch squirm.

"It is not merely your loss, but Brazil's. The world's loss. Vicente da Silva was one of our most well-known artists, if not most beloved, and although he was a—"

Ohhhh, no one loves you until you're dead and gone. "A practitioner of Quimbanda?" Oleander's voice held a note of happy venom.

Stiffly. "I was unaware of that."

Like hell you were.

"Signed works by Vicente are now worth a kidnapper's ransom." Formal. "This is something you must take into consideration. We'll get someone to work with you on the tax angle. You have tax obligations as an American citizen. I believe you retained your citizenship in Brazil? In any case you have cul-tur-alll obligations regarding this great art legacy."

Oh crap. She hadn't been in Brazil in nine years, it'd taken her three to get to the US and she'd been established, nicely thank you, as a proper Romni for nearly six. Her parents had been, in any case, Argentine citizens—actors on whatever stage would have them; it's true they died and left her to her own devices on Brazilian soil so she had considered herself Brazilian for many years, for lack of any alternative. Coming to the consulate here had been a mistake. Oleander sighed prettily, she twisted her hands helplessly. She stared past the woman at some non-existent something-or-other. Fuck this, she was thinking, after all she had a US passport; that secret security made her feel strong, besides they had no real address to connect her to. Inheritance taxes? And where was this tax money supposed to come from?

The woman behind the desk once again offered to make all the resources of the Brazilian Consulate at her complete disposal.

"Thank you very much." Oleander's voice shook. She hoped the silly woman thought it was grief rising to the surface at last, rather than the repressed rage it truly was.

With a little shudder of triumph, the secretary pushed the papers forward. Gently.

Oleander let her eyes rise to the ceiling, her hands, palm up lifted also. But she didn't reach for the pen. "Thank you very much." Again, her voice shook with just that little quiver, perfect. She spun softly on her heel, closing the door with care behind her, leaving the secretary staring, her mouth slightly open, "Stop! Wait! You must sign these papers!"

So. Oleander stomped down the stairs, berating herself for being a fool. Damn her own curiosity. Damn. Well. She was supposedly much richer. This she doubted. They simply wanted her to sign things. Bah. Vicente was not dead. He was a savage, too much attached to life. To revenge. How to have a heart-attack with no heart? Hah.

When Oleander arrived back at her rooming house, she hardly noticed the people in the lobby waiting for the fortuneteller to get to work. She called La Favorita to her, regally ignoring everyone, continued back into the kitchen. She put a bowl of puppy chow on the floor for Rita and tipped some dried herbs—peppermint, lemon verbena, chopped ginger and burdock roots into a ceramic bowl, added a pinch of opium poppy seeds, poured boiling water over it all, stirred it around a few times. Her mind was miles away, she'd read somewhere that Amazon Indians used Philodendron to stun fish. This was useful information. She was not sure for what. Her nose told her to add cinnamon. Orange peel. There was no philodendron handy. Too bad, she thought she could do something interesting, possibly important, with a little fish-stunning potion.

Everything that had happened was some stupid plot by Vicente—he'd certainly waited long enough. What did he want—to bust her out of her house, out of this city, out of who she had become? Force her to once again run? She thought of the porcelain woman at the consulate, wondering how people ended up like that? Smiling, Oleander thought that the secretary might be wondering how Oleander ended up like she had—and wouldn't the bitch just like to know.

Screw her. Well, she wasn't going to run anymore. Vicente wasn't dead, just playing some hateful game. Everything would become clear in time.

If she had time.

The smell of the tea was pungent, sweet/bitter, it changed slightly as the herbs soaked into the water. She didn't add any sugar, everybody added too damn much sugar to everything already. Life was sweet all on its own.

Julia poked her head in, made an *errrr* sound, Rita thumped her tail on the floor, Oleander held up her hand, "Five minutes." Julia swiveled out doing her best Oleander imitation. "I can read your palm for you if you'll step this way."

Fish-stunning philodendron? Francine, always on the lookout for potential concoctions, would like that. Oleander checked her watch, took a sip, not too bad, sort of uplifting. And grounding all the same. Good. Good. She needed uplifting. She tapped her foot. And grounding.

*   *   *

Upstairs, Francine had spent her morning examining the statue, working toward some final perspective. She didn't particularly like it, in spite of the artistry. Her hands itched when she turned it, slipped as if it was slimy. In spite of Ellis' dreams, it wasn't solid gold. The boy had no idea how much that would have weighed. If she had her old test kit she would have been able to tell if it was electroplated aluminum or some other technique. But she didn't. Her life had narrowed considerably over the last several months, her time was taken up with nausea, dizziness, cramps, fatigue; a metal-testing kit hadn't somehow seemed like something she'd be needing. Always the way.

She couldn't sustain a necessary philosophical head long enough to really concentrate. She brushed her hands against her jeans. Dope helped—sometimes it really helped to clarify. But it didn't clarify clearly. Clearly clarify. Oh fuck. Time's up. Run out. Finito. So much she never learned, she had thought facing death straight on would teach her a lot, sharpen her right up. But no, something puts the brakes on the learning process, her mind refused to bend into those comfortable curves.

The face looked like Oleander's face. Warped. Strange. The earrings at least looked to be real jewels. Rough cut emeralds? The statue was worth a small fortune. She wrapped it in a couple of her bath towels, put it back in the hidden side panel of her closet. She'd built in the stash when she moved into the house, half cut out of her closet and half out of the closet in the store room next door. For those things she needed to hide. Gina could spot it if she bothered to look, but no one else would find it.

Francine turned on her CD-player, lay back on her couch, waited for Raymond to let her know what he had on offer— he'd promised to get her something he called Chinese Numbah Four. He had begun naming his dope a couple months back, as if to impress her. This Numbah Four was theoretically very clean, very pure. As opposed to Numbah Three from two weeks ago which had been very clean very pure. Right. Fuck it.

She lay back and thought about nothing except the passage of time.

The phone rang. Ellis. Claiming he called to cheer her up. "So," she growled, "Start cheerin."

"Aw, Frankie. Why you make it so difficult?"

"Because, you idiot, it is difficult." He was going to try to get the statue back, she could hear it in his breathing. "You can't have her back yet. I said a month." Adamant. "I can't even get to where it's hid before then."

"Hey. I didn't say anything."

"Your voice been pryin into every corner. Here." She pointed the phone under the couch. "I'll give you a telephone tour of my house. Look over here. Look under here. Look in here. Ellis, believe me. It's not here."

"You don't understand, Frankie, I need it back. Everything is fucked up."

"Everything's always fucked up, Ellis. Ain't you noticed?"

He ignored that. Gratuitous insults seemed to be standard procedure lately. "I got to put it where it's supposed to be."

"My sweet ass. Ellis, I know you. I know you don't have the smallest idea where the thing's supposed to be, or what it's for."

"Oh? And you do?"

"So you might as well leave it where it is. At least it's safe with me." She lay back on the couch.

"You ain't sold it for dope, have you?"

"Eat shit and die, Ellis."

CHAPTER TWENTY

That Friday afternoon Gina found the front doors at Oleander's house locked, no one seemed to be around but she could hear voices from somewhere inside. She went around to the alley, walked through the tiny back yard, banged on the kitchen door, Thea answered with a distracted growl. "Oh, it's you. Keep an eye on the barbecues for me." And the woman trotted away.

Three smoking grills lined up along the next door building's blank wall, the coals were almost ready. A rickety table was pushed up against another building's back wall, a large mural was painted there of a sultry Cigana dancer. A little pit bull pup was outlined, unfinished, at her side. Maybe the artist would keep painting it over and over as La Favorita grew up?

No one came outside until La Favorita tiptoed over to greet her so Gina played with the pup for awhile, kneeling right down on the cement to roll around and work out some of the fancier moves of tag-you're-dead. But since the pup always won, Gina decided to go somewhere she might do a little better. She followed the sound of voices into the Kitchen of the Giddy Virgins.

She surveyed the scene, careful not to intrude: white-clad women bustling around, loaves of bread rising on the sideboard, pots of soup stock simmering, bowls of chopped vegetables and chilies. And three black-feathered hens, clucking and burping in a cage, one not too large but clearly majestic rooster strutting around loose and preening himself, getting underfoot. More women passed back and forth through the kitchen from the lobby, back and forth with sacks and bowls and big knives and platters and everybody was dressed in white with turbans and beads and bright dangly earrings. Gina stuck her hands in her pockets, took them out, stepped left then right dodging the bustle, finally she croaked: "Where's Frankie?"

No one paid any attention to her.

"Shit."

Queenie stomped through, nodded briefly, picked up the hen cage and trotted out the back door. Gina, for lack of anything better, followed her back out again. And the rooster solemnly followed both of them.

Julia, all in white, pale and jumpy as if she were in church, came out to stand slightly behind and to the left of Thea. Queenie put down the cage, put her arm around Thea, "It's going to be fine. Smooth."

Julia chimed in, "Just breathe easy, no sense in getting all nervous and stuff."

"Yah. Look who's talking? The little slicer who nearly puked the first time she saw a sacrifice." Thea humphed to herself, "Cut people up no problem, but when it comes to animals...."

Julia didn't answer, looking back and forth between them with large sad eyes. She turned her gaze at Gina.

"Hey. Don't ask me. I just accidentally wandered in here." Stepping back down the alley. "And now, I'm gonna mosey back on out."

Julia stopped her. "Stay. Please?"

Oh great gods in heaven.

"Just y'all don't faint, okay?"

"Put a bag on it, Thea." Queenie grinned, her wide mouth curling up into a wicked curve. "We'll just pretend we guttin that skanky-ass parole agent."

"She ain't half worth a pigeon."

"Now, tha's right, darlin."

"And not half so tidy either."

"Well, nothin tidy in this world seems to me."

"Babe, it's what we do."

"It's what we do."

Gina's lips turned down, she tucked her chin into her chest, "Damn."

Oleander came out then, followed by Frankie. She raised her eyebrows at Gina. "Good of you to come by. There's certainly enough work for everyone."

"What's all this?" Gina waved her arm in a vague looping gesture, taking in the square barren space, the grills birds babes and mural. The surrounding walls seemed to loom dangerously.

"Big Friday. Pomba Gira's havin a party."

Gina shrugged. "Always glad to be of help." She had no idea what was going on. All she wanted to do was talk to Frankie.

Oleander said, "It's not that I don't think you're the one to do it, Frankie, I'm just not sure that you should. You need to save your energy for keeping your own self alive."

"I'm the one who can do it quick, clean and simple. I'm the one got the training, long time ago, even before I hooked up with you. Who else you got in mind, Oleander?" She pointed at Julia with her chin, "She can't do it, no matter what anyone says, she hasn't been trained. Besides, she's working up to her initiation year." Francine looked at the other women standing around, "And it's clear that while in this very select crew of women we have some of the finer blade-masters in town," she grinned at Thea, gave a nod to Julia. "None of them have been trained for this. No matter how blood-thirsty any of them might be." She lifted her chin at the little crowd, spoke carefully, with an odd dignity, "I'm the only one who has *pinyaldo*, nobody else here is blessed to use the knife." She cut her eyes to Oleander, "Not even you."

Oleander looked at Francine for a moment longer.

Frankie said, "Carlos is a gem, a gentleman, one good man out of hundreds, he's a good friend, a sweetheart of a *padrino*, and he honors our Pomba Gira beautifully in spite of her not being part of the Cuban tradition. But he's out of town and if you want this done right, that leaves me the only one has the ceremonies to do it."

"You're right. Serve Ogun once again. But in the future we will make sure someone else is available for our monthly ceremony."

As they were talking, more women came out to cluster round-eyed in the corners of the small yard, wiping their hands nervously and straightening out their skirts and blouses. Francine smiled at Oleander, "Yep. If Ogun wants me to do this, then I'll do it."

Oleander dropped some coconut quarters on the ground, four white sides up. "Alright."

Gina looked around to see who was this Ogun. Then she realized Frankie was talking about herself, when she was that other self.

One night, in the far starry past, Gina came home late after a shift at some creepy bar, Frankie was in their living room dressed in green and black leather. She had her big machete and a sharpening stone, *sliiiirk sliiiirk*, Frankie'd looked up at Gina and growled, "Not now little one. Not now. Go back outside for awhile." Gina had scowled, "No way. It's cold and nasty and I'm tired and didn't make shit for tips." Frankie stood up then, holding the machete, "Go!" Gina went. When she returned they had a fight. Which had put some real cracks in their relationship.

Frankie tried to explain that she had work to do, as her "other self". As Ogun.

Gina thought Frankie was mean. Or nuts.

Gina had pushed the memory so deep, so deep into the forget-it bin, that she was surprised the memory made it back into the daylight. And now Frankie was going to do a reprise of that other self, that mean ass Ogun. Crap. Gina edged toward the door.

Francine pushed her thumb at Gina, "Gina can help me. There. You'll be my helper for this *trabajo*, okay?"

Both Gina and Oleander tipped their heads to one side, thinking about it. Oleander of course knew what it was they were thinking about. Gina, on the other hand, merely indulged in a familiar feeling of dread. "What the hell are you volunteering me for now, Frankie?"

"A little traditional ritual sacrifice." Grin. Sort of threatening. Sort of complacent. "Food for the Gods. Food for the celebrants."

Oleander sighed. Gina sighed. The little black hens sighed. The girls in the corner sighed. The rooster nodded his head. He'd been raised to be a hero.

Oleander dipped her fingers in a glass of water, began the chant to the ancestors, to the guardians of the gates. It was not quite what Vicente had taught her in Brazil, but she had adapted local customs, adding Lucumi spice to her basic brew. She spun the top off a fifth of Barbados rum, still muttering a chant she spit a little on the ground, handed the bottle to Frankie who sprayed a little on the ground then she handed the bottle to Julia, who spit, Rhea spit, the corner girls spit, and finally to Gina. Gina clutched the bottle and shot her eyes at each of them in turn, took a big gulp, swallowed. Yes. She hugged the bottle to her round little belly. She thought that robbing banks made more sense.

One of the black hens laid an egg. Glared at Gina.

"Oh." Gina took a long pull of the rum, sprayed it out like the rest of them had done. "Oh. Well, let's get to sacrificin. Jeez."

Oleander began a sing-song chant, "*I barago-oh, Mojuba… Oh mo-day ko-nee ko-see barago*…."

Oleander set out a wide black bowl in front of a little cement head. Happy cowry eyes, curly cowry mouth, little tiny cowry ears. Sharp rusty nail poking out the top of his head. Sweet. Dangerous. Weird. Gina looked at it, looked away. Looked back. The gremlin thing was grinning and winking at her. She muttered, "This is some good rum."

Oleander lit a cigar, puffed, passed it to Francine, who passed it to Gina who thought about keeping it but took a toke and passed it to Julia instead. Another cigar was lit and began to make the rounds. Gina thought it was incongruous to have all these cigar-smoking women dressed in whites. The cigars seemed more a prep for a poker game than a sacrifice. There was a low humming sound in the background, Thea and Queenie had picked up Oleander's chant and were riffing on it, shifting their weight side-to-side, elbows out, sort of bowing towards the little cowry head, towards the hens. Deeper bend to the rooster.

*   *   *

Oleander lifted the rooster then, gentled it by running her long fingers along the length of his sleek red feathers. She handed the cock to Gina, "Here, hold him like this." Right fingers grasping the bird's right leg, thumb tucked over the wing and tight to the shoulder, left hand the same. "Hold him into your belly. Breathe slow and easy." She caressed the feathers at the back of his head. She sing-song-sang something that sounded vaguely similar to the street corner song Gina had heard when she first saw Oleander, red gold and glowing.

Francine whispered softly, pulled the quiet bird's neck taut, smoothly she cut the windpipe cut the tendons between the tiny neck bones with one slide of the shiny knife, the rooster didn't even jerk, the blood slid smoothly down the blade into the bowl.

Gina stood still, clutching the dead bird, unable to let go, watching the blood pour into the bowl. Pour into the bowl.

Thea chant-sang, "*Bara su way oh mo yana alwana ma makenya ira oh we. Ehkay Eshu odara su way oh....*"

Francine lifted the creature out of her hands. Carefully, she placed the head in front of the bowl, pulled out three feathers from the body and handed the headless bird to Oleander.

"Thea? Please?" Thea took the creature from Oleander over to the bucket with an odd but appropriate reverence. She dipped it, began plucking, she gutted it, cut it into pieces, singing "*Mojuba*—blessings oh blessings oh" all the while. Oiled and snapped onto the grill, the pieces browned up nicely, then into the stew pot along with chicken stock, red bell peppers, redskin potatoes, peeled okra, handfuls of red beans, ginger root and a blister-hot jalapeno. Simmer. Smile. More food for the guardian of the crossroads. The little cowry-eyed gremlin licked his lips.

Oleander took one of the hens out of the cage and turning her back so the other hens couldn't watch, held the bird out to Gina who gripped it between her square strong hands, fingers gripping the legs, thumbs across the wings, and hen's ass squished against her belly. She noticed with surprise that her hands didn't hurt and her grip didn't falter.

Once again, the little hen didn't fuss or even shiver as Francine reached out, left hand deep on the neck, right hand snapped the head.

Quick.

Oleander sang.

And again.

And the third.

Oleander sang.

Bleed them into the smaller bowl.

Wash them. Pluck them. Split them, gut them. Wipe up the shit. The remnants of the blood. The goop and grit of the gizzard. Off to the side, away from the ritual space, Thea and Queenie wallowed in feathers and red black blood. Gray yellow shit covered their arms up past their elbows, an unspeakable black feather slime smeared un-mystical patterns across their once sparkling white ritual dresses. They sang, eyes slitted nearly closed, strong brown fingers moving the creatures from life, through death, into sustenance. Foundation for dreaming, for dancing, for living with honor. Sacrifice.

Gina couldn't see that she was going to be much good doing the whatever heebie-jeebie stuff Frankie, Oleander and Julia were into over by the blood bowls. She stepped over to help pluck the little corpses. She looked up from the nearly de-feathered fowl and muttered, "Some really funky old time religion you got goin here. You guys do this sort of thing often? Like is this the usual dinnertime sort of thing?"

Queenie wiped a gooey hand across her forehead, wrinkled her nose, speaking with a strange gargle in her voice, "Not. At. All." Grimacing, "Just keep plucking."

Oleander finished up the last three pigeons, dropping the entrails in one bucket, placing the organs on a platter, slicing the birds through the breastbone, flattening them open with a cleaver.

Pluck. Gut. Wash. Flatten. Somewhere in the process they stopped being pecking squawking hens, they stopped being gross corpses. Gina mumbled, "Are these gonna be eaten? Um. By people?" She figured the birds became food somewhere along the line. Food for humans and for gods. It occurred to Gina that they always had been sacred. "I couldn't say it beats all hell out of stealin dinner from the grocery store." She thought about it awhile. "Messy. A lot more work. But I don't suppose ya can get arrested for this?"

"Yeah you can. They find out, they arrest us."

"Well. Crap. Authority is insatiable." Gina set her jaw, worked harder. After all, it was a crime what they did, and she was all up on crime.

Chop them. Baste them with oil and garlic and cracked black pepper. Crumble dried red peppers. "Hey. Don't put yer fingers in yer eye!" Julia dusted the tidy little carcasses with a mixture of cornmeal and spices, Queenie placed them carefully on the barbecue. The smell began to change into something delicious.

"People like to think we're evil. Anyone not Christian. Proper white Christian. Yeah, if they got nothin better to do, they throw us all in jail."

Gina scowled. "I dunno. That's fucked up." Tilting her head to one side, "That's just typical bullshit bigotry up and down."

Oleander grabbed the hose and squirted everyone.

Gina, dripping along with the rest of them, said, "I hope tonight's big celebration isn't gonna be more of the same?" She chanced a look at the little cement head. There was a bouquet of flowers next to him, a little cup waiting for his portion of the stew, a big fat cigar with three black feathers curled around it. It seemed to her that the little cowry face laughed at her. "Shit."

CHAPTER TWENTY-ONE

On the bay side of North Beach, several vertical blocks up, in the eastern landscape where the city cliffs were sharp and steep all the way down, a broken street wandered among piles of rubble—abandoned foundations from homes long ago fallen into urban oblivion. There was an empty lot hidden behind some skinny Bay trees. No one remembered it was there, even the bums seemed to prefer other camping grounds. At ten o'clock at night the only sound was a low rumble of the light rail trains below. The salt tang of the bay whiffed by now and then mixed with old inadequate sewers.

The night was clear, glass candles burned at the base of three scruffy paper-bark trees, the multitude of tiny flames cast the only light; busy figures flickered, their hands lit up for a moment as an offering was placed by the trees then they faded back into gloom-pale apparitions decked with red and black ribbons. A sharp scent of damask rose, chocolate, vanilla and cigars drifted across the lot.

As Raymond approached the first line of spooky trees the whole thing began to seem like a really bad idea. He trotted up the street a few steps in front of James, moving at a rapid pace, speaking over his shoulder, nervous, he half-hoped his companion would change his mind. "Now, someone may object to your presence but I've cleared it with my people so it should be okay." He searched the other man's face, "Keep your mouth shut, be polite if you say anything. You have any problems," he tapped his massive chest, "send em over to talk to me."

Raymond didn't have the smallest idea what he'd do if James had problems. Run maybe. Raymond had attended actual rituals a couple of times. Scared the piss out of him. He understood from Ellis that this one wouldn't be the real deal, just a quiet night-time visit with the guardians of the crossroads. "Lightweight. Nothin to worry about." Ellis had spoken with a slightly superior tone as he held out his hand for the money, "It'll convince your friend that you're well-connected. That is the point isn't it?" Raymond had nodded, slipped him a wad of twenties. So far so good.

Ellis had no idea what was going to happen. He thought it would be the same sort of rum and madness dance and shake things around that he'd done with the old man. A little more dramatic, what with girls and all. He started over to talk to the drummer but stopped when he saw Raymond come up the hill followed by James. Ellis muttered, "Holy fuck" and did a quick-step back into the shrubs along the edge of the lot.

James was smiling. Raymond was sweating. James thought that Raymond seemed to be an emotional fellow—he hadn't realized that, but then, he supposed black people were like that. Primitive rhythms and rituals and all. James didn't expect any problems. On the other hand, he would be damned disappointed if he didn't get to see chickens slaughtered, he'd read enough about primitive rituals to believe that was the high point. He couldn't see any chickens. Nor any goats waiting patiently to get their stupid throats cut. He wanted to see frenzied people sucking blood. He needed some scary stories to go with his trinkets. He needed some potential connection to his statue. He needed—

Instead of any proper prelude to gore, he saw graceful women in wide white skirts with red and black scarves wrapped around their hips arranging steaming pots of chowder, roast chicken, plates of baked sugar yams, black beans, bottles of soda, and loaves of homemade bread on a small rickety table. Their movements were quick and happy. His mouth pinched in irritation, he growled to Raymond, "What is this? Some kind of a church social?"

Raymond didn't respond, he'd caught sight of Oleander strutting off to one side, her long hair flaming in the moonlight. She was a gypsy vision in red velvet, already half gone from her normal personality. He'd seen her a few other times as she shifted gears moving towards a trance state when she pulled cards for him. He didn't like that—once she was in trance, Oleander never seemed to have much tolerance for Raymond. Ellis hadn't told him there'd be any real magic worked. Damn the boy. Raymond looked around but there was no sign of Ellis.

"Uh, James? If you don't want to stay—"

"No. No. This should be fun." Condescending. His eyes were traveling the crowd, picking out beautiful women of all colors. "A bit tame for my taste, but fun."

Thea and Queenie swirled out of the crowd, small black one and tall black one. They stood in front of James, glaring. Thea said, "What you doin here white boy?"

James made *um-urk* sounds, looking thunderstruck.

Queenie sneered at him, "Why you here? What you think you doin here?"

Raymond sputtered, "He with me. He with me."

Thea and Queenie peered at him then bent forward, leaning on each other, laughing and pointing. "Ohhhh. Oh. He with youuuuu."

Oleander, quivering with the approaching possession trance, stood by a straw basket. She held up a bottle of rum, turned entirely around as if searching the perimeter, checking the space, she opened the lid of the basket and sprayed a mouthful of rum on whatever was inside.

The basket began to glow.

Raymond felt the hair on his arms stand up.

A distinct feeling of unease was hitting Raymond in the stomach. He looked around for a port-a-potty but the edges of the little clearing were beginning to blur. A young Latino man peeled the red and white cloth covering off his drum.

"This one moves as if he already hears music." Frankie, long legged in a pair of skin tight white jeans, green Eisenhower jacket, and many strands of green and black beads around her neck, bent over to talk to the drummer. He bounced and swayed tapping his drums. In a world of his own. Frankie would run the ceremony that night but he was the heart beat.

Frankie carried the energy of Ogun, the master craftsman and warrior, but Ogun would not entirely possess her, his energy hovered around her in the faint outline of a tall powerful man, sword and shield, shimmering in the air. She motioned to Thea and Queenie, asking them to patrol the edge where the lot fell off into scree and cliff edge. She said, "Don't let any damn fools wander off there. Nobody can fly no matter what they tell you."

The deadly duo smiled.

"We'll see. We'll see. I wouldn't mind watchin em try."

"Long long way down to the bottom, by the time they smash up down there they willa bin flyin."

"Hey it's not the trip down what kills you, it's the splat at the bottom."

They shrugged, as one.

Queenie spoke: "We got to go make a offering first, okay Frankie? Thea's fighting that parole violation for... uh well. There's an APB because we ain't uh...." Quick glance at Oleander and away. "Well. We ain't gone to see the PO for awhile."

Frankie looked grim. Oleander raised an eyebrow. Now was a fine time to tell her. Just a fiiiine time. "How long's it been?" Her mind rumbling through the possible ways to change things around.

"Since we been livin here wichu."

Lovely. Just fucking lovely.

"And I'm fixin to follow her back inside. Unless of course they's some miracle."

Oleander shook her head, the world seemed really short of miracles lately, but if anyone could pull the rabbit out of the hat, it'd be Pomba Gira. Then again, Pomba'd probably want someone to cook it for her then she'd eat it. Does Pomba Gira like rabbit? Who knows.

Frankie splashed the drummer's hands with rum; his eyes slid a little back into their sockets, he nodded his head, took the bottle from her, gulped it. Shaking his big hands out, shivering his shoulders, he hovered over his drum, talking to it. He began to tap gently: *Chik chik, chik uh chik chik chik.*

Gina stood off to one side, her arms clutched across her belly, her eyes watchful, hooded. She was curious. Hungry. After all her work holding and plucking the damn birds she intended to at least get to eat some before she had to go swamp out the stinky bar.

On a bright cloth at the root of the central tree there was a small wooden idol of a fellow with a huge erection, a feather sticking out the crown of his head. James took notice, he'd seen similar work in Nigeria, never bothered to pick any up (next trip), nearby there were a couple large cigars from Dominica, several packs of cigarettes made of colored paper, the ones with the fancy gold tips, and a fake Dunhill tortoise-shell lighter. To one side, many many bottles of rum, on the other, a couple little crystal glasses, several bottles of champagne. Three deep red, almost black, roses. Sticks of coconut incense poked out of notches in the trees.

James muttered, "There's a lot of people in white. Seems inappropriate for a black magic ceremony."

Frankie, glowing green in the candlelight, overheard, flicked him on the shoulder with her hand, "Don't be an idiot." Disdain.

He bit his lip. His eyes traveled the length of her body. He didn't notice the angles, the tracks, the skull-beneath-the-skin. The woman seemed to vibrate with an almost masculine muscularity, she/he seemed tall, tall and wide with a strange tang of sexual electricity. Ah, his groin tightened.

She laughed at him. As she disappeared into the crowd he caught a glimpse of a long well-used knife belted at her hip.

Hissing, Raymond muttered, "Told you not to fuck with people here. I didn't say nothin about no black magic. Get that straight? Black magic's somethin else altogether."

James shrugged, pursed his lips, started to reiterate his speech about how all power is the same *lalala*. His glance fell on beautiful Julia, all in white with a white turban covering her head. Kneeling down in front of the rose altar at the foot of the straggly tree, she drew cornmeal designs on the ground. His mouth dropped open slightly, he was a connoisseur of young girls and beauty. "That one looks ripe." He leered at Raymond, "Ready and waiting."

Raymond had no interest in girls, he shrugged.

Julia's breathing was deep, from her belly, she was shining with concentration, her movements were fluid, precise, trained. A perfectly round circle, drawn counter-clockwise without a flinch, a cross, three tridents flowering into curls of pre-historic squiggles. She sat back on her heels to survey her work. She didn't look directly at the cornmeal design, but a bit above, as if some of the corn flour was hovering there, catching and amplifying the candlelight.

Something was there, her designs sparkled and winked.

Julia looked over at Gina, a huge smile on her face.

Gina waved. She noticed how pretty Julia was, how the designs sparkled. It wasn't any big deal, that was just the way things were. She didn't know she was looking at magic, that maybe she was supposed to be awed or scared or overwhelmed. Mostly she wondered if the no-sex trip when you dress all in white applied to Thea and Queenie. Somehow she didn't think so.

"*Ago Ago-oh.*" A double metal bell clanked. "*Ago Ago-oh.*" The drummer backed the call with a series of strong whaps on his drum. A dozen voices joined the first voice, "*Ago ago-oh.*"

James frowned. He didn't like what he didn't understand.

The wailing became a compelling chant. Rough lines of people slapping their hands, singing, stomping, shifting. Clap, chant, step in a circle, clap, chant, step in a circle: *Vinha caminhando a pe ver se encontrava a minha cigana de fe. Parou e leu minha mão. (Exu) Me disse a pura verdade, E eu so queria saber, aonde mora Pomba Gira Cigana, so queria saber, aonde mora Pomba Gira Cigana.*

Gina squeezed her eyes shut. Open. "Hunh."

After an imperceptible eternity a few people began stiffening staggering shaking, spinning and dropping to their knees. The crowd seemed to double, triple. Clapping chanting pouring rum, spraying it, laughing with wildly distorted features—some individuals rushed around tangling with everyone, ferocious.

Pomba Gira zukong ee Ay ya Oh rey rey. Pomba Gira ai yey Pomba Gira ai yey Pomba Gira zukong ee ya oh rey rey.

It was chthonic madness: Terrors from the pit. James's eyes grew big. He stepped back from the crowd hoping no one would touch him.

The chanting grew louder.

Raymond got separated from James, pushed into the center of the crowd he came face to face with Oleander. Before he could say anything Oleander grabbed him by the arm, in a deep voice she commanded Raymond to "Sing. Sing as if your life depended upon it." A bulge-eyed glare. "As in fact it does."

"Oleander?" Raymond's own voice was tiny, a fragile creeping thing. "Is that you?"

The only response was laughter. Huge. Overwhelming.

Darkness descended. Raymond slumped to the ground, an inexplicable reverb happening between his ears. He didn't move for the next hour, he sat there, legs stuck out straight in front of him, an expression of childlike awe on his broad face.

This wild ritual was a party, a weird party for the spirits of the crossroads, a place and time for them to come dancing among their human children. A place and time for the living gods to give their children a taste of the divine. The sacred is not always gentle, delicate or pure.

"What did you bring me?" Oleander's voice was throaty, her smile sinister. She touched James's chin, one long carmine tipped finger drawing a line down his throat to the top button of his shirt. "You were supposed to bring me something. Why didn't you bring it?" An undercurrent of threat. Her fingers proceeded to walk down his chest, as if she were stabbing him, unzipping him. He tried to move away, fascinated but uncomfortable, he looked around for Raymond, for someone to explain. "You have lots of beautiful things, yet you didn't bring me anything?" Her dark eyes flashed at him, angry. James thought she was the most wonderful creature he'd ever seen.

Oleander/Pomba Gira sneered, "Your hands are filthy from touching things which don't belong to you. For what? To keep them for yourself?" Her voice was loud, cruel. "Where is it?" Her fingers worked his solar plexus, drawing all the strength out. "My present."

James convulsed with the desire to puke; retching ineffectively, he wondered what the hellish woman had done to him with a simple touch to his belly. He wanted to grab her, his hands clenched on air, his fear and rage finding no target. He badly wanted to talk to Raymond, ask where the bloody chickens were—chickens he could handle, but this other, this other was just too bizarre. He was unable to stand up straight, terrified by the discovery that his cock was quite hard.

Oleander/Pomba Gira stalked away, planted herself in front of Gina. "Where is it?" She pouted as she spoke, "That man denied me my present. Useless pig. I'll deal with him later. But you," she tipped her head to one side, "you of all people should know how to find it." She lowered her voice, grabbed Gina's hands. "You are a daughter of the wind. You know places no one else knows, you will go there."

Gina heard the whistling of the wind, her hair and shirt were ruffled by a light breeze, which seemed to whirl around her.

"I want what's mine. You will find it and give it to me."

Gina was in that neither-nor world, enchanted with her first glimpse of what seemed childhood's sweetest reality. She hardly heard what Oleander was saying, she certainly wouldn't remember it, except perhaps the delicious words that she was a daughter of the wind. That much she liked.

Pomba Gira lifted her shoulder, showed her pointed teeth in a grim smile. "Mine is the pleasure, mine is the power, mine is the rapture. Unto death. I could pluck you like a chicken, string your guts out from here to the corner and burn your heart before I eat it."

Gina had heard that kind of talk often enough from people — although usually they had an agenda Gina could figure out: Robbery, extortion, simple-minded terrorizing. She calmly pulled her hands from Pomba Gira's grip, placing her own on Pomba Gira's lovely shoulders, she said, "Yes, of course. But you won't. Don't waste your valuable time."

Pomba Gira stepped back then, amused that the little round bird had so confidently touched her, "Ah. You are one I shall watch."

Frankie came up then and carefully, gently pulled Pomba Gira away for a drink of champagne, motioning Gina back to the edge of the crowd with her hand.

Unperturbed, Gina faded back. She wondered if she could get some chicken soon. Rice and beans. And home-made bread. She thought she'd skip the yams. Orange vegetables did not agree with her.

James, rushing up behind Oleander, hand out, found that he never quite could reach her, his mouth had gone slack, a line of spit formed across his lower lip, he was spun in a circle, all unresisting he began to dance a bone-shaking hopping flopping dance. A large very dark man with a red T-shirt and a black leather vest came up to him and grabbed him, they began to dance together, hips rotating together, imitating each other's steps, hands on each other's shoulders they spun around, wobbling, fierce and inseparable. Their stamping shuffling feet appeared to be dancing on live coals, sparks flew, flames rose up.

Pomba Gira strolled away. She approached Julia, her voice was sultry, sarcastic. "Are any of these people my children or is this just a bunch of derelicts showing up for the food?"

Julia waved a red fan, her eyes didn't look normal, her voice came from a long way away. "They're not so bad."

Stormy. "That one. That one can't have any food. He didn't bring me any presents even after he promised." Pomba Gira gestured, imperial, at the unfortunate James. "I want what he owes me." Suddenly enraged she turned to Frankie, recognizing her as the child of Ogun, the finest warrior, she railed, "I want my statue!"

"It doesn't do you justice."

"Then destroy it." Implacable, "Destroy it."

Frankie's expression did not change, she was used to tantrums, both human and divine, she just nodded.

"You can tell my horse I'm not coming back," Pomba Gira's hands were on her hips, "until this matter is taken care of." Pomba Gira bit her lip until blood flowed down her chin. "Properly."

Pomba Gira/Oleander's face went blank, her knees nearly gave way. Shaking, Pomba Gira turned back into Oleander who took several deep slow breaths. Frankie held her arm, gently, so she wouldn't slide to the ground. Oleander returned to consciousness with a deep shudder. She moaned. Still half-tranced she looked for a victim. Her glance fell on James, puking into the shrubbery. "Who is that man? Why is he here? Who brought him?" No one answered.

Snapping her fingers, whip crack in the dark night, Oleander circled the group of dancers.

When she looked for the stranger again, he was gone.

Oleander leaned back against a tree, sipped some sweet water and pulled her fragmented personality back into cohesion as she tried to piece together the odd sensations she'd just experienced. She was no stranger to trance, not even to very rough ones, although she didn't court them, she could handle them. Still, she was uncomfortable, as if she were caught in undercurrents, walking along a rocky shoreline where the sand edged away flat and gray to a dull pewter horizon. It seemed familiar, yet was unknown to her. A small crease appeared between her brows. Her memory prickled, but that was all. Sometimes trance was like that. But never without cause.

The night sky was approaching its darkest most silent hours, the seductive drumming faded into memory, a faint echo like the small tapping beat of a second secret heart, the pale moon setting far away in the West gave little illumination; in the darkness someone tripped over the bell, at the sound of its plaintive tinkle a couple people held their hands over their ears, groaning.

"Eat! Eat, everyone! We need to come back to earth." Oleander's voice was rich, without the slightest tremor, giving no hint of the strange paths her soul still followed. She was once again answering to necessity, the strong woman with strong hands, wise eyes, and proud carriage. Her dark reddish hair was braided up once again into a complicated crown across the top of her head. The wild woman she had been was nowhere to be seen, except in the smoldering coals of her eyes.

A broad smile split her face as she looked over the crowd around the food table. Her little island was filled with happy people in various states of psychic post-coital collapse. Good.

The drummer seemed nearly comatose, draped like a limp rag over his drum, the red cloth half-on half-off. "Somebody please bring that man a plate of food. Or next time he'll kill us with his mad rhythms."

"He's not tired from playing the drum, Oleander, he's sloshed from too much rum."

Her voice cracked with authority, "The Orisha drink the rum, not you."

Sly voice. "I think maybe he started early on the rum. Before the gods got here."

Her voice was sharp. "Feed him anyway. The gods drank the liquor, the gods will take it away." She looked more closely at him. "Eventually. Meantime our drummer must eat." She sat down, arranged her skirt, felt in the pocket for her red and black lucky charm. It was gone.

Oleander had expected it to go away at some point, it was a warning charm. She wasn't surprised it was finally gone, but, no question, she would have been happier if it had stuck around for awhile yet. "Eat. Eat. We didn't waste our time cooking for you ingrates, did we?"

Gina muttered, "Bout time. I'm like to faint from hungries."

Frankie was leaning over a woman on the ground, a huddled lump of red and black at the far edge of Oleander's vision. Oleander snorted, "People who don't know how to come back to themselves should maybe not go so far away."

Frankie looked so fragile that the moonlight showed through her body, just a glow of skin draped across the frame of bones. The huddled lump looked even less impressive. Oleander strolled over, she needed to talk with Frankie, sooner rather than later. She recognized their Ogun wasn't going to get any stronger, and the thought caught in her throat. "Maybe Ellis, the world's greatest chauffeur, could give us a lift home? Julia can run the clean-up crew."

Tired. "That sounds like a good idea. Soon as Ellis comes out of hiding."

Oleander raised her voice again, speaking to everyone, "Make sure you're all the way back in your own body before you start home." She knelt down beside Rhea who was flat on the ground, as she lifted her up in her strong arms, Rhea struggled, muttering sadly about dying children. Everyone is susceptible to the shadows of trance, clinging to the freedom of being 'other', they wallow in the memory of power; rather than return to the smallness of the human condition they wander around neither here nor there—a distinct disadvantage in the modern world of cars and cops. Oleander hugged her closely, looking out over the small lot, beyond the scattered crowd, her eyes saw something else, perhaps an echo of pain which she couldn't quite place in time or space. "Hey! Julia! Would you please bring Rhea some water and a blanket!"

"I'll go get it."

"It's okay, Frankie, Julia can do it. Rest your bones. If Ellis shows up, we'll head back home." Turning away, Oleander grumbled, "Little bastard's more trouble than he's worth."

Julia fetched water and a blanket, trundled Rhea off to the food table. They grazed for a while, then Gina followed Julia as they both wandered back to Oleander and Frankie. Bringing them each a full plate of food.

Their erstwhile chauffeur nowhere in sight, the women sat together under a eucalyptus tree, nibbling the food they had spent all afternoon blessing. Oleander said, "Well. What do you think, Frankie?"

"At least this time it didn't rain. And no one took a header over the cliff."

"But, Frankie, we need the rain."

"Tomorrow it can rain." Small smile. "Turn the whole place to mud. Tomorrow. Not tonight." They spoke in soft voices, the words carrying no meaning, it was the waves of gentle sound, the simple sitting close together that was important. "This Big Friday ceremony was odd. Good. But odd." Frankie carefully did not mention the statue.

Gina said, around a mouthful of bread, "And the food's really good. A midnight picnic. Mmmm." She looked at Julia, the girl had been rushing here and back again, taking care that everyone was comfortable and happy, she still had energy and to spare. Gina was too tired for the strenuous flirting Julia always aroused. And she had to get to the Lizard in just a few minutes anyway. She settled back to admire the girl and watch the weirdness wind down.

"The energy was ragged. Scattered. I don't know that anyone did any healing work tonight at all. Maybe because there were strangers here." Oleander shook her head. "I think I got another warning. Do you remember anything? Am I just being dramatic? In a completely twisted way of course."

Frankie put her thin hand over Oleander's, "You're right, there was a warning." Her voice went radio-show spooky: "Trouble ahead," she snickered, "Trouble to the left of us, trouble to the right." Julia giggled. Frankie shook her head. "Ah, don't listen to me."

"Who better to listen to?"

"Gina maybe? Even though she doesn't know what she's seeing? I'm so tired, so much of the time. While I have plenty of appreciation for where I am, for what you've done for me, for all of us... but sometimes it gets wearisome, you know?"

"You're wishing to be somewhere else."

Frankie looked sad. "I may be a dangerous guest in your house."

"Hah!" Oleander snapped her fingers, "Frankie, my dear old friend, every single person in my house is a dangerous guest. In one way or another." She turned her burning coal eyes on Gina. "Else you all wouldn't be coming around. On the other hand, we're each pretty strong. Very strong." A lift of one shoulder. "Don't underestimate us."

Gina gnawed a bone. "Underestimate, overestimate. I get what the deal is about Big Friday. Clapping. Chanting. Goddesses. Gods. Cheerful demons saying inexplicable things. The good part was that it all led to rice and beans and roasted chickens at the end."

Oleander recollected part of the night's ritual. "Pomba Gira said She wouldn't come again?" Direct. "You wouldn't know anything about that would you, Frankie?"

Frankie thought about it, said, "No."

"Old choices influence the far future, that's why we worship at the crossroads, to keep our choices honorable." Oleander was grim as she thought about her old choices, worried about the ones she needed to make in the present. Then she smiled. "Oh hell, our friend Pomba Gira won't be able to stay away. She loves a good party." Looking at the friends around her she lifted up her hands, opening them wide to take in the whole world. "We'll just have to give her another party real soon."

"That's okay with me." Gina stood up, dusting herself off, "But I either get ready plucked chickens from the store or we work something out. Like, if I'm gonna be doin this kind of thing very often I need to know how much is the rent and when can I move in?"

Oleander laughed, then she turned her face, her smile shattered as she looked over at Thea. She was hugging the tall slender Queenie, her shoulders shook as if she were crying. Biting her lips, Oleander shook her head. Too many things were going wrong.

"Well, I'd love to stay and chat with you about many things, but I have to go to work," Gina said before she disappeared into the shadows. She was glad to be out of there. Confused. Tired. With a vague elation. Oh fucking well, it'd all become clear in the morning. Or it wouldn't.

Ellis tiptoed over, he'd watched the ceremony from the shrubs at the edge of the lot. He was filled with jagged energy, sparking in fitful bursts, he wasn't sure what he'd seen and what he imagined: Was it otherworldly visitations or just mass psychosis? He squatted next to Frankie, his mind tangled up with crazy Pomba Gira ripping James a new asshole. He wouldn't let himself imagine what she might have done to his own sweet self if she had laid eyes on him. Oh man, it had been so clear to him what she'd been pissed about, hollering about her present. His statue. Oleander was gonna tie him to a rack and hang him over hot coals! He groaned, his fingers curled into a knot.

"Easy there youngblood," Frankie's voice hissed in his ear. "Don't take your ideas someplace they can't survive, you hear what I'm sayin?"

Hissing right back, "You told Oleander. You gave it up— you rotten cunt junkie…"

Frankie pulled away, half-smiling, "Nope. I didn't do that. And for your information, my cunt is as sweet as a ripe pomegranate."

"What are you guys whispering about?"

"My sexual organ."

Ellis forced is mouth into a smile. "So. We had quite a time."

Oleander said, "Some of us had quite a time. You, on the other hand, hid in the damn bushes like some porno voyeur.

What's up with that, Ellis? Thought you told me how you know all about this stuff?"

"I was like a guard, you know. Keeping out the riff-raff."

"Ellis, you are the riff-raff."

"Hey."

"In any case, you didn't do the job very well. I don't suppose you know who that man was?"

"What man?"

Oleander hissed, "Ellis, you don't lie very well."

"Lie? Me? Ha." Indignant. Cutting his eyes over at Frankie.

Frankie stood up. "Come on Ellis." She pulled Ellis to his feet, whispered, "One of these days you might learn how to behave, in the meantime, quit being such a dope." She didn't mean it unkindly. "If you can't lie real good, just say 'Yes, Ma'am,' and leave it alone."

Ellis glared at her as she leaned on his shoulder. She insulted him yet needed his support. She said, "Don't look at me like that. Ya never realize how fragile the human structure is, until ya get old or sick or 'go missing' in trance. The other worlds are seductive, it's kind of a pain to come back to human frailty."

Ellis mumbled, "You guys ain't frail—look to me like y'all could rip someone's heart out just on a whim."

"What did you say?" Oleander's voice was sharp, heart-ripping in fact.

Ellis used his delicate voice, "Come on, Oleander, you know what I mean. That guy doesn't matter. You guys scared him good." Preening as if he was a party to the scaring.

"Scared?" Oleander, unmollified, fingered the red and black beads around his neck. "Scared? That's hardly the point. We're not some theatrical group. We're not doin this to impress OR to frighten. Listen Ellis, listen real good, okay? I don't know where you got these beads but I don't think you earned them."

"Wait a minute, it's not fair to be picking on me, I do my best. After all," he spread his hands wide, palms up, motor oil shining in the creases, appealing to her better nature, "My road is not an easy one." Approaching that smug whine he thought was convincing.

Oleander let her mouth fall open in mock surprise. "Oh? Your road? Not easy?" She growled, "Don't get me started."

The stupidity of it all overwhelmed Ellis for a moment, his mouth hung open, his narrow pink tongue pushed against his top teeth as he slammed it shut. He gripped Frankie's arm with a near-junkie panic of his own, walked a few feet away. "We still cool, Frankie?"

Frankie's mouth turned up on one side, "I am cool. But if you squeeze any tighter you're gonna break my arm."

He released his grip, muttering apologies, "I mean to say— you and me—we still gotta deal?"

Frankie lifted her chin in Oleander's direction. "When she's Pomba Gira she knows things, but Oleander doesn't necessarily know everything Pomba Gira knows. You follow?" She rubbed her arm, tipped her head to one side as she stared at him, "I told ya what the deal was. It still stands. However, let's you and I never discuss my cunt again." Mild. "Else I'll hand you your balls on a plate. You understand?"

His eyes were slitty as he looked at her. He didn't want to talk genitals. He had to return his statue to Pomba Gira.

Ellis curled his hands into fists. 'Wait and see' never worked out for him. But his time would come. He was man enough to overlook the petty shit. Yeah. Huffy, he muttered, "Any time you ready to go, let me know." He stomped off toward his limo.

They followed him in silence.

Standing by the limo, Oleander spoke off-handed, like it didn't really matter, "There's no comfortable place to go once you start mixing it up with the gods."

Ellis thought that was entirely unfair, after all, it wasn't like he ever chose to get involved in this horror show, it wasn't like anyone ever sat him down, told him what was up with any of it, it wasn't like he even had a bloody clue as to what was expected. Scowling, he opened the limo doors. "Okay Ladies, your chariot awaits you." And your chauffeur, as usual, is at your service too. Damn. "So get in the car, already." He would not think about it anymore.

Oleander was staring at him, a speculative gleam in her eye. Information which comes out in trance can be buried, but it will not stay buried for long.

He stared at the stars and hummed intensely to the world at large, "Don't ask me how I get myself into trouble, don't ask me how I do it."

"All right, Ellis, I won't."

"What? What?"

Oleander mused to no one in particular as she climbed in the limo, "When there's music people lose track of how it echoes into the silences. Our feet pounding the earth is what's real, not just in ceremony but in our lives."

Ellis stood outside the driver's side door frowning in perplexity. He had prepared to defend himself against what he expected to be an accusation. He took a deep breath, echoes of some high school text, sociology or something, rattled in his brain, he auto-piloted the words, happy to follow this change in subject. "You tellin me that ceremony and daily reality are the same? Damn. Seems to me they're entirely separate. Life just isn't like that whirling madness back there. We aren't primitives, our 'feet pounding the earth'. Dancing? Mindless oblivion? That shit won't make this fucked up world better."

Oleander's laugh was deep in her throat. "Oh? Primitives? Sexual libertines? Idolaters? And aren't we just exactly that?"

Ellis drove them home in unhappy silence. Damn them all to Hell anyway.

CHAPTER TWENTY-TWO

"Who were those people, man? That shit should be illegal." Belligerent, James rapped his knuckles on Raymond's workbench trying to make the big man pay attention to him.

Distant. "Probably is illegal. We live, after all, in a Christian country" Raymond said. He shrugged, illegalities were not his concern unless he was arrested. He frowned at the small carving he was examining. "Here. Look at this. Does this piece look old?" He held up the small dark wooden mask for James to see. "Supposed to be a Dan tribal passport-token a couple hundred years old." Raymond settled back, content with his knowledge of old African carving and modern copies.

James could have given Raymond the standard lecture, it came with the territory: Within the first three months traveling around collecting "antiquities" you either learned it or blew all your money on junk. The actual provenance of any particular item meant nothing to either of them other than getting a good price or putting their supposed erudition on display. "I don't give a shit about your counterfeit damn carving." James voice was ragged. "Sorry to be so blunt, old man, but if you paid more than twelve dollars American, you got ripped off. They're turning these out by the cart load."

"Mmm. I bought a cartload for twenty five. Each sells for between—"

"Never mind about that. I need to know who those people are, who is the woman who seems to be the cult leader?"

Raymond's basic protective instincts woke up. Not of course to protect Oleander, but to protect himself. "Hmm?"

"Who's the hot one with the body and the long hair?" He hadn't had a hard on like that in—in—well, a long time. "And where the hell were you?"

Raymond Arthur put the little carving down with regret. "I was involved in a business discussion with some members of the group, my apologies. I didn't realize you would feel abandoned." Gentle concern.

It isn't good for a man who depends on cold charm to be ruled by emotion, but poor James flared up anyway, his voice skittering toward the higher tighter vocal range. "Abandoned? I didn't feel abandoned." Not much. "I felt ripped off!" He fell back on intellectual pride. "That wasn't a magical ritual; it was just a buncha stoned barbarians. I know from magical rituals." He'd never been to one before. "Nothing went on last night that a psychiatrist couldn't fix." Huffy, he paced away, and back. "Drunken psychotics. Someone needs to make them take their Antabuse." James put an icy tone in his voice, "Tell me, Raymond, what do you really know about these people?"

Raymond didn't look up. "Give it up, James. No one's impressed with your routine today." He turned the little passport face down as if what might transpire might be too traumatic for one of such tender years. "You had the shit scared out of you. Admit it. Get over it." Raymond said that to people a lot. He, himself, tended to get over most of his frights fairly quickly, to the point where he never remembered really being scared.

James put his hands on Raymond's workbench. They were curled into fists. He'd been—he'd been—he finally thought about it directly: He'd been tossed right out of his mind and body into some nowhere place where he'd been threatened, insulted, and yes baby, scared shitless. Yes. And he didn't like it at all. He took a breath, about to deny.

Raymond short-stopped him, using his most tired, worldly tones. "Relax. You must know that most rituals of this type have a strong element of chaos." He picked his carving back up. "If I didn't know better, my gut would tell me this particular sculpture is authentic." His gut was large and hard to ignore.

"Fuck that. Listen." James took a long breath. "Someone stole a large statue out of my shipment from Brazil." Tension curled the edges of his voice. "It looks like gold, and it's jeweled. It's made by your friend the famous drunken Brazilian." He waved his hand at the drooping metal man in the shop's deepest shadows. "Not like that one. Mine is gorgeous. Utterly unique. Listen to me, man! A gold statue over three foot tall." He shivered over the potential value on the gluttonous West Coast market. "It's gone! But your psychotic lady friend was hollering at me about it. Claiming I owed it to her." James's patience was shriveled into nothingness. "Goddamn. It was stolen and those people last night know about it." He bent down, got right in Raymond's face. "And I suspect that you can put your grubby fat hands on my statue in fifteen minutes. You can make them give it back to me." His teeth clicked when he shut his mouth. "Just go over there and tell them it's mine. Mine."

Lifting his head Raymond was not happy to find James's pale eyes so close, boring holes in his face. He stood up, always an advantageous position. "No," he sighed. "It's probably not even in the Bay Area anymore." He sighed again, shaking his head. "Well, strange things happen." His mind was clicking at warp speed. The faster his mind, the slower his words; he spoke, mildly, "Where did you say you picked up this stolen piece?"

James ground his teeth. "I mentioned it when I was first here. When I asked about the old man's statue you have in back." James groaned, his head felt like it was filled with hot sand.

Raymond let his lips curl, he knew how to appear unimpressed. "It sounds like something Vicente would make. Is the image that of a gorgeous black woman?" He was guessing, "Maybe it looks something like our lovely friend from yesterday's little ceremony?" Raymond had seen several smaller statues that Vicente had done which favored his lost wife—but Vicente'd never have let any of those out of his hands.

"Well, I didn't notice a resemblance." Defensive. But now that it had been brought up, maybe.

Mild. "Oh, you might not have noticed anything, after all too many white people think we all look alike." A not quite accurate statement coming from Raymond, very few humans looked anything at all like him.

James ground his teeth. "It was stolen from me."

"Bingo." Vicente usually told him when he had a large piece up for sale. Raymond sucked on his cheek, Vicente hadn't mentioned anything about it last week when they'd talked. The man was a secretive old bastard. Raymond thought it was one hell of a coincidence. Why didn't people confide in him? They could accomplish so much more if they weren't continually working at cross purposes? People ought to just trust him. Raymond dressed his words in velvet as he spoke to James, "The woman you call my lady friend might have been simply talking gibberish, it's hardly likely that she knows anything about it." Well, he didn't say it out loud, but if he didn't know about it, then Oleander couldn't know about it. All information about Vicente or his art work came through Raymond—that was the way it had been from the jump. His lips tightened, and the arrangement would stay that way. He pushed his lips out, blowing. He would talk to Vicente soon. "That's one of the main things I've noticed at these rituals, lots of gibberish." Raymond felt the need to be very convincing, turn the conversation, "You're upset because there wasn't any blood. Isn't that what it is? You're a bit of the ghoul, eh?"

James's manner was brusque. "Three foot tall female figure, well above the standard workmanship from Northeastern Brazil. Extremely fine, extremely rare. Tremendously valuable." James couldn't see any change in Raymond's expression. "There's money in this." This statement caused no apparent impact on Raymond either, perhaps a slight stiffening of the man's shoulders, it was impossible to know. Like talking to a sack of—

"In any case," James regained control of himself, "Gibberish or no, I need to speak with that woman again. We didn't, ah, communicate as well as I'd have liked."

"Oh?" Raymond carefully printed on one of his cream colored price cards: Nineteenth century, Dan passport mask $150.00. He waved the card in the air to dry the ink. "People don't generally indulge in casual conversation at these things."

"Our conversation was not casual. She knows about it."

"Hmm." Dodgy. "I'll ask around, see if anyone can put me in touch with whoever it was." Prissy. Standing on the principle of confidentiality.

James laid a C-note on the workbench. "For getting me access to the ceremony." Stuck in his brain was the odd idea that a hundred dollars would get him anything. "The name of that woman."

* * *

Raymond stopped by Oleander's place later that evening, casual. He told himself he'd maybe talk to Oleander, maybe have her pull the cards for him, maybe they'd discuss Vicente, maybe she'd recall how much she owed him? Damn, he grumbled as he walked up the steps, he really hated to be cut out of anything. Besides, he had a delivery for Francine in his briefcase. That always got him a moment or two to probe for information. Francine had become less and less talkative over the past few weeks—if he could stick around until she got loaded she'd tell him everything she knew about anything unusual. Yes. There's the plan, Stan. Raymond was smiling as he opened the glass doors.

First thing he saw was Ellis pacing the lobby, "Hey." He reached in his pocket. "I lost track of you at the ceremony. Thanks for setting it up so nicely." His fingers closed on a bill. "Here's some money for your trouble." He handed the bill over. Ellis pocketed it in one swift move.

Raymond noticed after it was gone that it was the C-note James had given him. Too late.

Raymond licked his fat lips, motioning Ellis outside. "So. That money's also for you to keep me informed, you know."

Ellis looked at Raymond as if he was stupid. "That will buy piss all information."

Raymond fumbled in his pocket, he had no intention of pulling any more out, but the fumble was suggestive of more to come.

Ellis didn't seem to get it, he held his hand out again. Food. Gas. Cigarettes.

Raymond ignored the hand. "My man. You know, the guy who wanted to see the ceremony was very, ah very impressed." Raymond waited. Ellis edged off back towards the lobby. "He seems to have lost an important piece of art, offering some real money for its return."

Ellis stepped, slowly, carefully not hurrying, not hurrying not hurrying, towards the glass doors.

"You keep your eyes peeled, okay?"

"Sure thing." Muttering. "Sure thing." Jeez-uz kee-rist on a krutch. Could things get any worse?

Frankie came out then. Cool breeze. "Hey Raymond. I been waiting for you."

Ellis looked at Frankie, he had the sliding feeling that things could get worse. Hissing he stepped between them, his shoulders hunched, "You doin some deal with this sleaze bucket? What you plannin? What?" His fists were balled so tight the muscles on his arms were jumping. His eyes were pinpoints of dark red.

"You're wide of the mark, Ellis. This some private business. Get out of here." Frankie was tired.

He spun around, pushed his face into Raymond's. "Watch yourself dude. Oleander wouldn't like it if she knew you were bringing perverts to her ceremonies."

Raymond sucked his gold tooth, didn't bother to remind Ellis that he had been in on the arrangements, that he had just received a largely unearned C-note which, as a matter of fact, Raymond would much rather have not given him. Instead Raymond growled, "Watch your own ass, youngblood." He growled with a dangerous delicacy. Raymond pranced past him, taking Frankie by the hand, "Too bad the boy's always in a state." Cute. "One state or another." He gave Frankie the obligatory wink. "You know Francine, I'm curious about a coupla things?"

Sharp. "Curiosity's not my problem. You would do well to keep your curiosity to yourself." She stood in his way just inside the doorway, not letting him come all the way inside.

Ellis stomped off down the steps to his limo.

Raymond looked past her, his attention apparently engaged with the blood red walls. "Has Ellis's temper gotten worse lately, do you think?"

"What you mean, do I think? Of course I think." She held out her hand. "But not about Ellis's temper. Now, let's see what you've got."

"May I please come inside? It's highly unseemly to hand you things, wedged as we are in the front doorway."

Highly unseemly? Frankie stepped aside. She'd have his highly unseemly fried on a stick if he didn't come through for her with some serious dope. She thought she was inured to his annoying proclivities, his need to draw out every deal into something grander than it was in sordid reality. Time was getting short for her, and the less Raymond took of it, the happier she would be.

He opened his Moroccan satchel, pulled out a tiny shrink-wrapped square. "Pharmaceutical." He figured she'd be pleased, maybe talk to him a little about just what exactly was going on in Oleander's devious mind.

"As if I don't get enough bloody pharmaceutical drugs." Bitter laughter. "Oh hell, what's organic these days anyway? Feh. I want all you got, tell me how much I owe you and get your big sloppy butt out of here."

"You owe me an explanation about how come you're in such a terrible mood?"

"Raymond, you stupid fuck, I'm dying, I hurt like hell, I can't do anything I want to do, I'm fighting with my best friends, I can't sleep right I can't shit right I can't breathe right."

Hands up, pleading. "Ow. Ow. Okay. I'm sorry." He put the little square baggie on the counter. "There."

She smiled, peeled off a large bill. Turned to leave, biz-ness concluded, why linger?

"So. What's Ellis so bitchy about?"

Muttering, she didn't turn back to him, "He thinks I lost somethin of his, but I didn't." Frankie hardly noticed the tremor this information caused Raymond, she was busy balancing the square in her hands, her ability to know the weight of almost any baggie was uncanny. "This one," she held it up, "is light."

"Couldn't possibly be." He looked sly, "I weighed them out myself this morning."

"Crap." She took back her bill. "It's light." She replaced the bill with two smaller ones. Daring him to complain.

"Okay, tell you what," Raymond was thinking fast and mean, "I'll make it up to you soon. With some Especialidad."

Francine was maybe more trouble than he needed, she existed only, in his opinion, to keep him up-to-date. "Seems lots of people have been losing things lately. Wouldn't it be good," Raymond stretched his lips, "if I was the one to find them? Rather than someone who might not know how to properly appreciate them?"

"I've never doubted your ability to appreciate the finer things, Raymond. If anything seems to be lost and I hear where it might be you'll be the first one I'll call. How about that?"

"That would be good, Francine. That would be very good." He shut his satchel. "And don't forget, I will have something special coming in soon for you. I'll make sure you get it." His eyes were cold.

"That would be good, Raymond." Barely hiding the sarcasm.

"Please tell Oleander I stopped by. I'd like to set up an appointment for a reading in the next day or two?" He paused. "And remind her that some time ago she gave me a bottle of Gambler's Hand oil which worked so very well that I'm now completely out of it. I'd like another one."

"Right. Give us a call later tonight and Julia will give you a time."

Kiss kiss in the air to her retreating back, and he toddled off deep in thought.

"Bastard." Frankie went up to her room, put the kettle on the hotplate, heated up the strange brew Oleander had made for her to try out. She looked at the plastic square of heroin, opened it and eyeballed the dope. If Raymond had been weighing dope that morning he left his little finger on the scale for this one. Did he really think she was so far gone that she wouldn't notice? If it was bunk she'd kill him. But then again, if he came up with something really nice, she'd forgive him. Shrugging, she put the square behind a jar on her spice shelf, tried to figure her next move. Her next several moves. This was one checkmate she didn't dare fuck up. And she couldn't think clearly enough. Not nearly clearly. Not clearly nearly. Fuck. She wouldn't put her money on herself this time. But there wasn't any other way to bet.

CHAPTER TWENTY-THREE

Gina trotted into the lobby, "Howya doin Oleander?" She pulled several flowers out of the huge bunch in her hand, gave them to Oleander with a bow, like so. She was absolutely too through with sleeping in the crappy basement of the Lizard. Tonight she'd confront Oleander with her need for a place. Do or die.

"Oh, thank you very much." Oleander tucked the corners of her mouth in, dimples showing in her cheeks.

Gina shuffled her feet, "How is she today?"

"Not too bad. Brought her up some brew awhile ago, she was looking forward to your visit." Smile. "Besides, La Favorita is upstairs with her, she's eager to have another lesson in tag."

Gina kept her head down, rumpling around in a big shopping bag. "Rita's better company than most people. Here, I picked up a kind of Pomba Gira thing for you." Pulling out a red lace camisole, black ribbons woven through. Explaining, a guilty edge. "Maybe more of the ritual stuck than I cared to admit. This seemed like something she might like, you know?"

Gina had traded three bottles of Lethal Jack's rum for a dozen clean straight-from-the-manufacturer syringes for Francine but then she saw a guy she used to do business with back in the day hurrying along the street with an armload of hot clothes so she traded three of the syringes for the camisole, had to tell him twice that it wasn't for her and no she wouldn't model it for him. Damn. Now, of course she worried she should have stuck with the rum. Or kept all the points. The camisole seemed silly. "What you think?" Gina held it out, dubious.

"It's lovely." Oleander stroked it. "It's silk, you know."

Gina smiled, "Oh yeah?" Shy. Crease between her eyebrows. "I never know if I've blown it until I see the look on someone's face." Shrugging. "So. It's yours. Or hers. Whoever it fits. Okay?" She didn't say she'd like to be there when Oleander wore it sometime. Sometime not religious. There was a time—when Gina was feeling particularly suave, or maybe just loaded, she would have followed up the camisole with some clever suggestion, or maybe she would have simply been blunt. Oh hell, the woman really confused her. Anyway, Gina reminded herself, she had other business to conduct with Oleander. Housing. Sleeping. Fucking. Shit. She didn't know how to begin.

Oleander began to laugh. "Oh, Gina. Thank you, thank you." She did a little dance to the music playing on the stereo, some kind of shivery Brazilian thing. She held up the camisole as if it were her dance partner.

Bobbing her head, Gina kind of laughed too, not sure why; her connivings weren't always met with such delight. She wasn't, after all, any kind of professional conniver, it was more a matter of stumbling onto shit. She grinned, foolish, "Well. Hey. Glad you like it." She took a breath—the victim was primed, dancing with a silk camisole. Ready Steady Go. She opened her mouth.

James came through the front doors with a confident, worldly step. He gave both Gina and Oleander a big smile, introduced himself with that cosmopolitan edge which usually worked so well, elegant and sort of sorrowful, like European money devastated at the toll the latest war had taken on the youth of America. Or something. Bogus. He apologized to Oleander for not introducing himself when they spoke at the lovely little ceremony. Shook Gina's hand with a marvelous frozen gaze. Proffered his classiest card. To Oleander, not to Gina. Oleander did not take it.

Gina looked him up and down, cut her eyes at Oleander, the man was too rich for her blood. She was overwhelmed with a desire to go through his pockets. She clutched her bag of illegal syringes and stood her ground.

He turned his chiseled profile toward Oleander. The sun through the front windows sparked in his pale hair.

Oleander ignored him, carrying the camisole in her hand she stepped behind the counter, she put it away with care and slowly looked up.

"We met the other night at the little, ah, ceremony? You must remember me?" Pigeons couldn't coo as seductively as James.

Waves of suspicion came from Oleander; no matter, James was practiced at ignoring hostility. All in a day's work. Cream. "You said several things to me which I didn't understand. It was recommended that I speak to you rather than attempt to figure it out myself." His voice was deep, sexy, his posture was chaste, drooping.

"I'm sorry. I don't know what you're talking about." Freeze.

"Forgive me. My old friend Raymond assured me you could put my worries to rest."

No thaw. Two could do this dance. Throaty, "Perhaps your old friend was mistaken." She checked her watch. The gesture was intentional.

Gina went and sat on the couch. Crossed her arms. Glared.

James reached in his pocket, pulled out a thin silver chain with a double-ax bauble set in a black and red matrix. "At the ceremony you expressed your displeasure that I hadn't brought you any of my pretty things." He pressed it into her unwilling hand. "I picked up this lucky charm in Brazil. Wonderful country. I hoped this would take some of the edge off your anger."

Her fingers uncurled, she let the axes slide onto the counter. Barely a glance, as if it were a small insect. As in fact, it was. Another lucky charm. She'd rather it wasn't there, but there it sat. A cheesy piece of dime store crap. Her eyes flared up for a second, she turned her head away.

James hesitated. Apparently neither Oleander nor Pomba Gira would be so easily mollified.

"I don't know what you're talking about." Slight turn further away. She was a busy woman.

James leaned on the counter, his pale eyes abruptly fierce. "I must talk to you. Seeing you again today has erased all my previous visions of the future. It is an annihilation." He raised his hands, let them fall limp. His romantic mime was never very good. "My pride is at your feet."

"I don't want your damn pride underfoot."

"I have a problem." He looked around the little red lobby. His glance passed over Gina without a flinch.

Oleander glanced at her watch again. "I don't give a flying fuck about your problem. You have about another minute." She didn't need this man's attitude, bouncing between arrogance and self-pity. Annoying rich jerk.

"I'm an art collector, I've got some lovely pieces which I just brought back from Brazil." James laid his card on the desk, with a firm hand he wrote his hotel and room number. "I'd be honored if you'd stop by, give me your opinion."

Flat. "I don't give opinions. Especially about art objects."

"I'm sure I can meet your consultation price." He smiled. His charm was back on track, he thought he had her nearly convinced. "Unfortunately, while I'm an expert at picking beautiful things, I'm a novice at guessing their spiritual significance."

"It's not a matter of guesswork."

Too quick. "Yes. Yes. That's why I need your help." The sun through the glass doors caught him in its glare, giving him a halo. Oleander thought that was probably what Lucifer would look like on a bad day.

He continued, "Come. Look at them and if you are still unwilling to help, perhaps you can recommend someone else?"

He thought she wavered. He pushed his supposed advantage. "One of my best pieces has gone missing, a lovely golden Venus, about three feet high." Her face remained closed. "It seemed to me that you were perhaps speaking about it the other night, at the little ceremony."

"Wasn't me." Oleander sighed. She hated trying to explain, some people were simply incapable of accepting the information of their own damn eyes. This was going to get tricky. She resented it. She hadn't the foggiest idea what she'd said or where to find his stupid Venus.

"But it was you. You were irritated that I hadn't brought you something."

Oleander didn't wait for him to finish. "Stop. You're mistaken." James was unaccustomed to anyone telling him he was mistaken, the correct reaction was, he knew, to look apologetic for his mistakes, to hide his annoyance with the classic shuffle foot *aw*-sorry, but he was so angry that his expression wobbled, making him look goggle-eyed.

Oleander was fascinated, she hoped he would suddenly spin around and start to sing or puke green or something. She continued in a prim librarian voice, "At our ceremonies people go into trance. We say and do things which we in our own selves are not always aware of or even in control of. We are possessed by the living gods."

Gina still thought it sounded like a weak excuse for getting shit-faced and carrying on, but she kept her mouth shut. She vaguely remembered Oleander's Pomba Gira talking about some statue that night but she didn't see how it could be all that important. Besides, she couldn't afford to get side-tracked: she needed a place to live. This irritating man would have to leave. She stood up, ready to do her best imitation of someone big and threatening.

Oleander shot her a conspiratorial amused glance. "I'll be glad to look at your Brazilian wares, simply because these things interest me. If I have any opinion I'll discuss my fees at that time. If I wish to purchase any of them, we can talk about that too. But as to any comments you feel I made the other night regarding your lost statue, or anything else, I can't help you." Her tone told him to leave it there.

He wouldn't, of course, leave it there. He'd play her game for a while though. He sucked his bottom lip into his mouth, ran his teeth over it. "Then I will be happy with whatever time you can give me. How about this afternoon? Four o'clock?"

"I'll see how my schedule looks." She was untouchable. "I'll call you."

Smiling, he left.

Glowering at his back, Gina side-stepped to the counter.

CHAPTER TWENTY-FOUR

The next time Ellis drove Julia and Francine to the weekly hospital checkup, Ellis winked at Julia, making her smile-pretty-girl, but that was all she'd do, she wouldn't even loiter a moment with him to discuss, say, cultural education in the black community. Or the difference between dark chocolate and....He blamed her indifference on Frankie's presence. Frankie also seemed reluctant to talk to him, even casually. Her expression was a constant warning as if all he had to do was make one wrong step and his ass would be in the sling. He figured everyone was pissed at him just because when he saw opportunity, he took advantage of it. Hell, James didn't deserve that statue. For that matter, neither did Frankie. And she knew it. Shit. And then—and then there was Oleander, who in theory knew nothing of any of this. Ha. Right. Queen Bitch. Like anything that went wrong was his fault. Like he cared. Ellis slid behind the wheel of his cab, depressed. He seemed to have an endless capacity for doing the wrong thing.

Why was it that some women liked him just fine but others, well, others treated him like a pariah? It had to be something with the women, not with him. He pulled his cab up to the loading zone in front of the Lizard Lounge, hopped out, going to get himself a drink. Put all this shit to one side. Yeah.

He caught sight of Gina sitting in the dimmest back corner of the bar glaring at a pack of unopened cigarettes; he slid onto the stool next to her. "Open them. Or don't open them. They ain't gonna open themselves."

"The hell they ain't." Jaw set. Didn't lift her eyes.

"Okay. Whatever you say." Gina hadn't looked up yet. He pulled out his own pack, shook two cigarettes out, lit them both, handed one to her. "Suck on this."

Lethal Jack had the obligatory sign: No Smoking. Half the time he had a cig stuck to his lower lip. Sign be fucked—bars were for Smoking. Drinking. Conniving.

Gina heaved a sigh. "What's on your mind, Ellis? Why can't you ever just say what's...."

"How righteous is Frankie?" Couldn't put the question much more bluntly. "She stand up?"

Straight. "I've trusted her with my life. Junky or not, she's the most stand up person I've ever known." Gina's round eyes were sincere. They would have been, even if it wasn't true; what'd the man expect, she rat out her friend? But it happened to be true, so far as Gina knew, and in some of these matters, Gina knew pretty far.

Ellis relaxed. A smile began in the corners of his mouth. "But she likes to game people?"

"Does the Pope shit in the woods? Of course she does. She good at it too." Direct. "What's she got you walkin on coals about?"

"I can't tell you."

"Die then. Die." The man was useless. "Okay, Ellis. How about giving me a lift to Chinatown in that fancy ve-hicle of yours? I gotta date with a acupuncturist, a woman pretty as sunrise, says she can fix where it hurts." Gina smirked. "I don't believe her, but I like to watch her move. You know?"

Another one who seemed unmoved by his manly charms. "Gina, do you like me?"

"You givin me a lift? No charge?"

"Sure. What's that got to do with anything?"

"Then I like you fine." Gina bounced around the end of the booth. Spun her unopened pack down the bar to the bartender. "Hang on to those for me? I'm still debating about quitting." He stared at the cigarette smoking in her hand. She smiled. "Ah well. See ya in a few, Jack."

The bartender nodded his head. Didn't move from his stool next to the television. Replaying tapes of the Kentucky Derby from ten years back, when horses knew how to run.

The bar phone rang. "Hey, Shorty. Phone's for you."

Gina stopped. Didn't turn around. Shorty? Bloody hell. "You talkin to me?" Ha. Robert de Niro move over.

"Yeah. Yeah. Come pick up the stupid phone."

Gina grunted into the receiver. Said "Oh." And "Cool."

And "Well, not cool but I am grateful, you know?" and "I'm sorry, but glad, you know?" and "Okay, I'll be over some time soon to talk details." Hung up with a contorted look on her face.

Ellis raised his eyebrows. Gina ignored him, wandered outside.

"So? So?"

"That was Oleander, the lady of my dreams. She told me that two perfectly nice women, nutcases, true, are going back to the big home in the valley for wayward girls." Ellis nodded, a small gesture to let her know that he didn't understand. "Oleander says Thea and Queenie copped to a parole violation, I gotta place to live. Crappy the way things turn out."

"What's your problem? You gotta place to live. Be glad. Shit happens." He stopped and backed up a little. "Well they're really scary bitches, you know? I can't but think they'll um, do fine in jail, yunno?" He picked at his lip. "Well. It sucks. But then, it doesn't, yunno?"

Gina watched him try to find the moral in the situation. Fail.

"Put all that aside. What's important now is that you will be there with Frankie and you can jam her about, well, about stuff for me."

"It's better when you don't talk."

"But you still like me?"

Gina was proud that even though she might be fucked up at least she didn't lay out her insecurities on the street. "Ellis? Ellis? What's not to like about you? Come on, let's go."

He still didn't unlock her side of the limo. Somehow Ellis didn't feel like they were communicating real well. As he slid behind the wheel he realized that happened a lot with women. He leaned over to peer in the rear view mirror.

Gina banged on the door. "You are not a gentleman."

He sat for a moment staring straight ahead before he opened it. "You may be right." They drove in silence.

When she got out at Chinatown he asked her to reassure him once more about how trustworthy Frankie was.

"Trustworthy? I never said she was trustworthy. I just said she stand-up." A mean little smile on her sweet rosebud mouth.

CHAPTER TWENTY-FIVE

Botanical prints lined the lobby of the Criterion Hotel, their classic lines were indicative of an artist who never left the studio to look at any flowers, they were framed in marvelous carved and gilded antique frames—further indicative, Oleander thought, of an interior designer with more money than good sense. Indicative. The word came into her mind attached to the legal term 'indict'. It was a warning of sorts but she didn't know what to do with it. Her black suede stilettos sang as she swished forward in the hush of Persian carpets too recently vacuumed. She assumed the mantle of royalty, assessed the artistic merits of her environment: Touches of the Raj mixed with Swedish modern pale oak benches, beige linen wall paper embossed with something annoying. These lobby designers simply couldn't make up their minds, woke up one morning hollering, "Let's do it allllll. Whatever we want! We can! We're richichich." Oleander was a sucker for opulence, but this was simple, um, she paused, eyes narrowing, ostentation. Yes. Satisfied with her appraisal, she approached the empty front desk.

An elegant jockey in a fawn colored uniform padded on silent hooves across the hotel lobby to inquire how he might be of help. "Please." She pushed James's card onto the smooth counter top, "Please let him know I am on my way up to see him now." No name. Just a swivel on her heel and a sensual glide to the elevator. She heard the clerk mumble, "Right-oh."

As Oleander ascended in solitary faux-splendor, she speculated about the demented dreams of hotel decorators. Cultural misdirection. Her first words, when James opened his door, "Your hotel is striving awfully hard to impress."

His answering laugh was deep, sexy, insincere. "I told them you were coming."

Oleander wore an expensively cut dark gray coat over a pale green silk dress. Dead sexy shoes. A perfume she made for herself of oil of Oleander, Ylang Ylang, Cinnamon and Dragon's Blood. A serious scent for silly business. One long strand of red and black glass beads. She didn't carry a purse, the coat was designed to hold everything she might need including a couple hundred dollars sewn in the seam, a very small legally registered pistol in a reinforced pocket, a couple packages of condoms, papers to guarantee her a complete identity which was not the one she currently used. When Oleander was on duty, Oleander was thorough.

James turned to a vase on the dresser, brought her one red rose. The mark of a gentleman. The rose however had been neutered—it had no thorns. Oleander smiled to herself.

There was a silver bucket of iced champagne, a huge glass platter of prawns, a tub of hot sauce, nachos, guacamole. Arms at his side, small bow, "For you."

Well, how nice. How nice. Work could sometimes be very rewarding. Maybe.

His pirate booty was piled everywhere in the room, on top of the dresser, in packing boxes, leaning hap-hazard against the linen walls. Several lengths of hand-dyed cloth were laid across the bed.

Oleander opened her coat, pushed it back to show her curves, glanced over her shoulder, her face had a look of faint discomfort, she spun around in a small circle examining the room, the objects, the whole lavish spread of art and food. She didn't look at him until she'd finished her calculations. The man was desperate. Not a good thing.

Oleander sat in the wing chair, long legs crossed. She opened the conversation her own way. "That one in the corner is very nice. But it isn't Brazilian workmanship." She pointed to a well-carved wooden idol of a proud full-bellied warrior.

"You're right, it's not Brazilian although I picked it up down there. I think it's West African." He eased into his pitch. "I've become fond of it in the short time I've had it. Where do you think it's from?" The eager tones of a collector, "Do you like it?"

"Do you know what it is?"

He took a breath preparatory to launching into his usual bullshit speech which went one of two ways: He either said the religious iconography was lost in the mists of time, the art of primitive tribal cultures needed to be appreciated on aesthetic grounds, or else he made something up which seemed to fit the desires of the customer. He was very good at either routine but some deeper sense asserted itself in Oleander's presence, he said, "No."

He never managed to retake control of the conversation after that admission.

"I didn't think so. Do you care to know?"

He smiled his charming smile, spread his narrow hands wide. "What good would it do?" He went on. "I'm a merchant, I know quality, I know my customers, it's enough. I know how things are made, where they're from." A moment of candor, "Most of my customers don't give a good goddamn what these things were truly used for, any story I tell them is good enough."

Her eyes were cold as her mouth curled in a smile. "Profit makes everything all right?"

"You haven't had any champagne yet. Here." Pour. Hand off. Toast. "To getting to know you. And, perhaps, getting to know a little more about these marvelous pieces."

Oleander sipped. Bloody hell, the man had gone and gotten some decent champagne. She lifted her glass. "To a man with good taste in champagne."

At last some praise. "I'm delighted you approve."

"Oh, it's not that I approve exactly. It's simply that I can appreciate the gesture."

Clearing his throat. Diffident. "I've never met anyone who really seemed to know any of the actual religious traditions attached to this stuff." He put a twinkle in his eyes, "Perhaps you would enlighten me?"

"Enlightenment's far too big a job for me." The undercurrents were turbulent. "Someone certainly needs to fill you in a little on some of these items." Sidelong look. "At least then you won't come across as such a complete fool."

He smiled and swallowed at the same time, his throat closed and his mouth wiggled up and down with the effort not to cough. He managed a deep voice with a sort of squeak on the last syllable, "More champagne?" The sexual energy of the woman was driving him back into adolescence.

"Please. It's delicious." She sat on the edge of the bed, crossed one silky leg over the other. "The wooden fellow is Ogun, the god of war, patron of fine craftsmanship, father of civilization. Now, tell me about this lost Venus. I know you think I already know, but, believe me," her eyes were marvelous, discreet, oblique, everything she needed to be, "I don't know anything about it."

"It's quite lovely. Gold and jewels, not the usual ethno-tribal primitive work at all. It's supposed to be a representation of some Brazilian deity. A rather odd one actually." He wasn't looking at Oleander's face as he continued speaking in a superior seductive tone, "Something of a bar slut. Whips and chains. Great Danes." Ever the good host, he filled a plate for her with prawns, horseradish dip and nachos. His back was to her, he was unaware of the storm which passed across Oleander's features. "I picked it up in the northern provinces of Brazil. Recife."

"Um." She wasn't exactly surprised. "Tell me more."

He turned to look at her then. "Oh. Do you know the town?"

She mumbled, "Never been there."

"Picturesque, in a shabby way. The fellow who made it is a drunken old craftsman."

Soft voice. "Oh? What was his name?"

Shrugging. "I never knew. He was quite strange. And always drunk. He didn't seem particularly interested in doing any kind of business with me."

"I'll bet he didn't."

James missed her sarcasm.

James wasn't listening to her. He still couldn't recall all he'd seen that night at the beach. He placed the plate on the bureau next to her, paced the room. "If his name's important I can probably find it out, I still have connections there." He held up his glass, intoned. "To a fine craftsman." Took a sip. Noticed that Oleander did not join the toast. "The fellow had a real talent." Smile. "Just wasn't very sociable. You know?" James motioned at the plate. "Eat. Eat." He watched her nibble a prawn.

"How did you get it then?"

He hesitated. "You know, now that I think of it, it looked a lot like you."

She frowned.

"Well. Not like you. But like. You know?"

"No. You were telling me how you got it?"

Damn. "The old bastard threw it in the ocean!" Sullen. Like a little kid caught out. "I rescued the damn thing. He was just going to throw it away." He couldn't read her expression. "Well, let me tell you, I took especial care crating that beauty up and, as I thought, carefully shepherding it here." Dramatic pause. "But someone stole it from me somewhere along the line."

James sat on the bed, kicked his shoes off, leaned against the headboard. He took a deep breath, enjoying the smell of her. He could have sat like that for another hour. He mused, his voice thick, sexy. James hoped Oleander wouldn't make this difficult. "You're quite lovely. When you're not scowling at me—" Charm charm charm. "You really do remind me of it. Gold."

Oleander let her mind drift. She understood what impulse prompted someone to steal from this man James. But to steal the thing James had stolen? That stunk. She smiled, "Seems only fair, doesn't it?" She smiled. "You stole it, didn't you?" Delicate. So delicate he didn't notice he'd been cut.

"What?"

"What exactly did it look like?"

James closed his eyes, remembering. He described it as if it were rather more valuable than he knew it actually was. James told her it was solid gold. His voice went all honey, then he reached out to her with trembling fingers, bedroom eyes. "Tell me what you meant the other night when you said I was supposed to bring you something that was yours." His hand rested ver-y light-ly on her leg. "I felt devastated not to be able to give it to you." Women always liked to know he felt devastated, he wasn't sure why.

Oleander stood up. "I wouldn't know where to begin helping you." She pulled her coat closed around her, buttoned two buttons. Slid her hand in her pocket. "You know the story about the well educated merchant who went to visit a teacher, the teacher poured tea, kept pouring it into the man's cup, it spilled out all over?"

James frowned. "Um. Yes. No. Maybe?" What was the perplexing woman getting at?

"Your cup's already full. No more will go in."

"What?"

She laid her finger on his chin, electricity jumped between them with the touch, "You're too full of yourself." She poked him in the solar plexus, hissing, "Talk to me when you've made some room in there." Tap on his heart, his forehead. Then she held out her hand. "Thank you so much for showing me your stock, some of them are quite lovely." She smiled. "Some of them are even worth some money." Laughing at him. "I might be interested in purchasing one or two."

Dizzy, he grabbed for her hand, "Don't go!" His voice was husky. "I want to see you again. I must see you again." He fumbled, "I want to know what it is you people do, why you do it?"

Oleander smiled. "We people?"

James didn't like pleading, but her smile encouraged him. "I know you people know where my statue is. We could share it. You could teach me so much." Women liked to believe they were teachers, saviors. Madonnas.

In your dreams, James, in your dreams. Oleander could walk through that script blind-folded. "We'll see." Her mouth swelled slightly, she was very good at this sort of thing. "Call me in a few days?" She was gone.

James sat on the edge of his bed, his eyes glazed. His hand trembled as he fumbled for the bottle of champagne, he gulped it, thinking: If that woman would work with me we could make a killing, a fucking killing. He couldn't imagine anyone refusing.

CHAPTER TWENTY-SIX

Oleander knocked on Francine's door.

The candles were lit, the room had a warm old wine glow. Francine was languid, long, slim and lovely in an old green kimono, black squares embroidered along the hem. "You look like hell, Oleander. Come on in and have some tea." The kettle was already boiling. "What kind you want?"

"Philodendron." Growling.

"Ah." Francine glanced over at the huge plant encircling her window, "What's it good for?"

"Stunning fish."

"Sorry. The fish are all gone. Lobsang Souchong or my own concoction?"

"Either."

"Hmm. Well, the tea I'm brewing now is lavender, lemongrass, cinnamon and ginger. Good for the liver. And opium poppy seeds." She waved her hand, a slow dreamy circle over the tea pot. Her eyes were heavy, "Good for the soul." She pointed at a pile of oval green leaves, "I was going to add some Ska Pastora leaves, *Salvia divinorum*, you know? Just to see if they lose their power in hot water. But I can leave them out if you don't feel like hallucinating?"

"Sounds like it's Lobsang Souchong for me. I'm not up for liver de-tox or hallucinations right now." Oleander walked around Francine's room, noticing how everything was placed in a secret harmony, recognizing how much strength Francine drew from them. Thinking of that man and his nasty piles of treasure. La Favorita poked at the cupboard doors where Francine kept treats.

"Whatever suits you." Francine added four pairs of the green leaves to the pot. "Tell me what's on your mind, Oh Mistress Fish Basher."

"Well, first it's petty-ass parole officers."

"Thea cop to it? Queenie turn herself in?"

"Basically."

"You involved?"

"No. They're busted out of their old official address at that shooting gallery on Sixteenth." She shook her head, eyes hooded. "Stupid."

"And?"

"So I called your pal—told her she could come talk to me about living here."

"Gina's impervious to magic, or haven't you noticed?"

"Oh, that's not the problem. She's another one. Living too close to the edge."

"You worried you can't keep us from falling off?"

"Mmm."

"Well, you can't. It doesn't take a genius to know you can't save people, Oleander. Sometimes we just crash and burn."

"The point of this place is to save people."

"Good. Good. And we're damn thankful for it too. But that doesn't mean it's gonna work."

"People are vermin," Oleander growled. "The simplest thing and they have to make it so complicated—sometimes I think there isn't a good one on the planet."

"Even if that's true, and I've ascribed to that supposition for quite some time, what possible use is that information to you? You try to set up a place where we can be slightly less awful than elsewhere—and we still can't manage to be stellar human beings. You want to call it quits?"

"Not right now. I'm too mad. They can all burn in hell."

"I'd certainly be toastin my toes if I was already dead. Good company down there, or so I've heard. You should demand visiting rights."

Oleander sipped her tea, bumped around the room. "Been there. Done that. I guess Hell isn't quite where I'd like to send some people." She grinned, looking better for a moment. "My conception of Hell is a cozy bar with a fireplace and free snacks." She stopped pacing. "Okay. Enough. You know anything about what our dear Ellis might have been up to lately?"

Francine shook her head. She didn't even have to pretend disinterest, her odd tea concoction was already working. She murmured, "He in trouble again?"

"When isn't he in trouble?"

"Sleeping? He sleeps the sleep of the blessed."

"And well he should. Listen Frankie, you know anything about a stolen gold statue and where it might be?"

"What? Stolen from where?" Her voice was a soft, fading whisper.

"I hoped you would tell me."

The angel was beating her wings around Frankie's head. "I don't know, Oleander." Opium tea. "Or else, if I did know something, it's been temporarily dislodged." Ska Pastora dreams. "Is it as lovely as you, angel?" Sad smile. "I know the line's old. Never mind." Thin arms poking out of kimono sleeves. "Now when I drift, you know, I never drift far enough."

"Ah, Frankie," Oleander knew about Frankie's angels, "I know." Moving around the crowded room again. "Let me know, if you can, anything about that annoying statue."

"Oh, angel." Sad smile. "I entertain myself as best I can." When Frankie shifted every muscle quivered, her thin stretched skin seemed to shiver silver on her bones. "Either with my own secrets or with someone else's. I may know something about it, or I might not. Tonight's not the time for me to find out what I know. I'm planning my vacation. I don't intend to be here this winter. It's time I went somewhere warm."

Oleander squeezed her friend's hand. "I hate for people to leave the party before it's over."

Frankie's eyes didn't focus too well. It didn't matter. "The damned doctor you got me sure is an eager one, wants to set up an oxygen thing in here." Pause. "I know what happens next." Struggling to sit up very straight. "I ain't goin that route. No way. No thanks."

"Funny, I said those words to myself awhile ago."

"Oh? Sit back down, girl. Tell me, tell me alllll."

"I just had the silliest proposition." Oleander settled herself back down. "Well, maybe not the silliest, but easily one of the most arrogant. And he didn't actually present the proposition, but that's only because I left. I think I must look into it. Before he goes much further in his own mind—I need so much more information." Delicate shake of her head. "Let me start before that. Do you remember anything about my ex-husband? In Brazil?"

Frankie tilted her head to one side. "Tell me again."

"He's an artist. We worked together as Eshu and Pomba Gira until he, until he went ah, crazy and greedy?" She stopped, pinched her lip. "It's been a long time since I had any contact with him, longer since I wanted any. But it seems he's found me." Her hand flung out from her mouth as if to throw the words away.

Frankie wiggled closer on the couch. Nodded her head, eyes bright.

Oleander continued, "The bloody stupid consulate called me—I don't know how they knew where I am—to tell me Vicente's dead." She scowled, scratched with her fingers on the table, suddenly wanting a cigarette. "The bastard's not dead but no one listens to me."

"I'm listening."

"Oh. Right. So this arrogant white guy comes to me, acting as if I knew all about everything, he practically accuses me of stealing or harboring or something this golden Venus statue. Stolen from him." Sharp look. "You don't know what I'm talking about, do you?"

"Not a clue. But go on."

"Okay. I'm certain now that the statue is one of Vicente's, probably a Pomba Gira, and that he danced it in the ocean."

"Oh? Oh dear."

"This arrogant man, Jaaaames," she staggered over his name, "is a total dick, he seems to have grabbed it right out of the ocean, claims he rescued it when Vicente threw it away."

Frankie's face crinkled up, a cross between horror and laughter, "You mean he grabbed it after Vicente had danced it in the ocean? After some major spell-thing had been worked? And this guy is still in good health?" She grumbled, "Maybe we can exchange livers."

"He seems thin but well muscled and even graceful in a nasty predatory way."

"Oleander! You think he's sexy!"

"I do not. And we are far off topic here." She settled herself with a small flounce. "This man smuggled it into the States,

COME TO ME

and it's now gone missing. Raymond is looking for it now
too—in fact this business about Vicente being dead sounds like
something Raymond would think up."

"I heard the phone call. Didn't sound like Raymond."

"Oh, who knows what Raymond might sound like if he
expected to be well paid? Who knows what Vicente himself
might sound like? In any case, Vicente's supposed demise
makes all of his work terribly valuable. Even if he's not really
dead but only legally dead."

"The value of a piece of art is directly proportional to who
made it and who owned it and how they died. Ha."

"Yes. Vicente is known not merely as one of the finest
craftsmen in Northeastern Brazil, he's also one of the most
powerful sorcerers, all bitter blood and hatred." She turned the full
power of her impressive eyes on Frankie. "Male pride. A horrible
thing." Silence. Speculation. "Even before the ritual at the cliffs,
I've had the suspicion that something was looking for me. I think
it's hunting for me, like it was sent, oh, you know, to destroy me."

"You?" Frankie poured some of her own opium poppy tea
into Oleander's cup, "Why?"

"Oh. It's a long story. And a sordid one. The short version
is I left him. Stick around for a while and I'll tell you the long
version one day. In the meantime, the statue, if it exists, is
supposedly here."

"You believe this?"

"I believe something's gone rotten. Just the fact that two of
my wards are going back to prison tells me that something is
wrong. Listen, the man never gives anything up, never. And I
was one of his things." She looked into the middle distance, "He
swore he'd never give me up." She took a sip of Frankie's opium
tea, "Oh. Hey now, this really doesn't taste so bad. Peppery?
Will I start to see things soon?"

"As a matter of fact, you might." Cup lifted in salute.
"However," Francine sat up straighter, "don't stop tellin the
story now."

"Well. This big time culture vulture, James, ended up losing
it." She pushed her hair back over her shoulder, laughing a
little. "Losing it. Another one who hates to lose things. Having

159

just shared a bottle of champagne with the man, I would bet that he stole it from Vicente with no more knowledge of what he was stealing than a child."

Frankie held up her hand. "Stop."

Oleander stopped, a small frown growing between her eyes.

Frankie gave a re-cap of what Oleander had just told her: "Vicente. Big deal bad guy sorcerer. Gets his precious statue stolen. I don't think so."

Oleander's generous mouth pinched small, her eyes probed Frankie's face.

"Stolen by some over-sexed dude who just happens to lose it, who then comes right to you? And this guy is supposed to be an internationally famous dealer who does not apparently know or care that he's taken possession of a sacred, potentially dangerous, thing? And now he wants you, the object of all desire, to return it to him? And you, oh angel, you don't know where the hell it is." Francine's smile was voluptuous, "I like this better and better."

Prim. "I don't.

Eyes bright. Drifting. "Oh, but it's marvelous. Machiavellian. Follow the logic. There's an apparently beautiful thing floating around which is like some kind of psychic time bomb." Frankie smiled. "Like the Hope Diamond or something."

Grudging, "Well, it has the potential to bring disaster."

"Then it would be safe with me until we learn how to defuse it, you know what I mean? I'm the local disaster safety monitor. I'm already dead."

Oleander didn't respond, just looked at Francine very thoughtfully.

"You find it, Oleander, you bring it to me. " Frankie said. "I'll decontaminate the thing. Hell, I'll detonate it if that's what it takes." Low spooky voice. "It'll bring hard times to whoever has it, inspiring lust and greed in every heart." Frankie held up her hand. "It's a fine tale with a certain believability until I get to the kind of eeeevil he might have tried to work. Lust and greed maybe? Or what? What would he use to catch you?"

"Well. Lust is problematic." Oleander tipped her head to the left. To the right. Blinked. She played with her tea cup.

Turned it one way then the other. "And greed? Maybe. Maybe not." Rueful. Apologetic. "We don't know what he did after all. It may only seem to bring out these things. Its purpose may be something else entirely."

"So many sins. So small a vessel."

Sharp. "How do you know what size it is?"

Frankie blew her a kiss. "Oh angel, I don't. It's a figure of speech." She stretched, a slim green cat. "If the curse is aimed at me, it won't work. I'm not that kind of hungry any more. Now drink up, I've got nothing to do and I want to do it alone."

CHAPTER TWENTY-SEVEN

"Heard you want to talk with me?"

"What the hell's going on, Ellis?" Oleander's voice was pitched low, but it pierced. There were a couple customers crowding the coffee machine, grumbling about bills, health, the weather. "Come back into the kitchen."

Ellis already knew Oleander could be merciless when she copped an attitude. "Can't. Got to take Julia to her cooking class." His eyes lingered on the young girl, her hair starting to grow back, curly. Sensuous.

"My sweet ass." Oleander tried to stare him down. He became innocence incarnate. She didn't raise her voice, merely aimed it. "What you know about this guy James? The one you picked up at the airport." Glare. "You didn't tell me what really went down did you? You set it up so he'd be at the ritual didn't you?" Pressure. "Ellis, you have a hell of a lot of explaining to do."

"Sh. Shh. Keep your voice down, Oleander." He moved his chin at Julia, "You'll blow my scene."

Oleander hissed, "You don't have a scene, you rotten little creep. You may not have any balls either. Do you get my meaning?" Oleander looked him up and down. "The people I work with are trying to live a certain way. You are trying, or not trying, to live another way—an uncertain way. You aren't merely walking a difficult path, you are lying in the bushes next to the crossroads and you will be bleeding into a slow death unless you come up with some answers. And soon." Oleander tapped her finger on the bar. "What the hell you think you're doing with Raymond and his friend?"

"That man James? The one I picked up? He so fulla himself. Can't b'lieve anything that man says."

"He in good company with you, there."

Ellis held up his fingers, folding them down one at a time in answer to her questions. "Gave him a ride from the airport." Index finger down. "He had so much junk, such an attitude, was hardly room for me in the cab."

"With your ego I wonder you fit anyone else in there at all." Oleander sucked on a lemon peel, rubbed it on the edge of her espresso cup.

"Nah-hh. That ain't it. The man don't know what he's doin." Middle finger down. "He doesn't have any appreciation for the things he buys, except resale value. He doesn't know history or culture. People like that are dangerous. The man flips from one easy thing to the next."

"Ellis. Please. You want to talk about yourself or what? Tell me something I don't already know."

"My-self?" Rising note of incredulity.

"I just spent an unpleasant half hour with the man, he practically accused me of stealing his golden Venus."

Ellis looked at his shoes.

"Ellis. What you know about this?"

"Nothin. Wha'd he say?"

"You tell me." Oleander rolled her eyes. "Give it the fuck up, Ellis."

La Favorita padded into the shop on silent dangerous paws. She didn't charge Ellis right away, merely sniffed his shoes as if she would make up her mind sometime in the future.

Ellis grinned. Charming kid. "Don't worry about him, soon's he gets back within smellin distance of you, he'll forget the statue. Go for the real thing." He sniffed the air, "You sure smell good."

"Ellis. I'm going to geld you and gild your balls, I will hang them from the chandelier. Look up there, Ellis, can you see?"

He looked.

"See those little wrinkled things hanging among the crystals? Those are the balls of men who have fucked with me."

Ellis looked harder, he didn't quite believe her. He swallowed. Felt his face go ashy. Hand shaking, he lit a cigarette, thoughtful. "The man's up to somethin. You know? Think he's up to somethin big."

Exasperation. "Of course he is. What's it to you?" She reached over and grabbed his collar. "Where's the bloody statue? What's the bloody statue?"

Wailing. "I don't fucking know. Ask him." Petulant. "I try to do right. Look what it get me. Suspicion."

Oleander wondered, not for the last time, why she put up with Ellis at all—he was unreliable, a liar, a thief, he drove that limo like a lunatic, all he ever wanted was to have a good time. Screw young girls. Oleander forgot for a moment that was exactly what young men generally wanted. She looked over at Julia—caught her looking at Ellis. "Shit." Everything was falling apart. She had to believe in the damned curse when she looked at the potential wreckage around her.

Ellis had one of his bright ideas. He said, a small note of triumph in his voice, "I got it! James is hot for you, he usin this riff about the statue to get you interested." Impatient shrug, "It's a old trick." Worldly.

Oleander grabbed his shoulder, wiggled him back and forth. "Don't you be tellin me about old tricks."

"Wait and see." Chin up. "He got his nose spread wide for you. Let him and Raymond Arthur trade artifacts. An' you play him for the fish he is." Leer.

"What artifacts are we talking about now?"

Ellis shook his head.

"I need information." Oleander was cooing now. Sly. "If you won't give it to me, I'll have to find out for myself."

Ellis crossed his arms, curved one leg over the other, blew smoke rings at the ceiling. "Well, I guess you have to do that thing alone then since I don't know nothin about no statue." His cell phone went off. "Ex-cuuuuse me, I gotta call."

Oleander waved her hand at him. "Please." Her eyes dug huge pits in the back of his head.

* * *

James had called Raymond immediately upon Oleander's exit, to gloat. "Thanks for the tip, old man. I'm certain that the mysterious Oleander knows where my statue is. Only a matter of time."

Raymond said, "Oh?" Raymond didn't think Oleander had located it yet. If anything, she was just beginning to get curious about it, she'd call him soon, they'd talk. This time, they'd talk on his terms. Even though she considered herself some big deal magic-lady, he was the one who'd turned her into Oleander.

Raymond figured the statue was his. He'd been Vicente's representative to the northern art market since forever. Since Magdalena Caravalho had come north, it was him and Oleander, Oleander and him. James wasn't even in the running in this particular race. Ha. Raymond had only to make sure that he collected the money. The main snag was that he didn't yet know where this stupid statue was. Or what the hell it was. It was time for him to step up his game.

James was yammering on. "Oh?" Raymond mumbled again.

James laughed. Pompous. "Well you may say 'oh'. I'll have it within a day or two." He chortled. "The art market hasn't seen anything like me and Oleander in a long time." James hung up, rubbing his hands. Then he reached for the Scotch.

*　　*　　*

Once out of the traffic jam of the city, Ellis drove like a maniac to the old man's shack. The cell phone registered the old man's number, but when he'd called there was no answer, no voicemail. The time had come for that bastard to explain about—ah. Explain Things. Like how Ellis kept trying to get out there to the lot, talk to the old guy. Yeah. But every time he started driving, some weird ass shit would happen, that old guy at the crossroads or else fancy dancer broads leavin their purses in the limo or why he was under some weird compulsion to Do Something with the statue. He'd started to feel peculiar when he talked to Frankie, he recognized his own strange irrationality. Maybe it was cursed. Nah.

Ellis didn't feel badly that he hadn't gotten back in touch with the old man, I mean, he said to himself, it wasn't like we were really friends or anything, after all the old demon treated me like shit. Yeah. But still, he wanted to maybe reassure the old dude, just let him know he wouldn't let him down, that he was just doin things his own way, in his own time-frame, that was all. He'd tell the old dude how he'd gotten the crate like he asked but now he needed some money, he'd tell him how he was stoppin by to let him know he'd bring the thing any day now real soon, it was only a matter of time and no shit, he'd be right there with it oh yessir.

Nothing odd happened the whole trip down, there was heavy traffic, but that was to be expected, blue skies, light breeze. The neighborhood seemed shabbier than he remembered, he drove up and down the streets looking for the place longer than he thought he should, the fences, the wooden homes, the derelict warehouses all looked pretty much the same, one to the other, yellow gray boards beneath peeling paint. He began to swear at himself, how the hell was he lost, the whole area was only a coupla blocks end to end. Ellis sighed. This wasn't going to work.

He stopped the car. His mind rattled on for a moment. He wasn't goin to apologize. Shit no. He was goin to say, right out, that he wasn't bringin nothin til the old man came clean. Explained what it was all about. Ellis clamped his teeth together. He deserved to know.

He found the corner store where he'd bought rum and cheap cigars—it was closed, but he didn't need to ask for directions anyway, he finally knew where he was. A left. A left. Four corners. And a right, half way down the block, on the left. Easy as could be.

Ellis had a brilliant flash: he'd tell the old man he never had got the package. Made the pickup but had no chance to get that mysterious crate. Didn't know what it was. No clue. End of story. Too bad. The fuckin demon needed to talk to ol' James if he wanted anything. Yeah. Like that.

He didn't notice the beige Caddy turn the corner behind him, pull to the curb and park back there. No one got out.

Ellis frowned, the gate was closed tight with a piece of wire, there was no rum bottle leaning against it. That wasn't right. He fumbled it open and pushed through the weeds down the path. He took a deep breath, hollered, "Hey! Hey old man! I gots something ta say ta yas."

There was an acrid smell. He stepped beyond the crackling shrubs and behind the abandoned building into the back section where the old man's yam garden should start. It was clear in his mind: rich leaves then dry packed earth, the little barbecue pit, the rickety three steps up to the front door of the shack.

There was nothing there. A pile of old twisted boards off to the side. But no shack. No old demon. Nothing.

He walked forward swinging his head from side to side as if perhaps everything he remembered was still there, only hidden. He came to about where the shack would have been, there were some broken wooden stumps poking out of cement blocks. Nothing else. Looking left and right, "Where the fuck are you?"

His voice drifted away into dust. Feeling almost dizzy, he walked back along the fence and his foot sunk into some softer earth where the weeds were scattered, not growing. It was a long trench, dug and filled in again. A grave. He bent over and pushed his hand into the dirt. He pulled up a piece of red cloth which crumbled in his grasp.

Ellis didn't hear the soft tread of a careful man coming up behind him. He would only recognize the thunk of a tire iron when he came to consciousness again, face down, hands held behind him, wool cap or something that smelled sticky-sweet pulled down over his whole head, he lay on the ground in front of what he at first assumed to be a policeman.

Except, having spent his share of time in police custody, he sort of recalled that they didn't cover your face with knit caps. Nor theoretically, did they sneak up and bonk people. Well, sometimes they did. But he couldn't figure why they'd be after him. Well, then again, he could—his thoughts were interrupted by a jerk upward on his arms pulled behind him. His whole body was lifted, feet dangling free of the ground. His shoulders felt like they were ripping apart.

He decided not to say anything for a while. Except privately, intrapersonally as it were, to the gods, big and little, that were supposed to be so interested in his fate. He said (without saying): What the fuck was all this twirling sparring upside right side left side rum drinking dancing worshiping nonsense if you go and let my head get smashed in. My arms ripped off. What the hell was it all for any the fuck way! Then he remembered the red cloth and his foot sinking into a grave and how the shack was gone and he shut up. Even in his head, he shut up.

The man dropped Ellis again, he crouched over him, a small smile on his face. He knew he hadn't hit Ellis all that hard, the boy should be awake by now. He sighed. Hopefully the pretty boy wasn't dead. That would be a shame. He crooned, a weird mad tenor, a counterpoint to the bass wobble throbbing in Ellis's head, "I'm going to squeeze you like an orange, suck your brain empty like a coconut, scoop out the pith and seeds of your every secret. I'm going to leave you empty as a pumpkin jack-o-lantern without a candle."

He reached down, jerked Ellis upright again by his crossed arms. Hands like a pair of vice-grips hooked onto Ellis's thumbs. There was a sharp turn and a crack. Ellis screamed and tried to pass out. It didn't work. He remembered that it usually didn't work. His breathing came ragged and his attention wandered to the bits of grass still clinging to his face. He wondered where everybody was. All those spirits who were supposed to help him at times like this.

"Somebody's going to tell me where that statue is." The vise-grips moved to his index fingers.

Ellis could feel the little bones beginning to crack in his hands, his wrists, Jesus, all the way up his arms to his shoulders. He stopped thinking, stopped feeling. But rather than jibbering compliance, Ellis reared up and away, ripping his mangled arms free, back-kicking and shrieking, "It's beyond your reach, you filthy bastard."

The vise grip on his arms released, Ellis spun around, crescent kicking, swishing close without connecting. He couldn't see through the cap over his eyes, his arms wouldn't work to pull it off. Desperate he lunged again, "It's in the hands of the spirits now. The living dead!"

The man whacked him once again on the head, tossed him to the side of the yard. The man knew who the living dead were.

Ellis crawled upright, shivering, shamed. His hands were yowling howling useless pieces of shattered bones that he wished would just go away. Just go away. He finally passed out.

CHAPTER TWENTY-EIGHT

Raymond called James from his cell phone. No answer. He called a different number, no answer. So he called James again at the hotel, let it ring, the hotel concierge finally picked it up: "Room nineteen isn't answering, if you want to leave a message—"

Raymond hung up. Gently. He continued on to the Lizard Lounge.

When the Scotch was warming the occipital bones of his skull just nicely, Raymond made his calls one more time. The first number rang annoyingly again and again. What? The old bastard didn't have voice mail? Raymond gave a small exasperated grunt. Called James again.

James sounded about a half bottle past sober when he picked up the phone. It took Raymond ten minutes to flatter James into agreeing to meet him. Not as easy as Raymond expected, but he was tuned in tight to James, play the man like a fish.

James strolled into the Lizard, looking sharp, feeling clever; he'd taken a couple of Percoset to wipe his hangover, the drug gave him the feeling of being back on top. With the small buzz still hanging on after his encounter with the inimitable Oleander, he had a sort of drunk/drugged confidence. One or two of his ideas were bound to work out.

Gina trundled the mop bucket past the conferring duo on her way to the bar's basement, she saw a lot of people in the Lizard when she put in time during the day, she chose not to recognize any of them, even when they looked familiar. She'd worked hard on her mental sorting ability, filing people in tidy de-humanized compartments, keeping herself uninvolved. Untouchable. That way no one would know who she was or how she ended up at a crap place like the Lizard. Where the famous gathered. Oh yeah.

The big fat one could have been the usual kind of customer in the Lizard, an arrogant sloppy man who made a mess, didn't tip and threatened to complain to the management. Gina recognized him as the guy who sat on the ground the whole Big Friday Pomba Gira ceremony, looking bemused.

Gina's heart-shaped face didn't change expression—keep it one millimeter from drooling idiot and everyone left her alone—even when she recognized the other man as the annoying sleezer who was hot for Oleander. Her mouth curled down in disapproval: How dare they come into her bar?

Gina wondered, in an idle fashion, what kind of crimes they were into. She pushed her hands through her tangled hair, grouched that it didn't matter. She'd never see a piece of that action. Maybe one or the other of them would forget their wallets when they left. A lazy wish, Gina wasn't much interested in rigorous wishing. Other than that, wallets aside, she would be satisfied if they'd both just die.

The big man called their orders to Lethal Jack. "Two Johnny Walker Blacks, water back, thanks." She watched as Jack poured, he had different techniques for different customers: He poured the big guy's drink way light; arrangements must have been made to make it seem like he was drinking more than he actually was. Weird the way these guys operated. The other drink was the proverbial stiff one.

Lethal Jack nodded his head, "Okay Raymond. Two comin atcha."

Raymond didn't take his beady little eyes off of his drinking buddy. It looked to Gina as if he wanted to appear to be an unblinking but not necessarily unfriendly lizard as he slid a tenner on to the bar. He smiled as James drank. It was not a pleasant smile.

Gina thought they'd probably named the bar after that look. She revised her estimation downward of the one Jack had called Raymond. Creepy bastard.

James leaned back, the Percoset buffering the drink, he appeared casual, comfortably at ease, his arm hooked over the back of the chair, one long leg crossed over the other. Lucifer speaking to a lesser demon, "What's on your mind, Raymond?"

They looked to be settling in for one of those lengthy male-bonding bar-negotiation rituals. Gina poked under the bar stools a couple feet away picking up lemon peels and toothpicks.

"I heard from a friend of a friend, you know?" Sort of bored, "About your statue."

James gave his lopsided charming smile. "Yeah. Oleander has it." Smug, not looking at Raymond.

Gina slithered closer. She had a proprietary interest in Oleander, after all, that fine woman was going to be her landlady soon.

"She tell you she had it?" Raymond stretched his fat lips again in that reptilian grin Gina found so disturbing. "We've done business together for years now, right? Always treated each other fair, right?" From his tone even Gina could tell this wasn't exactly true. "So you can believe me when I tell you that she doesn't have it."

"Seemed to me that she has it. Maybe she's merely playing coy with you."

"Oleander? Coy? No way. Oleander wants it, but she doesn't have it." Dramatic pause. "And it's a good thing because if that woman gets her hands on it, you can fuggetabout it." Big breath, expanding his barrel chest. "Don't worry. Someone has it—someone who no one would suspect." Look left, look right. "Except me. I got it figured out." He sat back a little, didn't seem in any hurry to continue the discussion.

"Well. That certainly puts me at ease." James thought it would be nice if Raymond got run over by a train.

"It'll be a couple days before I've got it in the bag—I'll need a couple hundred dollars to set up the deal." He didn't look at James. But Gina did. She watched James laugh.

"You fat snake, you want my money so you can steal it? No fucking way." James pushed away from the bar nearly toppling over Gina. She kept her head down. "You work it your way, I'll work it mine." Standing up he wasn't quite steady on his feet.

"Wait a minute, James. You really shouldn't go off half cocked."

"What?"

Raymond lifted his drink, motioning to Lethal Jack to refill both their glasses. James sat back down. "Our lovely Oleander is actually the wife of the artist who made your statue and who is now officially legally dead."

"Who? What?" Gina gulped her way back into silence. "What?"

Raymond slurped his drink, his satisfaction would have curdled milk. "Vicente, her husband, is officially dead. Oleander is the legal guardian of all Vicente's work right now." Suggestive eyebrow lift. "The value of which has suddenly skyrocketed due to the artist's untimely demise."

"How d'you know all this?" James's attachment to his statue and to Oleander was growing by the moment.

"I've been Vicente da Silva's American rep for the past fifteen years. I know everything there is to know about anything anyone needs to know." Cool. "And that statue, as well as the rest of Vicente's oeuvre will all fall to Oleander unless we play this very carefully. I was hoping we could work something out with the man himself tonight. But it seems that since he's legally dead, he's not answering his damn phone. We'll have to do this on our own."

Gina tiptoed away, dropping mop and bucket, she slid out the door.

Then she ran like hell.

The two gentlemen art connoisseurs sat back and sipped their Scotch. Thoughtfully.

Raymond turned his glass, took a deep breath, sighing, "As a matter of fact," he glanced at James, "If you work it right you may be able to connect with the person who has it tonight." Raymond figured there were only two living deads he could think of. Vicente, who wasn't actually dead, or—his little flash of brilliance—Frankie. Soon dead.

It'd been simply a momentary inspiration that made him follow Ellis. He was sad that it had been so rough. Sad. But that was the way of things.

Raymond would send James to Frankie. He'd wait at his shop. Vicente should be showing up while James was trying to beguile Frankie out of the statue. He'd find out what was what. Frankie would be collateral damage.

James didn't bolt upright but only because he had trained himself not to make fast movements during delicate negotiations.

"Here's something which should make your negotiations smoother." Raymond handed James a small packet. "Francine has a fondness." It was received with the same slick gestures. The two men understood each other.

CHAPTER TWENTY-NINE

Thea wore overalls, a knit cap pulled down over her ears. Queenie sported a long red sheath dress and black spike high heels. Oleander put a silky black shawl over Queenie's shoulders, and said. "Six months?"

They nodded.

"I will come see you—I'll be Luella Black—don't forget to put me on your visitor's list." Her mouth was grim. Suddenly she smiled, grabbed them by their hands and swung them around the room in a fast swaying samba. She reached behind the bar and pulled out a bottle of Champagne, twisted the cork free. "To Pomba Gira!" She took a long swallow, passed it to Queenie. "To Pomba Gira! The Queen of Night. The Queen of Hell!"

"Oh beautiful whore, come walk with us now!" Thea gulped the sparkles down, passed the bottle back to Queenie. "Pomba Gira, come to me. Bloody fate, sweet destiny."

"Sweet destinyyyyyyyy." Oleander crashed the bottle down the steps behind them as the two women left for the police station and six months in County lockup.

Oleander put Rita on guard and slid into her little altar room. Once inside she did not waste a gesture or a word. Slam went the rum bottle. Snap went the lighter, fumes of thick cigar smoke wreathed around her, pouring like waves over the little cowry head. "What? What? You want to be homeless? You want to run and run again, making it up all over again every day every night? What? We had so much fun traveling around hungry and filthy? You're setting me up to do it all again? And again? And then what?"

Fuming. "What the fuck is the point?"

A voice, almost like the rasp of a snake through sand, "Shh-shh-shh. The battle is just beginning. Pay attention to your troops. Don't discount anyone. Shhh-shh."

"What? What troops?" Everyone was floundering, this wasn't a fucking war. It was a tsunami, a deluge of bad luck.

"Yes. Yes. Someone has stirred uppa ocean storm of trouble. Waves lappin at your door. Someone danced in the ocean. Someone slipped my wife up north."

Oleander tilted her head, listening to the hissing, remembering how she'd gone into the ocean on that sunny beach for a last swim, didn't even wash off, just got on the bus headed north. Putting Vicente and everything else behind her. All of it. Behind her.

"You're a big help you are." Oleander grunted. Hell, she didn't even practice her religion the way she had in Brazil—on purpose. No one and nothing should find her here. Obviously, something had. They were drowning. Everyone would drown. She smelled rotting seaweed.

Blowing smoke in a hard breath straight at the Eleggua, she wondered if there was a rescue boat big enough for all of them. The rest of her reply, rather more impolite and filled with swear words, was interrupted by Rita barking. Sharp. Oleander put the cigar in the ashtray in front of the cowry-faced cement head, slid the door open, stepped out and closed it again all in one swift motion. "What is it, Rita?"

As she came thumping up the street Gina had seen the black Caddy skewed at an angle about a block before Oleander's place. Gina slowed to a walk, breathing heavy; there was a lump sitting hunched over the wheel, she approached cautiously.

The driver's side window was cracked in but still holding solid. The door was locked. She took off her boot and whaled on it. Nothing but more cracks. Damn Cadillacs—built sturdy. The back door was unlocked however, so she slid in, rolled over into the front seat, landing next to the lump. It hadn't stirred. It was bleeding from the nose and mouth and the hands were all twisted up in his shirt, he'd tied them somehow to the wheel.

She reached across him, poked at the locking mechanism and pushed the door open. His fall onto the street was only stopped because he was still attached to the steering wheel. He groaned.

"Shit." Gina trotted around to the side, pulled out her knife, slit his shirt off him and crouched down so he fell onto her shoulders. Grunting, she staggered upright.

He began to wiggle, nearly fell off, "Don't fucking try to help me, Ellis." She wheezed, taking little shuffle steps up the street, "Just hang on and we'll get there."

Left. Right. Leftrightleftleftleft. It was easier to lead with the same foot, sidle up the street. She didn't know if she hoped someone would come and help her or not. This sloppy slide-step was hardly the dramatic graceful sort of heroics she did in her mind.

By the time they got to the bottom of the stairs Gina was no longer concerned with the look of the thing, she knew damn well she wasn't going to get him up there without help. Rolling him onto his back, turning his head so he wouldn't drown in his own blood or choke on his tongue or whatever people seemed to always be doing at times like this, she peered into his face. She couldn't tell if he was breathing. "Don't you dare die, you sorry bastard."

Rita barked.

Oleander came out, looked at the huddle of human debris and said, "Oh?" She was followed down the stairs by Julia. Gina tried to tell them to do things like help her up the stairs with Ellis and shut the Caddy door and a whole bunch of other things. She was gibbering.

Oleander took a close look at both of them, realized that Gina had simply been bled upon rather than contributing anything to the gore, she said, "Gina, you slip his arm over your shoulders, I've got this side, we'll get him up to Frankie's room. She's got all kinds of stuff there to deal with trauma."

Julia ran ahead, held the door, her bronzy skin gone muddy with concern, then she ran back, "Here, wait up, I'll pick up his legs."

Gina was just glad to do what they told her, she was pretty much out of ideas. She wasn't even sure if they were carrying a dead man. In which case bringing him inside was sort of stupid.

At some point someone went and tried to park the Caddy correctly but it seemed the steering was pretty fucked up. Someone else made Gina tea, put a cold compress on Ellis's head and did all those things sensible people do. Gina stared at her feet for a while. Noticing the blood spatters. Her stomach clenched. She stood up—she had things to say. But Oleander and Julia had gone off to get more medical supplies. Frankie was heating up water to make poultices for his head and rolling towels around ice for his hands.

"Is he dead?"

"No. Not hardly."

"Good." Gina stood up. "Well, Frankie, here we are again. How come we always end up with someone smashed up on the couch?"

"Remember how we'd make lame jokes about saving the world when we grew up?"

"Yeah. The ballerina and the butcher." Gina didn't like where the conversation was heading.

"Well, Gina, I'm not going to grow up. I've been everyone I'm gonna be, this time around." Francine scowled as her phone rattled. She got up slowly. Slowly went to her door. "You watch him. I'll see who that is and we'll continue this discussion. Some things I needa discuss with you."

Gina shook her head, looking down at Ellis she pinched her nose, hard, to stop the stupid shock tears. People deserved better than they got. She heard the door close and was left alone in the room with an inanimate comatose man and all of Frankie's things. Things. All around her. Murmuring at the passage of time.

"How's Ellis?" Oleander's voice was sharp, worried, not irritated like it usually was when she asked that question.

Dull. "Dunno. He's breathing."

"Where's Frankie?"

"Went to answer a call or something. A missed connection." Big sigh.

Oleander, distracted, didn't notice.

"Heard you had a rough time at the Consulate the other day." Small talk.

Gruff. "No I didn't." *And what do you know about it, little girl?* Oleander didn't say it aloud.

"They say your husband's dead."

"He's not my husband. And he's not dead. They just say shit."

"Well, yeah. They say that too. You know what I mean? Raymond, the big ugly guy who sat on the ground during the Friday ceremony? He was talking with that skinny white guy — the one with the hots for you? They seemed to know more about your business than maybe you'd like. And it sounded as if they were waiting for your husband to show—but then since he's dead, or not dead—maybe not. In any case he didn't show." Sometimes Gina had an uncanny knack for putting things in words in such a way that you only knew what she was saying if you already knew what she was going to say.

Oleander scowled. An awful lot of people were all up into her business all of a sudden. She glanced at Ellis. He was muttering, shifting his mashed up hands a couple inches to one side then the other. She gently took one of his hands in hers, tried to pry his fingers open where he clutched a piece of grimy red cloth. Ellis grumbled, "Only proof I have and you tryin to steal it."

His eyes opened, frightened, glaring. "There was a grave right there by the fence." He didn't recognize her. "You don't believe me do you?" Whisper. "It was all gone."

Oleander was so intent she quivered. "What was gone?"

But Ellis lapsed into silence.

Not taking her eyes off him she spoke to Gina, almost as if to keep herself occupied, "What did you hear them say?"

"The big guy, Lethal Jack called him Raymond, how well you know him?"

Oleander didn't react. Ellis's eyes fluttered for a moment as if he would say something, but he may have thought better of it. Or he may have merely passed out again.

Gina hadn't really expected Oleander to answer her, so she went on, "Well, he sure knows you. He said you didn't have this statue they both wanted—and that they hadda make sure you never got it."

Oleander didn't react.

Worried and frustrated, Gina wanted to shake her. "Huh. James referred to this statue as his, said you did so have it and you were gonna give it to him. Then Raymond said you didn't have it but he was gonna get it from who ever had it. He seemed to think he deserved it, said something to the effect that he'd worked all these years selling your husband's art work."

"He's not my husband."

"They both referred to this statue as if it belonged to each of them. They were maybe pissed that now you ended up in control of all the art because this Brazilian dude who is, or is not dead, is so your husband." Gina's voice got a little more life in it. "They weren't too pleased." Pause. "You're not a gypsy at all, you're a Brazilian."

"Romni. The word is romni. A Roma woman is romni. I took the persona of a gypsy before I knew enough about this culture—gypsy is a slur, you know. Don't use it to me. The history of the Roma is all sadness. Anyway, I'm not Brazilian. I was born in Argentina. And for your information," small haughty smile, "I'm a US citizen now."

Gina muttered, "Yeah. Me too. All the good it's ever done me." She continued, "What's with Brazil?"

"My parents died in Brazil when I was very young." It was a rusty tale with parts missing. "They had a dance troupe. So I kept dancing—and other things. Married a handsome clever man, I believed that together we could do anything. Everything. And so we did. But it wasn't enough." She searched Gina's face, not seeing anything but a reflection of her own. "Never enough for him. So I left again."

"What's with the statue?"

"I don't know. I don't know. And I don't believe he's dead and I don't understand why anyone is saying he is." Turning away, exasperated. "As if I wouldn't know if the bastard was finally dead. I don't understand what's going on."

"That's a new thing for you, eh? For me, it's a continuous state."

"I need to find out where Ellis got mugged." She grumbled, "We'll probably never know quite why—so many people would like to pop him." More loudly, "And what were those two in the bar talking about anyway?" Scowling, "When Frankie gets back, please stay with her, please don't let either of them do anything. You know, anything." Rita followed Oleander out with an apologetic wag of her tail to Gina.

"Gotcha." Gina looked at Ellis. He wasn't going to do shit for a long time.

The room was tight around her, airless, filled with objects Gina didn't understand, nothing familiar except for the barely breathing Ellis. Gina sat on the couch not crying, not worrying, not moving. She'd delivered her message. That had to be good. She'd brought Ellis to some kind of safety. That had to be good. But she didn't feel good. Maybe she should get some reward. Something.

Ellis twisted, arching his back and crying out, "Bastard." He tried to sit up. Glared at Gina. "Where's Frankie?"

"Downstairs." Soothing. "She be right back."

"Don't let her out of your sight. They know. They must know. They'll get it." Plop. Back out cold on the couch.

Weird.

Francine slammed into the room, "Asshole never answers. Calls me then never answers back." She scowled at Gina. "All dealers are the same." She stared at her hands, noticing the small shake, willing it away, unsmiling. Lifted her head, speaking without turning to Gina. "I'm almost done with it all, now. Soon."

Confrontation was pointless: Dig through the hidden stashes, grab the syringes and the dope then dash from the room so Frankie couldn't get at them. Yeah, right. "Who's your connect, anyway?"

"Why?" Slow. Not paying attention.

Nasty. "Well maybe I'll pick up your slack."

"Raymond."

"Raymond?" It was an explosion. "That sorry bastard has his filthy hands in everything now doesn't he?"

"Doesn't he what?" Honestly confused.

"Ah, forget it, Frankie. Just forget it." Gina's lip curled up on one side. She muttered, "Asshole." It was a general statement, not directed anywhere special.

The stupidity of their non-conversation was beginning to force itself into Frankie's awareness. "What the hell you talking about?"

"You tell me. Dammit. You tell me. Miss Oh I'm fixin to die and I know everything about everything and I'm gonna take all them secrets with me Francine."

"Huh?"

"What's the deal with this statue? What's the deal with this Vincent guy? Why is he pretending to be dead or whatever?"

Frankie looked blank.

"And, by the way, Ellis said they know. They know. And therefore you should be careful."

No response.

"And Raymond is involved up to his greasy green neck in all this. Jeez." Gina took a deep breath. If she blinked she could see the goddamn hungry angels hovering around them. Making bets on the time and condition of Frankie's immortal soul. Well, they can't have it yet. Not fucking yet. "You know what happened to Ellis?"

Frankie rested her chin on her fist. Stared at Gina. Started off slowly, gaining speed. "You found him, you get first speculations. No?" Frankie sighed. "Looks like he got jumped. Kid like that, quick on his feet, wouldn't be easy to take front-on. His wrists and thumbs are sprained maybe broken. And then someone gave him a whack on the head to help him sleep."

"To keep him from talking." Gina continued, "Well, he talked, told me everything." Chin tilted up. Firm as the proverbial rock of Gib.

"Who you trying to kid?" Frankie stood over Ellis, no expression on her face.

He moaned. She gave him another shot of morphine right in the bicep. "If the guy has anything to say, it'll be awhile."

CHAPTER THIRTY

Oleander, Julia and Gina moved the still semi-comatose Ellis down to Thea and Queenie's empty room. Oleander went off to the police station to check on Thea and Queenie, leave them some Commissary money. Gina fell asleep on the floor by the side of Ellis's bed, curled up in a ball around Rita; all three of them snoring with exhaustion.

Frankie wandered off down to the kitchen to maybe grab some soup or something, but mostly to be alone. It was oddly soothing to rattle pots and pans. A different kind of thinking is possible when you pretend to be busy. Or something. Francine took a deep breath.

There was a knock on the back door.

As Francine peered out the back door she saw James shifting from one foot to another. She remembered Raymond's number had shown on her cell phone—when she called there'd been no answer but she hadn't thought much about it, other than that Raymond was an asshole. Frankie smiled to herself, curious: Ah, has the mountain come to Mohammed? She flipped several locks. She carefully opened the door, James stepped past her into the room, "Hello? Frankie?" Non-threatening pose. "Hi. Um. Heard you were the person to talk to about ethnic art. I'm a collector, thought I'd introduce myself." Awkward on purpose. "My name's James." There was a shine of sweat on his forehead.

"The wandering art thief. Won't you come in? Oh. You already are in. Well, I must tell you I've heard nothing but terrible things about you." Francine floated back toward her place at the long table, picked up her soup, swirled it in her cup, not drinking, thinking hard. She said, "I would offer you hospitality if I was feeling better, but as it is...." Her hand flipped gently back and forth. "I don't think you'll be here long enough for me to indulge in courtesies."

"I'm not a thief." His indignation was met with one of Francine's most elaborate shrugs. "Really, I'm not. I collect and sell beautiful things. That's my job. But that doesn't make me a thief." Two steps deeper into the room. "It doesn't really matter if you believe me anyway." He tapped his long clean fingers on the table. Time to change tactics. "I'll bet you have some lovely things up in your room, but I'd never insinuate you stole them." Sly. "I'd like to see some of them sometime. Perhaps I can make you some real money on them. I handle a lot of things that are un-provenanced."

"Is that some kind of genteel threat?" Frankie laughed, a small sound almost like a sigh, "Don't bother threatening me about being a thief. You'd be right. I have all kindsa stolen shit." Francine scratched along her cheek, rubbed her nose. Delicate. "I used to be quite good at it." She flipped her hand around in the air again. Her own petty pilferings were of little account now. "But probably nothing I got is as good as what you steal, eh?" Francine's icy stare collided with his pale eyes in a direct challenge, "Of course you're a different kind of thief than I was. You probably have a degree."

James didn't respond except to slither deeper into the room toward the door leading into the lobby, eyes wide open darting around, looking hopelessly for his big golden statue.

"Men are not allowed back here. You are not here. Whyn't ya come back in the morning? I'll set up an appointment for you with Oleander."

Ignoring her. Measuring. Frowning. It wasn't anywhere in sight but he hadn't expected it to be, really. Anyway, the bitch clearly knew where it was, she knew what he was after. She was toying with him. He suddenly turned on her, grabbing her arm, his eyes dilated, his voice hoarse, "I know you've got it." James felt her skin slide in his grasp. With a sharp intake of breath he let go. "Oh." In the half-light he'd simply assumed she was slim, but when he felt the minute ridges of the bird bones beneath her skin, he realized it was a more serious condition than fashionable anorexia. Raymond hadn't told him that the woman, beneath her strong manner, was a walking skeleton. He shivered at the thought he'd touched someone diseased. AIDS? James wondered, too late, what else Raymond hadn't told him.

Francine flashed her teeth at him, held her arm up, there was a bruise beginning and a thin line of blood trickled toward her hand. "Hm."

James noticed a smear of blood on his fingers. "Did I do that? Oh my God. I couldn't have done that? Did I do that?"

She didn't even glance at him, she turned her back to him. She was smiling. "No. Yes." That feather light laugh again. She felt him tremble. "Perhaps I'll offer you a cup of tea after all? Calm yourself?"

"Yes, I'm sorry. Please. Tea would be very nice." He fished in his coat pocket, fingered the packet. He slid it onto the kitchen table. "Raymond sent this for you."

She took the kettle off the big stove. She hardly glanced at the dope.

Uncomfortable but determined, he scowled, resisted grabbing her again for fear of contamination. "He said you have it. That you'd give it to me for that."

She looked blank.

He stepped closer, fists clenched.

"I could be highly," she accented the word, "highly contagious." She gestured, boiling kettle in hand. "Besides having a kettle of boiling water." She lifted it in his direction with a macabre grimace, her teeth flashed in the dim light. "Some people just get sicker and sicker as their liver is destroyed, kidneys stop functioning, heart works too hard, then they can't breathe because the lungs stop." The line of blood slid down her arm another inch toward the hand holding the kettle. "Terrible things are spread by contact with blood. But you know that." Her eyebrow lifted. "I probably have AIDS. And hep and a million other things. MRSA." She was going to add chickenpox, but it seemed counterproductive. The guy had already gone greenish.

He stopped breathing, stepping back away from her. He needed to be quick. He stared around the room, there was no place large enough to hold it, there in the kitchen. He needed her, and he needed to get away from her. "I need to go look around in the rest of this building."

Francine rambled on in a dreamy ugly voice. "You're entirely right to be careful. A skinny guy like you probably catches everybody's cold." He didn't seem to hear her but that was alright. She poured, "Philodendron leaf tea. Very relaxing." She hoped he'd remember her saying that, later, and she hoped he would worry. She splashed some on the table. "Damn."

James clamped his lips together.

"Never mind. Drink up." Feral grin. "Tell me about this statue you think I ought to have." She didn't bother to clean up the spill, wondering idly how soon it'd eat through the varnish on the table and if James would notice and freak.

James concentrated on charm. "Actually, it's not as valuable as I'd thought originally. But there's a certain, um, sentimental value." Deprecating. "I realize it ought to be in the possession of someone who knows and appreciates it as a sacred thing. I intend to give it to Oleander."

"Right. Sure." Francine kept her voice light. "You're an idiot."

Confidential. "Together the three of us could make more damn money than you ever dreamed." He reached for his cup and took a big swallow.

"Do I look like someone who dreams about money?" Languid, teasing.

"You could use it to cover medical."

"There's nothing to be done for me. You ought to realize that. My needs are few and simple. Dope, darling, dope. " Francine watched him drain his cup. "It's time for my medicine, if you don't want to watch, you know where the door is." She reached for the packet he'd put down.

"You don't understand. This is terribly important."

Private amusement. "So's my medicine."

Desperate. "Listen, I'm willing to pay you well. I realize how things like this are." Riffled several stiff large denomination bills. "Here, two hundred dollars, no questions asked."

"How things like what are?" Her voice was cool, cool and bloody. Francine lifted the money out of his hand, a quick floating motion, delicate as a butterfly. The money disappeared into her kimono. She didn't say thanks, didn't offer to produce it.

"Where's my statue?" Glaring at her.

"What?" Francine rubbed two fingers together. Received two more hundreds. She said, "Raymond is a whore's asshole, sending such a cheap bastard over to me." She didn't know how Raymond twigged to her, but then, there was so much she didn't know; she was tired, so much she'd never know. Her voice was a soft rustling sound, "Raymond? Told you to see me? How strange." Leaves in autumn. She picked up her syringe, whispering, "Here hold this for me a moment, please, while I arrange my medicine."

He held it as if it might explode.

"Thank you." She didn't touch it, just pointed to the table where he put it down. She mixed a little of the dope up in some of the hot water, tied off on a fragile vein in her arm. That vein didn't work anymore but James wouldn't know that. "Yes. Odd that he told you to come here. He was just here, oh, not too long ago. Took your precious statue with him." The vein didn't get any bigger, but then she hadn't expected it to. "Funny. Didn't mention you at all."

James watched her, horrified, fascinated. His stomach was gurgling in a strange way. He lurched toward the sink, afraid he was going to throw up. Then he realized what she had said. He squeaked, "What? Raymond took it?"

Francine smiled, nodded her head once, hiccupped, "Yep. Just about oh, I don't know, maybe an hour ago. Maybe a couple hours? Told me you or someone would bring me this dope. In payment." She waggled the baggie in front of him, watched his eyes shift left right left with the motion. "Thanks." She proceeded to skin-pop it. Made sure a little blood got on his hand where he rested it on the table.

She fell to her knees. Her breathing jerked, her eyes rolled up. James didn't know if that was commonly what happened when someone shot heroin but he didn't think so. He didn't lean over to listen for her breathing, he didn't check to see if there was anything he could do, he didn't stay to see her skin shade to blue. Screams raged in his head as he dashed around the kitchen, shoving things around, looking in the closet. No statue.

He rushed at the door into the interior of the building. He stopped, staring at her writhing form. "Raymond took my statue?"

186

Frankie nodded, made television dying noises and rolled over onto her side, "*Glaaaah.*"

"*Glaah?*" James gave her a last, terrified glance and fled.

An enigmatic smile on her face, Frankie watched him go. She wasn't quite done yet.

CHAPTER THIRTY-ONE

James slouched in the doorway next to Raymond's shop. Shivering as he stood there, determination etched his thin face into a grimace: Nobody crosses me up like this. Nobody does me this way, and lives.

He continued, his voice low and seductive in his own ears, rambling on, listing the things which had happened to him since he found his Venus in the ocean. Intolerable. Unthinkable. He thought them anyway. The scrap iron in the crate instead of his statue, meeting the incredible Oleander, then Francine tumbling to the floor bloody syringe clinking as it fell out of her. Dead. Right in front of him.

He fumed, he didn't need to be a witness to that.

And it was Raymond's dope that killed her.

Around and around in his head. There was a certain comfortable inevitability every time he got to the ritual beginning again. Each circle gave him another reason to take another great gulp of Scotch, leading him to the final thought: If he didn't deserve to have it, no one did. No. One. Did. Which led to another gulp.

James played old hero movies in his head, the ones where the camera zooms in on him, triumphant, enemies at his feet. He didn't care that he had no scenes showing how he got to the foot-on-neck-scene.

He'd already attempted to break into the shop but he'd never really gotten down with any locks, he didn't understand that lock-picking is a learned skill, he figured anyone ought to be able to do it. It just wasn't his night. His expertise with locks was only for talking, like his expertise with his hands, as in hand-to-hand-combat—it existed in his head, nowhere else.

He'd jam the fat man up against the wall, yes he would, and he'd get his statue from the murdering bastard or he'd go to the police. Well. That was one plan anyway. Maybe something else would occur to him. He was trying, as he lurked in the darkness, to pack some reality into his mental picture of himself,

James-the-Brave. James-the-Righteous jacking up a quarter ton murderer.

Maybe he'd just offer to buy it back. He wasn't sure how effective physical persuasion was with someone who killed people. Killed people.

He could kill Raymond. Yeah.

On the other hand, he knew Raymond could be bought, no question. When a person has a price they assume that everyone else does too. James thought he should go back to the hotel and sell some of his artifacts and offer Raymond the lion's share.

Or maybe he would stay right there and kill him. He took shaky steps away from the wall, then back to it.

After Raymond told him where it was, of course, the whole thing's no good without that information. In any case, the local Gestapo would be interested in reliable information about Raymond and his group of weirdoes. Possession of stolen property, fraud, drugs, ritual murder (oh why not). Even if Oleander claimed her crew didn't do that—even if they swore they were all vegetarians, the police would take his word over theirs. Bunch of loonies. The public likes to hear what it wants to hear. So do the cops. The list grew longer the longer James waited for Raymond. He added public drunkenness. Basic bizarre and unacceptable behavior. Yes! Yes!

James wobbled against the wall. Residual paranoia. His fingerprints were all over that dead dope fiend's syringe. What had he been thinking! Ahhh, he hadn't been thinking clearly, but he was about to begin some real clear thoughts. And nothing would matter once he got his statue back. After he jammed up Raymond everything would be golden.

Damn Raymond.

He took another gulp of Scotch, prepared to begin his private movie one more time.

James smelled an expensive perfume as a dark-haired woman walked past, swaying as if she were drunk. She didn't even glance at him, a few feet beyond him she put one hand on the wall, leaned over with her back to him, bending to fix her spike-heeled shoe. When it was properly back on her well-shaped foot she turned to him, saying, "You look lonely." She smiled, opening her bright lips to show a flash of sharp white teeth, "You look like you just saw someone die." Her voice was whiskey sweet, holding the word die for an extra beat.

He jerked back, felt the rough bricks of the wall scratch against his shoulders. Her smell encircled him, there was a strange *wah-wah* wavering to his vision as if somehow he was seeing double, triple, blending, blurring—he began to fall forward.

Her finger pointed at him, aimed like a small silver gun right at his heart, "Give it to me." Her other hand was held out, imperial, unavoidable. She flashed red and gold, she was lovely, lovely beyond memory, enchanting beyond desire.

"Give what?" He breathed in sharply, noticing that once again he was getting an entirely inappropriate hard-on. He tried to speak, suave cosmopolitan words formed in his mind: Oh now lovely lady, you needn't demand anything of me, my heart is yours. Then he'd grab her and belt her in the mouth, throw her to the ground and fuck her longer harder better than anyone ever.

His mouth went slack as he heard the click of the safety come off the gun.

"Give it to me. Put it in my hand." The small silver gun lifted until it was aimed at the bridge of his nose. It didn't waver. Her large black eyes were calm, implacable.

His hand went to his front pocket where he kept his wallet. Slowly. His mind raced. He'd drop to one knee, grab the gun and butt her in the belly, then he'd throw her to the ground and fuck—

He handed her the wallet. She took his watch off his wrist with a butterfly flicker.

His world was filled with a woman's laughter, hideous, unstoppable, rolling over him in waves, battering him to his knees. When he looked up the street was empty. A trace of sweet cigar smoke and roses lingered on the wind. He threw up.

* * *

The sun was barely coming up, splitting the clouds into cheery red and gold streamers, oh yes, and the birds were singing as Raymond trotted up to his shop. Vicente hadn't shown at the bar. Raymond had sort of hoped that he wouldn't, the statue was a delicate thing to discuss. Frankie would be well out of the picture in a few days. Enough pure dope in that last packet to kill a horse. Eliminate them one-by-one. Whoever was left after Frankie, Ellis? Oleander? Well, he'd remind Oleander of all the favors he'd done her, promise to do lots more of the same, he'd guarantee it. They'd chat, smooth, the way he knew how to do. She would do the smart thing, hand it over. Raymond would protect Oleander from all the demons that haunted her if she would give him the statue. Yes. He snickered as he approached his shop.

"You bloody bastard!" James flung himself at Raymond, fists hammering. It was like smashing a cement bulkhead.

Raymond brushed him off, a dainty flick of an open hand.

"Give it to me!" James was gibbering, shrieking, flailing. With no real impact. James noticed, to his deep chagrin, there were tears running down his face.

"But I don't have it. Get a grip." Raymond moved James away from the front door of his shop, proceeded to unlock the several locks on the metal gate.

James shoved at his back, smacking him ineffectually, "You do. You do! She said so."

Raymond turned to face him. "Who said so?"

James's voice squeaked some but he got control, made it tough, harsh. "You do this shit to entertain yourself? Or what?"

Raymond held him off. Easy. One hand. "What you mean, 'she said I have it'?" Growling, "I ain't never even seen the damn thing. Who says I have it?"

"Frankie—"

"And you believed her?"

"She died saying it! People don't lie when they die!"

Raymond frowned. "Wait. Who died?" Frankie couldn't have died. Not yet. Not until he'd talked to her. Then she could die, then she would die. He had it all figured out. What the hell was James going on about? "Calm down, asshole. Explain yourself." How could she have died? There was enough dope in the packet to kill her, sure. But she wouldn't have done it all up right then? Would she? Crap.

"I went to Oleander's last night, you know, to see if I could buy the statue with the dope you gave me for Frankie."

Raymond paused mid-gesture, "Indeed?"

"Damn you anyway. Frankie was in the kitchen, she said she already gave it to you for the dope." Simple truth. "Then she stuck the needle in her arm and died." He tasted bile again.

"You bloody idiot!" Raymond slammed him into the door jamb, James stumbled and sprawled on the floor of the shop. "You have no idea what you're dealing with here, do you?"

James mumbled something. His mouth opened but no sound came out. Raymond's face wobbled, changed into a grotesque red/green mask.

Raymond's voice seemed to come from far away, "Vicente is a sorcerer! He's a great artist too, but that is secondary. Do you hear me? Do you understand?"

A line of spit dribbled from the corner of James's mouth.

Raymond said, "That statue, old man, is poison! I wouldn't touch it with a ten foot pole. It kills people! I didn't kill Francine, the statue did."

James shook his head but his vision didn't clear. He mumbled, "My statue didn't kill Frankie. Your dope did." He coughed, retching up nothing, remembering the blood dribbling on Frankie's arm, the syringe—poison. He stared at his hands. "And because of you, Frankie poisoned me." Rising, "I've been poisoned and I'm gonna die! And it's your fault!"

"You were meant to steal the statue down there in Brazil. Bring it here. Think about it, you asshole. There's no way you could've gotten your hands on it without Vicente wanting you to." Raymond paced away from James and back, "But then you let it go astray." He pushed his face forward, trying to stare into James's eyes, "You lost it. It's angry now. It will kill whoever has it. It's supposed to go to Oleander."

James looked at Raymond out of one eye then the other, still trying unsuccessfully to focus. "To Oleander?"

"Yes." Raymond smiled. "She's the one to blame for everything."

"Oleander?" James thought he caught the edge of clarity. "She made Francine poison me?" The world came into sharper focus. "She's the one killed Francine? Not you?"

"Yes. Vicente made the statue for her." Easy as taking candy from a child. "I suggest we make sure she gets it."

Gulping, "But it's mine!"

"Right, old man. Right. We'll offer to save her from its curse. And Oleander will give it up to us gratefully."

"To us?"

"Naturally."

CHAPTER THIRTY-TWO

Frankie locked her door. Placed a chair in front of it, tilted so it would crash if the door was opened before she'd finished. She popped the panel on the back of the little knick-knack cabinet Gina had made for her years ago. "Years ago. Ah well. I suppose I always knew it'd come to this." She tipped the hidden door out, arranged the bills she'd gotten from James in a tidy pile on top of the ones that were already there. Put it all back together. Set her little idols back on their shelves. "Years ago. Well, Gina will remember. Find the money." Small smile, "Do the girl good to have a wad of cash. Just hope she doesn't blow it all on dope." A pause, "Oh what the hell. Blow it on whatever your heart desires, Gina!"

She turned away from the stash cabinet, went to the sink and set up her syringe with the dope James had brought her. She pulled out the small chest that held her ritual tools, her initiation clothes and *collares*. Dressed carefully in the heavily embroidered jacket and pants. She put down the first of her three ritual blades, the long narrow flexible filleting knife, on the green cloth on her worktable. Then she unsheathed her big knife, a vintage Delaware Maid Fighter with the legendary R.W. Loveless signature etched on the blade. Green micarta hilt. Loveless. Yeah, she hadn't thought about that when she bought it long ago. She laid it to the left of the filleting knife. Finally she put her machete at an angle above the other two. Moving slowly, breathing a deep in and out from her belly, she retrieved the two glass candles she always burned, the ones Gina had noticed: One with the picture of the guy on the horse and the other with the black and red lady leaning in the doorway. Lit them and placed them, right and left. She unscrewed the cap off the dark rum, gulped a couple swallows and sprayed her blades. Lighting the cigar, she circled the room counter-clockwise, her steps getting longer, firmer. Her body getting larger. She swiped the bottle of Sapphire Gin from under the workbench, drank deep. When she cleared her throat it was with a strange grating noise, the hand she wiped her mouth with was large, thick, callused. The nails were short and blackened with motor oil. Her eyes gleamed reddish in the candlelight.

She slammed the fighting blade into the sheath at her waist and approached the closet, wedged her fingers in the small crack between the wall and the panel, the secret cabinet swung open. She dragged the golden statue out, unwrapped and lifted it onto the workbench in one smooth fluid motion.

Her hand went to her blade, hesitated, she reached out and grasped the machete, holding it above her head, the words of Pomba Gira rang in her ears: "Destroy it." She remembered her own voice, so far away, saying, "Lady, it does not do you justice."

She needed another drink. Drinking, she circled it again, sizing up the adversary. A thick rank smell began to ooze into the room—stale sex. Lonely, bleak and endless.

"Noooo—" Her howl was soundless, an infinity of pain going up against the specific nasty pain the statue was primed to emit. Once again she raised the machete, a great ripple of pleasure running from the blade down her suddenly huge arm into the powerful muscles of her shoulder. She could cleave the thing, split it down the middle, crack it forehead to twat. She would slice it diagonally across, left to right, shoulder heart hip, then straight through the waist, watching it crumple suddenly gutted. She'd take her filleting knife, skin it from the hairline, pop the eyeballs, slit the nostrils, slash the lips. She put down the machete, eyes gleaming, she would take all night, instead of a quick slashing smashing, she would use finesse. Like a lover. She tipped the statue on its side, her hands sizzling where she touched it.

She reached for the gin, for the filleting knife, for the cigar. She cut her thumb, sucked it, sucked the cigar, sucked the gin, spit the bloody mouthful on her filleting blade and approached the statue.

There was only a small vestige of Francine left to worry at the destruction of such beauty, the iron warrior Ogun had taken control, as he should, in this odd battle for the soul of a statue, for the captive spirit of Pomba Gira. Spinning, spinning, his bright blade ripped a hole between the worlds. When Ogun approached his prostrate lover there was a terrible smile on his lips.

His eye was caught by the crudely soldered base plate. He snarled. Francine cringed. The hands of Ogun, the hands of Francine rippling with precision took the filleting knife and began to slice away the solder, sliver by sliver. There was a hideous wailing, a wrenching of universes, black blood seemed to pour from the statue's eyes, Francine felt her own eyes brimming with tears. Ogun wiped his sweating face, the hand came away covered with blood. The bottom plate of the statue fell away, a mottled bundle of offal tumbled to the workbench where it lay hissing and steaming in the dim light. A curl of smoke began to rise, edging slyly towards Francine's heart, in terror her fingers uncurled and the filleting knife clattered to the floor.

With a wrench of will she grabbed the Delaware Maid— Loveless indeed—from the sheath at her hip, the touch of the cool hilt brought her back to herself, back to her Ogun self, back to the essentials of battle. She stepped away from the workbench without taking her eyes from the poisonous miasma writhing there between the legs of Pomba Gira—the abortion which was never meant to leave her belly. Not breathing she grabbed a bowl; then she used that pig-sticker to scrape the bundle into it, pinned the slimy filthy thing to the bottom with the point. The howling of her blade mixed with the nearly feline death rattle of the abortion. She edged her way to the toilet and flushed. Chanting to Eleggua she slashed her blade at the swirling mess. "Eleggua O Eleggua take care of this!" Her voice swelled and broke as she slammed the lid, flushing again. The tank rattled, empty of water. She imagined the lump growing fingers, claws? Gripping the toilet seat, pushing it up.

She continued chanting, wild, desperate. Hearing the final rush of water sucked from the bowl, she didn't look to see if it was empty. Flipping a chair over upside down on top of the toilet, she backed out of there. She washed her hands in the sink, not looking at the statue. Then she cleaned her blades in the only substance that seemed appropriate, her own blood.

Finally clean, she confronted the gutted thing, animated now by a milder malevolence. She drank yet more gin, became big boned and strong, once again Ogun set to work. He began cleaning the still reeking cavity. He hummed as he worked, a low toned resonating rhythmic song as if he worked the bellows of Frankie's chest like the bellows of his forge.

Frankie almost came back to herself when Ogun had finished and she looked down at the calm golden face, the whole thing undestroyed. Serene. Maybe a little sly? Memories came back to her in bits and pieces, but not clearly. Shaking, she wrapped the statue in her blankets. Her stomach began to twist.

Puking into the sink she managed to hang onto a few wisps of sanity, with each gut-wrenching jerk she pushed back the confusion of who she was: Ogun the mighty warrior or Francine the anxious tired-oh-so-tired woman. She rinsed her mouth out with water, tasting blood even after spitting.

Tottering, she staggered over to the closet clutching the statue, heavy now that she carried it with only human strength, but lighter without its noxious guts. Distanced from herself she watched her pale thin hands flutter out to seal the panel shut, fingers uncurling, delicate as petals, in front of her eyes. Her feet were far far below her, stepping through a field of shattered glass. It was herself, sparkling, that she walked over. Each breath chimed in her ears, a ringing singing melody from somewhere back in careless memory, from a time when she could not, would not fail.

She went to the sink, picked up her syringe, then knelt and rolled forward onto her couch. She filled the syringe with the dope James had brought. Then she dialed Raymond's number on her cell phone, there was no answer but she said, "We will talk. You bastard."

Smiling, triumphant, she lay back on her couch.

CHAPTER THIRTY-THREE

In the early morning hours Rita woke Oleander up, dragging her to Francine's door. With sad foreboding Oleander pushed on the door. It was locked. She hesitated for a moment, Frankie's door was never locked, Oleander noticed her hand was shaking slightly, she wondered what new horror would greet her, she called "Frankie?" She fished in her pocket for the master key, as she nudged the door open, the door bumped against a chair that must have fallen over sometime in the night. Oleander slid into the room around it.

All but one of Frankie's glass candles had burned down to almost nothing, it was very cold in there. Rita crawled, low to the ground, crying way back in her throat, over to Frankie's couch.

Frankie was dressed in her initiation clothes. The green military Eisenhower jacket embroidered with gold and silver thread, her dark blue dress pants with the double gold stripe down each leg, her white satin shirt. Her Bowie knife was strapped to her leg. The massive green and black ceremonial *collares* — multi-strand beads — were around her neck and draped across her chest. Ready. A promise to Ogun at her initiation.

No pulse at the neck or wrist, no respiration, no pupil reaction to light. There was a syringe on the floor next to a pool of spilled tea. Francine's other blades and her ritual machete were lined up on her workbench, vaguely dulled by blood. "Oh, Frankie."

Oleander held Frankie's hands for a long moment, tears rolling one at a time down her cheeks. She didn't wipe them away, she let them drip. At last she let go, cleaned up the tea, wrapped the syringe in a baggie, put the remains of the dope she found on the workbench into her pocket. She reached under the couch, pulled out the other kit hidden there, went over to the bureau, methodical, cleaned the top drawer out. She found two more baggies, still taped closed, dropped them in her pocket along with the rest of it. Grim-eyed, she would have someone look at the chemistry of the baggies, the syringe. Later. She covered Frankie with the quilt. As if she was asleep. La Favorita sat by the couch, straight and tall, guarding.

Oleander looked around. She noticed there was a burnt smell, something acrid, something more than spent candles. Oleander checked the closet where the toilet was, the odd stench was stronger there, but nothing she could name. A chair was placed, strangely, upside down on the lid. She left it there.

Oleander sat quietly at the edge of the bed. Pulled out a white cloth, a small handful of cowries, sang softly and flipped the shells gently onto the cloth: *Frankie is not finished yet.*

She went downstairs, called a friend at the hospital, asked them to send the coroner around: Looked like pneumonia. Respiratory failure.

While she was calling, Gina came downstairs, a look of fear on her face.

"I heard someone cry out."

"I'm sorry, Gina."

The lobby of the rooming house was dim, the wallpaper looked shabby, the place smelled of dead flowers and a tawdry kind of defeat. Gina's eyebrows knotted, her mouth quivered, other than that she was steady. She had dreamed of great loss during the night, woke on the floor by Ellis shivering with more than cold. Rita wasn't there when she had awakened.

Oleander hung up the phone. "I'm so sorry Gina."

Gina stared at her, steady. She would do her mourning alone, later, the screaming fit, the crying jag, in two days she would have gone through enough shock rage and bitterness to fill a month of grieving. She'd done it before. Just not recently.

Words over, beside, underneath, toward and away, words people have never learned to say, a sluggish dance, attempting dignity, objectivity: Death the ultimate objectifier. Obliterator. Wipes out language. No one can face all the dead faces they need to face in order to live without constant remembering.

Gina struggled to keep her composure. The hallway was empty of people, drab, cold, there seemed to be a fine grit over the surfaces. When Oleander stopped her in front of Frankie's door, Gina looked at her hard, then couldn't look any more, stared at the floor. "Tell me."

Oleander's voice carried tears. "The coroner will say she died from pneumonia."

Gina's jaw was locked, words stuck in her throat, she made a painful gargling sound.

Gentle. "She's still in there, they won't be here for awhile yet if you want to go in."

La Favorita barked, just once, sharp.

"Yeah, okay. I'll go in."

"I'm going to check on Ellis, be back to talk to you in awhile."

Gina knelt by the side of the couch, held Frankie's hand. Touched the heavily embroidered jacket, the beads, the Bowie knife. Rita sat next to her until Gina started to cry then the little pup put her big head down on Gina's foot. Then Gina really started to cry. That phase was all over by the time Oleander tapped on the door and came in.

Gina's voice was dull, tired. "How much Frankie owe you?" She didn't suppose she could pay it, but it seemed only polite to ask. Something to say.

"Nothin. Frankie's rent's paid up for months in advance. Besides, we never refund. See? Says so right there." Waved her manicured fingers as if at some fancy lettered sign. Imaginary fancy calligraphy. Smiling at her own foolishness. "Anyway, her rent will cover you for awhile. If you want, you can stay here, or in Thea and Queenie's room. Ellis will be mobile as soon as the sleeping potion wears off."

Gina blinked. Scratched her face, left her hand over her mouth. "Yeah. Huh? Just like that. Ya never know, do ya?" She blinked again. "It's an improvement over the basement of the Lizard. Just never expected to be livin here alone. You know?" Her mind slipped gears, wandered. Lonely. Too little. Too late.

Oleander held out her hand. "You won't be alone." The pain on Gina's face stopped her. "Unless you want to be." She moved toward the stairs. "You stay with her for awhile?" She paused again. "Julia wants to come and say good-bye if that's okay."

Damn. It wasn't okay. These people. These people let
Frankie die. Damn. Fuck. I let Frankie die. She glared over at
the slender body, as if Frankie was sleeping. "Sure. Okay."

"She was a good person."

"Yeah. Thanks. She spoke highly of you too." That sounded
lame. Shit. "Frankie had all kinds of sickness, but that don't mean
nothing. She was healthy." Gina bit her lip. "She was fuckin
healthy. Didn't have no pneumonia. But I guess that's what they
put on everybody's certificate if they poor when they die."

Frankie talked all the time about how she was going to check
out. And it wasn't pneumonia. Gina knew the plan: Cadillac
ride to the ocean, bottle of the best Champagne, whopper shot
of heroin, into the waves. Romantic. Like Frankie.

"Well, it could have happened any time." Oleander chewed
her index fingernail. She lifted her eyes from her nail, aimed a
sharp glance at Gina.

Gina didn't flinch. "Yeah, and so? Lots of junkies around.
Still alive." Feeble joke: "Alive and kickin.'"

Oleander didn't seem to get the joke.

"Oh hell, Oleander, junk don't kill people. Stupidity does."

"Seems like stupidity might've stopped by." Oleander
didn't look at Gina. "Even when they know what they're doing,
sometimes people just do too much, or, you know… it's not what
they think it is." Her large eyes flicked to one side, re-centered.

Gina said, "Not what they think it is? What you saying?
Someone puttin poison in our drugs again? The Mayor tryin to
clean up the City so the good executives don't hafta step over
loadouts and beggars on the way to the Opera?"

Oleander's eyebrows arched, a corner of her mouth
twitched. "Perhaps not the Mayor." Purring.

"Oh." Gina caught the innuendo, but she didn't know what
to do with it. "Perhaps not the Mayor."

Oleander smiled. Her mouth was never meant to be modest.

"You know what puzzles me, big time? There's no dope
or paraphernalia out." Gina wiped her hands on her jeans,
looked around. "The hell. There's always dope and works out
in Frankie's room. That's what she had a damn room FOR. So
she could get loaded in peace."

Oleander didn't say anything.

"There's no time between a bad shot and death to do the fucking dishes. Or maybe," she looked at Oleander, "someone cleaned up. Maybe she didn't die alone." Hopeful, "Might have been good for Frankie to have someone there? Dyin's a lonely business."

Oleander didn't say anything.

"Why didn't they call for help?"

"Maybe she didn't want help? Maybe she figured it was time to check out?"

"Shit." Gina mumbled through tight lips. "Whyn't she call me then?" Lost. "Say goodbye?" It was tactile, reach out, there's nothing there. Might as well pull the damn curtains, the show's fucking o-ver. Gina's fingers curled. "Were you with her?"

"No. But it might not have been a person exactly." She indicated the clothes Frankie wore.

Gina goggled as she stared at Rita. "No way."

"You're right. It wasn't Rita, she was sleeping with you until she came and got me."

The pup knew they were talking about her, she tapped her stubby tail on the floor three times, put her big paw on Gina's foot, then trotted over to the workbench, sniffing at Francine's machete.

Gina's anger edged forward, she forced it back, kept her face and posture quiet but her mouth curled down in exasperation, "Oh no. Not some spirit. No. No way."

"Ogun. You might not have liked that, but Frankie would've."

"Right. Cool. I'll go along with your batch of spooky creepy crawlies when they do the dishes—"

"And put the dope away?"

"Shit." Gina glared around the room as if there might be something there she could blame. Nothing.

Julia came in. Threw her arms around Gina and sobbed. Best thing anyone could have done. In remarkably few minutes they were all sobbing, then they stopped, grabbed each other's hands and said, "Coffee?" "Beer?" "Rum?" "Vodka?"

"Vodka. Yes. And lots of it, ice cold." They headed downstairs. To the familiarity of the kitchen, the heart of the household. Gina stared around her as if she'd never seen the place before. Three drinks.

Oleander stood up and smacked her glass down on the kitchen table.

The coroner had come and gone—taking the physical remains of the person they couldn't believe was actually dead with him. Leaving her Delaware Maid Bowie knife behind.

There was a sound of breaking glass.

Gina said, "Might as well get to work up there. Uh. Cleanin up. See what's what."

Rhea asked, "Want company?"

"No. Thanks." Gina swallowed her fear, on automatic. From now on all my conversations with Frankie will be just games in my head, Frankie will never come up with anything new, original to herself, never surprise me with a thought separate from my own thought, a perception different from my own, she'll just keep repeating and repeating the same lines, the same gestures. "Damn it all anyway."

The sound of the door closing as she left the kitchen was the sound of rattling danger in a B-movie dungeon.

Gina hesitated to open Frankie's door, she looked down the hall to see if anyone was still there, she waited for the incidental music. Salsa came from Rhea's room up the hall. Gina opened the door. No one was there. Frankie was dead. No weird spirits hovered.

No wild skinny broad clattered up to greet her, no fiery litany of the days and weeks of hell or paradise just passed. No one to tell her what to do or be or want. Francine was class down to her ass. But just now she wasn't at home.

Thinking: Frankie wouldn't check out without checkin in with me. Gina couldn't move past the doorway, neither inside nor out. She didn't know where to look.

Frankie's death was still something to plan, something for the deep future.

Frankie wasn't supposed to die yet. Frankie wasn't nowhere near ready to die yet.

Gina wasn't ready for her to be dead yet.

Wind lifting Frankie's hair, the sun caressing that once-bright face, those sad fleshless bones, dancing? Gina moved into the room, it reeked of Frankie, Gina was sniffing the air like a wild creature in a strange place looking for danger, for cover, for comfort; she called Frankie's name. Called her own name.

Calling out the names of all the dead. All the living. No one answered. Gina was the last person left alive on earth. "Last person left on earth," she whispered, so small, so heartbroken.

Gina pushed through the room to the small sink at the back, turned the water on full blast, stuck her head under the torrent. There were no towels. She shook herself dry like a dog, wondered where all the towels went to? To wrap the corpse? *Ugh, I got to stop this.*

Frankie's last supper, what? Prawns and ice cream? What music? There should have been a whole fuckin band. Did Frankie get to the beach yesterday? Any time recently? What did she do last night? Damn. The charade of it. Last wishes. She wondered if Frankie had left a will. Hell, her will wouldn't hardly be her last wishes, it'd be wishes from months and months ago, wishes no one expected to deal with so soon, wishes that might probably changed. Hell, Frankie's real last wish must have been to live. To live. Must have been to live.

Besides, what did last wishes matter? "I mean," Gina spoke aloud, "do the dead really check back about all this shit?" She felt a wave of nausea. Stomach always the weakest part. She wanted to believe but the faculty for belief was lacking.

Pounding on the sink. "Well Frankie, I hope you're pleased with yourself." Gina burst into tears.

Francine once suggested leaving all the left shoes to one friend, all the rights to another. So they'd meet up and swap stories and shoes. Her desk with everything inside it, just as it was, put out on the sidewalk for passersby to take what they need; see if anyone discovers the stash, eh? How about that for a lark? That was then, this was now and nothing was funny anymore. Gina couldn't remember what she was doing there, she started to sit on the couch, stopped herself. Looked at the couch, imagining the corpse, pearl gray, uninhabited.

Dead. Mute. Forever and ever. Gina put her hand on the couch, a light touch, leaned over to peel the Navajo rug off. Stopped. What was this sudden urge to clean, purge steam and disinfect? As if Frankie would return at any moment. Not hardly.

In defiance of all feeling she flopped her butt down, sighing. Sigh done, she fidgeted. It wasn't going to work. This is where Frankie died. Was it an overdose? Couldn't have been, Frankie knew her capacity, knew her dope. Knew her connect–Gina scowled. Raymond? Raymond? Why would the slimy fruity bastard give her crap dope? Made no sense to OD a solid customer.

Was it really sudden respiratory collapse like they said? Did that ever happen all-of-a-sudden like that? Bam? She remembered Frankie saying how she had enough dope to do it. She remembered Frankie saying they needed to talk.

So talk already you stupid dead bitch.

Gina bent to pull the bed out, examine the sheets. For clues.

The sheets were fresh, the edges turned down square. Precise. Gina shrugged, if Ellis had to stay immobile in the other room for a while yet, she guessed at least she could sleep in Frankie's bed without feeling/without feeling—dead people's sweat? Gina scowled at the bed, at its silence. Sweat. She ripped the bedding off the bed, she'd take it to the laundry. Or not. She slid her hand under the edge to the stash pouch where Francine would have kept a set of works. Empty. What'd Frankie do? Swallow the paraphernalia? Where the fuck was it? What was she missing here?

Gina ran her hand along the top of the wooden cabinet she and Frankie made years before. They put hiding places in everything, gave their life the fabric and texture of great secrets. Over. Never thought it'd end like this. Never in a million years. She rubbed the little cabinet's familiar dovetail joints, admired the smooth gleam of polished wood. She lifted out the bottom drawer, pressed the front left corner of the cabinet, the secret latch clicked open exposing a pile of hundred dollar bills. Faced. Just so. Francine kept her big money faced. She said: One day I'm going to have so much money so much so much it'll take hours to count it; when she did, she said, she wanted it to be all prepared, nicely. Like at some tight ass bank.

Gina put the money in her pocket. Took it out. Bounced it in her hand. Put it in her pocket. Took it out. Started to count it, started to sweat. JEEZ. She was driving herself nuts.

Francine had said: I'll pencil in flash pictures on the corners, a little girl turning somersaults.

Gina flipped the edge. Nothing. Tapped them straight with her other hand. Turned them, flipped the other edge. A stick figure kicked a bucket. Gina did it again. "Fuckin Frankie." Gina counted them. Twice. Whistled. "Fuckin Frankie."

CHAPTER THIRTY-FOUR

There was a knock on Francine's door. Gina shoved the money deep into her pocket, pulled her work shirt out to hide the bulge, shut the panel in the cabinet.

Oleander had tucked her hair back under a white headscarf, changed into a long white skirt and shirt. She said, "Thought you might like some company after all?" She looked at Gina's wretched little face, put her arms around her, didn't say another word.

After a moment Gina shrugged her away. "This sucks." Her voice faded. Gina wanted to step back into the circle of Oleander's arms, pretend everything wasn't the way it was. She wanted so hard to appear strong. Able to deal.

Oleander watched as Gina wandered, awkward, around Frankie's room, picking up one fragile thing, then another, putting them back. Gina's face took on an untouchable look, as if cellophane slid across her features, "What am I missing here Oleander? What is it I don't get?"

"Listen, Gina, don't worry about Frankie."

"What?" Why do people always say such stupid things? "I'm not worried about Frankie. Jeez. She dead. I'm worried about me. Death is an entirely selfish episode, you know?"

"Will you be too uncomfortable? I mean will it be too strange to stay here with all this stuff of Frankie's all over? I mean to say, we've got the other room? If you want."

"Talk about bad timing. I don't know how I feel about any of this." Drifting around the room, "It's not like there's any reason for me to be in this town, now she's gone. No special reason to be anywhere else either." Putting down a small green figurine, not gently. "Hell. I don't even know what half this stuff is."

Oleander turned around, holding a little toy robot in her hand, smiling a little. "Hey, you remember when Frankie wanted to join an organ donation group?"

"Frankie had a sick sense of humor. Had a list of people she hated, wanted them to get her eyes, her liver and stuff."

Gina laughed, made several useless gestures, talked too fast. "Told me, 'If they won't accept my organs then I got to be cremated, okay? I mean,' she said, 'that's firm.' She told me to sift through the ashes for her gold teeth." Warming to the story. "I said: Whyn't we just pullem out now? She went, you know how she talked, *Oh, Giiina*." Gina imitated Frankie's voice, her gestures, "I'm not ready to be spare parts yet." Trying to laugh, choking, "Then she'd go back to the organ donor thing, plotting how to pass off her toxic organs to politicians or judges, like one time she figured she'd just mail them to those fucks."

Looking for something to do, maybe something to drink. "Some people seem to die and come right back. At least that's what Frankie said. She said she'd had so much fun. I mean I don't see how she could think that way after dying for such a long time, but she did. Anyway she seemed pretty sure about the whole thing. But she didn't want to get reborn right away." Scowl at Oleander. "She said she wanted to like, well, explore the other side? I don't know, I mean, she was so sure there is another side?" Her voice got small. "Like if there was anything else to our existence besides stumbling around for years and then leaving a stupid corpse for some other stumbler to deal with." No tears. "Shit. Life sucks."

Oleander said, "Frankie didn't want to come right back. She wanted to be like the tooth fairy or something for a while."

Gina kept her face bland. At the moment she not only didn't believe in reincarnation, she would have splattered the damn tooth fairy against the wall. Shit. Gina always figured reincarnation blather was just one of the comforting things people say to each other, she sure hadn't expected to be discussing the merits of being a tooth fairy.

Oleander drifted around the room. "You know how when you're dying there's this bright light?"

"No." Gina made a small face, "I don't mean to be rude, but I haven't died enough times to recall."

"Well, there is, trust me. Some people are afraid, they look for a dark place to hide. You followin me?"

"Sort of." Reluctant.

"Well, you know what the dark place is, don't you? The next womb." Oleander spread her hands wide. Grinning.

"I'm not gonna put my money either way for-or-against."

Oleander put the little robot down. "Let's get outta this room, take a breather. You been in here long enough, girl. I'll make coffee."

"Or we could have some of Frankie's tea?" Gina turned toward the back cupboards. "Somewhere in all these weird-ass jars of mysterious brown leaves I know she had some lovely opium poppy seeds. Just what we need."

"I'm sorry. It's gone. You were right, I cleaned everything up before calling the coroner." Small smile. "He tends to either steal or report these things." Oleander looked out the window, quiet.

"Well. Coffee isn't going to do it for me." Gina's face started to collapse again. "I don't feel I can leave the room yet. Don't feel right about staying here neither." She opened the door into the hall. "One moment I decide to straighten everything all up," she pointed her hands at the walls, as if to encompass the whole room, Frankie's life, everything, "the next minute I think I should just leave it like a shrine." Gina decided to be blunt. "I think I'd like to get loaded. Really regally loaded. So, if you'll please just give me the dope you cleaned up then step outside I'll get to gettin to. I need something to, ah, take the edge off the day."

Oleander put her hands in her pockets. She blew a long breath. "I thought you'd want to do that. I can't give you the dope or Frankie's kit. I don't know how safe they are."

"What?"

"Her points are all contaminated, I didn't want you using one and getting sick like her."

"Like I'm too stupid to know that shit?" Raging. "Look lady, I was a junky before Frankie even knew from blow—" Stopped. Choked. Shook her head.

Cool breeze. "And I want to get the dope and the syringe analyzed. See if it coulda killed her."

Sullen. "So. You tellin me there's really no dope here?"

"Yes."

"What's Raymond's number? He was her connect, right?"

"Yes. And if his dope killed her, then he intended it that way and he will surely kill you."

"Huh?"

"If he killed Frankie, it was because she wouldn't do something, or give him something that he wanted. Francine left everything to you." Oleander pulled a copy of the papers out of her pocket, put it on the workbench. "Instructions are on file with my lawyers."

Gina didn't seem to hear, or maybe to care what Oleander said. She didn't bother to turn the paper facing her so she could read it.

Silence.

"To me?"

"You're supposed to deal with Frankie's goods. Personal property. Outstanding bills."

Death demands its due.

"Me?" Squeaking.

"Take your time. You're welcome here. Frankie wanted you to stay here."

Brittle. "No she didn't. I offered." Gina held her hands out, "Look. I can't do anything, I'm not good enough, no matter what I try. I can't do what I used to do, and I don't know how to do anything else. Frankie sent me away." She stared at nothing. "I come back barely in time for her to die." Her eyes were wild.

Oleander's voice was firm. "Let's get out of here."

CHAPTER THIRTY-FIVE

A man's voice rumbled in the shop doorway. "Oooo-leander? Where are youuuu?"

Anger flashed hot and cold across Oleander's face. She looked at Gina. Gina shrugged.

Oleander went down into the lobby, scowling. Gina followed her.

"Oh, good morning." Raymond's eyebrows were lifted in concern. His huge bulk filled the doorway. He wasn't quite all the way inside.

Julia stood in front of him, "I tol him he couldn't come in here." She rolled her lips over her teeth, panting with the effort to remain calm.

Oleander put her hands on her hips, "Get out. Get out."

He mumbled gently. Looked around, peered at Gina. "Have I met you?" To Oleander. "Have I met her?"

Oleander put out her hand. "Never mind." Her fingers curled. "Now, good-bye Raymond. I'll maybe call you sometime. But if you don't leave right now, I will never call you."

Raymond's nose quivered, he fussed to himself. He dragged his fingers through his short beard, adjusted the crocheted cap, made a forward kind of motion, like a stiff bow. He didn't say another word. His stomach pulled his striped sweater thin across the middle. He'd put on a garishly embroidered Indonesian vest, several strands of trade beads. His hands were thick with skull rings, bear rings, winged rings, and there was a large Rolex on his left wrist. He didn't budge. His eyes shifted taking in all the details as if taking inventory.

Oleander planted herself in front of him and moved forward, a small but palpable force. The big man said, "Is Frankie around?"

Sardonic. "Not at the moment."

"It's all very strange." He glanced around, his small eyes sparkled in his wide face. He nodded conspiratorially. "Francine called me late last night, but I didn't get the message until this morning…I mean. I suppose she'll get in touch with me soon?"

"Get out Raymond. She'll contact you when she's good and ready."

"Don't fuck with me, Oleander. I saw the coroner's van."

Julia glared at him her face wet with tears. "Get out, Raymond."

Rita, since no one was telling her what to do, made up her own mind, crouching low to the floor with her stubby tail shifting left right left with each careful paw left right left forward, she launched herself at him, alligator jaws closing on his beefy arm, using her own weight she spun him completely around. He staggered against the glass door, trying to shake her off, bellowing. Rita hung on until he slammed her to the floor.

"That dog ought to be put down! It's a danger—"

Oleander's right hand whipped out and connected with the right side of Raymond's face—backhanded. Her knuckles left an imprint.

"You fucking whore!" He grabbed at her hand but she snapped it free. "That's all you are. That's all you'll ever be."

Another deep growl rattled the windows, Julia picked Rita up and clutched her to her chest. Rita frowned—her job was unfinished.

Gina moved to stand beside Oleander. "Back off! Get the fuck away from her!"

Raymond braced his hands on the frame of the glass door. "You don't want to mess with me. You're garbage. Surrounded by garbage." His chin jerked at the people standing frozen in the lobby. "You can't imagine what I can do to you."

"You can't do shit. You played your cards and lost. There's nothing left in all the world for you." Oleander's voice was so cold the vapor of her words coalesced in the air.

He paused to take a deep breath, his hand wrapped around the door, squeezing. "Nothing? I still have copies of your fake papers. That bogus title to this building. The rights to all of Vicente's artwork." He leaned forward whispering, "One call, Oleander. That's all I need to make."

Oleander poked him right in the middle of his chest, his skin seemed to burn where she touched. Her eyes glittered. "Raymond. Remember? I know your every thought, your every crooked dream. Go the fuck away."

"One call and your world shatters." He jerked his powerful hands and the glass in the doorway cracked and fell slowly slowly onto the stairs. "Like that. Think about it, Oleander."

He stepped back, speaking through teeth tight from rage, "We're not done, you know." He continued down the steps with a small smile.

Oleander's bright lips parted to show the sharp edges of her teeth, her eyes flashed, curls of heat sizzled at the corners of her words, "Raymond?" Her body curved to one side, then to the other, swaying, she looked down at him, face tilted, purring, "You are very much done." The "n" in done seemed to reverberate in the morning air.

He got in his fancy ass car and drove away.

Oleander hissed, "Good bye, asshole. Good bye." She held out her hand, "Keep Rita inside please. I don't want her feet to get cut."

The rest of the women from the household shuffled around on the front steps, glaring at the empty street. Gina got the broom and began to sweep up. Not knowing exactly what else to do. Like, should she have tackled the guy? Yeah right. Sweeping was good she supposed. Shit.

Gina thought the whole thing had been pretty stupid. She went and got a piece of plywood from around back, screwed it into the doorframe, grumbling. "Probably not all that smart to have a glass door anyway." She looked at Julia holding the dog. "Would have been a good thing if we'd just killed him." Her head tipped to one side, "Except I really don't know what we'd do with that big whale of a corpse—calling the coroner twice in one morning might arouse suspicions. Still, why should he be allowed to live?" She paused, "Well. Other than to maybe sell me some dope."

She shrugged again, all she wanted was to get loaded. She'd try Oleander again, maybe she could be cajoled into getting up off the dope she'd stolen from Frankie's room? Gina hid a tiny smile at her use of stolen. Always a lot of stealin going on in the world. She thought maybe she ought to get in on it. All Frankie's dope can't all be bogus. And then, hoo baby, looook out.

Oleander turned, her eyes mildly shocked, mouth quivering over a smile "You don't want any of his dope, Gina."

Gina didn't answer, thinking oh-yes-I-do.

Oleander sounded tired. Sounded like the end of the world. "Good dog." She put her arms around Julia and Rita. "Best dog in the world." Rita licked her face. "Yes. You are a very good dog." Oleander started to say something else.

Julia muttered through clenched teeth, "Oh, I want to kill that man."

Gina nodded.

Oleander said, "Later for the killing, girlfriends. Later. We have a lot to do."

Oleander turned to Rita, pointed at the door, commanded, "La Favorita! On guard!"

Solemn as a tiger, Rita paced with slow menace around the lobby, almond eyes fiery, growling deep in her chest.

Oleander went into the kitchen, watched her hand shake as she picked up a small espresso-size coffee cup. She placed it on the tray, careful, then another. And another. A dozen or more. Then glasses. And on top of those a dozen small plates. And on top of that she piled cutlery and spatulas and…her hands stopped shaking. She picked up the tray, spun in a circle, a scream wild enough to pull the sun from the sky ripped from her throat as the piled crockery flew out in a circle of smashing crashing destruction littering every flat surface of the kitchen with shards.

Crunching across the floor, walking on hearts, stepping on bones. She opened the door, her arms filled with bottles. "Let's drink."

After a few shots she gave each of them some minor jobs to do—but no one, no one, she made it quite clear, was to sweep the kitchen. "We'll call out for Chinese, okay?"

Oleander wanted to slip off to speak with the little cement head in her altar room. She was gonna rip him a new asshole— well, she would if the little door guard had an asshole. She took a breath—later for you, buddy—and spoke as calmly as she could. "Listen to me, Gina. You needa be aware that there are some people who will benefit if you are not around."

The corners of Gina's mouth turned up. "Hey now. That's nothin new." Instead of sorrow or apology there was a weird cheerful upbeat tone in her voice. "Yep. All my stupid life everyone's said I was nothin but trouble." She paused. "You thinking I shouldn't stay here now, aren't you?"

Before Oleander could answer, Julia stepped up next to Gina. "Oh don't be silly, of course you should stay here." She turned to Oleander, "We mustn't let Raymond know Frankie left Gina in charge of her will, he'll be after Gina like a hog on slop."

"Hog on slop? Well, shit on a stick. That man gonna find out, but," Gina flopped her hand in circles back and forth, "but he can't know we know he knows."

"Then we can catch him tryin some shit—"

"And kill him."

Oleander smiled at the two of them. "There's a great deal to be done before we bother about Raymond Arthur. He'll keep. First you'll have to make a legal and financial statement as to the value of Francine's possessions. For taxes."

"Say what?"

"Death isn't free. The government collects taxes for every death."

"Hey, she's dead. Who cares if she has a bad credit rating?"

"You do. You're responsible as Executor for all her debts."

"Damn. Nothin good ever comes of anything now does it?"

"Frankie had more wealth than people think."

Gina remembered the wad of cash in her pocket. She'd be damned if she'd declare that. "Oh hell, Oleander, I never even file my own income taxes." She moved her hands in an outward gesture, an apology, an explanation, "Never really had much legal income, you know? And even if I had, I wouldn't want to give the government a cut—they never did nothin for me. Put me in jail. Feed me green eggs and ham."

Julia laughed, sputtered, "Oh, I'm sorry. I know it's not really funny."

"Don't worry, Gina. Raymond came a couple months back when Frankie thought she might be needing money, he appraised some of her things. He said that stained glass floor lamp over there by the counter was from the Thirties and was worth maybe three thousand dollars." Oleander watched Gina. "She's also got some other stuff in the storage room next door."

Gina had no idea what to do with that kind of information. She'd rather plot ways and means of dead-acing Raymond. "Right. Frankie kept three thousand dollar glass lamps layin around all the time. Right."

"There was a moment of hope when one of the doctors suggested a liver-transplant. I encouraged her to think about it." Sad. "She found out she couldn't afford it just about the time the doctor told her she wasn't eligible anyway." Sad. "The virus had done too much systemic damage already." Sad. Sad as if it was all happening again. Oleander's eyes were wide, for a moment it seemed as if she was unaware of the other people in the room. She spoke to herself, "Too late too many times." She came back to the present with a small jerk, "She collected things, you know. The things she used in her life she kept in her room. Things she had gotten merely for their beauty, or their artistic value, well, when she moved in here, she didn't have room for everything, so she put some around here in the lobby, the rest she stored. We'd go through them every once in awhile, seeing if someone would find them useful." In answer to Gina's unspoken question, she replied, "I don't believe she ever traded Raymond any of her things for dope."

"Someone? Useful? Okay. Even if Raymond said some of her stuff is worth that kind of money, is anyone going to actually pay that much?"

"In a word, yes. You are potentially a very rich woman."

"Me? Shit." She didn't know what to do. "Uh. Okay. So if you help me off-load some of her stuff, we see what kind of money we actually end up with? Then we do something with it. Together. I mean like, well, do you got a mortgage on this place?" She didn't wait for an answer. "I mean to say, we'll do something with the damn money." Stuck her lower lip out. "Something useful. What the hell was Frankie doing with expensive shit like that anyway?" Gina rubbed her hand over her face. Scratched her head. "But, it's all mine, right? I'm an heiress, right? And there's some folks who are going to want me out of the picture, right?" The thought cheered her. "Who, besides Raymond, exactly am I supposed to be afraid of?" She'd rather have Frankie back. Couldn't figure how to do that. Couldn't quite move beyond it. Bottom line: Gina was sort of glad her own life was in danger, seemed only fair.

"Only one I know of right now is Raymond. Like I said, he always expects a cut."

"What is it with that guy? He's a walking contradiction, all pudgy and violent." She scowled. "A contradiction. Besides, proper black men don't wear yarmulkes. Or yoga pants." Gina's hands flitted around her crotch, her head, her mouth wiggled in imitation of Raymond's expressions.

Julia hooted. "That's a Nigerian cap. Verrrry cultural." More laughter. Doubled over. "Why Gina, girl, what is your problem?"

Gina turned her back. "He culturally confused just like the rest of you."

Oleander snorted. "I don't think his problem is cultural. But it do seem like the big man's sufferin from a deep sense of loss."

Gina choked. "Can't tell me he sorry about Frankie dyin."

"Well. Maybe not." Smiling, Julia warmed to her subject, "But he already made a claim for some of her stuff." She turned to Oleander, "Is that statue in the store room?"

Mouth tight. "It isn't in the storeroom. Frankie did not have any three foot golden statue. There isn't anyone who has ever actually seen the damn thing. Forget the fucking statue."

Julia's eyes got round, her voice got little, "Okay, Oleander. Okay." She turned to Gina, "We'll be seeing more of Raymond for sure."

Gina shook her head. "Not me. I know how to deal with people like that." Kill kill kill. Then disappear. "Except I don't do that kind of thing any more." Actually, Gina never did. Kill anyone that is. But she always sort of figured she could. If it was necessary. Of course, with her best friend just newly dead, death was once again too close. Was it just this big huge hole or was there something more? Back to the practicalities, she turned to Oleander, "That coroner a friend of yours?"

Smiling, "Not really."

"Oh. Too bad."

Oleander shifted her weight. "As long as you're around and taking care of it, the will is pretty hard to challenge. Frankie set it up pretty well, she gave each of her blood relatives something so they aren't left out of the will, which makes a legal challenge more difficult."

"Blood relatives? Her family hasn't had anything to do with her in years. How will they know she's even dead?"

"You'll tell them."

"The hell I will. And anyway, they won't think Frankie had anything of value to leave."

"Families are weird that way. They will certainly try to get whatever they can, Frankie knew that, so the lawyer tied it up tight." Oleander wiggled her shoulders, remembering the scene at the lawyer's office when Francine drew up the papers. "She made it a point to give each of them things they really don't want."

"Like what?" Gina looked sideways at Oleander. "Oh no. She didn't really give her brother all her old dyke-porn books?"

"Well. Yes. And her sister was given full ownership of her underwear."

"No shit? Well I'll keep that in mind as I'm cleaning up." They began to laugh. Their laughter spilled out the doors, poured down the steps to pool in the street in front, finally it encircled the empty black Cadillac limousine. They remembered poor Ellis upstairs, all unknowing.

CHAPTER THIRTY-SIX

Oleander sent Gina and Julia back upstairs to check on Ellis, the others set up a table in the lobby. Rita prowled and growled. Not for the last time Oleander missed Thea and Queenie. As soon as she could she wanted to get them some more money for Commissary, make sure they had whatever supplies they needed from the streets. Fish out her Luella Black identity kit so she could visit. Scowling, she pushed open the door to her little altar room. Her Eleggua was going to get an earful.

As they passed Frankie's door both Julia and Gina instinctively slowed down, glanced at it, at each other, and kept walking. Silent. The reality kept closing in, claustrophobic, then retreating. Close or far there wasn't any real comfort anywhere.

Ellis was sitting on the edge of the bed as they came in. "What's going on?" His voice was thick with phlegm and blood and anxiety. "Why won't anyone tell me what's going on?"

The two of them stood there, wordless. Julia spoke first. "Um. How's your head?" She stopped, looked over at Gina for help.

Tears welled up in Gina's throat. Her mouth opened and closed, twisting. "Damn. Damn. Damn."

Ellis went very still, frozen in place. He whispered, "Who's dead? Tell me. Who's dead?"

"Frankie."

His eyes got big, then he squeezed them tight closed, fat tears ripped their way out the corners and down his cheeks. "Oh no. How? When?" There was a note of panic in his cry.

Whispering, "The coroner will say she died of pneumonia."

Whisper, "What happened?" Whisper because it was too awful, too frightening to say out loud. "What happened?"

Gina took a big breath, spoke in a neutral tone of voice, flat, she might as well get used to saying it, "Frankie's dead. We don't know how. We think she OD'd. Maybe a hot shot."

"What? You think someone killed her?" He stood up, shaky, they reached out to hold him. "Did they get the statue?"

"What the hell is it about this statue?" Gina glared at him. "And what did Frankie have to do with it?"

"Ohhhhh my head hurts so bad. I must have a concussion don't you think?"

Gina paced away from him, muttering, "This is too weird. Look, I'm glad to see you're up and about, Ellis, and I'd love to chat with you about statues and goblins and all the rest of it, but I've got," her hands waved in the air, big circles, "I've got taxes to file. I'm outta here." She slammed down the hall.

Julia, unintentionally using the same words as Oleander had, said, "You better come clean, Ellis."

He shook her off, jaw tight, "I gotta go look in Frankie's room."

"Not a good idea. I was just in there. There's no special statue. What you got to do is tell me what's going on. Who hit you?" She was immovable in front of the door to the hall.

"I gotta take a piss."

"Right over there, the door on the left." She called out to his back, "And don't try to crawl out the window either, you come back here and tell me what's going on." She paused, then hollered, "And don't forget to put the seat back down."

Ellis came out of the bathroom ashen and shaky, Julia rushed over to him immediately and put an arm around his shoulders, "Take a deep breath, Ellis, I'll help you back to the bed. Don't worry."

He liked her arm around him, hoped maybe it would be there more often. Then his guts twisted again and he nearly went down on his knees. When he was lying back on the bed, he whispered, "Is there someone I can talk to?"

"I'm right here. I'm here for you."

Embarrassed, "No. I mean, is there a guy anywhere?"

"Ellis, this is a women's shelter, you're the only guy around. What do you need?" Her face got business-like, "Look. There's no way you can embarrass me, so just tell me what you need."

"I'm pissin blood. Just blood all over." He looked small and young and scared.

Blunt, "Oh. Well of course you are. You got your kidneys stomped on. That's what ya do. Piss blood. It'll pass as you heal up. Don't worry." She smiled.

"How you know?"

She laughed, "I been through it, man. I been there, done that, lived to tell the tale. Now you just lay back and relax, I'll get you some healin tea."

"I'd rather have coffee."

"Don't be difficult, Ellis. I won't poison you." As she left the room she reassured him once again, "You're safe here, Ellis." She left the room.

The door popped back open and she stuck her head in, "Don't go wanderin around, now. You hear me?"

Ellis rolled the pillow up tighter under his head, considered his options. Julia said he was safe there. Safe? Oleander's house wasn't home, but—well, damn, it was the first place he'd felt safe, like Julia said: Safe. It'd been the longest time since that word had meant much to him. He needed to think about that. He needed to get enough strength to run the mugging through his memory again. Something familiar about the guy. A tone. A smell. Sweet. Sticky sweet. He almost remembered where he'd smelled it before. Almost. He fell asleep.

The next day Ellis felt somewhat better. Julia demanded to see the place where he got mugged. Julia said she would drive the Cadillac, "Your fucked up hands can't grip tha wheel."

Ellis rolled over to face the wall, "Not goin anywhere with you drivin. Shit."

They waited until Oleander had gone off on some secret lawyer-type errand with Gina, then snuck down to the Caddy. Ellis tied his hands to the wheel, the wind whistled in from the smashed side windows then with a whoopanaholler they fishtailed up the street. Ellis didn't tell Julia everything-everything as they headed south, just enough to give her the general idea. Enough to make him seem more heroic than he actually was. What the hell, the truth was never as good as the story anyway. He danced around the topic of the mysterious statue that everyone was not-talking about, didn't say much except that he had seen it, given it to Frankie to keep safe. "I didn't know she was gonna die."

Julia listened.

They wound slowly through the shabby streets south of the city, checking the rearview for a tail, until they came to the block where the shack had been. They parked two streets over. Walked casually. As casually as they could, considering that Ellis wasn't all that steady on his feet and Julia was as jumpy as a cat. "I wish we'd brought a gun. Or a knife. But then, my hands is all fucked up. I can't really handle either one very well right now."

"I can and I did." Her jaw was set, her hand closed on a long thin blade held carefully along her thigh.

"What?" Ellis lifted up his shades, looked at her, decided not to say anything else. Shit. He prayed to all the useless gods that there wouldn't be an occasion for either of them to—either of them to—

Fingernails on a blackboard.

The gate in the old fence swung open, hinges creaking. Must be the wind. Their footsteps were the merest rustle on the path, their breathing the loudest thing for miles.

They turned the corner of the abandoned building and there was the lot, weed-choked as if there never had been a shack. Julia's head was turning left and right, left and right, ready to slice up shadows.

"Here's where the grave is." Ellis knelt on the ground, poking his wrapped fingers into the dirt.

"You watch. I'll dig." She dug.

The dirt was soft, within a few inches she felt a lump, recoiled with a small 'oh', then began to scoop dirt away, chanting under her breath, "Please don't let it be a body please don't let it be a body oh god please."

She pulled out a roll of red and black cloth, it uncurled, exposing a half-full rum bottle, three black feathers and a small black plastic car with a huge rusty nail pounded through the roof into the driver's seat.

Her face shivered into a look of disgust. She pointed at the red stuff on the feathers, "Blood? People blood? Pigeon blood?"

"Paint. It's probably paint." Ellis didn't look closely at the junk, he sort of laughed, saying, "Oh well. Some kid's toy burial.

I guess I was just jumpy. Or hallucinating." He saw the look on her face. "What? What?"

Julia spoke slowly. "Ellis, what did you do here?"

"What?" He knew what she was getting at, he just didn't want to admit it.

"Look at this, Ellis. It's your car."

"Nahhh." He didn't sound convincing even to himself. His voice wobbled, "Didn't do nothin. Lived here for awhile with an old crazy drunk. Talked trash. You know." He remembered the nights when he'd flown through the sky with the old man, when he'd gotten small enough to curl up into a walnut shell. He glanced at the wrecked car, and away. "Let's go let's go let's get outta here quick now quick now. Come on Julia. There's nothing here. Leave that junk be. Let's go."

She didn't move, nothing except her eyes, back and forth between the car and his face. "We have to bring this to Oleander. She'll know what to do."

"What to do? There's nothing to do. It's just some junk. A derelict's crap hole. " He stared at the hole that wasn't a grave.

The wind picked up. The old trees rattled as if irritated. There was a tang of winter in the air, leaves burning.

"Ellis. You the biggest damn fool I ever know. I often wonder just how you earned those beads you wear around your neck." She sounded a lot like Oleander just then.

"Why's everybody always asking me that?" Plaintive. "Why'm I always the one at fault?"

She didn't bother to answer, took off her headscarf and, not touching the items with her hands, rolled everything up in it. "Come on. Let's get outta here. This place is creepy."

Perplexed, but not about to say anything more, he followed her back to the Caddy. Drove ever so ever so carefully back to the rooming house. His hands and head ached the whole way.

"Ellis. You know who hit you don't you?"

"Um. Not quite. It's like at the edge of memory."

"Was it that old drunk you lived with out there?"

"No, I don't think so. The smell was wrong. I mean, I thought it was him dead in that grave, you know? So the whole time I was getting pounded it was always someone else doin it. Like whoever had killed the old man." He turned the corner leading to Oleander's. "But now that he's not in the grave—I mean it's not a grave, you know? I still don't think it was him. There was a smell—he pulled a knit cap over my face. It had a smell I remember from somewhere."

"Well, then. Who'd want to do you like that?"

Torn between appearing to be a dangerous cat and honesty, he said, "I guess I don't know."

"And why they want to do it?" She growled, "I'm not stupid, even if you are."

"Mmmm?"

"It's something to do with that statue now isn't it?"

Ellis repeated, "Mmmm?" He pulled the Caddy slowly up in front of Oleander's house, got out slowly. Everything hurt and his head was ringing.

Oleander was standing on the front steps. Surrounded by thunderclouds, her voice rolled down at them like ball lightning. "What the hell you doin outta bed?"

"Oh." Ellis waved, sort of awkward. "Just the person we were looking for." He tried to wiggle himself behind Julia, "You explain, okay Julia? I got to go, uh, pick up someone." Stumbling back to the Caddy. "Far away."

Hissing. "Not on your life, Ellis." Her hand caught the back of his belt.

Oleander waited. Ellis thought that if there was music it would be playing some sort of doom death disaster riff.

Julia held out the headscarf with its ugly contents as if it were a dead baby.

Oleander took a sharp breath, "Where did you get that?"

"Where Ellis got whacked. It's his Caddy, innit? All destroyed. Big nail through the roof right into the driver's seat." Her voice trembled.

Ellis didn't know where to look.

Oleander heaved a big sigh. She should have known something like this would happen. "Come on in. Let's see what it is."

"See?" Julia smiled at Ellis. "I knew Oleander would fix it."

Ellis nodded. Glum. He didn't know what it was about a

cracked plastic toy that needed fixing. But when he tried to be realistic about the last twenty-four hours, no, the last several weeks, he realized there was probably something that ought to be fixed. "It's not my fault, you know?" Standard all purpose disclaimer.

"We'll see about that."

Before they could get inside, James came strolling up the street. "Hello! Hello?"

Ellis hustled inside the front doors, peering back at James. Julia followed him in, still carrying the ugly bundle. She looked over her shoulder with a frown.

James had decided to further his plan by going to visit Oleander. Take a look at the scene of the crime? Maybe let sweet Oleander give him some of her mojo. He was going to be charming. Wrap her up in his overwhelming charisma. Yeah. He had a flash of Francine on the kitchen floor. Took a sharp breath: collateral damage. He walked up the steps.

Confronted with the woman herself he found it difficult to play it quite the way he'd planned, he forgot what the point of his visit was, he went all jumpy and shifty, not nearly so cosmopolitan.

Oleander was beautiful, clear and cold as a winter's day.

Deep breath, James was a drowning man. "I'd love to have you do a reading for me. Perhaps we can trade for something I brought back from Brazil?"

"The big golden statue?"

Growling. "I haven't recovered that one yet. But when I do, you'll be the first one I'll offer it to." There. The bait was tossed out.

"Oh?" She said, "Won't that be nice."

James never knew what was really going on in any woman's head. "Yes. Of course." Standing on the lower stairs made James feel uncomfortable, and she blocked his way forward. He was making awkward gentleman noises when he noticed the skinny black dude hovering inside Oleander's front doors. "Hey! You're the cabbie what picked me up at the airport." He tried to push past Oleander, his eyes sliding into crazy. "You! What are you doing here? You little fucker."

Oleander watched, fascinated as Ellis didn't move. She could see he was making and unmaking a whole bunch of decisions.

Ellis settled back on his heels, bandage-wrapped hands loose at his belt, ready: Throw a jab. Then a right cross. Left hook to the jaw. Classic one-two-three. He stepped toward James. "No man. Wasn't me."

My god, Oleander thought, the boy is in amazing form today, she wondered if he had any use for the truth at all.

"You're all in on it, aren't you?" James glared around, hands clenched into fists.

Ellis's voice thickened, suddenly sharp, he growled, "I don't know you man. And I don't care who you think I am. We don't needa know what you think. It's time you left on out of here." Ellis shoved right up between Oleander and the angry man, shouldering James away from her. He didn't flinch from the pain. Maybe he didn't notice it at all.

"Don't you push me now, boy, I know my rights." James spoke in a self-righteous whine, shocked at how badly the world was treating him. Furious, he gritted an expletive as he staggered back down the steps. "You're all in on it. Raymond was right. He was right." Breathing through his mouth in scratchy gasps, he said, "You'll be very sorry, Oleander."

Oleander put her hand on Ellis's arm. But Julia slid past both of them, the long thin blade steady in her hand. Her face was blank, concentrated, her voice was cool, "Don't threaten her. Don't ever threaten Oleander."

James ran.

Julia, slipping the blade back into the pocket of her skirt asked, "Did that man actually threaten you, Oleander?"

Oleander smiled then, sunny as a summer day, "No, Julia, no one threatens me. Ever. That man is someone who can't threaten—he's got nothin to threaten with. He fell in love with beauty a long time ago, forgetting what a harsh mistress she is." She turned the wicked beams of her smile on Ellis. "Somewhere along the line he figured he could buy it. Sell it. Steal it. Make it his own."

Ellis headed back down the steps. "Can't be done."

"Ellis. Get back up here." Oleander's voice caught him with one foot in the air. He froze.

Julia handed her the bundle. The broken plastic car didn't look like a smashed child's toy when it was laid out on the counter along with the bloody feathers and half-empty rum bottle. Oleander bit her lip. "And where did you say you found this?"

"Didn't say." Eyes shifted.

Julia picked it up, covering his ass, "It was out where Ellis lived before he came here." That didn't seem like it would be too damning.

Oleander opened the panel at the side of the bar. Rita, wagging her tail and bobbing her big head, rushed over, she wanted to go with everyone into the secret room, she always found something interesting in there. "No, Rita." Instantly Rita was forsaken, forlorn, gloomy and utterly pit bull pitiful. "You have to stand guard with Julia while we go inside." Ah, that was okay then. Rita strutted over to the doors and sat down, glaring fiercely.

"Go on in there, Ellis. Jeez. It's the altar room, not jail." Julia prodded him to follow Oleander.

He'd really rather stay with Rita—better to be bit by the dog you know than to follow a crazy woman into some closet. The panel was all the way back. Ellis saw candles sparking patterns on walls hung with bright pieces of cloth, small tables with figures waving their arms with grotesque good cheer, soup tureens, knives, sacks of herbs, heaps of stones, a black three-legged cauldron bubbling on one side of the weird cave. Distracted, he stood in the doorway, shuffled his red tennis shoes as if his feet were burning.

"Hurry up, come on in."

He still stood there, goggling.

"Please, Ellis?" Oleander tugged his arm, pushed him gently down on the floor. "You do know how to show respect, don't you? You must have learned that much?" Her eyes were kind even though her words were sharp.

Ellis heard another voice, it sounded a little like the old man's, "Fellow doesn't know what he knows." A strange whistling filled his ears as he rolled forward into the room.

Oleander had her arm around him when he sat up.

He said, "Um." Brilliant.

Oleander was doing things over the cauldron, filling it with water from a bottle labeled 'Thunderstorm Rain'. She added handfuls of herbs and then dropped the car into it. "Well Ellis, it's late in the game, but it's time we brought you up to speed here. We can do the rest of the necessary ceremonies later, I suppose." Oleander's eyes burned holes in his chest. "Give me those beads!"

He discovered he was reluctant to hand them over. Peremptory bitch. Who did she think she was? His bruised hands hovered over them, protectively, "Why?"

"You're vulnerable, Ellis. Wide open. No more protection around you than a naked lady in the park." Her mouth turned down. "We're going to re-work them. Re-work you." She continued, "You have brought danger to yourself, to my House."

Sullen. "Well, it's not like I meant any harm." Ellis muttered, "It's not my fault."

Oleander smiled, a shaft of odd moonlight, "No. It's not your fault. You were put up to this." She shrugged, "Everyone falls for the okie-doke sometimes. You know. And I think you were conned by a master—if you get my drift?"

The little cowry-mouth in the cement head whistled. Ellis, startled, turned to stare at it. The cowry mouth smiled at him and winked, seeming to hum. Ellis slowly took the beads off his neck and over his head. He held them out, solemn, to the little cowry-face creature. A small chuckling seemed to fill the room.

"There is energy in the world, I know it sounds new age but that's not what I mean. Energy, or maybe the word might be intention—it fills objects, it infuses the air, the sunlight, and it inhabits, or perhaps co-habits with people, plants, animals. In that sense everything is a living thing. Are you following me?"

Ellis wanted to say: No. No I'm not. This is stupid. He nodded, once, sharp: Yes.

"The energy you carry belongs to Eleggua. The Eshu."

Words words words. Ellis shut his mouth.

"It is, of itself, neither good nor bad. But it works in the world in ways we perceive to be helpful or detrimental." She dropped some white blossoms in the cauldron, it boiled furiously, subsiding as she spoke, "There is evil, real evil in the world." Oleander glanced at him, then away. "Someone who carries the same Eshu energy that you do is in a position to do you tremendous harm if you are not protected." Fresh green herbs were added, the boiling brought the black car to the surface.

Ellis recoiled, dropping the beads in a circle around the cement head.

"Tonight we will bless those beads for you all new. You won't be so easily manipulated ever again. You will acknowledge Eleggua." She paused for emphasis, "You will accept the responsibility of being a man." She made him stand up, she stripped him down to his underwear, and poured some greeny-smelling water over his head. It dripped down to his shoulders, he shivered, but the liquid dried very fast. Oleander handed him a pair of white pants, a white shirt, and a white sweatshirt.

Once he was dressed, Ellis lay flat on the floor in front of her, saluting not Oleander but the powers she carried. Oleander leaned forward, tapping him on his shoulders, saying, "Child of Eleggua! Pomba Gira raises you up." She hugged him, "Ben'diction."

Ellis stuttered, enclosed in those voluptuous dangerous arms, "Ben'diction."

Like a child he let her seat him next to the whistling cowry head. Catholic confession was nothin compared to this.

Oleander pulled out a straight razor, Ellis looked up at her towering above him, his eyes filled with despair. She was gonna cut his damn throat. Oleander didn't smile at him or offer the least reassurance. She began to shave his head, catching the long rough locks as they fell into a white towel. She sang to him.

Bald bald bald, Ellis was gonna be bald. "I hope you know what you're doing."

She grinned at him, "Holy cow, Ellis. Hold still. It's hair. It will grow back." She relented and answered his question. "This shaving is generally done at different time. As part of a greater initiation. But I've discovered it's really helpful when the poison has gone deeply into you."

The whistling of the small cowry faced creature filled his head. He felt oil being rubbed on his scalp, a sharp bitter sensation. Then cool. As if honey were poured from some celestial vessel down and down over him, covering him in sweetness and gold.

Oleander said, "I'm leaving you alone in here to listen to your Eleggua. Don't touch the cauldron, it's cooking away the evil. And whatever you do, don't fall asleep."

He didn't have the energy to protest. In fact, he thought muzzily, it would be very nice to be alone for a bit.

Oleander stood up and spit into the cauldron, snarling, "Nobody threatens us. Nobody. Hear me?"

Ellis didn't see her leave. He was listening to Eleggua. Listening to a whistling voice tell him stories.

CHAPTER THIRTY-SEVEN

Oleander appeared next to him with a cup of coffee. Ellis stared at her as if she was an apparition. He was at the stage of thinking everything was an apparition. The lovely coffee however was rich. Real. "Thank you. I was a long way away I guess." He frowned, remembering. He was bald! "Hey. What's going on?"

Oleander's eyebrows lifted a quarter of an inch, the corners of her mouth likewise. "You're finally getting the initiation you thought you'd had."

"Didn't think no such thing about what that old man did." He scowled. "Was just all—you know how things are hazy when you try to remember? Now I'm sore, beat up, mostly nekkid—and bald. That's initiation?" But as he swallowed more coffee he began to feel that it was all sort of cool. Except for the bald part. That was going to seriously cramp his style.

"Welcome to our House. You know we make an earthly paradise every time we celebrate the spirits, demanding that the world be holy."

"What?"

"Of course we are all merely dancers, and why not? There is something wonderful about rhythm as well as everything else, isn't there? You know," she twinkled, "feet pounding the earth in primitive rhythms?"

He remembered their earlier conversation. Deluded egomaniac bitches all of them. Oh his head hurt—he was coming down off the night's high. His hands shook so hard he nearly dropped the cup. He looked up at her, sorrowing as the world imploded on him. "Yeah, okay, sure. Wonderful." His lower lip stuck out, a child's pouting mouth in a man's face. "Sex is grand, dancing is grand, driving a stupid limo and having hallucinations is grand. It's all just grand. Thank you for reminding me. The world is a wonderful place." His stomach felt icy, shaking. The coffee sloshed in his cup. He knew the world was a cesspool, a violent vicious corrupted piece of crap.

Oleander and the rest of them thought they made it somehow better by their stupid ceremonies.

"Pay attention, Ellis," Oleander took the cup away from him. "Initiations and celebrations remind us magic is real. Even when the world seems too much for us."

He shrugged.

"We all participate in the spark of power. This is one way we learn to recognize magic as it happens in our daily lives."

"Everyone except me," he mumbled. More loudly he said. "Everyone but me gets off with this magic business, but me, all I get is weirdness." The beads around his neck had an odd glow around them.

Oleander nodded. "Yep. Weirdness. Flex your hands now — how they feel, hey? All better?"

"No. No they ain't." Nobody cared. It was all just Ellis do this and Ellis do that and never a thought about what he wanted. He put his head into his hands and clutched at his face—he realized his hands didn't hurt. He looked up at her, glowering.

Laughing, she helped him to his feet. "Come on, have some breakfast. Then you have to go up to the room. You need to sleep."

"Sleep. Yeah." He planned on hiding until his hair grew out. That be about a year. "Breakfast sounds good. Thanks."

Breakfast was casual, eggs and bacon and more coffee. Ellis stuffed his face, didn't talk to anyone (bald bald bald) while Oleander tended to household business—she wouldn't even let him hide in his limo: "Go upstairs. I'll be up to talk with you in a while."

He slept. Oleander woke him. "Hey. There's some things we need to talk about. You know Frankie's gone, right?"

He sat up. "Oh man. It seemed like, uh, it wasn't true. Oh man." He pushed his knuckles into his eyes, they were all watery.

"It's true. And we've got a great deal to do. For her spirit. For our hearts." She paused. "For revenge." She took another deep breath. "Will you please tell me who mugged you Ellis?"

"Dunno." The same series of questions, over and over. He retreated as far away from her as he could, curled against the wall knees to his chest.

"Come on. Yes, you do." Implacable, her huge black eyes ripped away little strips of his self-respect, "Don't pretend to be stupid. You know."

Sighing, "I almost know. There was a smell about him. Sweetish?" Shaking his head, "They say the last sense you lose is smell, and it may be true. The last thing I remember was a smell. Not sweat. Not perfume." Scratching the back of his neck, he repeated, "Dunno."

Oleander looked up at the ceiling as if perhaps an answer lurked there maybe somewhere around the light fixture. She brought her eyes back down to earth, "Eh, I got an idea." She took three little vials out of her pocket. "Close your eyes." She waved one bottle under his nose, rosewater.

"No. It wasn't roses. It was bitter. No, wait, not bitter. It was sharp. Not unpleasant really, except in the circumstances."

She waved another vial, Kolonia 1800 vetiver.

He opened his eyes, surprised, "Huh. Yeah, that's close. But it seemed more musky."

Oleander nodded, "I sell this to half the men that come in here. But that narrows it down." She measured him with her eyes, waiting.

He grumbled, "I'm not gonna hang around here sniffing all the guys who come in. Shit."

"How about this one?"

"Nope. Though—the old man might have smelled like that sometimes."

"Florida water. Lots of people who work with spirits use it. But usually they're good guys."

"The old man wasn't a good guy."

"You always knew that, didn't you."

Ellis shifted away. "I gotta get up and do things."

"That's another thing we need to talk about." Oleander pulled a long white skirt out of her shoulder bag. "You will not leave this floor without this."

Ellis said, "What the hell you talking about now, Oleander?" He retreated to the window, hands behind his back.

"This house is for women only. At least from a distance you can't be a guy. No one must know you're here. No one. Do you understand how important this is?

"That's it! I'm not wearing a skirt. No." He thought maybe he'd never leave the room. Until all this was over. Maybe they'd bring him food? Fat chance. "For crap sake." He shoved his hands in his pockets. "For crap sake."

She put a white sweatshirt on the bed, a white knit hat next to it. And the skirt. "Keep your jeans on underneath, you'll feel more comfortable I think. Be careful walkin in the skirt—unless you've done drag?"

"Get out of here, Oleander. Just get the fuck out of here."

He slithered out of the room, down the hall. At the top of the stairs he checked that no one was in the lobby, headed for the kitchen. But they were screaming again in there, Julia had burned the stew. He looked for someplace to hide, bolted for the door. Goin to hide in his limo.

It was gone.

He rushed back into the kitchen. "Hey what happen'ta my ride?" His eyes stung. "Um. Is something burning?"

Julia looked stricken, "Oh, shut up. I burned the stew." She waved her hand at the other women in the kitchen, "Again. They've got it under control now. I've volunteered for clean up." She didn't even seem to notice the stupid skirt.

She turned to Oleander, "What are you going to do about Ellis?" Her eyes slipped to the frantic angry young man.

"He's a grown man. He can take care of hisself." Oleander knew, as she said it, that it clearly wasn't true.

"Oh right. Witness how well he takes care of himself."

He interrupted. "Hey! I'm right here!" This house was a shrew palace. "And where's my ride?"

"Hauled it to the shop this morning." Oleander's voice was flat. "This rooming house for women only. Our chauffeur took off."

"What shop? My beautiful limo." Ellis groaned: His limo. His hair. He was a captive in a women's shelter. In a skirt. He might as well dieeeeeeeee.

Julia said, "Don't be a creep, Ellis. It's only temporary until you straighten everything out."

"Straighten everything out? Me? That will take for-fucking-ever."

"No it won't. You need something we can provide. Safe harbor." Julia shrugged as she looked around at the dangerous kitchen harpies. "Well. You know what I mean."

Oleander was having a hard time not laughing at both of them. "We already discussed it."

Ellis scowled.

"Women only here. Wear the skirt. Or get castrated." Oleander walked away, snickering.

Ellis glared at everyone. He could tell they were barely holding back laughter. He took a big breath, hitched the stupid skirt up and said, "So. I'm not the chauffeur. I'm just a mechanic. Can't cook. What the hell do I do around here?"

"Wash up. We goin to start settin up for the spirit session."

CHAPTER THIRTY-EIGHT

Ellis, Julia and Rhea walked over to the Lizard and picked Gina up. Picked her up bodily. She had been sitting there at the bar for two days, drinking. She couldn't seem to get drunk. They all walked together back to Oleander's. It was oddly comforting, a rag-tag band of pirates wandering down the street together. Gina put her arm around Ellis's shoulder, looked up into his face, mumbled, "Ya lookin good in ya skirt, dude."

Ellis shrugged. "Should be pourin down rain, but the fuckin sun's shinin. Like everythin is fine."

Gina turned blearily to Rhea. "Is everything fine? The hell's goin on?"

"Tomorrow they're crematin Frankie. We're havin a session for her tonight."

"You notify her dipshit family that she gone?"

"Registered mail. Oleander's lawyer took care of that. The family's just glad we came up with enough to pay the funeral people so they didn't have to. Yolanda is a very clever lawyer. I don't think we'll be bothered by Frankie's family."

"One enemy down, how many to go?"

Rhea smiled. "It's never ending. Haven't you learned that yet?"

"So far I haven't even gotten a shot off."

"Come on. Let's get on to the next phase."

"Oh. God." She swallowed. "I guess burning is better'n worms. But now there'll be no-resurrection-in-the-physical-bodyyyy."

"We'll talk to Eleggua."

Gina, grumbling to herself, asked, "Who now?"

"The gatekeeper. The door man. One of the celestial guides. We'll tip him good tonight so Frankie will find the way open."

"What? What way? Tip who?" These people slid into absurdities at the drop of a nickel. Gina refused to talk or look at anyone the rest of the way back to the rooming house.

When they got there, Oleander offered everyone coffee.

"What is it with you and coffee?" Snappish. "What I need is heroin. Alcohol isn't working. I neeeeeed oblivion." Gina repeated 'oblivion' to herself, in a whisper, as if it would be some comfort. It was not.

"I can probably manage that in awhile. If the chemist says the drugs aren't poisoned, I suppose you can have Frankie's stash back." Oleander looked at Gina. Frowning. "I just don't know how well you're doing."

"And it ain't properly your business, now is it?"

"Gina. I'm sorry. But, yes, it is my business."

"Fuck." Gina curled her hands into fists, opened them again. "Look, I'm not upset that you're concerned about my welfare, you know? I think it's kind of sweet. But then on the other hand, I'm a grown up and you gotta respect that."

"Fair enough."

Julia came out of the kitchen, wiping her hands on her white skirt. "I made some soup. You want? I've gone veggie and I think my cooking's improved."

"You gonna be a professional chef now?"

"Instead of a professional whore?" Julia laughed at Gina's expression. "Not likely."

"Shit." Gina didn't care what she became. Gina didn't care about anything. Gina didn't care. "They're going to burn Francine tomorrow. Burn her. God. I'm not hungry."

"You need food, you're getting pale."

Hard girl to refuse. Gina tried. "Course I'm pale. I'm a white girl."

Tolerant. "Come on."

Gina pulled her chin in. Looked sideways. Didn't say anything except "Hum."

Oleander led the way into the kitchen. What the hell, Gina thought she'd willingly follow the sound of Oleander's slingback shoes straight into a hurricane. Into hell. Right. That was for tonight. Gina wondered if she could ask Oleander to wear those sexy black stilettos....She remembered the mortician asking "What would you like to have done with the cremains?" Cremains? Gina gagged.

"We need to get some of Francine's things together for tonight."

Weary. "I know. I know. I'm supposed to make a big-ass list for the tax people. But you know, Oleander, I just don't want to, right now."

"Not for the tax people, Gina. For the ritual."

"Ohhhh. The ritualllll." Gina nodded. "The ritual. Of course." How many damn rituals were they gonna fuckin have anyway? Do I really want to know?

"And you need to write something for the Saturday obits."

Gina moaned.

Oleander tried to reassure her. "Don't worry. I know the routine, I'll help you."

Gina planted herself. Fists balled. Face screwed up, breathing fast. Too loud, "Not only do I not want any of your goddamn help, I don't want anything to do with any of this." Fists waving. "I don't want to do any of it." Wailing. "I don't want Frankie to be dead. And not all burnt up neither." There. Gina stood in the kitchen glaring.

Julia had her arms across her chest as if she was hugging herself, or squeezing hard so she wouldn't cry. "Of course. You're right." She smiled a little at Gina who still stood rigid. Julia said, "I loved Frankie too." Her voice was round, silvery.

Small. "I don't want her to be dead." Gina scrubbed her face, "Shit."

Julia touched Gina's arm. "Food won't bring her back, but it will help us to do what we need to do."

Gina fidgeted, stepped back a pace. Stepped forward. Who the hell were these people? "What all you need to do? I thought I was the one supposed to be in charge." Gina didn't know from cremation, last wishes or dispersal of worldly goods. Didn't want to know. Was happy just fine with things as they were. Fucked up as they were. It was bad enough Francine was dead, let alone having to deal with all this other crap.

"Well then, you gotta take care of it, either working with me or with the lawyer." Oleander's voice was cool, firm, not smoky like it usually was.

"Don't like lawyers. Not even beautiful ones. Especially not beautiful ones. What's a woman who looks like that have to go and be a lawyer for?"

"She should just be decorative?"

"Point taken." Gina looked back and forth between them. "Okay. Okay. I'll stop having fits every time I look up from my own knees. Let's go eat burnt vegetables and talk about something else." For lack of anything better, she asked, "What's with tonight's ritual?" Maybe they'd tell her she could pass it up?

"We got to have a ceremony, prepare to send Frankie on her way. Make sure she has everything she needs."

Gina stopped once again, digging her heels in, she muttered, "Frankie's dead, dammit all. She don't need shit." No one paid any attention to her.

They all survived dinner, but it didn't seem to Gina that Julia was going to make it as a professional chef.

Ellis didn't get too close, Gina looked like she might hit him, he said, "You gonna get some of Frankie's stuff together for her? Then tonight we'll talk to the ancestors." He shrugged. "Apparently everyone cries a lot."

"Right. Talk to the ancestors. Beats banging my head against the wall." Now even Ellis was getting into it. "And what the fuck you know about it, bald guy?" Gina turned away from him, saying, "I really don't want to hurt anyone's feelings."

"Don't worry. You won't," Rhea said.

"No. I mean I don't go for all this spirit shit." Gina caught herself. "I don't go to funerals as a general thing, you know? And I don't have anything to say to any ancestors. Where I come from death is handled by someone else, mothers mostly. Mothers take care of all the detail work then some priest with mustard stains on his chasuble finishes it up." Gina knew. That's how it was. But usually the corpse wasn't someone she loved. Her stomach lurched.

Ellis gave his best dazzling innocent smile. "But this ceremony's ours. For Frankie." If it went the way they said it would, then Frankie herself might appear and THEN he could ask her maybe, on the side, casual like, so maybe no one else would hear, what the hell she did with it. That would be very cool.

Gina grumbled, reaching for bad-tempered comfort. "Uh. Right." Sure. The whole scene was too bizarre for Gina. Gina swallowed, tasted bile. She kept her mouth shut. Edged toward the stairs, thinking that the smart move would be to wait until they were all involved in the spirit session—whatever it was, she hoped it would be elaborate—grab up her duffel bag and Frankie's money. And book. Gone. Wide open spaces. Yep. She squared her shoulders, suddenly feeling much better. Been a long time since she hit the road with cash in her pocket. Uh huh oh yeah. "Well," casual, "I'm going upstairs to, ah, rest for awhile."

"Heya. When's it starting?" Rhea appeared at the end of the hallway, in white sweats, a barbell in one hand, a hairdryer in the other. "Hey *hermana*. Hangin in?" She held up the barbell and her muscles stood out in ridges.

Gina said, "Hell no." She thought Rhea looked like a crazy angel.

Julia hollered up the stairs, "About an hour. There's soup down here. Non-fat version for you in the small pot."

"Good. I'll be down in another twenty minutes, I gotta stretch out, you know. Take me awhile."

"Gotcha."

Julia and Ellis wandered back toward the kitchen.

"It's really kind of wild being the only guy in a house fulla women."

Oleander overheard, tapped him on his shoulder, "Don't get any funny ideas, Ellis." Sighing. "Don't get any ideas at all, okay? Just do what you're told. Just for a while. Just this once in your life. Oh hell. I don't know why I bother."

Oleander hollered up at Gina just as she reached the top of the stairs. "As Francine's representative, you need to be there tonight." The voice of authority. "I'll knock in about forty-five minutes."

"Sure thing, Oleander." Man, these people knew how to cramp a girl's plans. Forty-five was tight but she could do it. She would do it even if she had to climb out the goddamn bathroom window.

Rita bounded up, braced her big paws on Gina's thighs, big smile just for her. Gina bent over and scratched behind her ears, rubbed upandown her broad puppy chest. She'd miss the pup. Gina tried to keep on hating everything. Oh Frankie, what have you gotten me into? Gina wanted a cigarette. Rita tugged at her hand, throw the ball, Gina, throw the ball. Gina said, "But I don't have a ball." Rita wagged her tail, looked up at her with those tiny sparkling almond eyes as if to say: Oh that's okay then. I'll just come along and keep you company while you pack.

CHAPTER THIRTY-NINE

Alone in Frankie's room with just Rita for company, Gina sat on the floor. Every bone hurt. She laid out her money in piles on the floor. Eyeballed it. Niiiiice. Even Lethal Jack had been remarkably sympathetic, gave her a hundred dollars to send off Frankie. Or spend on herself. He didn't care, "Just do something to ease the pain. You know? Got to ease the pain however you can."

Gina grabbed her feet, moved them up and down, her own ritual, flex release flex release, as if letting them know they were going to be doing some traveling. Got to put some serious distance between me and—and whatever this place was.

Gina looked around. Time to separate the valuable from the sentimental from the trash. Think, Gina told herself, think of this stuff as potential income. A couple really lightweight items would fit in her bedroll, the rest she'd leave for Oleander and the girls. Her head pounded, her eyelids felt stuck together, glue in the corners. She was tired of talking to herself, tired of listening. Irritated, she swore at Frankie for not being there. Dumb bitch. Dead.

Gina groaned aloud as she tottered to her feet, "Fuck fuck fuck." She shuffled over to the couch, flipped her bedroll over with a practiced flick. Dropped the little bronze warrior in, Frankie's filleting blade—the Bowie was too butch for her. What else?

Her brain was fried. She stretched, hands over her head, reach for the sky stranger, ugh, bend forward hands flat on floor, stand back up straight and glad of it. Supposed to do it nine-ten times. Once was enough. Shit. Stretch to the left, stretch to the right. Oh what the hell's the point. She glared around the room, at all the stuff: Quit calling to me, I'm gone already.

Rita went over to the cupboard, scratched on it for treats. Gina gave her one, happy for a moment at Rita's simple pleasure.

She moved to the closet, pulled Francine's clothes out. Might be something in there useful, but most were too tall for her, too narrow for Oleander, might fit Julia but who knew if the girl would wear a dead person's clothes? Besides, the poor beauty was stuck in white until the Pope gave her dispensation. Or something.

The memories threatened to kill her.

She started to shut the closet door, peered at it again, the size of it was off, the proportions were wrong, the door was set right at the edge of the wall, no frame as if the wall had been built after the door. That's not the way they did these things when the building was put up. She rubbed her hand on the side of her nose. Weird. Even in a funky remodel, nobody made closets set like that in relation to the door, she shrugged, she stepped back, wrong size in relation to the room. Gina couldn't help it, she was trained to notice proportional relationships. It was a habit.

Shit. She couldn't concentrate. Everything was off-kilter, it wasn't the closet, it was her. She was all twisted up. There'd be time enough to blow Dodge tomorrow. By then maybe she'd figure out what to do. What to do? She promised herself to hit the road. Do whatever she wanted. Whatever the hell that was. Damn. She had a pocketful of money, she ought to go spend some of it. On anything she wanted.

Same old same old. All she wanted was to be happy. Hah. She picked up an armload of Frankie's clothes, shoved them hurriedly back into the closet. They smelled like Frankie. Gina hurt. Like a little child, beaten for no reason. She remembered Oleander telling her to bring some of Frankie's clothes to the ritual. Like—what? A sharp outfit? Crap.

There was still plenty of time before the stupid spirit ritual. She didn't need to spend any time dressing, she wasn't going to wear whites. Right. She wouldn't be around long enough for it to matter that she didn't have any whites anyway.

"Come on Rita. Let's get outta here." She couldn't leave the city yet, but she would get out of that particular place for a while. She couldn't score heroin at the moment but she could get shit-faced. Maybe she'd be late for the stupid ritual and so what.

"Rita, I'd love to take ya with me, but I dunno what I'mma do exactly."

La Favorita tipped her head to one side and sat by the glass doors as if to say, 'Don't worry, I'll wait for you to come back. I'll be right here.'

Gina walked out of there like she was on a mission. If anyone saw her leave, they didn't say a word.

CHAPTER FORTY

Ellis took a long pull off the rum bottle, poured some into the street. "You got a bad attitude, you know that, Gina?"

"Got the only damn attitude I know how to have." Grim, drunk again and self-pitying, she moaned, "Once a convict always a criminal. Lemme tellya Ellis. We ex-cons are nothin but trouble. Day in, day out." Gina would've gone on crooning day-in-day-out but Ellis handed her the bottle.

The air was crisp, the streets were empty; the smart people in the neighborhood were home asleep, or making dinner for the kids and watching TV; the local bums curled into alleys and doorways with the last of the light—catch a few winks before performing penance all night, scrounging for a safe place to crash, something to eat, holding vigils and trying to score, they were in no mood to witness solid citizens pursuing quasi-legit interests. Or semi-solid citizens consuming vast quantities of booze so early in the evening.

Gina sucked in a great breath of air, realized she was sitting on some dim street corner, drunk, all because she didn't have the courage to stay in Francine's room. Ex-Francine's ex-room. "Shit." There were a whole bunch of half smoked cigarettes and some chocolate candy wrappers in the gutter. She had a sinking feeling that she'd participated in their demise, but couldn't remember. "What's all this?" Hand waving wobbly at the junk at her feet.

Ellis stood up, shook his bones into place like some old man. His voice was scratchy. "Possibilities, that's what that is. While the possibilities ain't infinite, now we know things aren't as circumscribed as you thought they were the day before yesterday. Or the day before that." Ellis himself might not have used a word like circumscribed, but then he wasn't entirely himself.

"Say what?" Listen to the man. "Circumscribed? Circumcised? What?" Gina took another swallow. "What d'ya think about when you think about the future, Ellis?"

"Use to be I couldn't think about it. You know: Is that light at the end of the tunnel an on-comin train?" He laughed, checked his watch. "Got to finish with the past somehow before ya can think about the future. Speaking of which, I got to get some coffee in me, we're gonna start the show in a little while."

They stood up, held onto each other doing it. "Hadn't expected to meet up with a corner drinking partner this evening."

"Lizard's just over a couple blocks. Coffee there. Better'n approaching Oleander, huh?" Gina wasn't steady on her feet, "Maybe we should catch the bus?" She looked up the street searching for the phantom bus, there were signs that said busses stopped on various corners in the neighborhood but no one ever saw any. There were, Francine had told Gina, drivers who set out on the route never to be seen again. Gina kept an eye out without any expectations. She didn't expect to have expectations any more. If there was a light it was a train for sure. For sure not a bus.

Ellis lit a cigar, "Better not see Oleander until we have us some coffee. Right."

Gina shrugged her shoulders, listened to the cartilage crunch. Sniffing the cigar she glared at Ellis. "When you smoke those things you talk like a pompous old man, you know that Ellis?"

Ellis puffed out a big cloud of smoke, "Ya do what ya hafta do."

"You obligated ta smoke?" Sarcasm.

"Life no easy task." Strutting in front of her. Stubborn.

"Dyin's no piece a cake either." Hah. Suck on that sucker. Hell, Gina thought, I don't mean to be this bad-tempered, alcohol must bring out the very worst in me. Gina scratched her cheek, thoughtful, "What you doin out here anyway?" What she wanted to know was what had she been doing out there.

He leaned back against a brick building, his wiry body relaxed, his gestures economical, his voice soft, almost sweet, "Wanted to do a *despacho*, an offering. I realized it couldn't wait 'til after the spirit session. And then you came along. So you been helpin me set it up."

Words tumbled in her head like small annoying acrobats. "*Despacho?* Set what up?"

"Well. James been coming around, trying to rattle everyone's cage about something Frankie had. You and me, we just put the whammy on him."

"Whammy on him? Wait." She looked at him with a perplexed expression, "Wait-a-minute. I don't put whammies. I'm a straight forward sort of person, I just pick up a equalizer and bop em over the head." Well, she thought woozily, I would if I could.

"Nah. That's not the way to deal with someone like James. Trust me. We got to find the statue before he does."

"You too, huh, Ellis? Frankie kicks off leaving a room fulla knickknacks and everyone suddenly remembers they lent her their grandmother's silverware." She was too loaded to tell him off properly so she leaned against the bar door, waited for the world to quit rolling up and down; Ellis leaned against the opposite side. "Besides you and James and Raymond, who else is after that elusive thing? And what's your special claim to it?"

He carefully didn't answer the part of the question about who else might be after it, the old man's interest in it was a private kind of thing, Ellis told himself, just between the two of them. "I gave it to Frankie to hold for me. Until people stopped, you know, wonderin where it had went."

"How did you end up with it to give? And what in the world made you think people would stop chasin after it?"

"I picked it up at the airport. Slick as owl shit. Yeah. You keep an eye out for it as you go through her stuff."

"I won't ask you how it was that you just happened to pick it up at the airport like maybe it was some confused tourist, okay? You just keep in mind that I haven't seen it. Don't think it's likely that I will." Smug. "But, hey, if I do find it, you'll be the first one I'll call. You're probably easier to deal with than the rest of the scumbags who seem to be so interested in this statue. You sure you gave it to Frankie?" Eyes focused on the middle distance.

Explosive. "Damn! Of course I'm sure. Right there in the kitchen."

"Then maybe it's still in the kitchen?"

Mournful. "Nope. I checked."

"You checked." Shifting. "Tell me, what's the deal tonight? I mean, now that we're both official tenants or whatever, it'd be nice to get an idea about how the place really functions. Like can you get the spirits to clean up? Do floors and windows? And if not, what good are they?" She thought for a moment. "Will they tell us where it's hidden?"

Uncomfortable. "Maybe. I dunno. Probably should ask Oleander, I dunno too much about it. She can run it down for ya. It's secret, you know, but you seem all right to me." His gesture indicated that was a very good thing.

Gina stepped back. "I seem all right? Well, thanks. What am I supposed to do? Jump in the air hollering: Oh lucky day! I'm not possessed!"

"Be a good start."

"Shit. I know I'm all right, but I have real serious doubts about the rest of you. Your opinion doesn't get you no discount in my book."

Gina pushed into the Lizard. "Evening Jack. I'm back again. Just when I think I get a grip on things, start to be satisfied with what-is instead of what-oughta, someone gets in my face with opinions."

They climbed on the stools, elbows on the bar. Two sets of glazed eyes stared at the coffee machine.

Lethal Jack clicked down two big cups of sober-up in front of them. He hadn't been a bartender at the Lizard for most of his life without learning to read what people wanted to drink before they asked for it. "Time's tough. Even in a skirt."

Ellis laughed. "Protective coloration, dude. Coffee's on me."

Gina growled, "Only if you promise not to talk to me."

"You a hard woman."

"Advice. That's what you're givin me, isn't it?" Angry. "You waited for me, didn't you? Plied me with rum." Gina stopped to think about the phrase. It sounded like uncontrolled melodrama, well, that's just what life was. "It's all a stoopit fuckin melodrama. Yes. You plied me with rum so I'd listen to you spewing out shit from your superior spiritual wisdom. Well, I don't need your advice, thanks. I already looked for the meaning behind the meaning of everything. And it's...." She took a gulp from her cup. "Coffee. The root and foundation." Muzzy voice. "Coffee."

"Every time we come to a cross-road, a point of decision, there's a chance to straighten out our lives." Ellis ignored Gina's expressions of disgust, he plowed forward, "What's important is not so much whether you go left or right or forwards or back the way you came, but what you base your decision on. The foundation." He was rather pleased with that.

"Coffee is the foundation of civilization." More swallowing. "Thanks Jack, do it again?" She kept talking to Ellis, even though he was sliding in and out of focus. She leaned on the bar, muttering, "You think I oughta be one more person with a thin skull? Alien radio-waves bombard everyone all the time, people with thin skulls get their brains scrambled. You want me to join the flat-earth society or what? I don't give a shit about the shape of the goddamn world."

Irritation. "I think you need to open up to new experiences."

Raving. "I haven't had a new experience that wasn't a total fucking disaster in living memory."

Soothing. He actually patted her shoulder. "Relax. You'll learn something."

"I'm not as interested in learning as I am in—" She thought for a moment. "In having the freedom to change my mind." Gina clambered down off the bar stool, dropped the bill Jack had given her the day Frankie died, on the bar. "Can you change this so early in the evening, Jack?"

"My pleasure." Lethal Jack didn't bat an eye. He'd given her the hundred, he'd break it down for her, she might just end up spending it all back right here at his bar. And if Gina needed it, he'd give it right back to her, he just liked the girl. He just liked the girl. She had heart.

Gina fell into a corner booth on her way out. Thought she'd maybe sit there for a while. Like all night.

"Come the fuck on, Gina. We have to get back for the ritual."

"Ritual. Right." She wobbled to her feet. "Stand back now. I gotta go ritual."

CHAPTER FORTY-ONE

Raymond and James stood on the street a block up, grinding their teeth at each other. Ellis pushed Gina flat against the side of the building, he gave her a warning look, he was suddenly a lot more sober than he'd been and it sure wasn't the coffee. He ducked into the side alley, pulled her along behind him and scrunched down behind the dumpster.

"Was it your plan for that man to, like, pop up everywhere we went or something?" Hissing, "Some kinda whammy you put on him, Ellis."

Eyes big. "We put." He hadn't expected or wanted such immediate response. "I just don't want to meet up with him right now, okay?" He bit his lip. "He already recognized me as the guy who picked him up at the airport."

"Oh? You picked him and the statue up?"

"Shut up, Gina."

The two men weren't keeping their angry voices low as they approached the bar.

"So. Where the hell is it? It's not at Oleander's, so it must be with you."

"I haven't got the damn thing. Honest." Raymond pulled his thick lips so narrow it looked like he'd swallowed them. "Listen. If I had it I would be glad to sell it to you, but I don't have it. And I don't want it. If it fell on my doorstep I'd step over it." Waving his huge arms up and down, a flightless bird, he muttered, "I'm sorry I ever tried to help you."

"Frankie said you traded her that dope for the statue."

"I can't believe we're going over this again."

"And then she died. Right there in front of me!" James folded his arms and glared at the other man. "Listen, I don't care if you are a murderer. I don't even care that I watched someone die from your lousy dope. I want what's mine." His voice went thin. "Vicente's dead and Francine's dead. It's worth way more now than before. If we," James thought his use of 'we' was clever, "get our hands on it now, we'll make a fortune."

"James, I don't appreciate your calling me a murderer."
Remaining calm. "And I realize you've been through a lot of
trauma lately, but I think you've taken this whole thing too much
to heart. Besides, I thought we agreed to give it to Oleander?"
Solemn. "I think that's the best thing. Anyway, it's more likely
that she already has it. I certainly don't have it, no matter what
you think Francine said."

"I heard her clear as clear."

"And if Oleander doesn't have it, and I don't have it, then
it's in with Francine's things." His mouth compressed, "Or it's
gone altogether. And that'd be just fine." Raymond's gesture
was resigned, "I don't want anything more to do with it."
Pious.

"Easy for you to say, you've never seen it. Or you have it
and you gonna make a set? With that other statue you have?"
He stopped, frowning. "Cut me out?"

Gina and Ellis exchanged glances. Gina whispered, "The
hell?"

Ellis shushed at her.

Raymond was running out of patience, he struck a noble
pose. "Nothing to cut you out of."

"It's my statue." Whine.

"Do you have any idea who Oleander is? You want black
magic?"

"Black magic? Bullshit." His breath came in ragged gulps.
James was tired of being victimized. Manipulated. "Hell. I don't
need you. I don't need your help." He walked a couple steps up
the street. "I'll share it with Oleander."

Raymond's voice mocked him, unimpressed with the
cheesy drama. "Was the piece signed?"

James stopped, didn't turn, didn't answer Raymond's
question because he didn't know.

"When you get the piece back, it can be signed if you'd like
it to be. Double the value, ya know? Since I handle all Vicente's
work in this country I can certainly authenticate it for you. For
a fee." He smiled. Mean.

James didn't turn around, he said, "Oleander will
authenticate it for me." Ha! Ha!

Raymond's voice was an oily blade. "But why would she do that little thing for you, hey, James? Especially since you watched her friend die, and did nothing." James came back up the street, right to where Raymond stood. James was shaking.

Almost kindly, Raymond said, "I feel I should tell you a little more about what I believe you are dealing with here. Sorcery. Quimbanda. Yeah. Black black blackest magic. A powerful force which springs from a primitive perception of reality. Fear and hate and blood and bones in a cauldron. It's all cursing, killing. You know, a bit of someone's hair, some graveyard dirt, bat's eyes. Death."

"Crap, Raymond. You don't believe in this."

"Not a matter of be-lief." Raymond drew the word belief out, ironic, deprecating his adversary's experience. "Matter of fact."

"Get the statue back to me and I'll give you fifteen percent when I sell it."

"I haven't got it. And fifteen percent is an insulting offer." Cold. "When I get it, I will do you the favor of not reporting your part in all this to the customs agents I know." He lifted his chin, glaring down at the shorter man.

James blinked. "Report me? The hell you will, Raymond." He looked where his watch ought to be. It wasn't there. "Jesus." His life was turning all to shit. "I'll to go to the police. And to the Museum trustees. And to the Small Business Bureau. They will be excited to hear the truly damning information about certain barbaric practices you're involved in."

Flat. "I am not involved in Quimbanda." Raymond's eyes had taken on a funny shine, the whites glowed red, his shoulders hunched up. "You have no basis to claim that."

"Au contraire." James translated it, snotty, "On the contrary. There's fraud. Possession of stolen property. Your shop is a front for dealing death—Quimbanda or heroin." James was pleased with himself.

Raymond's face darkened, growling noises issued from his mouth. He thought how easy it would be to draw James across his knee, snap James's long spine.

James continued, blithely, "Dealing drugs! Which lead to a fatality. Your friends can all go to jail with you. Animal sacrifice. The Health Department. Animal Control. SPCA. Public drunkenness. Procuring. All that and more!"

Raymond's large fist, the size and weight of a prosciutto, slammed into James's mouth.

Gina watched James collapse on the pavement, Raymond stepped over him and sauntered off down the street into the bar, dusting his huge hand on his pant leg. She raised her eyebrows at Ellis. "Time to get to gettin, Ellis?"

"Feets do yore thing."

On her way past the unconscious man she flicked her hand carefully over his pockets, two twenties, no wallet, no watch, she grabbed his penny-loafers. "Walk home barefoot. Scumbag."

They were several blocks up the street when the police cruiser passed them, lights and siren pumping. They were too far away to see James loaded into the back seat.

*   *   *

Everyone was already crowded into the kitchen, the long worktable covered with a simple white cloth. There were photographs of Francine, lots of white roses. A small carved gourd, Francine's silver candlesticks and a couple brass vases filled with palm fronds, a white dish with bluish opium poppy seeds. Gina stood perfectly still just inside the door, not even breathing.

The lights were dim and filled with writhing wisps of incense smoke. Oleander was seated on a low stool, holding a crooked branch in her hand, nine ribbons knotted on top, each with a small brass bell. About a dozen people sat on the floor around her.

Someone was speaking, Gina didn't know who, didn't care. She heard Francine's name mentioned, everyone in the room turned to look her way, Gina shifted around, no place to hide, the voice resumed again. Then silence.

Gina argued with herself, ponderously, in two voices, or three or four: It's too weird/no, it's not, you've been through stranger shit/ oh yeah when/put a bag on it, Gina, this kind of thing's a comfort in grief. No, no it's not/ people need to express their spirituality. She thought maybe people shouldn't have such strange spiritual needs. It's all a crock. Frankie's dead and nothing anyone can do can ever make it better. Where's the fucking booze? Did that man really see Frankie die? Where? When? He oughta die himself. Oughta die. Die.

The lights dimmed. Someone lit nine white candles on the end of the table with Francine's picture, the flames sputtered then steadied. The only sound was the gentle persistent tapping of Oleander's branch. The eerie chinking of the brass bells. "Francine, can you hear us? We love you Frankie. We're sending you light to guide you."

Someone set nine glasses of water on the table. "And here's refreshment, pure water to help you on your way."

Gina scowled. Pure water? Light to guide you? Give me a fucking break. She wondered if there'd be big trouble if she put the opium seeds in the water, drank it up.

Choked-up voice, "And money. Lots of money." Julia lit a handful of Chinese 'Hell-notes', ten thousand dollar ones, everyone watched them burn. Gina's mouth dropped open. "Here's money for your journey." It curled into ashes. "And light. And water for sustenance. Don't worry Frankie, there's friends all around you."

Shaking the poppy seeds in the white dish, Ellis said, "And something for sleep when you get tired." He sprinkled a pinch in the water glasses. Gina liked him very much for that.

"Gone. Gone. Gone beyond. Gone beyond. Beyond."

Gina felt the hairs on her arms raise up.

"Beyond. Beyond. All hail the traveler."

The chant was taken up by everyone in the room, thunder solemn it echoed: "Gone. Gone. Gone beyond. Gone beyond. All hail the traveler." Again. And again.

Gina caught herself rocking forward and back in time with the chant, imagining Frankie somehow borne away on wings of a raven. She stopped herself. She would not become part of this cheesy cult, no matter how seductive. Julia slipped next to her, put her arm around her waist. They rocked back and forth together.

"Bendic'cion. Blessed be the path you travel. Blessed be your comings and your goings. Blessed be. Blessed be." Ragged voices repeated the phrase. Sniffing back tears.

All the time in the background, not stopping, not losing rhythm, Oleander kept tapping her stick. Gina's heartbeat had synchronized at some point to the rhythm of the tapping, her mind slipped gears, some of the anger faded, the rigidity slipped from her body, her eyes slipped to half-closed. She hadn't realized how tired she was.

Much of the rest of the night was a blur, it seemed to Gina that the long table was filled with food, that it was much longer than the room could hold, there were foods of all kinds, bottles and bottles of champagne or something, course after course, a whole lot of people came and went, laughed and argued and sang songs. They were numerous, dressed oddly, different races, talking all different languages, they were familiar, yet unfamiliar. "Who are all these people?" Gina tried to ask but no one seemed to hear, or she couldn't form the words, or no one near her understood whatever particular language she was speaking just then.

It was all very bizarre. Not unpleasant. Just odd.

People went off, arm and arm, still talking; other people sat down, served each other, served themselves, talking, laughing. Gina wondered what all this had to do with Frankie anyway.

Then Ellis told her Francine hadn't arrived yet. It'd probably take awhile.

Gina decided not to tell the man that Francine was dead, that she wouldn't be arriving any damn where. It didn't seem appropriate to remind all these happy intense people that Frankie was dead. Dead. Dead.

Oleander handed her a Kleenex.

Gina blew her nose, "Never been able to cry without my nose running." She told herself that there were simply some things she just wasn't meant to understand. She had another shot of tequila.

Later, much later, it seemed that people were looking at her again. She heard herself saying, "It's right here. It's been gutted,

Frankie took the poison out of it, but the curse is in the shape itself. She couldn't bring herself to destroy it. But if we finish what she started nobody else will die. If we don't, the curse will just spread and spread. But we can't kill the thief. We can't kill the maker either. We can only make the spirit right in the statue." Gina, talking, not knowing what she was saying, spoke very sadly, "And the other one. Needa be together. Then the spell will be broke. But we can't kill the thief or the maker. I'm sorry." She sat up straight, hiccupping, said, "What? What?" sort of confused and frightened, then slipped slowly to one side in a faint.

CHAPTER FORTY-TWO

Gina woke up slowly in the dark, lying on Frankie's couch, covered with a soft quilt. There was a steaming pot of coffee on the side of the little sink. A plate with a sliced peach and a bagel. Homey. She stretched, unfamiliar luxury. Good. She tottered up, poured a cup of coffee, tore off a corner of the bagel, leaned against the counter and took stock. Stock. Whatever. She went over to the closet and pulled Frankie's clothes back out. Might as well get things in piles for give-away. She'd set things up so it'd be easy. Then she was out of there. Out. Of. There.

More coffee. Good. Peach. Good. Big sigh.

She looked at the closet. Frowned. It really didn't look right to her, the proportions were all wrong. The closet size was off by more than a foot. What the hell do I care? Glaring at it she scrabbled her strong stubby fingers against the side wall, found a tiny nail; it didn't seem to be a new job, the style of it was from the thirties, bootleggers? Maybe earlier. How pleased Frankie must have been when she found it. Gina wanted to believe Francine found it, something about the idea that Frankie had another secret pleased the shit out of her. She eyeballed it, there better fucking be some dope hidden back in there. Oh yes.

Gina smiled as she fished Frankie's flexible steel filleting blade out of her bedroll; she pressed it between the protesting boards all the way around the nearly invisible partition, the panel finally groaned forward, quarter inch by quarter inch until she could wedge her hands behind and pull.

Behind it was something about the size of a small mummy, shrouded in layers of terry cloth towels—so that's where they went—which took up nearly all the space in the compartment.

With shaking hands Gina lifted the mummy out of the closet's secret hole, laid it on the couch. It was about three feet high, more than a foot and a half around. Heavy. She peeled a layer of towels off the upper end.

A jeweled band cut across lustrous enameled black hair; removing the next layer of towels exposed a smooth forehead the color of coffee with a little cream; the artist had given a sardonic curve to the eyebrows. A pair of dark seductive star-eyes gazed up at her, implacable as the night sky. Gina lifted the towels off as carefully as if she were uncovering a living creature. Cheeks and nose haughty as Cleopatra, mouth sweet, avaricious. Chin, neck, shoulders as pure as a medieval icon. When all the towels had been finally pulled away the curvaceous red black and gold thing lay exposed on the couch: An incredible female, glowing, voluptuous, the perfect Madonna Dominatrix. The foundation and fulfillment of every desire.

Whoa baby. Gina had never seen anything remotely like it. Her hands stung.

Gina shook herself, suddenly aware that she'd drifted off into a reverie, blank as a burger flipper in a fast food joint. Visions of blackbirds, people in red and black, spinning and spinning. Spinning.

Unnoticed, the flat oval plate that Frankie had removed from the bottom of the statue slipped into the back crack of the couch.

Gina shook her head. Shifting. She didn't want to look at it anymore. She wrapped it up, put it back in its hiding place.

Breathing deeply as if she'd just run a long way, or was about to run a long way. She didn't know what to do. She still needed to do something. Keep moving. There wasn't enough time to figure things out, there wasn't enough time. She paced to one edge of the room and back, shaking her hands. Tell Oleander? Tell Ellis? Who did it belong to anyway?

To her?

Things to keep, things to throw out, things to give away, things to sell.

And what should I do with a statue, lovely as the dawn, and twice as dangerous?

The proverbial knock on the door. Enter Oleander. Staring, one at the other. "Oh. How are you today?"

"Thanks for the coffee. And."

Watching watching. "You're welcome." Waiting.

"Here. Sit down. I'll pour you a cup?" Nervous.

"Thank you." Oleander arranged herself on the couch.

Gina fiddled with the pot, with the cup, for crying out loud this was too weird. "Here." Gina turned around with the cup preparing to hand it to Oleander.

Suddenly Oleander held an oval flat plate in her hand. Her face was pale, drawn. "What's this?"

Gina's eyes opened wider, in honest shock. "I don't know. What is it?"

"These lines, these lines here, are a very fancy curse. These other lines here, surrounding them, are a less fancy but far more nasty curse. This part here seems to try and make the curse cycle infinitely, continuously re-establishing itself until some time when it has finished its work."

Leaning forward, looking but not touching the oval, "What's it supposed to mean?"

"Hatred. Revenge. The usual puke and shit of someone who needs to find someone else to blame." She stood up. "You have no idea how this came to be here?"

"No." Gina had no idea. Well. Maybe a small idea. But then maybe she didn't. So she didn't say anything.

"Come with me then, and I'll show you how we deal with things like this."

Shivering, Gina tiptoed down the hall behind Oleander.

She took Gina with her into her little altar room, spit rum on the little cowry head, preoccupied she handed the bottle to Gina. Gina spit. The cowry head seemed to wink at her. She really didn't like that, she took a few short breaths and tried to reestablish herself, as herself.

There was a black cauldron with a couple dead blossoms floating on the surface of some murky water. In the depths was a black car. Oleander added the oval plate. The water seemed to bubble red, Oleander seemed to glow red, for just a moment.

Gina managed not to see whatever it was that she was seeing.

"We don't kiss nobody's ass. Not for money. Not from fear. Nobody." She sent a glare to her cowry face cement door guard, "We send this crap right back at them. Won't we?"

Gina, thinking she was the one addressed said, "Sure. Whatever you say."

Oleander smiled, a brief flash, she scooped out the dead blossoms, added another handful of fresh ones to float on the surface of the bubbling water.

CHAPTER FORTY-THREE

Gina wandered out onto the late afternoon street, mumbling to herself. Oleander watched her go.

Gina stopped and looked for Ellis's limo. It was an impressive car. But it wasn't anywhere around. Maybe Ellis had taken it out for a little drive. There was a curse on the car, or so Gina had been told. Curses. Right. Cauldrons that boiled up all on their own. Statues popping out of secret compartments in her dead best friend's closet. Her feet headed themselves toward the Lizard where there was nothing out of the ordinary except that she could afford to pay for her own drinks and therefore Jack would probably pour for free. She hoped there wouldn't be any more idiotic men brawling over mystical bullshit, claiming there was thousands, tens of thousands of dollars to be made. Gina shook her head. Maybe Jack would let her in on what happened after James had gotten cold-cocked on the sidewalk. Maybe the bastard was dead. Dead would be good.

On the corner just before the Lizard, Gina saw an awkward woman, sort of glowing red/black in the fading daylight. There was a short slender girl dressed in gang-banger baggies, kneeling down fussing with something in the gutter. Flowers. The glint of a bottle of rum. They were in conference. Cigars were being smoked.

Gina's steps slowed. This was too close to where she had come in several weeks back. Seemed a good time to not come in again—

"Hey! Gina!"

Oh great gods in heaven, the demons had seen her. She shuffled backwards quickly, trying to remember a nursery rhyme or something to make them go away.

"Gina! Cool! Come on!" Julia stood up, impatiently waving her over. Gina noticed she had hair, long thin blonde braids bouncing around her face. Had to be a wig poking out from a knit cap. Very strange. And the other woman was Ellis. No braids but some stupid turban or something on his head.

Gina wiggled her fingers at the braids, at the clothes. At the dorky turban.

"Disguise." Julia was proud of herself.

"Oh." That was all Gina could think of to say, "Hey." It would have to do.

"We just finished the *despacho*."

"Not another one? How many of them things do you have to make, anyway?"

"Here. Have some rum to bless our work. Ellis told me what you guys heard goin on between Raymond and James."

Gina took a big gulp of rum. Maybe they were going to kill someone. Seemed only fair. She tilted the remainder of the bottle into her mouth. Killing time. "I'm ready."

Arms around each other they set off down the street, none too steady on their feet, tangling up every once in awhile, but their staggering progress seemed only right. They were brave. And ready. "You bring your blade?"

"Yeah. You got one?"

"Yeah."

Ellis tucked his skirt up, his black jeans showed. No one cared. Raymond's shop loomed up ahead.

Gina was having a marvelous time. True night had fallen as they staggered around. The stars were shiny and briiiiight—

They slipped and slithered along the street. "How you guys plan on doing this?"

"Gonna break in through the side second floor window. Check the place out."

"Lay in wait and jump him."

Oh boy. Just like old times. Gina didn't even much care if she was arrested. She wasn't doing much of anything anyway. Not that she could recognize. It was all sort of blurry. Getting arrested would give her a chance to catch up on the local jailhouse gossip, catch up with Thea and Queenie, catch up on some sleep maybe. It would all depend on where she was housed. She was kind of looking forward to it. It would get her out of the stupid situation she was in.

"Oh well. Take care of the fat man and then—What are we after? Anything that strikes our fancy or what?"

"The gold statue."

"And the other statue."

"What other statue? Jeez." There were altogether too many damn statues.

"What are we gonna do with them when we get them?"

"Give them to Oleander."

"Oh." Gina thought about that. Blearily. "And what's she gonna do with them?"

"Dunno." They were all tilting towards each other in a completely loopy fashion, whispering. "But I know she'll do whatever is right. Something."

"Well then. Hate to bust your bubble...." Gina wasn't sure how she was going to tell them, she started over: "Hate to...." She couldn't figure out how to go on. Then quickly, all-of-a-piece, she said, "Hate to bust your bubble. But it ain't in there."

"Oh? You heard James say how he heard Frankie say she traded it to Raymond for dope."

"And you believe him?"

"Um. Well. Yeah."

"Um. Maybe not?"

"Good. The man lie like a rug." Gina took a big breath.

In the half-dark doorway of Raymond's shop they noticed an old bum squatting there.

Ellis grabbed each of them by the shoulders, too tightly, dragging them back deeper into the shadows. "Shhh. Shhh. Holy fuck."

"*Oh Elegba nisa La Roi-ey so kuo, ohhhh Elegba nisa la roye so kuo ai-yey.*"

Whispering, "Do you hear that?"

Thin, a whisper on the wind, "*Elegba nisa La Roye, so kuo, ohhh Elegba nisa La Roye so kuo ai-yey.*"

"What?" They stared at the bum, the source of the strange singing.

As if on cue the shivery voice sang it again, "*Elegba ai-yey, Elegba ai-yey, Elegba la roye so kuuuuuuu-ohhhhhh ai-yey.*"

Julia knocked on the wall three times. "That's the song of the guardian at the gate."

"That's the old man. The one I stayed with. He's the one wanted me to get him the statue."

Not hardly breathing they stared at the humming shadow in the doorway. The door to the shop opened, and the crouching man stood up. For a moment they saw the man outlined, but he looked tall, taller than the height of the door, and jaunty in a tuxedo. A top hat. He was smoking a large cigar.

He continued into Raymond's shop as if he was familiar with the place.

CHAPTER FORTY-FOUR

They had, all three, backed away down the alley, praying to whatever gods might give them succor, might offer them safety, oh man at least hide them from the red red eyes of that weird old man at Raymond's shop. Ellis's eyes gleamed, "That's where it is for sure. That old bastid's goin to steal it."

Gina muttered, "Uh. I don't think so."

Ellis thought about that for a while. "What you mean, Gina?"

Julia said, "You think that guy was robbin the place?"

Ellis exclaimed, "What need do he have to rob? That's the king of the demons, there."

"No he's not. He just some tall guy, smokin."

"Bullshit!"

"What you think, Gina?"

"I think he was over-dressed for whatever it was he was gonna do. I think it's not our night." She grumbled to herself that she never never seemed to get a clean shot at robbin any place any more. "You guys go on and head home. I got some things I want to think about." Gina's tone of voice didn't leave them much room to argue. "I'm gonna go hang at my old work place." She left them, and stumbled off towards the Lizard, after all the sun was finally coming up, she figured Lethal Jack would be there. "Like I'm not drunk enough already." Finish off the day with some vodka. Something.

Gina walked into the bar.

"Hell, Shorty. You look like hell." Lethal Jack actually sounded concerned.

"Set me up with a tall glass of ice cold vodka and don't talk to me for a while, okay, Jack?"

"You know, Shorty, sometimes alcohol won't help."

"Shut up and pour, you old geezer."

He busied himself, poured her drink very light. Didn't move away. "You know that skinny art dealer guy, friend of Raymond's?"

"Mmm."

Lethal Jack said, "You saw him get creamed last night, eh?"

"Mmm."

"You know what else happened? Raymond comes in here, after cold-cocking the man, and cool as cool, asks to use the phone, calls the police, tells 'em some homeless guy tried to attack him."

"No shit?" Gina was talking just to talk, she could have cared less about those two bastards. She had problems of her own. Damn.

Jack was having too much fun with his story to notice her lack of enthusiasm. "When the cops come, James is just coming around, starts hollering at Raymond. Finally realizes what's going on with the cops and all, and tells Raymond to tell the police who he is." Pause. "Raymond looks shocked, shocked-I-tell-you, shocked, and says to the cops he's never seen the derelict before in his whole life." Pause. Small smile at the meanness of people. "Then, our boy James gets thrown in jail, then he was let go and sent over to County hospital where they tell him he has a concussion—"

"How you know what they tell him?" Gina asked.

"He came in an hour or so ago, bangin on the bar, demanding I find Raymond. I tole him no one around here's seen old Raymond. Then James is swearin he gonna kill the bastard. Crying. Not only did they find he had a concussion, no big deal, but James seems to have taken the whole thing much further. Kept wiping his hands on his pants, said he'd woke up knowing he was gonna die."

"That's common when you wake up hung over in jail."

"He said he was doomed. He swore he was gonna test positive for Hep. For AIDS." Lethal Jack had to bend forward to see the expression on Gina's face. "For TB. Hey. You're pretty poker-face about that news. I thought maybe you'd be pleased."

"Now, why's that?"

"I know you don't like him. I mean, first of all, he's just the type you really don't get along with." Tilt of his head, "Not like me. We get along good don't we?"

"Jack, old man, are you hitting on me again?"

"Would it do any good if I were?"

"Not on your life."

"Then I'm not."

Gina said, "Let me get this clear. James came in here, out for Raymond's blood, as it were, and told you he had suddenly come down with the same disease that Frankie had, or didn't have. Right?"

"Bingo."

"So, how'd he get all them diseases?"

Hands spread wide. "Don't ask me. I'm not privy to all the particular secrets of any particular gentleman's soul. Only the general secrets, and even those, I tend to keep pretty much to myself."

"Well. Damn." She swallowed big. Put the glass down empty. Didn't feel drunk. "Do me another. With some alcohol this time."

He came back with another glass, "I don't suppose you'd like to meet up with Raymond's friend?"

"Now? Not especially. I left my knife back at the house. Although slicing him seems a risky procedure now that his blood's poison. Or what d'ya think?" Half-smile.

"Then, since our friend made noises about checking back with me," Jack rubbed his thumb and middle finger together, "this morning, I suggest you drink and book."

She drank with one hand, fished in her pocket for money with the other, "Thanks, Jack."

"No problem, Shorty. I just like to see your face sometimes, you know?"

"Don't get too used to it. I don't think this town agrees with me."

"Well. You got to do what you got to do. But it's only wisdom to take a good long look at what it is you got to do, and then just go and do it."

"Just go and do it? Simple as that?"

Jack nodded, watched her walk out the door.

CHAPTER FORTY-FIVE

She wandered the streets, saying goodbye to various corners she'd never really said hello to. The night had passed into morning somehow, she wondered if all her life would be like that—empty, grim, empty—Her steps slowed as she approached Oleander's rooming house, her resolution remained firm—at least she reassured herself that it was so, but her desire or ability to tell Oleander what she needed to tell her was getting sort of wobbly.

Distracted by her own thoughts, she was looking, not seeing, at the stairs as she climbed up. Slow, reluctant, unhappy. Near the top step her eyes focused on blood smears. "Now what the fuck's happened?"

She heard Rita howling.

The red curtains were pulled across the glass doors. Gina pushed into the lobby holding her breath.

The chandelier shed a dim murky light on the small group of people gathered there. First she saw Oleander, dressed in a blasted black dress, a slash of red cloth burning around her shoulders. Then she noticed Ellis, or someone who sometimes was Ellis but at the moment he seemed to be quite someone else. Someone older, ageless, timeless, glowing with a dull matte-black shine. The several candles around the edge of the circle sparked off his mirror shades. Everyone else was in white, silent.

Rita padded over to her, solemn, she pushed her big head into Gina's thigh.

That's when Gina noticed the dead rooster hanging from Oleander's hands. She stuttered, "What the fuck?"

Oleander said, in a thick smoky voice from somewhere far away, "Time is running out. You know anything about that?"

"Me?" It was a squeak. "Me?" Gina shook her head, "Like I know anything about these things?"

"You know more than you've said."

Doom. Big breath. "Well, whatever. Anyway. I got something to say."

"Go get it."

"Oh. Yeah. Right." She hustled up the stairs, wondering just how Oleander knew she'd found the statue? Maybe Ellis realized it from what she almost said back at Raymond's shop? No matter. The deal was done. She pried and tugged and pulled and the wood creaked as if it didn't want to come free. Funny, the first time she'd opened the secret stash it had come out pretty smooth. She gave a final jerk, the wall panel fell on top of her. "Ah, shit."

She grabbed the statue in both arms. Heavy. Heavier than she remembered, as if it really didn't want to come out of its hiding place. Heavy. A rancid stench seemed to fill the room. Heavy. As if to choke the breath out of her. She talked to it, "No you don't, you damned inanimate object. I don't go for that shit. No you don't." She ripped the towels off, her fingers seeming to burn where she touched it. She growled at it again, "Don't you try any of that shit with me, you stupid bitch. I'm not no believer." She wrestled it free of all its coverings, squeezed her eyes against the glare of the gold. A stabbing pain shot through her shoulders, shocking her in its intensity. For the first time she realized that for a while there she'd been virtually pain free. As if her body had gotten a glimpse of hope, or something, and now that too had gone. Shit, now was not the time for her body to start acting like a walking piece of crap again. Jeez.

As she backed from the room, tottering towards the stairs she felt the statue wiggle with a shiver as if it were alive, it shook nearly free of her grip. She set it on the floor and gave it a good cuff with her left hand. "Fuck you, bitch. We goin down those stairs!"

Julia appeared with a white pillow case, popped it over its gleaming head, "Need help?"

"Nah. Piece of cake. I've carried nastier things in my life." Puffing.

Halfway down she remembered muscling the palm tree for Frankie. Her throat filled with tears. She couldn't see.

Julia guided her, Gina was grateful for the hand on her arm, catching her as she stumbled down the stairs until they hit the bottom. "Holy mother of god but that's a rotten hunk of metal." The stink filled the lobby.

Oleander approached, pulled off the pillowcase and lay the dead rooster at the feet of the statue. She looked it up-and-down. "It doesn't do me justice."

Gina grumbled, "Phew. Doesn't do a rotting fish justice."

Ellis came over, put his arm around Gina, his voice was deep, an eerie reverb, "Justice. That's what we're doing here right now. Justice."

"Well, get to justifyin, old man, so we can breathe in here, okay?" Gina moved well away. Nobody seemed to be who they ought to be and nobody was saying thanks for her delivering it up. And since nobody was paying any attention to her anyway she thought maybe she'd just sort of tiptoe away.

"Don't leave this room." A voice which could not be refused. "Nobody can leave this room until everything's clean. Until we're all clean again." Oleander began a low humming chant, Julia picked it up, then to Gina's surprise, Ellis joined in.

They'd brought out the three-legged cauldron with the plastic car in it along with the oval plate and God only knew what else. The little cowry-faced guy sat placidly next to a sack of herbs. Three bottles of rum. Nine red roses. A pile of cigars. Julia was lighting the cigars, handing them out to everyone. "You too, Gina. And you've got to finish it."

"Yes, ma'am." Gina toked, her eyes were running so that she wasn't ever sure just what she saw. It seemed the statue stretched and grew, maybe it was just the shadows dancing on the blood red walls, then the water in the black cauldron began to bubble, Oleander threw herbs into it and the roiling water subsided. The battle chant coming from Oleander and Ellis, joined by the rolling growls of Rita and the counterpoint of the other voices never let up.

Oleander picked up the rooster, placed a large hot pepper where its head would have been, tying it on with a strip of red cloth, she sprayed it with rum and added it to the cauldron. The water overflowed, hissing. It evaporated before it hit the floor.

Another bucket filled with some kind of liquid was brought forward, fresh herbs were dropped in, others were burned and dropped in. Sage was lit. Rosemary crushed. Sacred rue shredded. The pith of La Reina de Noche, *brugmansia*, was stirred into the brew. And still they smoked the cigars. The first bottle of rum was entirely gone.

Gina mused, partly to save her private vision of the way the world was supposed to be, as opposed to the way it seemed to be just then, that she'd drunk a tremendous amount of liquor to be feeling this sober. She wondered if there was any amount of liquor that could get her drunk any more ever? She took several hefty swallows from the third bottle. Perhaps that would do the trick. If there was a trick left in the world.

"Gina?"

"Hmmm? Hello?" She had not planned on being involved any more than she was, figured puffing on the cigar ought to be proof enough of her good will. An unspoken indication of her positive attitude towards all and sundry involved in this—in this whatever it was. "Yes?"

"Will you sell this?" Oleander was a black flame, invincible, irresistible, a column of fire from floor to ceiling. "How much do you want for it?"

"What?" Gina would just put one foot in front of the other, little by little the job would get done. She had a feeling that at the end of this particular ceremony there wouldn't be any barbecued chicken, red beans and rice. But, if they all survived—was there a question? Well, yes—at some point in the sunshine future there would be food again. Not, she hoped, that sad dead black rooster. She wanted to ask, just to make sure, that they weren't going to cook it, but instead she said, "Ain't mine any way."

Pomba remarked, "How much is it worth—to you or you or you?"

Gina stepped forward and put her hand on the cheek of the golden statue. The sting when she touched it wasn't as intense as it had been upstairs, but it was still enough to make her grit her teeth and swear. "Bitch."

Oleander dipped a white cloth into the cauldron, reached out and washed Gina's hands. It was an immediate comfort. Gina said, "I wouldn't take no amount of money for the thing. Honest. Don't want it. Don't wanta sell it neither."

Oleander/Pomba squeezed the rag out, dipped it back in the herbed water, "Ellis?" She washed his hands.

Ellis said, "No, Ma'am. Thank you Ma'am. Me, I don't want no part of it."

She went around the circle. The smell was a small stink as she neared the end of the proceedings, a nasty glimmer in the corners getting pushed out and away.

Pomba Gira smiled. She murmured, "And my horse? She could sell me and buy—oh all sorts of good things. Take care of—oh all kinds of people. Then Oleander would be someone in the world. Do good things? Yes?"

Pomba shivered as she let Oleander become Oleander again. "No." Oleander spoke firmly, "No. There is no good can come that way. Frankie died to take the curse off. It's up to us to finish with it." She sighed, then laughed. "Into the kitchen with my golden friend! She will guard our dinners from burning, our rice from vermin, make our morning coffee sweet and rich. Rich!"

Everyone spread to the edges of the room with hands full of sage, rosemary and rue, blowing smoke, spitting rum, throwing pennies, stamping their feet. It was as if a lazy ocean wave broke, gentle as a sigh against the sand, and then receded. The dreams of wealth and power faded.

CHAPTER FORTY-SIX

Apparently the fringe community of magical adepts and supplicants found the few days that Oleander's shop was closed after Frankie's death to be nearly unbearable.

"At nine a fuckin clock in the morning?" Gina stumbled to a side window and peered out at the motley crew. "Stop bangin on the door. All the voodoo priestesses is still asleep." She turned to Rhea, morning exercise weights strapped to each wrist. "What is up with these people?"

Rhea lifted her hands above her head, dropped into a crouch and popped off some fancy shadow boxing moves. She turned her back to the door and said, "Starts early some days. It's either the phase of the moon, or it's payday. Welfare comes the first and the fifteenth. People take care of their immediate needs— sometimes it's dope, sometimes it's food or rent, or something for the kids. But a lot of times it's magic. Money spent on wishes, on wonders, on something to make dreams come true." Rhea fiddled with the switches on the coffee machine, the whoosh and burbling counterpointed her words. "Not such a bad thing. Oleander never knowingly takes the rent money, you know. Anyway she gives a lot more than she gets. It's bad the way she doesn't always get paid." Shrug. Smile. "But good karma."

Gina smiled back. It felt good to have just a normal conversation with someone in that household. Then she paused, normal conversation did not generally concern itself with buying wishes, or karma. Oh well, she'd take what she could get.

"The worst is when some old fraud wanders in, trying to out-voodoo us." One hand stretched heavenwards, Rhea intoned in a fervent sweaty voice: "Oh Lord, I feel Satan. Yes, Lord! I feel Satan all around me." She made a goofy face. "Get behint me Satan!"

Gina didn't say anything, after the past few days she could sort of see how someone might make that assumption.

Rhea continued on, "I want to tell them to shove their stupid Satan where the sun don't shine and take their funky ass on outta here. Maybe I should explain to them how there's no room for Satan in any household that works as hard as ours to be helpful. But it just pisses me off. Couple weeks back, Julia did the best thing I ever saw to some cranky young preppie dude. When he started with his Come to Jeezuz I can feeeel the eeevil vibe routine, she starts in to tremblin and moanin, groanin *oh no ah ah*. Like she's coming? You know? And falls into the poor guy's arms. Sucker didn't know what to do. I used to just kind of lean on the counter, cross my eyes and drool, but it's a messy procedure and sometimes they wouldn't leave the store, like they hang around waiting to see what my next trick was gonna be."

"What happens when someone tries to out-voodoo Oleander?"

"You know what? That never happens." She put three cups on the counter, bent forward to stretch out her back. Lifted her leg up behind her head in some uncomfortable contortion. "Yoga." Back to normal. "Got to keep at it or I'll just calcify, you know? You take anything in your coffee?"

"Black, thanks." Gina wondered if Rhea was flirting with her.

"So. How'd you end up with the statue?"

Oh. Not flirt. Nosy. Ah well.

Oleander appeared before she could answer, all three picked up their coffee cups, clicked them together. "To a normal day."

"I'll drink to that."

The banging on the door rose to a frenzy. The huddled masses longing to have their fortunes told were an early rising impatient bunch.

Rhea opened the doors and the morning began with a flurry of activity: Measuring herbs, fixing candles for the vandals, whispered questions, oblique answers, esoteric speculations on the omens of the day. Gina backed into the kitchen clutching her coffee cup like a shield against the weirdoes.

The Pomba Gira statue had been placed by the stove, an apron tied around it and a dish towel draped over the out-stretched arm. "Banished to the scullery cause you been bad?"

Seemed sacrilegious to Gina. Then she realized she'd just addressed it as if it had ears. Which it did, actually, and with some honkin big green rocks too. She reminded herself that even so, statues couldn't hear. As a general thing they couldn't. But this one specifically, this one probably listened with a mean attention, gonna Get whoever spoke nasty to it. Ugh. Gina turned away, noticed Julia fiddling with pans in the sink, "You suppose she hears what we say to her?"

"Maybe. But I don't think she understands English."

Gina had that new and familiar sense of carrying on a conversation some degrees off plumb.

"You want me to make you some eggs?"

"I'm afraid of your cooking."

Smile. "And well you should be. Ellis went to get bagels and stuff."

"In the curs-ed Caddy?"

"Yeah. Might as well find out sooner rather than later if the cleansing last night worked."

Cold. These people were cold. "Couldn't someone like sniff around for eeeevil or something? Cold blooded to send a fellow out to maybe get an I-beam through his head."

Lips compressed. "An I-beam probably wouldn't go through his head."

Ellis bundled in the back door, arms filled with two huge sacks of groceries. "I made it!" Beaming like he'd done something terrific. "And you'll never guess what!"

"Wait. Wait. I got it. You crashed the limo?"

"Hell no. The Caddy runs like it just hadda tune-up. Wish you'd found that statue earlier, maybe a lot of the strain woulda been less."

"Like it was my fault you didn't get to keep it for your ownself?" Gina ducked her head and watched him from under hooded eyelids.

Big sigh. "As it turns out, I'm real glad she's not mine. What a crazy thing, huh?" He peeked at the statue next to the stove, "How long's she gonna be there like that do you suppose?"

Julia threatened him with the frying pan. "What happened, Ellis? What happened? What did you see while you were gone that's soooo important? Why can't you ever just tell us what happened without looping around and making this big deal—"

"Okay. Okay. So I drove by Raymond's shop and there was a fire truck and the roof was all fallen in."

"The roof on the fire truck?"

"Not the roof on the fire truck, smart ass. On Raymond's old shop. Place was all burned up." Pleased with himself, as if he had something to do with it.

"No shit?" Gina subscribed to the general idea of payback. The general idea. She wasn't into that school of self-absorbed philosophy which stipulated that people could change destiny, that someone could put the whammy on someone. People didn't DO that. "Was it the tall guy in the top hat, you think?"

Oleander came into the kitchen, wide smile on her full lips. "What happened, Ellis?"

People didn't do that kind of thing, except for maybe Oleander.

"Raymond's shop burned down. And Gina says that Lethal Jack said that James said he'd suddenly gone positive for Hepatitis. Or AIDS or something."

Not a glimmer of surprise crossed Oleander's placid features. "Well, if any of that were true, perhaps there would be some justice in the world. I wouldn't count on it though."

She swished back into the lobby.

"What she mean by that?"

Gina spoke in her best gloomy voice, "Nothin good come of wicked thoughts." She smiled, tight. All her wanting to kill-em, when she knew damn well she wasn't going to, seemed feeble next to the actual come-around. "Then again, seems like we should just say thank you for small favors."

Julia said, "Well, I'm keeping my blade sharp. In case."

Ellis strutted around the room, waving his bagel, "In case what, girl? We done won this war."

CHAPTER FORTY-SEVEN

There was no visible moon, at new moon there never is. Beginnings take place in secret, unnoticed, in the dark.

Clap-shuffling in a circle at the top of the scruffy hill, Oleander's strange little family moved as sinuous as a snake to the sensual throbbing of the drums. The black pigeons chuckled in their cages at the foot of the glowing statue. Their blood would not be shed tonight, it was a feast of chocolate and roses, of telling fortunes, true and false, a special time for dancing, sweating, making promises they would only remember, and keep, the next time they were this delirious.

Gina stood beside the statue, she folded her arms staring at the edges of the cliff with her habitual discomfort. In some obscure way she felt responsible for it. It had been left to her, even if it hadn't exactly been Frankie's to leave, she'd left it. And so Gina was there, sort of like Frankie's representative, alternatively smiling and scowling. She couldn't figure out what to do with her face—she'd surely never seen a happier or more sincere bunch of idolaters.

Julia and one of the other women patrolled the cliff edge, Ellis crouched by the entrance from the street; one by one, everyone else shucked their human skins and danced possessed by gods. Then Oleander's Pomba Gira approached her statue, sprayed it with champagne, blew the smoke of a sweet cigar all over it. Pomba Gira turned then, gestured grandly for the dancers to approach. Each one must drop to the ground to greet her first, then salute her statue—the kitchen witch. Pomba Gira laughed at that.

Gina was pulled forward to kneel, huddled in on herself, awkward—oh well, she figured it was maybe better to kneel before a golden bitch statue than make a scene and upset the cross-eyed semi-human entranced lunatic-whoever-they-weres.

As everyone was kneeling in a ragged circle, Pomba Gira began to sway towards the statue and away, the smoke from the small brazier shifted in the wind to swirl around them, growing thicker and thicker until it completely obscured them from any outsider's view. The drummer tapped with his stick on the side of the drums, a sharp complicated click-clacking like the crackle of eyes snapped open, mouths shut. It was nearly time to pick up the statue, to dance with it, bless it, welcome it into their sacred family as a guardian. As a symbol of hope.

The drum rhythm quickened and everyone began to chant-sing *"Pomba Gira, Come to me! Pomba Gira ai-yey! Bloody fate, sweet destiny—Pomba Gira, Come to me…"*

Suddenly a snarling man burst into the circle, grinning like a feral cat he slammed his foot into the nearest hen cage. He stomped the little hen as she fluttered to her aborted freedom. He moved with assurance toward the statue.

Flashing in red and black he was Eshu the fortune-crossed spirit of broken dreams, the post midnight street slurry of every ghetto.

Gina, reacting simply to some big asshole approaching the statue, was the first to respond. A flying jailhouse tackle from a crouch, screaming, "Don't touch our statue!" It was a sweet move, but ineffective. She bounced off him, feeling her shoulder crunch into her collarbone, she ate dirt. "Damn."

The man was tall, taller than imagination, and proud. His teeth flashed silver, his eyes were obsidian sharp, his thick black hair flamed around his smooth mahogany face and hung down to his thick shoulders. He was handsome, arrogant, strutting. He posed. He put his hands on his hips and growled, "What is all this?"

Oleander's Pomba Gira slid smoothly, imperceptibly between the man and the statue as she slid equally smoothly a little ways back into Oleander. There were two formidable women who glared out of her eyes, an implacable Goddess and a worldly-wise whore. "Vicente. I knew you were not dead."

"And too bad for your morals about it. You had your chance to get control of my whole fortune, but you hesitated. You had a chance to come with me again, but it seems you have chosen otherwise?"

Oleander/Pomba Gira put her hand over her mouth, perhaps to hide a smile, she shook her head, less in answer to his pompous question than at the follies of men.

He understood the gesture as one of confusion, his voice was liquid fire, "Now. It is too late for your small choices. I have come to take what is mine." His hand snaked out, tangled in her hair, pulling her toward him. "All of it."

Oleander/Pomba Gira didn't even seem to notice that he was man-handling her, she twisted, a coil of smoke in his hands, free. She met his pride-filled stance with smooth elegance, at her full height she actually seemed to top him by a few inches. "I don't think so." It was impossible to tell who it was that said it, the voice came from the scraggly trees, from the dance-pounded earth itself.

"And I don't think so." Ellis, moving before he made any decision to do so, crouched down at the foot of the statue, fingers delicately touching the ground, here and here, a homage to the Orishas and the ancient rules of combat. "You played with me, you played with all of us. No regard for how we might feel about things. All's you care about is what you want. Always it's only what you want. Now we play for reals." He tilted his head to one side, blew on his hands and reached them out, slow, as if in supplication, to the angry man.

"*Ie, maior e Deus. Ie, maior e Deus, Pequeno sou eu.*" The drummer didn't have a *berimbau* to play the traditional challenge songs of capoeira, but he could sing them: "*Ie, God is great and I am so small. Everything I have, everything I know comes from God. But although I am small before God, in combat I discover my own greatness.*"

Ellis crooked his body, twisted his head, awkward, shy, pleading with the angry man to come with him into the world of capoeira. 'After all', his movements seemed to say, 'You were my Master in this, you taught me all I know, yes?' Then, he groveled, cajoling with the traditional circular postures, 'Come on. Show me how little I know.' Behind the formal gestures which open a blood match there was a tiny frantic scrambling somewhere deep in Ellis's brain: What the Hell? How damn fucking foolish can I be? Jeezuz.

The world shifted, they could feel the muscles of the hilltop flex and relax as the red and black man crouched down, touching the earth, there and there. His eyes were red mirrors, his thin lips disappeared into his razor smile, he rolled into the circle with a smooth and lazy *au*—the cartwheel of someone who expects the match to be short.

Ellis turned upside down only a moment behind the Master, thinking: Oh now I'm really in deep shit, I'm going to get creamed. He was upside down then thinking: That ruddy bastard, I thought it was him buried in that grave and I was sorry. Right side up, crouching, foot sweep, hands up to block the kick that came from somewhere high above him, rolling, the circle bulging as he rolled. On his feet, spinning back, catching the Master's leg with his own, pain screaming to his groin, down and rolling again, away toward the edge, the circle re-forming deeper into the scrub. He remembered the fighter's mantra: Keep your eyes on your opponent. He thought, fragmented, that he certainly would if he could find the bastard. Crouch, shift, spin, roll, the man blurred appearing in a new place, Ellis lost him, he was at the mercy of the Master, no longer blocking the blows which came at his face kidneys knees ribs, his face kidneys knees ribs—a barrage of flicks, knife foot, hammer hands pounding him from all directions, pushing him towards unconsciousness. Keep your eyes on your opponent. He blinked blood out of his eyes.

His mouth filled with the taste of iron and he remembered: capoeira is treachery. Focus. A Master is supposed to win the game with grace and skill, but Vicente was battering him, proving his Mastery with a butcher's thoroughness, an arrogant viciousness.

Capoeira is treachery.

Ellis crouched, then staggered up, his left leg buckled but he moved to receive the killing blow with dignity. His arms outstretched, face filled with terror, he swayed gently as if bowing to an inevitable breeze.

The sound of trucks on the roadway far below were the rumble of the sacred *berimbau*, "In myself before God I am small, but in the circle I discover my greatness."

Vicente feathered forward to deliver a crushing *bençao*, the straight leg kick to the chest called 'a blessing.' He smiled with a calm benevolence his red eyes denied.

Within the crack in time as Vicente delivered the blessing, Ellis flung himself backwards, sliding over the edge of the cliff. He caught onto a boulder with a shuddering sigh.

Vicente's momentum carried him forward, he made no cry as he plummeted out into the night air over the edge, there was only a short animal grunt as he hit the scree thirty feet below and continued rolling into the dark.

Ellis frantically hung on to his boulder, sweat made his hands slick, he was terrified he would follow Vicente into oblivion far below.

Pomba Gira ambled over and peered down at Ellis with other-worldly eyes. "You're not really very good at this are you?" She held out a strong hand to him.

Bloody grin. Reaching up for her hand, "Well. I won the match now, didn't I?"

CHAPTER FORTY-EIGHT

James was at Oleander's door the following morning. He was unshaven, his white linen jacket was a vaguely grimy wad of cloth drooping off his shoulders. He carried a large package under one arm.

Ellis met him at the door, eyes narrowed. "Dude. You look like shit." His own face was battered from the beating he'd taken the night before, one side bruised green and blue, the other just beginning to scab over where he'd scraped it eating dirt. He folded his arms.

"I'm here to see Oleander." James tried a steely glare, it faltered momentarily, then he noticed Oleander in the lobby behind Ellis. "I have an appointment." He stepped forward, Ellis turned only slightly to let the other man squeeze past.

"Ah. James. You brought me a present." Oleander smiled, a lazy cat in the sun.

James shifted his package, left to right, mumbling, "Is there some place we can talk?"

Her gaze was level, "Right here seems fine to me." She didn't offer him coffee.

He cleared his throat, tempted to ask for coffee, fearing he would be refused.

"Or would you prefer to go in the kitchen?"

"Kitchen?" His voice squeaked. James wouldn't even begin to chase down all the conflicting reactions he had to that question. Did Oleander know he'd seen Frankie die? Seemed pretty impossible to him—he glared at her for a moment, debated challenging her right there. To what? Truth or Consequences? Arm wrestling? Abstruse anthropology? Precognition—or was it post-cognition? He shuddered, grumbling to himself that his health was too delicate to challenge anyone. He whispered, not quite pleading, glancing over his shoulder at Ellis who still stood there with his arms crossed, "Please. I need to talk to you."

She went behind the counter, placed her hands flat on it and leaned forward. "Put the package down right here. Should I open it now?"

He nodded glumly. Lately nothing seemed to go the way he planned it. He had a short moment of self-discovery, realizing that since he'd picked up that strange golden Venus nothing had quite—he slammed the door on that thought. "Regrets," he said aloud, "are useless things." Hesitation, "I'm sorry we couldn't have been friends."

Her smile was small, but real none the less, she said, "James. Thank you. But we could never actually be friends." Smile a little bigger, "I would eat you up and spit out the bones."

Happy to play the game. "And it would be my pleasure to be destroyed by such a lovely woman."

"The world is filled with them." She peeled a layer of brown paper off the proud wooden Ogun from Nigeria that she had admired in the hotel. "Ah. Now this is a surprise. How thoughtful." She lifted an eyebrow at him. "And this is payment for?"

James grunted. Fidgeted. Sighed. Looked around the lobby to discover that not only had Ellis not moved from his cross-armed position, but he'd been joined by that demonic pit bull dog, both of them stared at him from tiny glowing red eyes. The embodiment of evil.

Rita sat, bright and sharp, grinning. She thought perhaps she'd be able to throw this one down the front stairs all on her own. She'd been practicing in her dreams. She glanced over at Ellis, sly. Now that he was an accepted member of her family she didn't think about chasing him so much anymore. She growled a little, back in her throat, low and rumbling. The sound was far larger than the size of the puppy would lead one to expect.

Ellis smiled at the effect it had on James.

"Uh. Could you put that dog on a leash or something?" His voice slid, once again, into those higher registers he imagined he'd left behind with acne.

"No." Oleander nodded Ellis to wait in the kitchen. As they passed by, Rita made a feint for James's cuffs. He jumped straight up.

James scowled as he heard Ellis and Rita laughing. He rubbed his face and said, "Ah. Um. You managed to keep Francine alive even though she had this…terrible disease?" No reaction. He plunged forward, all-in-one-breath, "So I was wondering if you could, you could give me some of the herbs or whatever you gave to her?" Still no reaction. In desperation, "I think I have what she had. I know it." Long, slim hands clasped together as if in prayer, their elegance was marred by torn nails and scuffed-in dirt on the knuckles. "I don't want to die. Please, Oleander, help me?"

Oleander took a step back, "What?" She started to snort with incredulity, picked up the wooden statue and turned away to hide the expression on her face, turning back she put the statue down nearly in the same place. Frowning, hand over her mouth, she said again, "What?"

Exasperation. These people had no idea, no idea of the seriousness of his condition. "I am certain I have hepatitis C. Or AIDS. Tuberculosis for sure." He shivered. "I need the medicine you gave to Frankie! You've got to give it to me!"

Oleander's mouth opened slightly, the corners of her lips quivered, "Oh, James. You don't have hep. Or anything. You stupid man. Where did you get that idea?"

His mouth opened and closed, wordless. Guilty.

"Have you even been tested? Oh don't tell me, I can imagine well enough." Her grimace was a full-blown rose. "You haven't, have you? Idiot. Frankie's blood on your hands… It won't kill you." She stepped out from behind the bar counter. Step. Step. Moving toward him. Grim. "Even if you did catch some deadly disease, there's nothing I would do for you. Nothing." Step. Step. Right in his face. "Frankie kept her own self alive. You don't have what she had." Long deadly stare. "You don't have anything she had."

James had slumped inward as she spoke, torn between anger and hope, gripping the edge of the counter, sliding away from her. Part of him wanted to believe he was disease free, the other part wanted to holler that he did so too have hepatitis! And AIDS! And all kinds of other undeserved curses riding on him. That blasted woman had splashed blood all over him before she died. He swallowed. Damn the woman. Damn them all to Hell. He whined, "TB is rampant in the County jails."

Oleander wasn't done yet. "You do have a terminal disease. The symptoms are arrogance. Stupidity. Greed." She kept advancing, pushing him back towards the lobby doors, back into the world. Not the one he'd inhabited before he met her—a colder darker place. Her voice was filled with venom, "You lie, you steal. This isn't a problem, really. But you do it pretending to yourself that it's okay. Because you're somehow different. Better than the rest of us."

A feeble voice in his head was screaming: But I am, damn it! I am!

"You are different."

Vindication? From Oleander? James stopped his retreat, his back against the doors.

"You're a completely value-free organism polluting the shores of our lives." Every word punctuated by a step forward until she stood inches away. "A craven slobbering fool who pisses his pants when he should be brave. You're the man who chokes on his own vomit when he thinks about how utterly useless his life is." She opened one hand, slapped it flat on his chest, with the other she opened the door behind him. "You're a whining slimy sack of shit pretending to be a man."

She shoved. James spun around and nearly fell. "I don't have to listen to this." Shaking, snot and slobber running down his chin.

There didn't seem to be anything more to say. "Good-bye. Good-bye." Oleander waved with an odd jerky flip of her hands, then she clenched them sharp into fists. "Good-bye!" She jerked her fists downward. Her hands opened, spilling something.

A huge pain ripped through James's chest as he stumbled down the street. His long jaw wobbled, his whole body shrunken and sagging on the left side. He looked over his crooked shoulder every few steps, his mouth opening and closing, a mewling noise wheezing out. He got smaller and smaller until he limped awkwardly around the corner.

Ellis had come out to watch him leave. "What did that scumbag want?"

"To give me this." She went back inside, held out the little Ogun.

"Oh no. Another poisonous thing?" Ellis actually recoiled.

"No, Ellis. This one is just lonely, hasn't had anyone to talk to for a long time, maybe we can help it out."

"I don't trust that bastard."

Oleander didn't say anything about pot calling kettles, she was trying to give Ellis a little bit of leeway in some things, but she spoke tartly, "James isn't evil, he's just an ordinary guy consumed by extra-ordinary passion. He's got a hole in him that nothing can fill. You're familiar with greed, I think? James is merely human and that's not enough for him." She raised the corners of her mouth, a sure sign she had said something profound. Ellis stuck his hands in his pockets. "He doesn't need our hatred, his curse is to live his life always unsatisfied." She said, "He's a greedy fool. He's paying for that. But he's not the walking evil you'd like to make him into. There are others to fill that role."

Ellis didn't say anything, the fool-part seemed to hit a little too close to home for him. The 'others' part sounded ominous.

"Best leave it alone, Ellis." She rummaged in a chest for the white cloths they would use for the tables that night. "Funny how the Ogun statue would just show up, eh? Right on the day we're planning dinner for Frankie. For our Ogun on the other side."

"I don't know so much how I feel about this other side shit. Mostly I just have a big empty spot where Frankie should be." He rubbed his face. "Fuck it. Maybe we might dance the Ogun statue? Maybe tonight? For Frankie? We don't have to go back up to the hill for it. Besides, listen to me, Oleander, nobody wants to go back there any time soon. Like we all worry that maybe the ghost of Vicente will come clawing its way back up the cliff."

Oleander snorted, "Nonsense. Vicente's no ghost. He didn't die last night."

"The man's immortal?"

"Not in the least. But that cliff didn't kill him. Only reason he hasn't been around to harass us this afternoon is because he's ashamed." Grin. "Immortality has many forms—let's give Vicente a really embarrassing one, okay? We'll tell the story again and again how you tricked him."

"Oh. I dunno about that, I was just lucky I think. I sort of wish I hadn't done him like that. If he ain't dead then he's really after me now. Jeez."

"Ellis, he was after you from the moment James loaded Pomba Gira in the crate."

"Oh hell. Don't tell me that." Ellis wandered off mumbling about doom.

There was an excited bustle in the lobby. Feed the dead. Feed the living. Always seemed to be feedin someone around Oleander's house.

Gina hid out in the backyard tending to the barbeque while Rita ran circles around her feet, waiting for some good bits of chicken to drop to the ground. Oleander came out, stood staring at the food on the grill, preoccupied.

"What's on your mind, hey?"

Oleander realized there was no use in a preamble, she said, "The chemist got back to me today. The dope in the syringe wasn't right." Oleander had two baggies of Francine's stash in her pocket, she gripped the larger one. "One is ordinary, tested about sixty percent heroin. He listed the other forty percent for me, it was, you know, not quite fully processed opium bi-products and typical street crud. Nothin in there to kill anyone." Her movements were fluid, but she hesitated before she handed the baggie to Gina, "Still, I'd rather you didn't want it, you know?"

Gina ran her tongue across her lips. "Well, I might just like to have it." Her tongue pushed at her cheek. As she held out her hand, she said, "What you mean the stuff in the syringe was not right?"

"It wasn't actually poisoned. But, it might as well have been. It was pure."

"Pure?" Gina thought about that. "As in 'pure'?" She eyed Oleander's pocket, still heavy with something. Gina damned herself for being a greedy cunt—but if that was yet more of Frankie's dope, she wanted it. She wanted it all. She wanted it pure. Not necessarily to do herself, but she had a few ideas about how remarkably useful something like that could be. Pure? She licked her lips again, thinking hard how she could get Oleander to give it up.

Julia overheard, "Wait a minute. Pure? That gonna kill you if you don't know."

"Raymond knew she didn't use regularly. If his usual dope was sixty percent or less then he knew she'd OD, sure as shit. But I really don't know what was on his mind." Oleander's mouth quirked up at the corner, "Some fortune teller I am, huh?"

"Doesn't matter now, does it? She's dead and he killed her."

"Well then, was that what James was goin on about back there at the bar? He saw her die?"

"He did not. Not unless the man's got more contact with the spirit world than any of us ever suspected. I think Frankie just pulled a fast one on him."

"I'm sure he wouldn't see it quite like that."

"It's hard to know just how he would see anything. You know? So much shit in his eyes."

Rhea poked her head around the corner, "C'mon guys, let's eat."

Oleander said, "Everyone take a little of the food on your plate and put it on the plates here in the middle of the table. Feed the dead. When we feed the dead, they taste it. They taste it. What they taste is love." She spooned little portions from everything on her plate.

Everyone was fairly sad and solemn in the beginning, each wrapped in their own thoughts, putting them out little by little, memories, sharp as shards of broken glass passed around gingerly for inspection, for healing. The food was good, the wine and beer flowed like wine and beer, the talk got louder, funnier, wilder. There were moments when everyone was rocked back laughing, they'd look around for a second, wondering if laughter was appropriate, "Hey, this is Frankie we're celebrating here."

The clock moved around to midnight, they put all the lights in the room off, nothing but darkness and the sound of a lot of people breathing together.

Oleander started the chant for the blessing of the midnight Eshu: *Hey Bara go. Mo-juba. Hey Bara go. Ago Mo-jubara. Omo dey koni kosi Bara go. Ago mojubara El-egwa Eshu onah.*

All the lights on the lower floor had been turned out, but as the praise chant for the turn of midnight began, the chandelier glowed reddish, blinking with a strange pulsing glitter. Gina moved closer to Oleander, watching as the Pomba Gira possession took her over, then Gina stood on tiptoe, whispering, "Give me what's in your pocket. Give me what's in your pocket Pomba Gira, dear. I have need of it this night." She wasn't sure if it would work.

Pomba/Oleander turned those great spooky shining eyes on her, her blood red lips parted in an awful smile, her hand went into her pocket and she pressed the bag of pure dope into Gina's hand.

Gina did a quick fade from the room.

When the lights came back up there were a couple extra pie-eyed people not quite themselves standing in the middle of the room. Julia/not Julia stood, eyes glazed, implacable, her blade out, she held it low, half hidden in her skirt. She muttered, "I'll kill the bastard. I will." The voice was not her own.

Pomba/Oleander spoke, carefully with a lot of gentle thrust, "No. This is not your work."

Julia shook her head, smoky, sultry, she said, "You people refuse to take care of unfinished business. So it's first blood for me tonight. I'll do it since you won't. After I'm done you can do what you wish with the carcass." She shook her head again, reaching up to touch her long hair she felt a skull with a harsh stubble of hair just beginning to grow back. Pomba Gira was horrified. "What have you done? What have you done to my hair?"

Oleander shook off the possession trance, spoke as herself, kindly, "You're in the body of a young girl in her first ritually pure year. She can't even kill a rooster."

The unearthly voice of the possessed woman rose in confusion, "This can't be so. This can't be so!"

Oleander rolled over the incipient hysteria in flat tones, a practicality which was impossible to disagree with, "I'm not saying you couldn't kill him, Pomba Gira my love, I'm merely pointing out that this one can't."

"If the horse had been allowed to work with me first instead of that insipid Oshun, I surely would take him out." Pride.

"Yes. Perhaps you would. But that's why this year is not devoted entirely to you. This *yawo* is still not ready to receive you." Oleander put her arm around Julia's shoulders, "You will be made welcome to this horse. Just not tonight."

"I will take another then." Julia slumped forward into Oleander's arms, tears rolling down her cheeks.

"Soon, Julia, soon. Just not tonight."

Julia's breath came in long slow gulps.

A voice with too much reverb interrupted, "If you are all done with your dramatics, it's time we deliver the leftovers to honored dead." Ellis was not himself either.

Gina peeked back into the room from the kitchen. Hah, she thought: Turn out the lights for a moment and the kids become other people. High-handed autocratic demanding ones. She touched the baggie in her left pocket and reached for the phone.

Oleander wasn't finished with Julia, she merely nodded to Ellis/not-Ellis, motioned for someone to light him a cigar, returned to Julia, saying, "It's only a few more months and you can start to work with Pomba."

Julia, recognizing that it was a good time to try for a bargain, said, "No more kitchen duty?"

"Everybody has kitchen duty."

"Not Ellis."

"You want him in the kitchen? No? I didn't think so. The Eshu's job is to be the messenger. And the garbage man."

"And chauffeur," Ellis/Eshu butted in, "And chauffeur." He strutted around the room, blowing smoke rings, "And a damn fine chauffeur I am too. With a fine set of wheels."

Julia, entirely back to herself, looked around the room, "Where's Gina?"

"She left soon as the lights came back on."

Ellis/Eshu snorted, "She left as soon as the lights went out. That one is a clever one. Don't let her fool you with that dumb act she does."

Gina returned looking like the cat swallowed the canary. "I think we might have a visitor, you know, to pay his last respects to Frankie."

"No shit? You called Raymond?"

"Well, it wasn't me." She tipped her head to one side, rolled her shoulders, slid one foot forward and intoned in a smoky voice, "You sssay you're Frankie's friend. You want to show me how much of a good friend you are? Ssso, come sssay good-bye properly."

Oleander nearly busted a gut, the imitation was so close. "And he went for it?"

"Damn straight. I hung up with the fucker squeaking: 'Oleander? Ooooleander?' It was great."

"Now all's we got to do is—"

"Julia. This was Gina's call. Not yours."

Gina figured that it was Frankie's turn to make the call. The damn dead bitch better come up with something. Or not. Gina wasn't going to trust that Frankie would really show up to take care of matters. The theory was that the ninth night after someone died was the last official time the shade spent hanging around their earthly digs, after that they mostly went off to do whatever dead spirits do, maybe check in once and awhile, raise some hell at the old homestead (none of them ever did a lick of housework, that was obvious) maybe get reborn, work towards Buddhahood or Ogun-hood or Robinhood. Whatever. Gina wasn't quite clear on that part of it. In any case it was ninth night and Frankie's last chance to put in a starring appearance. Or not. Frankie could just spend the next part of eternity mourning lost chances.

In a few moments everyone drifted out towards the street, aiming for the corner. They were smoking cigars, singing quietly. If they had looked back they would have seen that they were accompanied by the faint glimmer of a tall woman dressed in military dress blues.

Ellis carried the remains of the dinner, part of which he had placed carefully in a couple plastic bowls that he left by the side of the front steps for the local homeless to pick up. He wondered, half-heartedly, if the old man—he continued to think of Vicente as old, even though that had just been part of his act—was homeless and would stop by for something to eat. He grinned. Then sobered up again. Somehow he doubted anything much would touch Vicente, not even a thirty-foot fall off a cliff. The wily old cat probably landed on his feet.

He balanced the rest of the food from their feast on a large paper platter which they would drop at the corner runoff drain for all the honored dead. Ellis, as Eshu, had specially blessed the food for the dead, after that, the living were prohibited from eating it.

Gina put a couple slices of cream pie for the dead on a separate plate.

Ellis had stepped into the street just as Raymond drove up. "Oh hello, Raymond. So sorry about your shop."

Raymond didn't look particularly the worse for the wear, he didn't have the drawn features of someone who'd lost nearly everything. "No matter," he said with an airy wave of his fat hand, covered with rings, "the insurance will more than take care of it." His cheeks chipmunked out in a toothy grin. He started to get out of the car but Ellis, sniffing the air catching a scent of vetiver oil, blocked the door from opening. Raymond looked up, surprised.

Ellis murmured, "It was you. It was you. I shoulda known."

Gina ambled over and gently shoved Ellis aside, he walked around to the other side of the car while she leaned into the window, butt stuck out in an imitation of a perky whore. "Here." She grabbed a slice of pie, handed it over to the soon-to-be-dead. "Here's a little coconut cream pie from our memorial dinner for Frankie. I know you woulda been here if you'd known earlier, so we saved you a piece." There was a glimmering of that silvery warrior woman at her elbow. She watched as he took the pie, as he nodded his confusion and thanks, she said, "Take a bite. It's delicious."

"Well, get the fuck out of the way so I can properly pay my respects." He shook his head and pushed on the door. Gina held it shut. He slid to the other side, pushing on that door. "Damn you, youngblood. Get away from there."

Gina crooned, "Oh don't mind him. He's still mad at you. But just taste the cream pie. Frankie's favorite you know."

Scowling, he bit into it. Nodded his head.

Food for the dead. Food for the dead.

Gina smiled, her hand slipped to the top of the seat as he moved back behind the wheel, she flipped the open packet of dope all over the back seat and the floor. Fabulous China White Numbah Whatevah spilling all over the place. "We know how you felt about Frankie. Glad you could share at least in this much with us." The pure heroin glowed there, down the back of his shoulders, powdery silver white on the floor, shining in the glare from the overhead streetlights.

Raymond started again to get out, but his door was kept firmly closed.

The two demon children stood there grinning at him, teeth and eyes gleamed red in the streetlight glare.

His lips curled up in an insincere smile, "What the hell? I was invited and now I'm not? I don't have to put up with this bullshit. Thanks for nothing. Hey, Oleander?" He craned to get a glimpse of Oleander, of anyone other than the two menaces, but he only saw a vague glimmering, the view was completely blocked as if he were in a tunnel. "Oleander?"

"You're done here, Raymond. We'll make sure Oleander knows you stopped by."

He drove off, shaking his head to clear his sight, licking his fingers. He was angry and a little uneasy about what had just happened, after all he'd gotten a call telling him to come and he came but then they just sort of sent him on his way? Oh well. Shrugging, he looked into his rear view mirror.

A tall woman, a really unnaturally tall woman, like maybe ten feet tall or more, all dressed in armor, strode down the street after his vehicle, pointing a bright sharp sword directly at the car.

Raymond, mouth in an 'O', stepped on the gas, not taking his eyes off the apparition.

Gina said, "Um. Do you see that?" No one answered her as they all stood, utterly still, watching Raymond get chased off down the block by a ferocious shining woman.

Raymond's car sped up, as if perhaps he was trying to out-distance the apparition. The tires smoked and squealed as he took the corner too fast, he hit a slick spot on the pavement, there was a blast of headlights shining back at them, then the lights splayed away again, around off the buildings and parked cars to each side, spinning spinning. Crazy. Sparks spit from his exhaust when it scraped the curb, the engine choked and screamed as he attempted to regain control. It wasn't slow motion the way these things are supposed to seem, it was sudden, quick speed, double time, the car spinning, going straight, blink and it's bumping, crashing, smashing to a halt against a chain link fence. Took no longer than a breath.

No one moved. The sound of sirens began far away faintly wailing, crescendoed as the cop car approached the corner.

Oleander whispered, "We better set out the platter and go back inside before the cops come ask us if we saw the wreck."

"What did we see, Oleander?"

"What goes around, comes around."

CHAPTER FORTY-NINE

"Hey." Julia was nervous. She said, "I think we should take a look at Raymond's ol shop. Something maybe there we could use." She sort of shrugged and wiggled. "Get it now or do without."

Ellis looked at her sideways. "Say what?"

"Just seems to me we're not done with him."

"Fucker's in the hospital, then he goin to jail. Seems done to me."

Scowling, Julia scratched Rita's head and said, "C'mon Rita, we've got work to do."

Ellis said, "Wait. I wanta come too. What're we doin anyway?"

"Ellis. You just drive, okay? Don't do—don't do—oh, don't do anything stupid, okay?"

He pouted. Why did these people always caution him that way? Why didn't anyone ever give him credit for being able to take care of business?

Julia was laughing at him. "Oh yeah. Please wash your Caddy while I go change, okay?"

Once the Caddy was shiny and bright, Ellis washed up, changed his shirt, grabbed a walking stick, spun it in a little salute as Julia came down the stairs. She wore a long red velvet skirt, a big sleeve blouse, and a sequin shawl. Her head was wrapped in a bright gold scarf twisted and knotted like an African Queen. Or a Cigana Fortune Teller. Gold hoop earrings, dramatic makeup.

"What the hell we doin, Julia?"

Rita pranced at her side like a show dog. Julia smiled, slow, her voice was a sultry reverb imitation of Oleander's. "Let's go, Ellis." Her eyes did an Oleander flash.

Ellis gawped at her. She turned her head so he wouldn't see her giggle.

He drove. Didn't say a word. They pulled up in front of the lot where Raymond's shop had been. There was a big sign: COMING SOON PAYLESS SHOE SOURCE.

"Moving right on up in the world." Julia still had the reverb.

A workman was busy clearing the debris from the sidewalk where it had been dumped after the fire. There was dust in the air mixed with the sodden fumes of burnt out wallboard. Julia took a breath, let it go, "Okay Ellis. Let me work it, okay?"

"Okay, boss lady. Okay."

The lovely woman and a slim dapper man got out of the handsome black Cadillac limousine and stood carefully on the sidewalk looking at what was left of the shop. They were accompanied by a large brindle pit bull pup on a braided leather leash. The workman shoveling debris into the dumpster liked dogs, he crouched down to say hello to Rita, virtually ignoring her human companions, "Hullo pretty girl?"

Rita sat, noble as a princess, and held up one huge paw, delicate as the dawn.

Julia realized her job was already half done, thanks to her clever dog. She smiled, "Anyone seen the fella who usta run this place?" Her glance was sharp, a deep mysterious black, her voice was smoky, redolent of midnight dreams and secret passions.

The workman stood up, taking a good look at her for the first time. He liked dogs fine, liked pretty women more, "Nope, the guy's gone for good, in the hospital or in jail. One or the other. We just got the contract to clear the place out." Proud. "We're Build-Rite Construction. Gonna put uppa real nice building here. What you need?"

Ellis stepped around to the side, let Julia do her thing. Poking carefully, he investigated the dumpster, bits and pieces of not really very ancient clay artifacts, burned and broken statues, twisted metal office furniture. A pile of water-soaked gooey books. Everything ruined beyond use. He pushed his walking stick deeper into the crap, finding nothing much but garbage.

Chatting, Julia and the construction worker walked into the front of the building. She was laughing at something he said, moving her shoulders in a subtle precise fashion, he followed her happily as she moved deeper, partnered by Rita, admirably on heel. She sifted through the rubble with her eyes, and with those other mysterious talents she had. Like La Favorita, she used a delicate sort of psychic sniffing. They made their way to the back, an area the workmen hadn't yet gotten around to cleaning out.

Using every nuance she could muster, Julia said, "I'm looking for something, a sculpture. It belonged to my family. It was on loan as a display piece here. We're hoping it may have survived the fire." She pulled out an official looking document, State Historical Society or something with a lot of words in the title. One of the women temporarily crashing at Oleander's rooming house was an expert at that sort of thing. It had only taken her a half hour with the computer and the copy machine. "Is the foreman around?"

"Nah. He's off havin a beer up the street. Let me see that? Seems straightforward enough, you know?" He handed the paper back to her, "You find what you're looking for, just get it outta our way. One less piece of junk for us to move. Our instructions are to clear this place out. Clean. We got to start construction next week." He wiped his face with a grimy hand. "It's always a bitch, pardon my French, to clean up after a fire."

"Thank you so much." She reached in her pocket for a cigarette, he was quick to light it for her, pleased to do even that small service. The smoke ring floated around his head, a blessing he was not entirely ignorant of. He was smiling as he walked away.

Ellis came back, wiping his hands, shaking his head. He murmured quietly to her, "Nothing in the dumpster. Nothing worth anything at all that I can see. You sure it's here?"

"Never know til we look. Ya gotta pay attention when ya getta di-rect clue. More'n once. You know, the ooga-ooga vibe. Seemed to me that there was something to it. Vicente always needs to have the last word. Even after goin offa cliff. I'd like to shortstop him before his next move."

"I keep hoping that fall from the cliff woulda made him leave us alone."

"Dream on. He'll never leave us alone. But I think there's something here might keep him away."

"Dream on yourself, Julia. If he ain't dead then I'll bet he's sneakin around our house right now, plottin something." He wrinkled his nose at the mess, unaware he'd called Oleander's house 'our house'.

"I thought of that. Oleander's got it covered, don't you worry. Just keep looking."

"Looking. Right." He poked at a burnt-out shelving unit, "Oleander know we here?"

"Noooo. But that Vicente's always one step ahead, one step to the side. Perhaps we're not as clever as he is, and the Good Lord knows it's not safe to have any dealings with him." She put an arm around Ellis, "But there are more of us than there are of him. Anyway, we're in this up to our ears and elbows."

"Yeah and what if the roof here has been rigged to fall in on us?"

"It will miss us then. Now pay attention to what's here. You actually worked with him, you oughta be able to sense what we lookin for."

"Well, Gina went a couple rounds with him, even though her flying tackle failed, at least she fought him to something of a standoff. And she didn't die. Do you suppose she'll ever come back?"

"Not my job to suppose. But, if I was a betting woman," she made a gesture, palm down palm up, "I'd say she'll be back before the year is out."

"We be just too much fun to stay away from for very long, huh?"

"I think she'll miss Rita so bad—she come back just to see how La Favorita the wonder dog has grown."

Rita pushed her nose at a blob of rubble. Ellis moved a shelf so it wouldn't tumble down on the dog. There was a creaking sound, Rita gave a small snarl, there was a whiff of smoke, maybe from Julia's cigarette, maybe from the blob itself.

"What's this?" Ellis pushed the rest of the shelves aside, stepped past the sodden books that cascaded down, reached around and stood the blob roughly on its feet. "Oh crap. Here's another statue to dance. Just what you wanted, Julia."

Under the grit and grime there seemed to be a battered but still cocky matte-black metal man standing there, leaning a little to the left where a falling shelf had bent his leg. About three and a half feet tall, including his rather flattened top hat, the statue wore mirror shades, red tennies, and a small sardonic smile.

"Well I'll be damned."

"Most likely. Most likely."

Julia grinned at him, smacked him on the shoulder, "Looks familiar, hey? Well, let's load the little fucker in the limo and bring him on home where we can keep an eye on him."

CHAPTER FIFTY

Friday night, Oleander and Julia, both dressed in glowing red satin, walked to the corner nearest Oleander's house carrying a bottle of rum, some cornmeal, three red roses and a couple good cigars. Rita prowled alongside, measuring the world. Julia's dark curly hair was grown out long enough to bounce around her shoulders as she moved, she squatted in the gutter drawing a design which sparked and glittered in the streetlights, she laid the three roses across her work. Oleander lit a cigar as Julia stood up.

The cigar was passed to Julia. She blew awkward smoke rings. Up the street at the top of a slight rise the silhouette of a tall elegant man appeared, he strolled casually, as if he had all the time in the world, down to the women. Silently they handed Ellis their bottle of rum. Turning turning turning they greeted each other, solemn and precise.

Rita barked three times, sharp.

The streetlights flickered.

They heard the sound of determined footsteps coming up the street. The short woman trudged closer, huffing and puffing, a large canvas sack over one shoulder. She slung it to the ground in front of them. It clinked in an interesting fashion.

"Was wonderin if there was a room I could crash in for a few? Lethal Jack still has his cellar but you know, I'd rather not."

"Welcome home, Gina, welcome home."

Gina ducked her head to hide her smile, bent and gave Rita a hug.

*　　*　　*

Just before midnight a small group of people are spinning, spinning at the edge of a cliff, spinning to keep the stars in their places, and fate on its course.

White doves fly up into the sky and disappear into the moon.

Someone tosses a half-pint bottle of rum over the edge, it never hits earth.

THE END

In late fall of 2015 Patrick Marks, proprietor of The Green Arcade, and Francesca Rosa, co-editor of Ithuriel's Spear Press, interviewed Sin Soracco in an undisclosed location on the Russian River, Northern California.

Patrick: Sin and I worked together on reprints of her two earlier books, *Low Bite* and *Edge City*, both collaborations with Oakland's PM Press. Sin, your latest book, *Come To Me*, now a collaboration with Ithuriel's Spear press, has a lot in common with the earlier books—

Sin: Ya, the same person wrote 'em.

Patrick: Besides the fact that the same person wrote them, the settings are all in well-known California locations. *Edge City* is set in a North Beach belly dancing club and *Low Bite* in a California women's prison. *Come To Me* is a real San Francisco book. And the *Edge City* character Reno, is similar to Gina in *Come To*—

Sin: She is an ex-con, as are a number of the women in *Come To Me*. But I certainly hope that Reno is a distinct individual from Gina. Partly because I have been writing Gina stories for a very long time. And I wrote one Reno story—well, she was my protag to give a sense of what it's like to *just* get out of prison. And now she's gone on and had her own little character life somewhere else, but I haven't written about her, she didn't interest me nearly as much as Gina did. One of the things I was thinking about the three books as well as the short stories is I write transgressive fiction. And it's kind of a guilty pleasure of mine to write stories that people who are smug self-righteous assholes will not enjoy reading. [All laugh.] I like to send up people who are self-righteous. In that sense it is transgressive. None of my favorite characters, including the villains in *Come To Me* have the traits and patterns in common with what's considered ordinary white people.

Francesca: Working class people are very marginalized in our society and I think you bring them to the forefront in a way we don't see much in who's writing fiction and who fiction is marketed to.

Sin: Yeah. Not merely working class, but outcast class. I try to keep overt politics out of my books—but for a number of people the politics were really just in-your-face, partly because I set *Low Bite* in a prison and my heroes were convict women. And then in *Edge City* my protag again was somebody who at one point was not particularly normal, but even so, I'm always surprised when people say, "I don't know any of these people." And I'd be interested to see, as I am again writing about a doubly marginalized group of women, whether people are actually so silly as to say, "Well, I've never met anybody like anybody in your book." I'm like: You don't get out of the house much then."

Patrick: If you hung around North Beach and other neighborhoods during the time that *Edge City* takes place, these are places we in San Francisco can recognize—so, how do you think place plays out in *Come To Me*, like where people go, who they are?

Sin: I have parts of buildings I know that are utilized in the various places where people are. The distance between places sort of shifts around though. For example, the distance between Oleander's *botanica*/women's refuge and the Lizard Lounge tends to stretch or get closer. As I was working on the book I finally decided that distance is all in the mind of the people who are going someplace. So, where might Oleander's house be? Well, it's pretty easy. South of Market, Mission-ish because there's bars within walking distance.

Francesca: It's also where the Santeria/Quimbanda community is located—

Sin: It's not Quimbanda. The only Quimbanda worker in the story is Vicente.

Patrick: Can we stop here for a second, and get some background? So part of the backdrop of this novel is a community of people that are living in what we might call a safe house, and the house leader, we could call her, is Oleander. Can you explain their situation for us?

Sin: When Oleander hit the City she was dedicated to making things better. One way to make money in the City, along with her various other talents, was to set up a magic shop, a *botanica*, where she tells fortunes and sells herbs and candles and all of the classic afro-diaspora-religious materials. The building had space upstairs so she made it a women's refuge. Most of the women who stay there work with her in matters spiritual, are members of a community that is, essentially, in

San Francisco, Santeria based. There are a number of purely Brazilian houses in the area also, but I work with a Santeria house, so that's what I lean on. When the Afro-Brazilian spirit Pomba Gira came with Oleander to San Francisco, the first people she encountered were working in the Afro-Cuban not an Afro-Brazilian tradition. So she modified her original practice. The women who have needed shelter with her have not been from Brazil, they have mostly been Latinas, Cubanas, or local black women whose easiest entrée into the world of the spirits was through Santeria. So while Oleander was baptized in Candomblé to Pomba Gira, she is comfortable working with the similar spirits of Santeria.

Patrick: In *Edge City*, music and the culture of the belly dance were extremely well delineated and there was accuracy in terms of describing the dancing and the rhythms and the relation of those to the rhythm of the writing. And that is one of the strengths of the book. In *Come to Me* the description of the community and their rituals moves the story and the rhythm of the story along. I was wondering about how careful and well, accurate the spiritual practices are. Did you vet the story?

Sin: A *padrino* friend read the book and he liked it. In any case I do not bust any of the secrets of the religion, and it is a secretive religion because it has to be. Especially as this particular nation becomes and more theocratic, fascistic, autocratic towards not merely people of color, but people whose belief structures are denigrated by the larger Christian community that really holds all of the power.

Francesca: I would also add that the way that San Francisco is changing—if something can't be commodified it is considered to be irrelevant, marginalized or has no use. I really like the way you invoke that community in this book and in *Edge City*. You really bring forward these worlds.

Sin: I think that those communities are the only way that any of us are going to survive, with some connection to like-minded people, getting together to do joyful stuff. The problem with Afro-Cuban or Afro-the-diaspora religions--which are ecstatic spiritual practices—that very ecstasy is what this culture finds most threatening. Because if people discover fundamental human joy, then they are bound to look at the world differently than someone who is purely caught up in the commodification of their life. I think it's more obvious now in San Francisco—it's shriekingly obvious—but it's always been like that. What has happened, I think, is that the greater nasty political world has made it more and more possible for that point of view to take precedence in terms of how even how the "little" people live their "little" lives. But the religion survived SLAVERY so both the people and the ideas will survive gentrification and the neo-liberal agenda.

Francesca: Tony Robles, the Bay Are poet and activist says, "San Francisco has become an app."*

Sin: Ha! That's good! Back to the idea of utilizing the religions of the African diaspora in my fiction. It was something I had wanted to do for years. I love the religion. I got into Santeria because of the music. And the rest of the spirits and philosophies were kind of secondary to the music. As time went on, I learned more and met some people that I absolutely loved. I have been involved in that community now for decades.

Francesca: How was someone who is not from that background—how were you welcomed into that community?

Sin: I'm a weirdo. I'm a hardass. And I actually knew something about the religions beforehand and I was also fortunate in that I was trained in various western magical traditions. So there's a lot of stuff about magic that I was comfortable with. I had also lived with people of color for a lot of time. And my *padrino* lets me slide on a number of things and unlike someone who *likes* the hierarchy and structure of the religion, my *padrino* realizes that I am an anarchist, bone-deep, by my nature. There are certain things that I do not like to do. However, in a ritual setting, I am as good a devotee as you will find. But in my personal deep spiritual work--years ago, I said I don't take bullying in my life. Not in my spiritual life either. I have a *padrino* who never bullies. Over the decades we have become very close, and I am delighted that he is still in my life.

Francesca: Is that community still able to survive in San Francisco? With the extreme economic stress?

Sin: Yes. But a lot of people have moved out. Remember that *santeros* must have certain ceremonies throughout the year. Some of these ceremonies have lots of drumming, singing, dancing, trancing.

Patrick: There goes the neighborhood.

Andrew (Sin's partner): In the City there are still many many many practitioners. Remember, it's a secret religion. Survived slavery. Will survive this too. That's a major point.

Sin: Yes. However, it is often difficult for ceremonies to be allowed in certain neighborhoods.

Francesca: And it's getting much worse in places like the Mission, which were strongholds of Latino culture now getting very waspish.

Sin: We were very fortunate when we were working in the Mission in that the people who were our direct neighbors, on one side I had known them since before I was born. They were friends of my family and they were from Central America. And they *loved* the drumming. We always made it a point to stop at ten, because they had kids. And the people on the other side who were Latinos thought it was great. So we never had the least bit of trouble, dead center in the Mission.

Francesca: When was this timeframe?

Sin: We stopped only three or four years ago.

Francesca: As you know there have been enormous changes in the last few years.

Sin: Recently, practicing their religion in a predominantly Christian neighborhood, in a predominantly wealthier neighborhood, people have been harassed. The new people who have bought in want things to be just like in the suburbs, only in the o so exciting urban atmosphere, and therefore, it's got to be tidy. Tidy in terms of color, in terms of noise, in terms of cars and parking.

Francesca: And they want the people of color either wearing aprons and waiting on them or standing behind musical instruments.

Sin: I think that it's too easy to say that this is a color thing. It's a broader hate-filled attitude. We are still missing some of that—but we are talking Bay Area here.

Patrick: Yeah. My new phrase is: "Think locally, act locally."

Sin: Act out! In the Bay Area we can also see that there is a smug self-righteous attitude, aimed generally at anyone who is not from the same economic class. It's always been that way. But now the divide is so huge.

Francesca: And it's hard to hang on.

Sin: When you realize that the firefighters and the schoolteachers and the nurses, who are all good guys, cannot afford to live in the communities they serve, you know something has gone wrong.

Francesca: And the retail workers and the non-profit workers and the artists and everyone else.

Patrick: One of the scenes in *Come To Me* that I think is so fantastic, the largest ritual that we see—like you say a very ecstatic and joyous occasion, takes place on Telegraph Hill. We know where that is, and the juxtaposing of all these characters we have gotten to know doing this amazing thing, right splat in the middle of all of Telegraph Hill against the backdrop of well, insane real estate, is well, fantastic.

Sin: They are in this derelict lot—

Patrick: Which they are still fighting over. I used to go up there when I was a bike messenger, up the backway. Also, there's been a lot of shedding. A lot of the Hill has fallen. But let's get back to the book. I wanted to talk a bit more about Gina and her development. It really isn't a bildungsroman—

Sin: Ellis is the only character that might apply to. I wanted us to see a rather wonderful young man come into his manhood. It sort of happened within the story and when I would go back and try to put the stupid book together, I tried to keep an eye on his trajectory from drunk as a lord to still drunk as lord but very much taking control of being a young black man. That was important. Gina is always changing—

Patrick: But we see the world through her eyes, mostly, we discover what is going on in the house through her.

Sin: Now, there's a reason for that. Gina is one of the people who is brought into Oleander's world. Who is not a trained, not a participant in magic. Virtually everyone who works with Oleander *gets it*. They trance, they see spirits. Gina's is the outside viewpoint. When everybody is going, "Wow, this is so cool," Gina is going, "I was told there was going to be rice and chicken." I felt that it was very important to have her be a viewpoint character, so that somebody would not simply throw the book across the room. I had things I wanted people to experience through the book, and if I shut them out by speaking too much within the religion, they would feel that these ideas I tried to sneak in would have nothing to do with them.

Francesca: Could you talk a little about Francine. She is such an evocative character, although she's very mysterious. Like her illness.

Sin: I never quantified her illness, because in the years of working with Frankie there were too many possible illnesses. She is the ideal idealistic junkie artist. And is very very very smart. And very good at what she does. And she is a combination of a lot of people I have known who were battered by the culture, and their attempts to contribute to the culture, especially in terms of artwork, were continuously put down, or delayed, or they were ripped off. And a huge number of those people became junkies because they were in so many ways too fragile to survive; except for-- most of the junkies I've known have ended up being tough. And Frankie is both fragile and very tough.

Francesca: And also like people deep into speed, even though they are so much more wired.

Sin: I had a good friend who told me he had just turned fifty and he was cleaning up. And he came in where I was working, and I said, "You're looking good." And he said, "I'm having kind of a rough time, you know, I'm trying not to do any crank." And he goes, "You know why?" And I said, "Well, I could think of a number of reasons *why*." But he said, "Nobody likes an old speed freak."

Patrick: O my god, it's so true.

Sin: It's much easier to age on junk, if you don't die young.

Patrick: The speed and the coke—so easy to get those infarctions and keel. Junk is healthier.

Sin: I agree. And I think Frankie would agree. For people I have known, who lived, again, a life *aside* from most of society, and I kind of wanted, like you said Frankie is an evocative character, I want people to see her and go, "I know this person. And I like this person."

Francesca: When I was reading it, she was the haunted character who brought back many people I have known.

Patrick: Where is she within the community of the house? She seems removed, but also seems to know everything.

Sin: She's major. She made *santo* a good seven to ten years before this story starts.

Patrick: So she was already involved when she and Gina were first together?

Sin: Gina has the memory of when she and Frankie were living together. Gina thought this all pretty stupid. She remembers coming home from work and Frankie is growling and sharpening her blade and says, "Wait outside." And Gina thinks, "What the fuck, I live here." And it's like, no no little girl, you can't come in right now. At that point Frankie was doing her own thing. She was called, like I was, to the music, to the creativity, to the altars, to the clothing, the relationships. It's all religious theater in the outward appearance. It's beautiful.

Patrick: And speaking about outward appearance, I wanted to talk about the concept of the gypsy and the cultural put down of calling Roma people "gypsies."

Sin: What I originally had was that Oleander claimed the Gypsy Woman Oleander as a safe mask. And because she was no-one and was here illegally, and didn't know much about the society, and Pomba Gira is seen, in the community, as the stereotypical fabulous gypsy. In so many ceremonies there's not a lot of the Roma in it. It's very stereotypical. And beyond that, many of the spirits, who are vast, are shrunk, so that a human can have something of a shorthand. Ogun is often seen as the classic blacksmith; he is so much more than that. Ochossi is the personification of all native peoples all around the world, and is often seen with the classic feathered headdress. Again, it is a shorthand. A mask. One of the most obvious masks is the African spirits wearing the masks of western saints. So Oleander takes the mask of the Gypsy Woman Oleander but as she stays in the culture here, she begins to see this is a slur. Oleander is masked. She is born in Argentina. It is very likely that she is Roma. We don't know. She is masked. Vicente is masked as the old man. Frankie is masked both as the child of Ogun and the dying junkie. And she is so much more. Gina is by trade and personality, masked as being stupid and insignificant.

Francesca: Or highly pragmatic.

Sin: But she also wants people to *not* look at her. Julia is living in disguise. What I'm playing with, which is part of the whole gypsy tzigane Roma game, is the idea that a path to survival in this culture is in fact that of the hidden self. And people who maintain and people who break down throughout the book. Of course the greatest masking of all is within the various afro-diaspora religions hiding behind the mask of saints. And the eventual changes within the African religions, which happened because of the incorporations of Christian and Native spiritualties.

Francesca: I also wanted to ask about the animals.

Sin: Animal sacrifice. This is a religion where you make offerings. And you make sacrifices. It is not always an animal. It is not always a blood sacrifice. The idea is that you have set up a relationship with the universe and that you don't get to simply say, "I need, give me, I've been good, I deserve." It is an ongoing daily relationship with the universe. Sacrifice, offering can be tobacco, honey, booze, coffee, a song. It can also be the blood of a creature that was living. These sacrifices are not done often. They are not done particularly happily. I have Francine doing *pinaldo*, having learned and been blessed with the ability to do the sacrifice. For a very long time females could not sacrifice four-legged animals—the goats. A male had to do that. Females could not play the drums. It originates in a very old hierarchical culture, sexually differentiated in terms of acceptable roles. Of course this carried over into the religion. Fortunately, for people like me, who say, "This is the twenty-first century (or whatever the hell it is)." I don't want to hear about any anti-queer bullshit— because there's a lot of queers in the religion. I don't want to hear that a woman shouldn't be playing drum. Of course, this needs to be discussed. Don't hand me the line, "It's traditionally and culturally demanded." Because all the cultures are changing, for the better. Of course, the crypto-fascists are turning for the worse.

Patrick: So do you think this is one of the cool things about the Bay Area? More acceptance?

Sin: The discussions are going on nationwide. There are incredible movements towards social acceptance of various kinds—we've got transsexuals within the religion, we've got queers and bisexuals and people who will fuck anything that moves.

Francesca: But weren't intersex people in ancient cultures considered special as if they were able to more fluidly be able to open the door to the other side—

Sin: Yes, Eleggua is the doorkeeper.

Patrick: And how does this all come down to you as a writer? Beyond *Come To Me* what are you thinking of?

Sin: We began this all with transgressive and those are really the only stories that I am deeply enamored of telling. If I don't offend somebody, I am not doing my job. I've got a Gina and Frankie story from years before *Come To Me.* I've got a number of little stories about more Gina than Frankie at this stage because I'm gonna try and encapsulate Frankie past-tense, because she *dies* in this book. Besides that, there's *Eating Butterflies*, a novel that is going to be as big or as little as it is. It takes place in San Francisco, maybe two or three years before *Come To Me* opens. And I got a couple short stories I was asked to write. And Andrew and I are writing *Frankenstein Club* for my website/blog Soracco Stories.

Patrick: Francesca, I've wanted to ask you—what attracted you to want get involved with co-publishing Sin?

Francesca: Well, I read *Low Bite* and *Edge City* and I was really amazed at her ability to evoke a place. *Low Bite* really got that prison—when I was reading it I felt like I was right there. And then when the character gets out, well, there is this quality of drawing people into a world. The reader suspends judgment, which I think is a real skill. The characters seem very real to me. Particularly when I got to *Edge City*—I've lived in San Francisco since the seventies and am extremely attached to the City, and in North Beach and in the Mission there is a quality that is immaterial but that is very much there in those places. *Edge City* really captures that North Beach energy—I used to go there a lot in my twenties—I love North Beach. And that was just *there* in *Edge City*. I was very impressed by that. So when the opportunity came along—Patrick opened the doors of The Green Arcade to many of our book launches. So this I thought was great, do a joint publishing project with The Green Arcade. Plus be able to publish Sin. And we have already started a mystery series at Ithuriel's Spear with John Goins and Susie Hara—and I am writing a mystery now. I love the noir genre and with our city evaporating before our eyes, it just seemed like a rare opportunity to be able to embody someone who has really captured the City into our series.

Sin: Thank you.

Francesca: I mean it.

Patrick: Nice way to end.

*Tony Robles' book, *Cool Don't Live Here No More: A Letter to San Francisco,* was also published by Ithuriel's Spear, in 2015.

SIN SORACCO lives at the undisclosed location in the woods by the river with her partner Andrew, Poppy the Newf and The Gentleman cat. In These Weird Times the job is to reach for joy when ever where ever—screw the theocratic oligarchs. And so on. Subversion and Stories: Bring the bastids down.

Ithuriel's Spear Press

Ithuriel's Spear is dedicated mainly to the literary arts. We publish San Francisco and wider Bay Area writers and translators. Our books are distributed by Small Press Distribution in Berkeley CA and can be purchased through www.spdbooks.org. Follow us on Facebook at Ithuriel's Spear Press. Visit our website at www.ithuriel.com. Previous titles in our mystery series:

A Portrait in the Tenderloin by John Goins
Finder of Lost Objects by Susie Hara.

We are pleased to be part of this joint noir collaboration of Sin Soracco's *Come to Me* with:

The Green Arcade Press

Credo of The Green Arcade:

The Green Arcade specializes in San Francisco and California history, the built and the natural environment, politics and social justice, with an eye to the interesting and varied in art and literature. The Green Arcade is a meeting place for rebels, *flaneurs,* farmers and the creative.

The Green Arcade Press
1680 Market St.
San Francisco, CA 94102-5949

www.thegreenarcade.com

Previous Titles by Sin Soracco

Novels:
> *Low Bite*
> *Edge City*

Anthologies:
> *San Francisco Noir* (edited by Peter Maravelis)
> "Double Expresso"

Prison Noir (edited by Joyce Carol Oates)
> "I Saw An Angel"

LADYLAND: Anthologie de Littérature Féminine Americaine, 13e Note Editions
"Must. Gentrify. Now" (short story published in French)

Blogs:

Seth's Blog | CrimeWAV.com
"Must. Gentrify. Now" (mp3)

Website:

Soracco Stories
http://soraccostories.com/